BEHOLD A PALE HORSE

FORGE BOOKS BY FRANKLIN ALLEN LEIB

The House of Pain
Behold a Pale Horse

BEHOLD A PALE HORSE

Franklin Allen Leib

FORGE®

A Tom Doherty Associates Book
New York

This is a work of fiction. All the characters and events portrayed in this novel are either fictitious or are used fictitiously.

BEHOLD A PALE HORSE

This book is printed on acid-free paper.

A Forge Book
Published by Tom Doherty Associates, LLC
175 Fifth Avenue
New York, NY 10010

www.tor.com

ISBN: 0-312-89064-8

First Edition: January 2000

Printed in the United States of America

0 9 8 7 6 5 4 3 2 1

To my loyal friend, Catherine the Great, who sat on my table and watched me write. When I typed rapidly, she purred, and when I stopped, she stared with the intensity only a cat can maintain. Get on with it, she seemed to say.

Cat, 1980–1999. *In pace requiescat.*

History is an account,
mostly false,
of events
mostly unimportant,
which are brought about by rulers,
mostly knaves,
and soldiers,
mostly fools.

—*Ambrose Bierce*

And I looked, and behold a pale horse: and his name that sat on him was Death, and Hell followed with him.

—*The Revelation of St. John the Divine*
chapter 6, verse 8

I

FORETELLING

1963

1

THE SHOOTER DREW himself up beneath the sixth-floor windowsill, peered over carefully. The window was open only a fraction, but hot wind blew against his cheeks and raised dry dust around him from the neglected floor of the shabby old warehouse. He looked down across an oblong of thin grass surrounded by swaying trees. Crowds lined the sides of the roads away from the square; policemen patrolled the plaza itself. Red, white, and blue flags fluttered, reminding him of the wind, the swirling hot wind that could move his bullet inches in the two hundred meters between his position and the head of the man he had been hired to kill.

Hired, not yet paid.

The shooter had taken the job on such thin promise of reward only because it had given him a chance to escape the poverty of his homeland. Even the expense money he had been given was more than he had ever earned, and he was here, overlooking a place in a bigger city than he had ever seen, with a chance to use his gift against a head of state, a young man of promise, of courage; a man dangerous enough to others that they would pay for his death.

But he felt a setup. He would be abandoned; it was a bad contract. The shooter had been called Paul by the mission priests, and when he went into the business of shooting rogue, cornfield-destroying elephants and wounded rhinos and lions driven mad by pain of gunshots from high-paying poachers from Europe and the Middle East. He named himself Cobra when he moved on to killing African dictators, captains, even sergeants from the slums of coastal cities who threw a leopard skin across their shoulders and called themselves general, president, king, invoking ancient gods of the tribes of the country that were barely remembered.

The shooter recalled brutal and corrupt despots he had taken without regret, but as he squinted into the sulfurous urban haze and rewrapped the rifle sling more tightly around his left forearm his conscience gnawed at him. He had nothing against the young leader who would soon pass under his sights, and he was more than suspicious that he would not be paid.

Nevertheless, they had got him here and given him a chance of a lifetime. It was a chance to become a legend, even a god, never to be forgotten, but never to be known either outside of the shadow world of mercenaries. Cobra fought down his doubts. He had thought of a way to have all the fame, the notoriety of the shooter who got to this young man despite the tightest security in the world. He could do it and be true to his conscience—he had one, he reminded himself, nodding over the clumsy Italian Mannlicher Carcano rifle his "employers" had given him, sighting the lead vehicle of the motorcade in the antiquated 8x telescopic sight—he would show them he was as good as he said, many times as good as they believed, greater yet because he would not accept the money they had no intention of paying.

But it could all go very wrong. He knew that real professional shooters had backup, alternate routes of escape, alibis. He had none of these.

He opened the bolt of the Mannlicher action. It was smooth and silent; he had spent many hours rebuilding it and reseating the barrel to tolerances the rifle had never known even when new. The rifle was a piece of shit, discarded even by the Italian Army after their quixotic Ethiopian campaign. The load, light at 6.5mm, was so slow it dropped three meters in three hundred.

Cobra had opened the brass cartridges and discarded the dry old powder and corroded jacketed bullets, then carefully reloaded the best brass with match grade, even-burning powder over new-milled primers. He cast new bullets himself, soft-nosed with a shallow depression at the tip, a bullet to kill, not wound. Cobra pressed five rounds into the box magazine, careful not to damage the soft noses on the aligns. He closed the bolt and climbed onto the gray metal desk he had shoved up against the windowsill and assumed his shooting position. The first vehicle, carrying the president's guards standing on running boards, leaped into focus in the old telescope.

The shot itself was absurdly easy. He had trained himself on the windy savannas of Matabeleland, tracking wily old elephants no man could approach within their sight, scent or hearing. He had killed animals at over seven hundred meters. He had killed the communist leader Lumumba in the Congo at nearly a thousand, albeit with a far superior weapon. At this short range, even despite the awkward long-throw of the rifle's bolt, he could place three rounds in a circle three inches across in just over three seconds.

Cobra rested the forearm-stock of the rifle on a bag of fine sand, in a groove he had fashioned with his thumbs. His weight rested on his elbows and spread knees. The steel top of the desk hurt his bare elbows, but cushioning of any type could introduce slippage, movement, imprecision. He held the rifle on the bag of rigid sand and the bone-bipod of his elbows. No flesh, no pumping blood would move the weapon. The lead vehicle slid out of sight and the president's car appeared, an open Lincoln. The range was six hundred meters and closing. Cobra's contract called for a head shot because the subject was known to wear a vest of light body armor made of a new composite. Cobra could have taken him easily as he rode toward his position. The subject's face, recognizable around the world, smiled as he waved to cheering spectators. His eyes almost seemed to meet the shooter's.

Cobra relaxed his muscles, drove away the pain in his elbows, knees, and groin from the hard table, and began to count his breathing down, reaching for a nearly trancelike state that would cancel all error-inducing movement in his body. The Lincoln glided around the corner and slowed; the president turned his head and once again seemed to meet the shooter's eyes. Cobra focused on his chosen target, a pinpoint in comparison to the head he was meant to shoot. His trigger finger began to tighten as he took a half-breath and let it out. He increased pressure as his heart paused, held it when it beat. The target waved and bobbed as the president gestured; it was an impossible shot but one Cobra knew he could make. The subject's face reappeared in the scope as the black target touched his mouth and the shot broke perfectly.

Fidel Castro's cigar exploded mere centimeters from his face.

Cobra rolled off the table as the crowd fell into shocked silence punctuated by anguished screams. He wiped the rifle clean of fingerprints and threw it under the table, picked up the sandbag, dumped it out, and folded it into his pocket. By the time sirens and barked commands reached his window, Cobra was running down the stairs of the Almacen Municipal de la Habana and into backstreets empty of people who had crowded into the plaza to cheer the Maximum Leader of the Cuban revolution. Cobra slowed his pace a block away; police and military vehicles raced toward the plaza behind him as he walked unhurriedly toward the harbor, where his patrons were supposed to have a boat waiting. Cobra grinned to himself. They certainly wouldn't pay him now, and he didn't expect to find the boat, but he had to play out the hand.

2

The news of the attempt on Fidel Castro's life caused powerful men to be called out of meetings all over Washington. Great men of both parties came together and nattered about dangerous adventurism and the rashness of President Kennedy's inept national security and intelligence staffs. The Attorney General angrily summoned the Directors of Central Intelligence and the FBI, and the heads of Army, Navy, and Air Force intelligence and demanded an explanation: who ordered an attempt on Castro? And who fucked it up? Answers were few and Robert Kennedy resolved to see his brother the president about bringing intelligence and counterintelligence activities under tighter White House control. Robert meant to handle the matter personally.

* * *

THE CUBAN LEADER was not seen for forty-eight hours after the shooting. Eyewitnesses had reported that his head snapped back at the shot and that he had slumped to the floor of his limousine and been covered by the body of his own brother Raul. Rumors that Fidel was dead or gravely wounded were denied by the Cuban Revolutionary Council and Radio Havana, but no explanation was offered for the Leader's disappearance. The radio played funeral marches and Fidel's old anti-American speeches.

Two days after the incident Fidel appeared on the balcony of the presidential palace. He looked drawn and shaken as he waved to a hastily gathered crowd of supporters, but his voice was firm as he announced that the assassin had been captured in the harbor area hours after the shooting and had admitted under interrogation that he had been brought to Cuba illegally by *gusanos,* hated exiles who had fled the justice of Socialist Cuba, and paid by the American CIA.

HOW CAN YOU be sure you were paid by the CIA?" Lieutenant Carvahal of the Servicio Nacional de Infomaciones, Cuba's secret intelligence service, asked the man who called himself Cobra.

Cobra blinked at the harsh light that made his questioner a dark silhouette. He was strapped to a heavy wooden chair, naked. Fine salt water dripped on him from a leak in the ceiling; the taste confirmed he was in one of the stone dungeons below sea level beneath the seventeenth-century Spanish fort called El Morro. He wasn't sure how long he had been there; the light was never extinguished. He had never been fed more than sweetened rice and for the rest there was a ragged hole in the cane seat and a smelly bucket under the chair. Police had knocked him around when they caught him in a dragnet on the quay where he was to meet his Cuban-exile escort, the same that had landed him from a fishing boat on the beach in Matanzas Bay a week before on a night with no moon. He had cursed them on the empty dock as he waited for the police; they came so quickly they had to have been tipped.

He shifted, holding the gaze of the Cuban policeman. His buttocks were rubbed raw from the remnants of cane seat and he felt dizzy with hunger and chilled by the constant drip, but he had not been beaten since being put in this room with its too-bright light. He had answered all their questions truthfully; he owed nothing to the men who had lied to him and left him and he wanted to live a little longer. "I can't prove it, I told you. The man who sought me out in Salisbury and arranged my passage through Luanda and Lisbon is known for handling CIA contracts."

"Exclusively?"

"No."

Carvahal considered the man. He was fine looking, even aristocratic in bearing despite his discomfort. He spoke well, an educated voice beneath the flat Rhodesian drawl. "Who was this man?"

I told you that, Cobra thought. I've told you several times. "He's a Russian, Lives in Durban. Uses the name Rokovsky."

"Why would the CIA use a Russian?"

"Why would a Russian want your leader dead?"

"It's conjecture." Carvahal turned away. He wanted to believe it, so would Fidel. "There's no evidence at all."

Cobra shrugged. "This Russian hired me before, three years ago. I wasn't called Cobra then and I don't think he remembered me."

Carvahal looked at the man's dark face. He seemed eager to please but two days under the seawater drip loosened minds as well as tongues. "You didn't say this before."

"You didn't ask."

"Well, what then? What did the Russian hire you to do?"

"Shoot a rebel. A communist rebel, Patrice Lumumba."

Carvahal started. The world believed Lumumba had been hit by the CIA; the Americans barely denied it. "Did you?"

"Yes. A very long shot."

"You didn't miss, as you claim you missed our president?"

"No."

"What was the difference?"

"Lumumba was an evil man, a traitor to his people." Cobra caught a glimpse of the interrogator's narrow face as he leaned in to catch the answer. "Besides, I got paid."

Lieutenant Carvahal stood and pushed his own chair aside. "You'll be shot, of course. The council has already decided."

"I missed intentionally."

"You insist on that. No one believes you."

"Let me show you. Let me make the same shot again, for my life. Then you may think of better ways for me to make amends than merely by dying."

Carvahal nodded. It was exactly as he had argued to Colonel Rosas, the commander of the National Service of Information. This one was far too useful to be left in a shallow grave next to the ancient stone walls of the castle.

"You speak well. Where were you educated?"

The man called Cobra smiled. He gaze was frank, open.

"Southern Rhodesia. Matabeleland. The bush, north of Bulawayo."

"Let me guess," Carvahal said. "Mission school, Jesuits."

"Yes."

"Of course." He left the prisoner, wet and stinking, to think of more ways to be grateful.

3

ROBERT KENNEDY RECEIVED the Director of the FBI in the Attorney General's office in the Department of Justice Building on Pennsylvania Avenue. Hoover was half an hour late despite his own stern requirement for punctuality. He was a short, portly man, dressed in a well-made suit of an old-fashioned cut. He ignored Kennedy's outstretched hand and looked around the room curiously as if to imply that he had never been in it before. The director normally took his meetings in his own much larger office on the opposite corner of the building; he did not expect to be summoned by a mere attorney general even though the man was technically his boss. Hoover dismissed attorneys general for what they were: politicians soon to be gone while he and the FBI remained to protect the nation. He finished his tour around the office and sat in the middle of a soft couch.

RFK perched one hip on his desk. He considered himself a tough lawyer, never reluctant to use power to help his family, especially his brother, the President of the United States. He thought Hoover was a dinosaur and he hoped soon to be rid of him; in the meantime he feared the old man. "Thank you for coming up, Director."

"What is it?" Hoover demanded sharply.

Bobby scratched his scalp behind his ear, a nervous tick. He stopped himself when he saw Hoover watching; clasped his hands in his lap. "The Castro thing."

"Botched. Pity."

"Who authorized it? The president—"

"General," Hoover interrupted like a schoolmaster. "Operations of this type occur when opportunities arise. Castro is a communist and an enemy of the United States; when a chance comes up to assist an operation against him, we may assist in an untraceable way."

"Who's 'we?' "

Hoover waved the question away like a gnat. "It's informal. Surely the president and the Attorney General do not wish to involve themselves directly." It was not a question.

"Director, the president and only the president can make foreign policy. He hasn't authorized this, and he wants all such activities halted at once."

Hoover leaned forward, his pale cheeks coloring slightly. "He does, does he? Flush with the success of his Bay of Pigs campaign? Giddy with his triumph over Khruschev's missiles that nearly led us to total war and remain in Cuba still?"

Bobby choked on his anger. "What if Castro takes it into his head to retaliate? Strike, even at the president himself?"

"The President of the United States should not shrink from the threat of a petty despot. General."

Jesus, you arrogant son of a bitch! Kennedy swallowed and controlled his voice. "Director, the president wants this business stopped. At once. Castro is trumpeting CIA involvement and we know that sells all over Latin America."

"The CIA may have got sloppy. As usual the Bureau will clean up after them."

"Who sent this assassin? Who paid him?"

"Looking for someone to blame? Hell, General, the Miami Cubans do this stuff, we just try to keep a rein on them. Surely the president is in no position to offend the brave Cubans who have been victims of his . . . caution."

Kennedy stood and took a step toward the director. He knew the director meant cowardice. Bobby's face flushed all the way to his hairline. "God *dammit,* Hoover—"

"*Director* Hoover." He remained seated as Kennedy towered over him, his fists balled. "Yes?"

"Even *you* can't say absolutely anything in this office!"

"No disrespect was intended," Hoover said with an insincere smile that said just the opposite.

Kennedy turned away. "Who's CIA's man in Florida?"

"His name is Fernandez, but he's not on CIA's payroll, or any other government agency's."

"Get rid of him."

"What, to show your displeasure? No. Fernandez does useful work."

Kennedy turned back. He felt his color rising again, his hands trembling. Hoover was insufferable. "Director, I just gave you an order."

"You can't fire him, General," Hoover said blandly. "I've just told you he doesn't work for government."

"But *you* could fire him."

"Yes, if I thought it advisable. I don't.

"You're all but daring me to fire you."

Hoover laughed, a single bark. He slapped his hands on his fleshy thighs and pushed himself out of the soft couch. "General, you can't know how far I go to protect you—and of course the president. So many secrets are on my files it would be perilous indeed to entrust them to the care of a *political* appointee."

"Blackmail?" Kennedy rasped.

"Not at all," Hoover said blandly. "I serve the nation; I work with each administration in its turn. The president needs steady advisers in shaping his policies; not only on communism and Cuba, but on his ambitions in the area of civil rights."

Bobby Kennedy believed Hoover kept secret files. "You have information that could damage the president."

"Safely locked away. Protected, General, by me personally."

Kennedy shook his head in disgust. How the old bastard was enjoying this. "I don't suppose you'd show me."

"Files? Your brother's? Yours?" Hoover chuckled. "Of course. Though the one you should enjoy the most is that of your favorite Negro preacher, Martin Luther King Jr." Hoover turned to leave without waiting for his boss to dismiss him.

"Director," Kennedy said sharply. Hoover stopped with his hand on the doorknob and turned slowly. He did not reply. "I *will* have a look at the files. Today, please."

Hoover gave a little bow. "Of course. Yours and the president's."

"Dr. King's too," Kennedy said sadly.

Hoover turned and went out, leaving the door open behind him.

4

COBRA BLINKED IN THE harsh Havana sunlight. The lamp in his cell had been extinguished hours before, he assumed to disorient him. It had worked; he stumbled as he was marched across the stone-flagged courtyard to a waiting 6×6 truck. He was tossed in between two rows of seated soldiers. His hands were cuffed behind his back and he was blindfolded with a white handkerchief. He closed his eyes to rest them as the truck lurched forward with a clash of worn gears. Lieutenant Carvahal had told him he would be shot within the prison, so the movement away had to be a good sign.

He reckoned they had been driving for about an hour over badly broken roads, never very fast. The truck stopped with a jerk that caused him to slide to the front of the bed and bang his head. Soldiers handed him down and the blindfold was pulled off. Hands held his as the handcuffs were unlocked. Lieutenant Carvahal stepped from behind him, putting the cuffs in a belt holster. "Come along, *Cabron,*" he said. *Cabron* was Carvahal's little joke; it meant goat instead of cobra; it also meant cuckold.

He followed the lieutenant down an irregular row of parked trucks, most resting on rusted axles, stripped for parts. At the end of the row was a dusty parade ground several hundred meters long. Carvahal led him up a steep grandstand to a dilapidated covered booth at the top. Inside on a rude bench was the Carcano rifle the Cuban exiles had given him weeks before in Miami. So Carvahal has convinced his bosses to let me show them how I hit the cigar instead of the man, Cobra thought with a glimmer of hope. He hoped the bright lights of his cell hadn't damaged his eyes, especially his depth perception; he'd heard that could happen. He looked at the weapon and then at Carvahal; the lieutenant nodded. Cobra picked the rifle up and jacked the bolt open. Empty, of course, and dirty. "May I clean the rifle?"

Carvahal smiled slightly. "There is a rod, rags, solvent, and oil in the holdall beneath the bench." He watched as Cobra swiftly field-stripped the weapon and cleaned it with care. He removed the scope and cleaned it and its mounting, unscrewed and reseated the stock. He worked twenty minutes in silence, then set the rifle carefully on a rag spread over the bench. "What would you have me shoot?"

"The same, Cabron. One shot for your life."

There was another grandstand at right angles to the one where they waited. Cobra saw two truckloads of soldiers pull in front of it, a dusty Buick in between them. The soldiers jumped down and formed a loose perimeter. Two men in green Russian-style fatigues left the Buick and climbed the grandstand halfway and sat. They and the soldiers looked expectantly toward the covered booth. So, Cobra thought looking at the burly man with his heavy black beard and his slighter companion, Fidel and Raul have come themselves to see if I can do it again. For some reason he found the Castros' presence calming. "What's my target?"

"Are you ready to shoot?"

Cobra turned the rifle toward Carvahal, the bolt open. "I trust you recovered the cartridges that were in this weapon when I left it."

Carvahal reached into a leg pocket in his fatigue trousers and withdrew a cardboard box. He laid it on the bench. Cobra flipped off the lid and found four cartridges nestled in oiled cotton. He picked up two and examined them; they were his and didn't appear to have been tampered with.

"What else do you need?" Carvahal asked.

"A table, and a sandbag to rest the barrel. I made the shot prone."

Carvahal snapped his fingers. Four soldiers struggled in with the metal desk from the warehouse. The sandbag Cobra had carried when he was taken had been stitched and filled and was placed on the desk. Carvahal allowed himself a faint smile. "Everything shall be as you made it, Cabron."

Cobra looked across the dusty parade ground. There was very little wind, but a shimmer of heat, especially over the paved road that ran around the perimeter. "I had sunglasses when I was arrested. Polarized."

Carvahal produced them from a pocket with a flourish. "El Lider Maximo is waiting, Shooter. He is anxious to see a reconstruction of your sparing of his life."

"You haven't told me what I'm to shoot." Cobra climbed up

onto the table and kneaded a groove in the sandbag with his thumbs. He placed the rifle on the bag and set the cartridges beside it; he made no move to load.

"A man will be driven by in a jeep. The limousine is undergoing modifications suggested by your enterprise; an armored bubble just like the American president uses. The passenger in the back seat of the jeep will be smoking a cigar."

"Who is the man?"

"A volunteer. An American, actually, but don't kill him; we have plans for him."

"Just like that."

"Yes. The first run will be free; you can see the target and gauge the range. It should be very close to what you had in the plaza."

I was higher, Cobra thought, and I walked the plaza many times. Worries. What do I do if the subject doesn't turn his head as Fidel did?

"Take your shot on the second pass, just as the jeep turns away, as you did in the plaza." Carvahal drew a Russian Makarov pistol and pointed it at Cobra's head. "Be careful not to train your rifle *this* way at all."

Cobra looked beyond Carvahal to the brothers Castro. They seemed to be sharing a joke. "All right. Let's begin."

Carvahal grinned. "Good shooting, Rhodesian. Believe it or not, I hope you make it." He withdrew a whistle from his pocket and blew three sharp, shrill blasts. Almost immediately a jeep with Cuban flags on the front bumper emerged from among the parked trucks and drove across the far end of the parade ground, about five hundred meters away. Cobra loaded a single round and locked the bolt as Carvahal watched, holding the pistol two meters from his temple. Cobra picked up his subject easily in the telescopic sight, a big, dark-complected man with a thick black beard, dressed in fatigues and flat-crowned cap, lighting a big cigar as the jeep moved off. He looked very much like Fidel. The jeep reached the far corner of the field and turned toward the grandstands. Cobra measured the speed with his eye; the Cubans were playing him straight, at least so far; Carvahal might have a reason for wanting him to make the shot, but what of Fidel?

The shooter forced his breathing to slow. He had had hours in the warehouse to lower himself into the near-trance state, heart rate and breathing to minimums so his body would impart no movement to the rifle. He always allowed himself time to ready his body and mind but now there was no time. He could feel his blood pumping as he slid in behind the rifle and braced his weight on his elbows. The image in the scope moved slightly but perceptibly in time with the pulse in his cheek. Deeper, deeper, he willed himself. Nirvana, a place of perfect harmony, stillness. Nirvana in Sanskrit meant no wind.

The jeep turned left in the middle of the parade field, about two hundred meters away, simulating the short block of Avenida Jose Marti in the capital's central plaza. When it turned again as if in front of the cathedral, he would fire. Cobra saw it all and saw nothing. Not this time; he'll drive by again. The image continued to move in time with his vital rhythm. The American's face was clear as he sucked vigorously on the cigar. He was very young and seemed at ease. A very brave man, Cobra thought as the jeep turned away. Brave or perhaps uninformed.

Just there. A shot across the jeep would take the cigar cleanly. Cobra's breathing slowed and his world became the crosshairs and the black cigar that looked finer than they did. Cobra allowed his elbow bridge to relax as the jeep turned at the top of the field and made ready for its second run, but he maintained his mental focus. He heard Carvahal ask a question but didn't answer. Carvahal blew his whistle twice and the jeep came on.

Cobra came up in his elbows, the rifle balanced lightly on the fulcrum of the sandbag. The image was crisp as the jeep made its first slow turn. On the first pass he had noted the rough places in the road that caused the subject to bounce; he hoped the second turn would be on smooth pavement as it had before. The jeep was still on "Avenida Marti" when he began squeezing the trigger, adding pressure in each still period of his heart. The subject's profile was clear, the cigar jutting at a rakish angle. Cobra was shocked wide awake by the shot when it broke, but his eye never left the scope. The cigar disappeared.

Cobra stood on the desk, leaving the rifle. The jeep jerked forward and swerved as the driver panicked; the subject rolled out of the jeep flailing his arms and legs in the dust. He jumped to his feet, his false beard askew and missing his hat. He looked around at the grandstands. "Holy jumpin' Jehosaphat!" he bellowed in English. "What the fuck was that?"

Uninformed, Cobra thought. He stepped down from the desk. Fidel and Raul rocked with laughter as the American continued to dart his eyes around in search of his assailant.

The laughter of scared men trying to look brave, Cobra thought. Carvahal picked up the rifle and cradled it under his arm. "Wait here, Cabron."

Cobra sat on the edge of the desk as Carvahal climbed down the steps of the grandstand and walked over to the knot of giggling soldiers surrounding the Castro brothers. The jeep remained in the middle of the field, its motor idling. The American calmed down and stood limp, his head bowed. Cobra yawned. He always felt very sleepy after a shot broke; he supposed because his shallow breathing and slowed heart rate deprived his brain of oxygen—sometimes he was almost too lethargic to execute his escape. Today there could be no escape.

Carvahal presented the Carcano to Fidel, who examined it quickly then handed it to his brother. Carvahal saluted and trotted back to the grandstand beneath Cobra. He was breathing hard when he reached the booth. "Congratulations, Cabron. You're to live again."

To what end? Cobra wondered idly. He covered a great yawn. A show trial and back to the dungeon?

"I'm to take you back to the capital, get you cleaned up, and let you rest. Tomorrow you will fly to Mexico City, then on to Dallas, Texas."

"What do I do there?"

"Go to a certain hotel and wait. A man will find you and give you a job to do and some money. Not much; we're a poor revolution, but enough to survive."

"Who is this man?"

"He will call himself Howard Fernandez."

"Afterwards I'm free to go?"

"To disappear. Cobras know how to disappear."

Cobra was flown from Havana to Mexico City on a small Tupolev transport in the red, white, and blue livery of Cubana de Aviacion. There were several other passengers, mostly officials of the revolution dressed in the obligatory green fatigues. Cobra wore civilian clothes Carvahal had given him, a seersucker suit and cotton shirt, a knit tie, and cheap shoes. The clothes fitted him poorly; the label in the suit said "Sears, Roebuck and Co., Chicago."

The only other passenger in civilian clothes was the young American who had ridden the jeep smoking as Cobra aimed and shot. He was seated forward with more senior officials; he glanced back at Cobra a few times but made no attempt to approach him. Cobra kept to himself, glad to be out of Cuba, content to wait to see what would happen next.

The officials departed in Mexico City but Cobra and the American were escorted across the airport to a Viscount turboprop of Aeronaves de Mexico. The American was a big man, handsome with a dark, smooth face. He looked very young, younger even than Cobra, who was nineteen. Cobra looked at him with an African's practiced eye and felt certain the man had Negro blood, just a bit. The man winked at him and grinned as Mexican officials gravely studied his new Spanish passport, provided by Carvahal in Havana. Cobra noted the American used a green U.S. passport, perhaps even his own. When they boarded the plane, the American sat across the aisle but said nothing until the doors closed and the Viscount began to taxi away from the terminal. He leaned over and beckoned with a finger. "Name's Rupert J. Tolliver. You the shooter damn near blowed my head off." Cobra didn't offer a name for himself, but shook the proffered hand. "A demonstration for Fidel. No offense intended."

"Hell, none taken. Damn glad you can shoot some."

"I take it you weren't warned."

"Fuckin' Cubans! Said they was shootin' a movie an' old Fidel gets carsick."

"What were you doing in Cuba?"

"Just visiting my conscience, friend. Where I come from up yonder in Texas it's so God-an'-country you got to carry a flag an' two Bibles an' pray for a third, but I think this damn Kennedy feller is about to get us into a war, if not with Cuba, then in some far-off Godforsaken corner of Asia. I reckon a young man's got to stop that if he can."

"What will your government do if they find out you've been in Cuba?"

Tolliver winked again. "They'll not likely draft me into the army, and that's a fact."

Ah, Cobra thought. Where have all the flowers gone?

"You ain't American, are you, boy?"

"No." Cobra turned to look out the window.

"Where, then?" Tolliver pressed.

Cobra patted the phony passport in his coat pocket.

"Spain."

"Sure," Tolliver guffawed. "Well, boy, when you get back to *Spain,* remember my name. My ambition is to be President of the United States one day."

Cobra grinned. The kid was so silly he was fun. "I'll remember."

5

PRESIDENT JOHN F. KENNEDY dropped the red and white FBI folder on the floor next to his rocking chair with a slap. His brother sat opposite him in the living room of the family quarters in the

White House. A fire crackled low in the grate; the first chill of autumn was early in Washington, only the fifteenth of November. "Bobby, we knew Hoover had files."

"He threatens to use them against you, against your reelection."

"Yet he gave them to you."

"Copies. Excerpts."

The president rubbed his sore back beneath his suit jacket. "So what? Marilyn, poor dear. It was long ago."

Bobby leaned forward. "It was last month, Jack, in this very room."

The president chuckled. "Hoover can't know that."

"He does. Also Judy Campbell, and he knows of the connection to Sam Giancana."

"More 'n we did, at the time. Hell, Bobby, I like a little pussy. Every red-blooded American would cheer if he knew."

"Men, perhaps. Fifty-six percent of the men in this country voted for Nixon, Jack. Women put you in the White House."

The president took a sip of scotch whisky. "You really think he'd disclose this shit?"

"You willing to bet he won't?"

Jack grinned. "What's he got on you?"

The attorney general held his own file in his lap. "Nothing to compare."

"Come on," the president said playfully. "Let me see."

Bobby reluctantly passed the slip folder across. "I'm not the president, Jack."

The president opened the file, leafed through, and tossed it on top of his own. "What about Dr. King?"

"Enough shit to destroy him and everyone who has befriended him. We'll have to distance ourselves."

"He's a good man, Bobby. Smart. Reasonable."

Bobby shook his head. "There's just too much, Jack. Hoover has us by the balls."

Jack lit a cigar and rocked. "I'm not letting that old bastard run me out of this house, Bobby."

"We have to trap him. Find some way to discredit him, arrest him away from his office, then seal it and get the damn files."

"Arrest John Edgar Hoover?" The president chuckled. "Neat trick."

"It has to be done. We have to do to him what he's doing to us—to you."

"What? Snoop? What's he like, Bobby, little boys?" Bobby didn't answer. "You know something, don't you, little brother."

"Something better you did not."

The president rocked forward and stood up, once again rubbing his back. "OK, Bobby, find out what you can. I've got to fly down to Dallas to make a speech, rub Lyndon's tummy in front of the home folks. When I get back we'll decide what to do about Mr. Hoover."

6

COBRA MADE HIS WAY to Dallas and checked into the dilapidated rooming house Lieutenant Carvahal had told him about. He roamed the city center as he had been instructed, eating and drinking little, conserving the meager advance the Cubans had provided. He bought some new clothes, and every afternoon he waited in his room from five to seven to be contacted.

On the third day of his unproductive vigil, he was startled from a doze by a soft knock on the flimsy door to his room. He opened it, and a big middle-aged man running to fat with an improbable reddish wig and glasses with thick lenses and heavy black frames slid into the shabby room without a word. He was carrying a black case with the silhouette of a tennis racket stenciled on the side. This he placed on Cobra's sagging single bed, as he waved at the shooter to close the door. "You're Cobra." The man made it a statement not a question. "Call me Fernandez."

"Mr. Fernandez," Cobra said, leaning against the wall as Fernandez settled heavily on the bed next to his case. The rusty springs of the mattress protested. "I was promised money."

Fernandez withdrew a plain white envelope, badly creased, from the inside pocket of his worn leather jacket. He handed it to Cobra, who opened the flap and peered inside. Hundred-dollar bills, a thick stack encircled with a rubber band.

"You're to do a job for that. It's full payment in advance, because my masters want you to disappear immediately after it's done. Needless to say, if you think to run without performing your mission, I'll find you."

Needless to say, Cobra thought, pocketing the money. His total wealth had hit a lifetime high. "What's the job?"

"In due course. It's easy, really. You're backup for a guy who's going to take the shot. You're only there in case he fucks it up."

"When do I meet this guy?"

"You don't. He'll take the fall; a lone crazy. That's why you have to make your escape." He popped the catches on the black case. Inside packed in foam rubber cut to fit were the components of a Mannlicher Carcano 6.5mm bolt-action carbine with an 8x scope, the twin of the rifle he had been given on his way to Cuba.

Cobra picked up the stock and the barrel. "I've seen this type before. Piece of shit."

"It is, but we've got cases of them, untraceable. Shot, if you have to take it, is less than a hundred yards."

Cobra shrugged. "Lay it out for me."

Fernandez did. Cobra was to conceal himself in a stand of shrubs on a low hill overlooking the city's central plaza. The target would be riding in an open car, perhaps with a bulletproof bubble protecting him, perhaps not. The primary shooter would take him from behind from a high hide. Cobra was to shoot if the first guy missed, if the shot didn't look fatal, or if the plastic bubble was in place, blocking the primary's shot. Cobra would be shooting at his target from ahead and to the target's right. "Seems straightforward enough, except maybe the escape from so close," Cobra said, patting the money folded into his hip pocket. "Payment seems generous. Why?"

"Because we have to be sure, and because the target is the President of the United States." Fernandez heaved himself up from the squeaky bed and left without another word.

Two days later, Cobra carried out his end of the contract. He had scouted his position carefully, noting the only interference with his gun-target line might be spectators lining the route, but he had enough altitude on what later became known as "the grassy knoll" to see over them. He had located a manhole over a reeking sewer and opened it; that was where he would dump the rifle. He had of course cleaned and reset the rifle and the scope. He had no access to reloading machinery so he had to rely on store-bought ammunition, absurdly easy to buy in Texas.

The Saturday of the mission dawned cool and cloudless, what passed for autumn in Dallas. There was no protective bubble on the Lincoln. Cobra saw his target clearly in the telescopic sight, and he saw the man's head snap forward as the primary's round hit. The round seemed to exit through the man's throat, a probably fatal shot. Cobra put his in anyway, snapping the president's head back, exploding the skull. Cobra dumped the rifle, reseated the manhole cover, and walked away.

He made his way to the bus station and took the first one out of state, to New Orleans. He wanted to leave the country, for Europe or Latin America, but the Spanish passport the Cubans had given was such a shoddy forgery that it was literally falling apart. He had no other papers; no birth or baptismal certificate a travel agent said could be used to obtain a Mexican tourist card, no social security card and no driving license, so he couldn't work. He had no way to reach the Cubans or Mr. Fernandez, and after he saw the pictures of Lee Harvey Oswald being gunned down inside the Dallas Police headquarters, he had no desire to.

Early in 1964, he was nearly out of money, alone, and scared. Five thousand dollars went rather easily when one had to move every day. The newspapers said people had heard shots (he knew of course there had been only one) from the grassy knoll, and there were newspaper photos of people pointing.

He was tired of running. He did the only thing a healthy young man with no identity papers could do.

He joined the United States Marine Corps.

7

Rupert Tolliver heard about the assassination while deer hunting on a disused ranch in the Hill Country in south Texas. The ranch was owned by some cousins, all much more rabid Kennedy-haters than Rupert. Rupert hadn't liked Kennedy's politics or his much-admired style, but he bore the president no personal animus. He was chilled to think that he had a loaded rifle in his hands the moment the president was shot. He was very quiet when the news was repeated over and over, heard over a little transistor radio in the deer blind. His cousins whooped and hollered and got into the whiskey early.

Tolliver thought about the unblinking, hard black eyes of the shooter from Cuba, the one with the Spanish passport who had got off the plane with him in Dallas barely a week ago, and felt colder still.

II

THE JOURNEY

1

December 1999

JULIA EARLY LOOKED out the window of the American Airlines Boeing 767 at the Mississippi River far below. So many exiting things were happening to her for the first time, and this airplane, the biggest she had ever seen let alone ridden in, carrying her on the final leg of her journey from the dry Texas Hill Country to a new life in Washington, D.C., was the biggest thrill of all.

It seemed like she had been traveling for a week. She'd cleaned out her desk in the tiny office across the street from the Governor's Mansion in Austin and had been given a big send-off by the other junior staffers on the campaign committee. With Governor Rupert Justice Tolliver safely reelected, all the staffers would be going to new jobs, many like Julia's arranged with the help of the governor's office. It was sad to move away from good friends, fellow crusaders, but wonderful to be going to a wider world.

Julia drove home to Uvalde to spend Christmas with her mother and to leave her jeep. She packed the few real city clothes she had, hoping she had enough saved to buy some more professional-looking suits appropriate to her new job as a management trainee at Capital National Bank, Washington's oldest and most venerable. On a chill third of January she took an all-night bus ride to San Antonio, then a little American Eagle plane to Dallas, now at last the big Luxury Liner on to Washington.

Julia was one of the original Justice Girls—Governor Tolliver used his middle name in preference to his first— recruited from his home county during his first run for the statehouse four years ago. She was eighteen at the time, just beginning at the university, when the fiery orator and former television preacher revealed that God had told him to go to Austin to do the people's business, to clean out the stable of influence-peddling and outright corruption that Texas politics had become—some said always had been since the days of Sam Houston, old Big Drunk himself. As a preacher Tolliver had been a spellbinder, but as a politician he had shown a greater gift, and his oddball candidacy spread out from the Hill Country like wildfire as he thumped and roared and vowed to make government work for all Texans but especially for the "left aside": poor redneck farmers, disenfranchised urban blacks, Latino refugees cruelly ignored by the prosperous Mexican-American middle class. His energetic campaign had taken Texas insiders by storm, and Tolliver overwhelmed a promising Republican congressman in the primary, then the incumbent Democratic governor, and preached his way all the way to Austin. Julia had seen the entire campaign, first as a cheerleader warming up crowds on high school football fields and later as a campaign aide stuffing envelopes and working the phones. In the second campaign she worked in fund-raising and saw a different side of the business of politics.

Julia accepted a soft drink from a passing flight attendant with thanks. She opened her brand-new briefcase— presented by the governor himself at her going-away party and withdrew the letter from the bank's chairman, a famous Washington insider and adviser to presidents, Colonel Alfred Thayer. She smoothed it on the soft leather and read it for the hundredth time. Management Trainee with a salary of thirty-nine thousand dollars a year! She knew it was the lowliest entry position for a college graduate, but it seemed such a long way from hardscrabble sagebrush Texas. The colonel (or whoever wrote his letters) took noncommittal note of her preference for the bank's international department. Julia knew most of the bank's business was overseas, that was one of two reasons she had chosen it over larger New York rivals. The other reason was that a girl bitten with the bug of politics wanted to taste the crackle and hum of government at the national level.

She turned to the second page. At the bottom below Colonel

Thayer's round signature: cc Governor Rupert Justice Tolliver. She guessed she owed him, but she had given hundreds of hours to the campaigns with no promise of this or any reward. Tolliver was a complex man beneath the thundering prophet of his public persona; controversial, though he didn't seem to care. He was gentle and caring in public but given to arrogance and rages behind the scenes. His staff loved him and feared him. Julia believed in him because he seemed relentless in pursuit of the corrupt, the deceitful, and in his word, the ungodly. She knew he took a drink now and then to relax and she'd heard the rumors that he stepped out now and again on his beautiful cold-eyed wife. The staff, even the guards from the Texas Ranger Executive Detail, called him Sunflower and her Stoneheart. She was his strength, he always said on the hustings. Be careful, she frequently charged the Justice Girls. Julia wondered. Tolliver had always treated her like a lady—well, a pat on the bottom now and then, a squeeze, but nothing more. One of the girls from San Antonio had left the campaign with appendicitis and never returned, and of course people talked, but people will talk about anything.

Julia folded her letter, closed her eyes, and retraced the plans she had in her mind for a little apartment in the leafy district she'd been told lay southeast of the Capitol.

RUPERT JUSTICE TOLLIVER sat in his spacious second-floor office in the Greek Revival Governor's Mansion in Austin, brooding and doodling on a yellow legal-size pad. Ezekiel Archer, his chief of staff, lawyer, a deacon in his church and some said his conscience, stood beside the desk with an armful of legislative briefs. "Justice, you don't hardly seem overjoyed at the prospect of four more years as the people's high servant in Austin."

Tolliver grunted. "Glad to get on with the people's work, Zeke, 'course I am." He looked up at his old friend and wondered when he'd next have a chance to hold Archer's black-eyed Mexican wife in his arms. Texas and its politics, especially the dreary legislative shit like the folders in his aide's arms, were suddenly boring old news. "What d'you have there?"

"Markups on the crime bill, the extension of local-option prohibition, a new gay rights bill—"

"VWR," the governor said, knitting his fingers behind his head. Veto Without Reading.

"The gays are going to keep picketing and complaining, Juss. Might be better to throw them a bone."

"Fucking faggots. Hurry on, God's righteous plague."

"You're going to have to moderate those views if you've got national ambitions."

Tolliver looked sly. "Who says I do?"

"You're fixin' to run for president, Juss."

"Maybe." Tolliver drew more doodles. "This office does seem a might confining after four years of horse trading and horseshit, but I can't see why I have to change my view of faggots that comes straight from the Lord's book."

"Leviticus twenty-thirteen, if memory serves."

"It does."

"If you won't change your views, change how you say them."

Tolliver ripped the top sheet off the yellow pad and crumpled it. He threw it at a wastebasket three feet away and missed. Archer set his briefs on the edge of the desk, picked the paper up, and smoothed it. " 'Send Justice to Washington.' Very original." Tolliver's slogan in his first campaign had been "Send Justice to Austin."

Tolliver scowled. "Man be a damned fool throw up a sweet perch like this 'n to go to Washington, take shit from a bunch of Jews and damn Yankees."

"But you want it."

Tolliver grinned. "Think what I could do with the presidency as a pulpit. The damned liberals would be dancing and spitting like raindrops on a hot skillet."

"You better go if you're going, Juss. Election's in thirteen months, New Hampshire primary's in four."

"Forget New Hampshire. That pursed-lipped Irishman, Senator Joseph Bow-to-Rome Donahue, will win that. If I go for it it'll be grass-roots, back of the pickup, Friday night speeches and Sunday church suppers." Tolliver jumped to his feet and clapped his hands like a delighted child. He was a big man with a dark, craggy face that reminded his friends of Abraham Lincoln and his enemies of the devil himself. "We go forth into the south, Brother Archer."

"America isn't Texas, Juss."

"Who says it isn't?" Tolliver walked to the window and looked at the domed Texas state capitol four hundred yards to the northeast. It looked very much like the Capitol in Washington. "You saying the American people wouldn't vote for a redneck preacher who'd tell 'em the truth? You think the American people are any less weary of corruption and greed and influence-selling in the halls of Congress than the people of Texas were when they sent me here with a shovel and a broom?"

Archer smiled. Juss is already writing his speeches, he thought. Tolliver had indeed ridden to his first inaugural in the back of a farmer's stake truck holding a coal shovel and a push broom promising to "muck out the capital." Sophisticates in Austin and Dallas snickered at the rube gesture and legislators made angry speeches about the disrespectful symbolism, but muck it out Tolliver had. "People in the rest of the country don't love God as we do, Juss."

"We are privileged to love God, Zeke. Others need only learn to fear Him."

Archer shook his head. Juss was naive, but wasn't easily dissuaded. "The city liberals will be nipping at your flanks as soon as you break cover."

"Let 'em try, Zeke. They'll snap and I'll snap back, and when the bitin's done we'll see who's got the teeth marks and on what parts of their bodies." He picked up the briefs off the corner of his desk and pushed them back in Archer's arms. "Do whatever you think is right with this tiresome stuff, Ezekiel. I got a crusade to think up."

2

THE MAN CALLED COBRA sat under an acacia tree on his farm on a plateau north of Stellenbosch in the Cape Province of the Republic of South Africa. He had a laptop computer on a small, somewhat rickety, folding table, a pitcher of gin slings, a bucket of ice, and his tattered journal. He'd bought the vast, dry farm with its quite promising vineyards in 1981 from an old white man who had given up on the racial politics of apartheid despite the gradual emergence of men of goodwill on both sides of the deep color divide that went back generations. He had the money from his campaigns with the legendary Major Mad Mike Harris, boosted by a handful of diamonds from his last and most profitable shot, the elimination of a Russian nationalist extremist. The job had involved killing a retired general and presidential candidate in Russia's elections of 1994, probably the most heavily guarded man on the planet. The shot had been over a thousand yards on a winter's day with light wind and snow in the swirling urban canyons of central St. Petersburg. Cobra had been well paid by the Russian government, and even better by the Americans. Neither knew of the other's involvement. Or so Cobra believed.

Cobra felt he had earned his retirement. This year he would turn fifty-one years old, but it had been a hard life of danger and war and wounds, both physical and psychic. He liked the quiet life of the country; his workers and tenants, all inherited from the seller, needed minimal supervision, and riding among the vines and across the open veldt gave him pleasure of owning, actually controlling, a vast open place. Cobra had spent too much of his life hiding in small spaces, waiting in damp darkness.

The farm was self-sustaining, not really profitable, although South African wines were finding increasing interest in overseas markets. Cobra had more than enough money invested in Belgium and Switzerland to last out his days in modest comfort if he was careful. Others had made more in the business of hunting men, but none that he knew of was alive to sit in the cool shade of his own acacia tree, writing his memoirs.

The memoirs could not be published until after his death, if ever. He had considered casting the story as a novel, written under a pseudonym, of course. Perhaps he would, but first he had to get the story written down, fleshed out from the laconic notes he had made after each job. It was tedious work, but he had nothing but time.

He set the laptop aside, took a sip of gin, and closed his eyes.

3

CAPITAL NATIONAL BANK arranged and paid for a room for Julia in a quiet women's residence hotel near the campus of George Washington University. She could stay for three weeks at Mary Custis House while she got organized and found an apartment of her own. Her supervisor, the bank's head of Recruitment and Training, a rather grave middle-aged man named Reginald Hollis, assigned her a desk in a large bay in the Credit Department on the eighth floor of the bank, then gave her a packet of personnel forms to fill out, and told her to find a place and get settled; her formal training cycle wouldn't start for a month.

Hollis walked Julia through the Credit Department—the bay where her desk was in one of four long rows leading from the windows on the north end facing the Willard Hotel to a blank wall in the center of the building. Seniority began at the windows and ran inward; Julia's desk was hard by the wall. All the desks faced east at a row of offices with frosted glass walls. Hollis had the corner office, and the other two were occupied by the head of Credit Analysis, Doris Masters, and the bank's International Economist, Gerry Brain. Neither was in, so Hollis took Julia along each row of desks and introduced her to the "window rank"—the heads of each region—and her fellow trainees, all of whom, like her, were to begin in Credit.

There were twenty-four trainees and eight empty desks. The young men and women were from nine different countries and eight different states. Julia was the only one from Texas, or anyplace in the Southwest. Everyone seemed bright, friendly, and best of all, relaxed. Julia was herself nervous, but the group seemed not to notice.

"Got you over at Custis?" a pretty auburn-haired woman named Judith Langtry, from London, asked.

"Yes," Julia said. "I just dropped my stuff and crashed last night, rushed over here this morning."

Judith rummaged in her desk drawer, came up with a wrinkled business card. "Here's a rental agent the bank puts us on to," she said, handing the card to Julia. Capital Realty. "They're nice, and have nice listings. Why not give them a ring, go round this afternoon? Then let's get on to lunch."

Julia sat and dialed. She appreciated Judith's warmth. She was one of only three other women in the program, the others a very pretty, haughty-looking Frenchwoman and a shy, tiny woman from Hong Kong who looked about fifteen years old.

Mrs. Wilson of Capital Realty welcomed Julia to Washington and congratulated her on her employment with Capital National Bank. She would be happy to show Julia some rentals if she would come by the agency at two o'clock. The office was only three blocks away, on 12th Street. Could Julia give her some idea of price range and location?

Julia had no idea of what she should pay, and no knowledge of Washington beyond what she had been told about Southeast. "I just started here at the bank," she confided to Mrs. Wilson, then whispered her salary that had seemed a huge amount down in Texas.

"Hm." Mrs. Wilson said, sounding disappointed. "Come in, we'll talk. Would you consider sharing?"

Sharing? Roommates? The suggestion was unexpected and disturbing. Roommates were bad enough in college, where at least you knew them. Julia couldn't imagine sharing an apartment in an alien city with a total stranger. How high could rents be in Washington?

Judith stood in front of her desk, her Coach bag over her shoulder. "Lunch, then? Hilda's joining us." Hilda Chu was the beautiful Chinese child.

"You bet," Julia said, standing. "I'll get my coat."

"You won't need the coat. Unless you're of independent means, you can't afford a restaurant within a mile of this place. Lunch for our lot means the dreaded, but subsidized, ninth-floor employee feedlot. Come on."

Julia followed Judith and Hilda to the elevator. Jesus, thirty-nine thousand a year was a lot of money! Wasn't it?

The ninth floor proved to be a cafeteria, busy with mostly young men and women, all in banker's drab. The food was institutional and uninspiring, but certainly cheap. Julia followed Hilda, who selected a salad with gray tuna fish and hard-looking tomatoes, and Judith, who took a wrapped hamburger and coleslaw. Julia was hungry and went for Salisbury steak, mashed potatoes, gravy, and string beans, all in shades of gray. Hilda took hot tea while Judith and Julia each picked a diet soda out of a bin of shaved ice. The three women found an empty six-place Formica table next to the windows overlooking F Street. The afternoon was dark and it had started to snow.

Dreary day for apartment-hunting, Julia thought, sawing a piece off the Salisbury steak, fighting to control it as it slipped around the plate in greasy gravy.

"We should have warned you about the daily blue-plate special," Hilda said with a giggle. She modestly covered her mouth with her hand as she laughed. These were the first words she had spoken to Julia after "hello."

Julia got a morsel to her mouth, dipped in mashed potato. It wasn't all that bad to a woman from the world of chicken-fried steak, just mortally overcooked. "I have a lot to learn of local customs. I hope you two will help me."

"All I can tell you about the food is that it's worse than English pub grub, and I honestly wouldn't have thought that possible," Judith said around a mouthful of hamburger that looked as though it had been stepped on. She turned the conversation to the bank, the training program, and the capital's extravagant social life. Judith had a quick wit and a raunchy sense of humor, and Julia hoped the Englishwoman would be her guide and her friend. Hilda said little, and seemed a little embarrassed by Judith's descriptions of Hollis, the other bank officers in Credit, and the other trainees. Judith fixed Julia with a curious stare. "How'd you get on with dotty old Mrs. Wilson?"

Julia hacked another bit of slippery meat off, added mash, and chewed it. It was so tough that she was unable to answer for half a minute. The beans were cold, fibrous, and tasteless. "She asked how much I wanted to pay. I didn't know, so I told her my salary. She didn't sound impressed."

"Rents are fierce in the District," Judith said. She and Hilda exchanged glances.

"How much should I have to pay?"

"In a decent area? Southeast, Georgetown? Mrs. Wilson will show you. Up in the north corner, less, but it's awfully dark up there if you get my drift."

Julia knew most of the District was black. She nodded.

"A one-bedroom could run two thousand a month, unfurnished," Judith continued. "Across the river in Arlington or Alexandria, or over in Maryland, much less, but it's so inconvenient getting home after the parties, and so hard dragging back into the office the morning after."

Two thousand a month. After taxes she would be making about twenty-six hundred a month. Her heart sank. God, roommates, how awful. She gave up on the tasteless meal and glanced at her watch. "I'd better go. I'm due over at the realtor at two."

Judith stood and held out her hand. Julia shook. "Run around with the old trout, but be cautious. She'll show you lovely flats you can't possibly afford, then run you out to the student ghettos way up Connecticut Avenue, find you a *fabulous* studio for only a thousand a month, but you must put your deposit down this instant or all will be lost. Do yourself a favor: before you agree to anything, even if you like the garret, call me here, or call Hilda; run it by us, as you Yanks say."

"I will," Julia said. "Thanks." She rode the elevator down one floor to Credit, got her new Burberry raincoat, and went out into the snow.

Three hours later, tired, chilled, and wet through, Julia called Judith from the "fabulous" flat Mrs. Wilson—a big, forceful woman who obviously thought showing low-priced rental apartments a task far beneath her—was pressing her to rent "before it was gone. A matter of hours, dear." It was a dreary studio on a trash-strewn street, as predicted, on upper Connecticut Avenue.

"Hilda and I have talked," Judith said warmly. "We weren't entirely candid with you earlier; we had to size you up. Washington is a difficult town."

"What do you think I should do?" Julia asked, fighting to keep despair out of her voice.

"Today? Nothing. Hilda and I would like to show you our place. Georgetown, good location, two bedrooms each with two beds so that if a girl gets lucky—well, you know. Come have a look; if you like the place and us as we like you, perhaps you'd like to be our flat mate."

Julia kicked off a ruined shoe and rubbed her ice-cold foot. Across the room Mrs. Wilson stared malevolently. "I'd like very much to see your place. And I do like you both."

Smart politicians, Julia thought, as Rupert Justice Tolliver often said, knew the difference between attainable pretty good solutions and unattainable perfect ones.

Julia went to Judith and Hilda's apartment off Wisconsin Avenue in Georgetown as soon as she had showered, changed and thrown away her ruined new shoes at Mary Custis House. The two-bedroom flat was small but airy, and nicely furnished with pieces made of real solid wood. Nothing fancy, but better than the sticks in the furnished places Mrs. Wilson had shown earlier. Julia could see that both women were tidy and clean in their habits, as she was.

She had two glasses of wine and a slice of pizza from the corner shop, and agreed to move in. Her share of the rent was nine hundred dollars a month.

She moved in the next Saturday, received a credit for the time not spent at Mary Custis, and was taken to lunch by her new boss, Larry Taggart. He was a gay man in his late twenties, well out of the closet, and was in charge of the Americas and Caribbean. The other three areas were Asia, the Middle East and Africa, and Europe. Julia hoped to end up in any of those, but the training assignment was said to have no influence on one's later territory. Larry, earrings, ruffled shirts, and all, was silly but charming, and she could tell he knew credit. Her first real day on the job he gave her the guidelines for credit analysis, her computer access code, and three annual reports to spread and review: Banco Ganadero in Peru, Cayman Islands Trust Company of Grand Cayman, and Uvalde County Savings and Loan Society of Uvalde, Texas.

"Get right on the last one, sugar," Larry said. "No one here or upstairs has any idea how it got in here to begin with."

4

February 2000

Rupert Justice Tolliver sat in his darkened office with Ezekiel Archer. Each had a large cut-glass tumbler of Jack Daniel's whiskey in his hand; a bucket of ice and pitcher of water were on the table in front of them, between their feet. A television in the corner, its volume turned low, carried an account of the New Hampshire primary. As expected, Senator Joseph Donahue from

Connecticut had finished first in a field of five, but with only 29 percent of the vote.

"Piss-poor," Tolliver said matter-of-factly. "That priest-ridden boy didn't knock anyone out; didn't even scare anyone."

"What's it gonna be, Juss?"

"How many primaries we entered in?"

"All of 'em, 'cept California, where our 'Draft Justice' committees are still gathering signatures, but that one's a way's off yet."

"We'll get there? Hard to win without California."

"We'll get there. As soon as you declare, the signatures will come in."

"Then let's do it." Tolliver popped his feet off the coffee table and stood. "Let's run for president, Zeke."

Archer stood and shook the big man's hand. "Thursday afternoon, on the steps of the Capitol across the way? I have your speech ready."

"Good. Let's get her done. I'm gonna enjoy this, Zeke."

JULIA IMMERSED HERSELF in the dry credit files and the often more interesting correspondence files that went with them. Her compulsion to make a good impression, to show the better-educated and more sophisticated bankers and trainees that she wasn't a hopeless country bumpkin, earned her a bit of chaff from Judith, who berated her as a grind who was missing too many "required parties" and making the others look lazy. Julia laughed off the criticism but it hurt; the truth was she felt genuinely inferior.

Fortunately the computer was her ally. She quickly mastered the bank's analysis program, a template on Excel, and made a few improvements that allowed her to highlight anything that deviated from the canned ratios automatically. Despite Larry's request that she begin with Uvalde County S. and L., she ran the two other banks first, because the files were current and in good shape. Both Banco Ganadero and Cayman Islands Trust were well within guidelines for the credit Capital National Bank allowed them, lines of credit for settlement of money transfers and letters of credit used to finance trade.

The file of Uvalde County was a different matter entirely. There were great gaps in the information, missing annual and quarterly reports, 10ks and other securities filings, and income-tax returns. The account with Capital National was opened three years ago, but statements indicated little activity until only a month ago, when balances suddenly went from a few tens of thousands to over $10 million.

Julia thought all this odd, and she remembered Larry's offhand remark that neither Credit nor the account executives—"upstairs" he called them—knew where the account had come from. Capital National dealt only with the largest and best-managed banks in the world, and with almost none in the United States outside of a few giants in New York, San Francisco, Chicago, and Houston.

She completed the spreadsheet as best she could, noted that Capital National cleared payments for Uvalde in Europe, the Caribbean, and the Bahamas but did not extend it credit, and wrote a memo to the account officer suggesting that current statements be requested from Uvalde. Her memo came back, initialed, with a notation that she flag the file and review it again in six months.

Shit, Julia thought, as she returned the file to the library. A flagged file meant she had to stay on top of it as long as she was in Credit, even if, as she hoped, she was soon assigned to more interesting areas. She noted the flag in the computer and on the file itself, and decided to forget about it.

LIFE IN WASHINGTON WAS gradually becoming less frightening and more fun. Julia counted herself lucky that she had moved in with Judith and Hilda; if she had found her dream flat she probably would have never left it due to shyness. Julia and Hilda shared a room, because Judith, in Hilda's words, handled the sex for the three of them. Judith was so full of energy and joie de vivre that the two more retiring roommates met people and partied whether they would have chosen to or not.

Washington, Julia discovered, was a city filled with young people from everywhere else. The people her age were all attached to the Congress or wanted to be if they were American, and to embassies if they were not. Most of the Americans and some of the foreigners were harried, overworked, and underpaid to the point of being downright poor. Power and influence were the currencies they craved and traded in; if one had the right "rabbi"—a powerful congressman or senator, the right committee staff assignment, or the right embassy posting—one could eat, drink, and party for free. People who actually worked for "the government," the executive departments, were "lame"—without power.

It was a game for men, but some women played it with the best. For the rest of the women in the Georgetown-Capitol axis, one had only to be pretty and willing. Judith laughed and proclaimed at any occasion that these women had power of a far older time.

A separate class of beings, with their own brand of power and influence, were the journalists. The senior people, the network anchors and the "face" reporters who covered the White House, the Capitol, and the Pentagon, were gods, but they were older. The younger reporters, especially the freelancers and stringers for minor out-of-town papers, were far down the pecking order, the hungry ones, the seekers, hoping to become Woodward or Bernstein, to develop the ultimate story, the ultimate inside source, before they were chased back to Des Moines or Nashville by abject poverty and despair.

Julia loved it all. She was pretty enough and bright enough to be a "prestige bird" on any man's arm, or quite welcome solo at parties and events given by embassies and lobbyists, the two groups who fed the capital's hungry in the hopes of influencing a vote in what was described as "the world's biggest purchasing office." Judith was in it for expensive fun and was willing to trade on her own beauty to stay in the game; Hilda was precious and unattainable; a strategy Julia thought would be more lasting, while she herself became immersed in the politics, the deals discussed, the trades made, the secrets exchanged. She once heard a bargain struck between a lobbyist for the Sugar Growers and a staffer from the Senate Agriculture Committee who had actually wrapped themselves in a velvet curtain at the Belgian embassy.

She had peeked behind a curtain at another party and seen a congressman giving oral sex to a prominent woman reporter for CBS as she leaned against the window and moaned with ecstasy. Sex and information and money were power in Washington, and power was everything.

The crazy thing to Julia, who had learned about security in the Justice Tolliver campaigns, was that these men, doing deals and trading secrets that were certainly unethical and perhaps illegal, liked to do it in front of Julia and any other pretty woman they hoped to impress. Influence and power paid off in money and sex; the equation ran both ways. Julia heard a story about a presidential adviser who had let his prostitute girlfriend listen in to his conversations with his boss, and had no trouble believing it.

She met a number of men she liked, but avoided serious entanglements. It was too much fun playing as many games as she could. One man who seemed less predatory than the others, less determined to impress rather than charm, was Charles Taylor, a man about ten years older than Julia who had had articles published in a number of second-rank news magazines and the *Washington Times*. He implied he reported for the *Times,* but Julia soon learned he was freelance. Charles approached her one Friday evening in early March in a function room at the Mayflower Hotel, a cocktail given by the American Trial Lawyers' Association Julia was attending with a junior counsel to the Food and Drug Administration. "Congratulations," Charles said. "You must be pleased."

She was puzzled. "I'm sorry; did I miss something?"

"You're from Texas, right?"

"You bet."

"Your Governor Tolliver declared his candidacy for the president. Hours ago."

"Governor *Tolliver!*" she yelped. "I worked on his gubernatorial campaigns."

"Maybe you'll have to go back," Charles said, suddenly looking very interested in the pretty but clueless banker-trainee. "Though I'd miss you."

"Oh, I don't think he'd ask me back. I was a pretty low-level volunteer."

"But you do know the man," Charles said. "Few do." He looked around to see if anyone more important was open for chat. Julia recognized the move; it was so Washington. Charles turned back to her with a big smile. "Would you like to blow this pop stand and have a little dinner?"

5

1965

COBRA, NOW CALLING HIMSELF Jack Chance, the name he had given the marine recruiters, shipped out to Vietnam in early September.

He had distinguished himself in basic training, especially in marksmanship, something far more highly regarded in the Corps than in the army. He had considered taking a little off his shooting, not drawing attention to himself while the FBI was still looking for leads to the assassination of President Kennedy, but in the end his pride wouldn't let him. Marines shot the M-14 to qualify at three hundred and five hundred yards, iron sights, no scope. The ten-ring was as big as a basketball. Cobra failed one drill because he had fired so accurately that after five rounds only a single slightly jagged hole appeared in the center of the bull's-eye. After that he always made a neat little ring about two inches in diameter until the drill instructors told him to stop.

After boot camp and Advanced Infantry Training, Cobra was sent to the Second Battalion, 26th Marines, at Camp Pendleton, California. In a rare example of the armed forces assigning someone a specialty for which he had aptitude, Cobra was trained as a sniper, qualified on scope-mounted accuritized M-14s and Remington 700 bolt-action rifles, and assigned to the battalion's Reconnaissance Platoon.

Three months after Cobra joined the battalion, it lashed up and shipped out to Okinawa, and after training there with other units destined to join the growing Marine Amphibious Force, shipped out again to Da Nang, the northern seaport in what the South Vietnamese army called its First Military Region. The marines called it simply I Corps.

Da Nang was a place of utter confusion. The port was being completely reconstructed to accommodate the American buildup, as were several airstrips. There were marines everywhere, along with all their supplies and equipment, much of it just dumped by the docks or runways, unclaimed and unguarded. The proud line infantry troops of the 2/26 were pressed into service as stevedores and construction laborers. Many men, tough enough in the dry California desert, suffered from hard work in the humid heat of the tropical jungles and steaming rice paddies that surrounded the red knee-high mud of the marine bases sprouting outside the city. Cobra was used to working all day in the wet heat of the forest-choked river valleys of North Matabeleland, and Vietnam felt almost like home.

The mission of the marines was to secure and guard the American facilities that were being put in place to assist the South Vietnamese forces, the Army of the Republic of Vietnam, or ARVN. The ARVNs were supposed to do the actual fighting against the Vietcong, from bases beyond the American enclaves and throughout the country. In practice, the ARVNs tended to camp as close to the American bases as possible, often so close that the VC could lob mortar shells and rockets right over the ARVN positions and into the Americans'. Shelling occurred almost every night, and some nights enemy sappers would slip past the ARVNs and the American outposts and drop satchel charges in fuel and ammo dumps, vehicle parks, and personnel tents. Given this reality, it was no surprise to the marines that as soon as their numbers in Da Nang were great enough, they were sent out on their own patrols to hunt the enemy's supplies by day and to disrupt his movements, find and kill him at night.

Cobra was a twenty-one-year-old lance corporal when he first killed a man legally. He found the kill oddly satisfying because this, of all of his victims, was firing back at Cobra and his squad. The VC was in a cave serving a heavy Russian-made 14.5mm KPV machine gun; Cobra easily recognized the sound. The gunner killed two marines with his first burst, and pinned the squad down next to a heavily forested, weed-choked stream with single rounds that rained down splinters and bits of leaves on the frightened men who were trying to screw themselves into the mud.

The terrain was flooded paddy on one side of the strip of high forest that followed the stream, and rugged jungle-covered hills on the other. The gunner was somewhere in the limestone cliffs. Nobody could see him, or even the smoke from his weapon. Cobra knew from sniper school that VC snipers fired their weapons dry, with virtually no lubricant in the barrels. That shortened barrel life but prevented the telltale brown smoke of burning gun oil. VC ambushers did not fire tracer rounds to avoid giving away their positions.

None in the squad had ever been shot at before that evening, not even the sergeant. The lieutenant, the platoon leader, was with them, and he wanted to call for artillery. They were close enough to the firebases inside the Da Nang perimeter, but the line wasn't good: the VC gunner was between them and the big guns.

Cobra crawled over to the fallen tree trunk that sheltered the LT and the sergeant. "I can get him, sir," he whispered.

Both men jumped. Lance Corporal Chance was known in the platoon for his ability to approach unseen and unheard, but the random flat cracks of the big Russian gun had them both on edge. "How, Jack?" the sergeant asked. "We can't see him."

"I can track him by the sound until I get a picture. I need to move up and to the right, I expect."

The sergeant and the wild-eyed LT looked at him uncomprehending. Cobra knew that a weapon made two sounds when it was fired, the first the bang of the shot going off, the noise of the cartridge exploding, expelling the bullet from the chamber. The second sound, much louder, was made by the bullet breaking the sound barrier after it left the barrel. The sonic boom was directionless, but the first sound could lead a trained ear to the weapon. They taught that in sniper school but Cobra had learned it years earlier. "All right," the LT said. "Sergeant Perez, send one man with Chance for security."

"I'd just as soon go alone, sir," Jack Chance said.

"No. The gunner out there is unlikely to be alone, and neither should you. Sergeant?"

"I'll go myself, sir."

The lieutenant shouldn't have allowed that, but he did, and Sergeant Hernando Perez followed Cobra as he climbed the riverbank, listening intently to each single round. The sergeant carried his M-14 and seemed to Cobra to make as much noise as a buffalo dragging tin cans over rocks. Cobra knew the LT was following the book, sending a rifleman to cover the sniper's back, but Lance Corporal Chance was used to operating alone and undetected. He carried his heavy Remington Model 700 with the big Redfield variable power scope and moved in silent concentration, timing the reports of his opponent's machine gun. If that gunner was alone he wouldn't be for long, and the pinned-down platoon was a sitting duck for a few rounds from a light mortar.

Cobra stopped, raising his hand to halt the sergeant, who was much too close behind him. He pulled his rifle in front of him and rested it on a fallen branch. A muzzle flash had preceded the last boom, a light no brighter than a firefly rising in an African early evening. "I see him, sergeant," Cobra whispered. The machine gun cracked, another single shot. "A muzzle flash, in the cave, there."

"Where?" the sergeant puffed. "I don't even see a fucking cave."

"There," Cobra said as the machine gun cracked again. He cranked the telescopic sight up to nine power and looked through it at the tiny cave he guessed was at least four hundred yards away. Through the scope he could see two shapes in the shadows; he thought a gunner and a loader but knew he was guessing. He worked the bolt, chambering a round. The Remington fired the same ammo as the M-14 but Cobra, like his opponent, never loaded tracers. He centered the vague shape he thought was the gunner in the crosshairs and waited, gradually increasing finger pressure on the trigger. When the VC fired, the big KPV would buck. When the gunner settled in again, Cobra would take him. The only sound in the clearing except the incessant buzz of insects and the shrieks of birds was the heavy, labored breathing of the frightened sergeant. Cobra blotted out all sound.

The machine gun fired and a second later Cobra did. His blurry target disappeared and Cobra saw the other man, his face turned toward him in the telescopic sight. Cobra worked the bolt, chambering another round without ever losing the sight picture, and drilled the face right through the center. The man fell on the tripod-mounted machine gun and Cobra saw it tilt forward and slide out of the cave. "Let's go, Sergeant."

"Jesus, you hit anything?"

"We'll know soon enough," Cobra said, slinging his rifle and turning back down the slope toward the squad. He went carefully, crouched over, but not crawling as he had on the way up.

The KPV machine gun did not speak again.

6

1966

Rupert Justice Tolliver leaned over the table in the political science building at Houston Christian University. His dark-complected face was twisted with anguish as he looked at the old professor of political science who was his faculty adviser. "I got a draft notice, Professor Johns," Rupert said. "Two weeks before graduation, I got a draft notice."

The professor stiffened. He respected young Tolliver's drive and ambition, but disliked the boy because of his excessive drive and ambition. "Couple years in the army won't hurt you, Rupert. I was in for War Two and I always felt the experience aided my understanding of God in the real world."

"I don't want to do it, sir," Rupert said, shaking his head. "No, sir, I do not. Can't see dying in some Asian swamp because Kennedy and Johnson couldn't leave well enough alone."

Professor Johns had admired President Kennedy, an uncommon view in south Texas. The Hill Country where Tolliver came from was Lyndon Johnson country. Johns wondered idly whether this big, strong-looking senior was a coward, and whether he ought to help him at all. Benefit of the doubt, he thought ruefully. Always benefit of the doubt. "You talk to your local draft board?"

"Yeah." Tolliver shook his head again. "Get me a wife and a baby real quick, or get into graduate school. They got deferments for graduate school because they have so few applicants down the Hill Country, but I have no money and haven't even applied anywhere."

"What do you want to do with your life, young Rupert?"

"Politics, sir. I want to change Texas and the nation."

Johns smiled. "You've done well enough with me, although I

doubt either one of us has demonstrated politics is a science. You could apply to law school; most legislators are lawyers."

"With no money and no time? I gotta go take a physical in four weeks."

"Maybe University of Texas at Austin might take you as a master's candidate in political science; they have that program."

Tolliver fidgeted. "Is there anything here? Anything I could get done quick?"

He is a coward, Johns thought. "Only graduate program here at Houston Christian is the divinity school. You got a calling, young Rupert?"

The professor's question had a barb on it but Tolliver swallowed it without notice. "Perhaps I do," he said slowly. Then he jumped to his feet, his tanned face splitting with a slow grin. "I surely and purely *do* believe I hear the Lord calling!"

Professor Johns shook his head and swallowed the taste of disgust. "I'll make some calls for you."

Tolliver thanked his adviser profusely and left. Two weeks later he had his admission to divinity school, and his draft deferment, and three months after that he began his studies for the ministry.

How bad could it be? He asked himself. Johnson's damn war couldn't go on forever.

AT FIRST IT WAS bad, deadly boring. The curriculum was the Bible, and little else except writings about the Bible. The rantings of St. Thomas Aquinas, the commentaries of the great monks of the middle ages who protected the church. And the church's implacable enemies, the heresies. The Cathar, or Albiguensian Heresy of the Middle Ages. The sins of venal popes and priests, the Reformation and Counter-Reformation, the black Inquisition.

Then back to the Bible, to see the clear message of Jesus, and the errors of everyone who had come after, injecting alien creeds and even gods and saints, intermediaries to salvation the Lord had never spoken of.

Rupert couldn't help himself. The message was powerful, and it began to soften his shell of cynicism. Perhaps he had been called.

7

March 2000

JUSTICE TOLLIVER TOOK a sip of water and looked out over the crowd standing in a cold rain in the Louisiana State Fair Grounds outside Baton Rouge. His throat burned from nonstop speechifying; his booming voice sometimes reduced to a tortured croak. His eyes itched from lack of sleep and the blue cigarette smoke drifting up to him from the crowd. It would be a very long day, beginning here at ten A.M. and ending in Texas at ten at night after speaking in Florida, Tennessee and Missouri. Tolliver had been crisscrossing the South for a week since his disastrous showing in New York that had the pundits branding his campaign a failed joke despite his surprising come-from-nowhere win in South Carolina a week before. Tomorrow was Super Tuesday, primaries in Florida, Hawaii, Louisiana, Massachusetts, Mississippi, Oklahoma, Rhode Island, Tennessee, and Texas. Tolliver gave himself no chance in Massachusetts or Rhode Island. Senator Joseph Fucking Donahue of Connecticut had taken the Liberal Northeast: Vermont and Delaware in addition to New Hampshire. Donahue had even taken Arizona and South Dakota, conservative states that should have gone for Tolliver if he had had any money or organization in either one. Donahue had 110 delegates to the 37 Justice Tolliver had won in South Carolina amid dark murmurs in the press of intimidation and vote-buying in rural districts. But then on the same day Donahue had won Colorado and Minnesota, Tolliver had won in Maryland and Georgia, and Justice had 111 delegates to Donahue's 169.

Two days later, Donahue won New York when the Republican establishment, in the firm grip of Senator Armand Cresta, had frozen Tolliver right off the ballot. Going into Super Tuesday with a total of 408 delegates at stake, Donahue led Tolliver by over a hundred delegates.

Most of Super Tuesday was in the South. Tolliver knew he had to win in the South.

He took another sip of water and put down the glass. He rounded into the big finish of his stump speech. Whatever topic he focused on in any given speech in any state, he varied the finale very little. It came from his preaching, and he believed it came from the heart. "My fellow Americans," he rasped through inflamed vocal cords, "my fellow patriots, my fellow Southerners, my neighbors of Louisiana. Hear me."

The crowd began to call out and applaud. A lot of faithful were gathered here in the piney woods country of central Louisiana. This was redneck country, or as they said hereabouts, peckerwood country. Joseph Donahue was that very morning chasing votes in the Frenchified Catholic south, corrupt New Orleans and the Cajun swamp parishes. Tolliver doubted he'd get many to listen, but Justice knew the majority Baptists, Evangelicals, and Pentecostals were his.

He'd selected this spot, this crowd along with all the others he would address on this crucial day, because their size and enthusiasm would make good television, good for the evening news shows throughout the South, where the voters would send him onward to triumph or back to Austin in shame.

"We're here not just running for political office, even though it is the highest office in the land and the most powerful on earth under God. We're here as cleansers of a failed, corrupt, loose-moralled government, an administration polluted by dirty money, a government of broken promises. A government whose highest officials are under investigation by more independent counsels than I can remember, a government for sale to the rich and godless interests, from Asian banking cartels with ties to dictators to the tobacco lobby that seduces your children, to the self-enriching trial lawyers to the sleek, well-paid officials of teachers' and public workers' unions who want to do everything other than teach your kids right and wrong and letters and figures, and clean and police the streets of your towns and cities. Hear me!"

"We hear!" the crowd boomed. Great television.

"Now Ronald Reagan, a great man and a great Republican, said speak no evil of a fellow Republican, and maybe in his time that was right. But now, and sad to say, my friends, our party has fallen from President Reagan's vision of a stronger, more prosperous America, an America of hardworking, God-fearing people. Our Republican Party is back to making deals, going along to get along, porking up the budget, raising your taxes and congressmen's and senators' pay. Who sits at the center of that web of Republican corruption but the sly, slick senator from Connecticut, Joseph Donahue? Do I speak ill of him? I do not, but he is not my friend or yours.

"My friends, my fellow patriotic Republicans, we have to take back our party so we can clean it up before we begin the larger task of cleaning up the government in Washington."

Justice paused and allowed the cheers and applause to swell. A few piercing rebel yells caused the cheering and clapping to grow louder. Fine television.

Justice raised his hands. "My friends," he shouted into the still-cheering crowd. "Send Justice to Washington and I will clean up the mess! I'll muck out the Congress. I'll end the corruption in the White House. I *will*, as God is my witness!"

"Witness. Witness," the crowd roared. Tolliver looked around. Ezekiel Archer beckoned him to exit stage left. Tolliver had had a small Secret Service detail since his win in South Carolina, but his main protection was provided by the Witnesses to Justice, a group of powerfully built young men in conservative blue suits, white shirts, and plain red ties with military-style short haircuts. No mustaches or beards. Many were off-duty or vacationing Texas Rangers, and all were from Tolliver's church in Dallas. They were unarmed but they were tough, and eight surrounded the candidate as he descended from the bunting-draped stage into the crowd. The Witnesses let people reach the governor's hands and good-looking women got close enough to kiss him, but the guards were so careful to keep hecklers or even reporters shouting questions away that the boys on the press bus called them the Witness Protection Program.

Tolliver felt exhausted, drained by his communion with the crowd. "Where we goin' now, Zeke?" he shouted at Archer, while shaking four or five hands at once.

"Orlando, Florida, then a helicopter hop to Cape Canaveral. Donahue's due down kissing the rings of Cuban bishops in Miami about the same time."

Progress through the happy crowd to the buses was slow, but Justice could see that the TV cameramen kept pace, and smiled at the lenses as he shook hands and said what he said in answer to any question: "Thank you and God bless you for your support."

Movement abruptly halted. The Witnesses drew in closer, bristles standing out on their thick necks. Six black men in suits, one with a bullhorn, blocked the governor's path to the bus. "Hypocrite! Racist! Fornicator! Liar!" thundered the one with the bullhorn, a very fat man in a gray silk suit, a black shirt with clerical collar, a large gold medal on a chain around his neck. "For shame, Rupert Justice Tolliver. You call yourself a man of God yet you preach hatred as surely as you do practice it!"

Justice looked around in panic. Sure enough, the television handheld cameras had swung over to the angry black preacher. "Jesus, Zeke," he whispered to Archer. "This is bad television!"

The friendly crowd seemed to shrink back. Young white men dressed in dirty jeans and work boots, some wearing cut-off leather jackets and some carrying chains or baseball bats, swarmed out of the crowd and attacked the preachers, wrestling or beating some to the muddy fairground.

Spectators began to scream as bats rose and fell. Justice felt hands—Zeke Archer's—grab his shoulders and propel him forward into the fray. "No, no," Justice shouted, pulling one of the attackers off. "Let my brothers speak."

Archer grabbed him again, as did two Witnesses. He was half dragged, half carried the rest of the way into his bus. The driver released the brakes and the bus rolled slowly forward, parting the crowd. Justice sat in a back seat, shaken and sweating from the encounter. One of the cameramen who had jumped on behind him came back and shook his hand. "Wonderful, brave gesture, Governor," the cameraman, who was black, said. "You saved those men."

"Thank you," Justice said, grinning modestly and relaxing. Who the hell set that up? he wondered. Bad television into good.

Yet in a strange and unexpected way, he felt he had done right.

ON THE PLANE TO FLORIDA, he got Ezekiel Archer alone. "Who was it back there who thumped those niggers, Zeke? Coulda been a disaster."

"You handled it beautifully, Juss," Zeke said softly.

"Yeah, after you shoved me into it. I still want to know who those greasy bikers were with their bats at just the right or wrong moment."

Zeke fidgeted. "I don't know. I'll ask the Mormon." The Mormon was Jim Bob Slate, head of the Witnesses, not a Mormon at all but one of Justice's flock. He was called the Mormon because he never smoked, drank alcohol or caffeine, or cursed. "I'll find out; you think about what you're going to say in the State of Florida."

Zeke left Justice alone in the private compartment of the chartered airliner. The candidate chewed his lower lip. Who set that up?

JULIA EARLY WATCHED the eleven o'clock news in her apartment. Her roommates, Judith Langtry and Hilda Chu, were out making the rounds in Georgetown, but Julia had a cold. Wrapped up warm in a thick terry bathrobe, she ate ice cream and drank herbal tea. The little Sony flickered, its volume muted through the sports. Julia was drowsy, and reached for the remote to shut it off when suddenly the sportscaster's face was replaced by Governor Justice Tolliver's. Julia turned the volume up. Tolliver was stepping off an airplane, waving and shouting. The caption at the bottom of the picture said Austin, Texas. The governor began his stump speech and the TV station cut away to the black woman anchor. "Governor Tolliver made eight campaign appearances today, crisscrossing the South in what some in this town consider a last and desperate effort to break Senator Joseph Donahue's momentum toward the Republican nomination. Earlier today, the governor had to intervene personally in a violent clash between bat-wielding supporters and a small, peaceful group of African-American clergymen who confronted the governor, saying he practiced hatemongering." The anchor looked to her left and twenty seconds of tape appeared, showing the shoving crowd and the black preachers warding off blows from the bikers. Then the governor was in the middle of the camera's lens, his face bouncing as the cameraman was jostled. The governor pulled one of the attackers away, said, "Let my brothers speak," and was himself hustled away.

The anchor's pretty face returned, her expression somber. "The governor's spokesman deplored the attack and disclaimed any knowledge of the attackers."

Ezekiel Archer's narrow face appeared on the screen. "We're just glad no one was seriously hurt."

The anchor's image returned. "Now, the weather."

Julia turned off the television. The Washington establishment despises Governor Tolliver, she thought, wouldn't even give him credit for stopping a violent act. All her friends dismissed Tolliver, as they were mostly Democrats or Donahue Republicans, Julia tried to defend the governor, but people looked at her like she was a drooling idiot, so she stopped. She knew Tolliver was a good man, a little rough around the edges, but compassionate. She believed he loved God, as she did. She hoped he would do well in tomorrow's primaries.

She put out the light and went to sleep.

8

Before dawn on Super Tuesday, volunteers gathered at Protestant churches large and small across the states of Florida, Louisiana, Mississippi, Oklahoma, Tennessee and Texas. All the volunteers were young and clean-cut. The men wore khaki pants and the women skirts of the same color. They all wore shirts with the broad blue and white stripes that were a trademark of the Tolliver campaign. Most, but not all, of the volunteers were white. They drove their own cars or cars lent to the churches. Hand-painted signs taped to the doors read "FREE RIDES TO VOTE." The volunteers wore no buttons but did carry literature. They were given lists of streets to canvas, and told only to render an opinion of the candidates if asked, then offer their flyers listing Governor Tolliver's positions on key issues of the day. As day dawned, fine and warm across the South, the volunteers fanned out to neighborhoods and began their good work.

The whole effort had been organized by Jim Bob Slate, the head of the Witnesses, the one nicknamed the Mormon. He drove a van himself in his hometown of Houston, and assigned himself a black neighborhood. By the time the polls opened at eight A.M, there were already many people out on their carefully painted front porches. Some were women with small children, and more were elderly. Jim Bob drove slowly, leaning over, greeting people, asking them if they needed any help getting to the polls. Many people looked right through him, or away. One white-haired black man sitting with an old black woman with palsied hands called down to him. "What you doin' here, boy?"

"Offerin' to take you and the missus to the polls so you can vote. Y'all registered?"

"Damn right." The old man stood up. It was five blocks to the school where they voted, and he supposed he could make it, but not Millie, his wife.

"Republican, I do hope," Jim Bob said, leaning across and opening the door.

"No. We be democrats." He turned to his wife. "Set back down, Millie, we'll have to wait for the church bus."

A small crowd had gathered. Jim Bob got out of the truck and smiled at all of them. "Well now, sir, I offered you a ride to the polls. How you vote is your business and yours alone."

The old man looked at him with ill-concealed suspicion. "Who you work for?"

"Governor Justice Tolliver, the next President of the United States."

"He done some good things here in Texas," the old man conceded. "He don't much care for the Colored."

"Well now, sir, I've got no mind to contradict you, but Governor Tolliver cares about all God's children. It's his opponents who lie about him and say he doesn't. Only yesterday he risked his life to prevent some bad boys from molesting a delegation of African-American preachers in Louisiana. Waded right in and pulled them boys off, walked right in under their clubs."

"I seen that on the news," a young woman with a baby said. "My man and me, we voted for Tolliver for governor."

"Well come on down and vote for him again."

Soon Jim Bob's van filled up with happy voters, high-spirited as if being taken to a party. Jim Bob closed the doors and promised to come back and get more people as soon as the first group voted.

He grinned to himself as he drove off. If this worked in this neighborhood, it would work anywhere.

* * *

Justice Tolliver sat in his study in the Governor's Mansion in Austin. There was a television on in one corner with the sound off, but he wasn't watching. He stared into a low fire flickering in the grate that, with the television picture, provided all the light in the room. He had taken a new bottle of Jack Daniel's and a bucket of ice with him as he left dinner with his wife and Ezekiel Archer just as the polls were closing and the news shows began. He had instructed Archer to see he was undisturbed until all the results were known, and then he was to bring them personally. The bottle of whiskey was half empty and Justice was slumped deep in his armchair. His head ached and his nerves jangled. He would not look at his watch but he sensed it wouldn't be long before he knew what the South thought of his upstart challenge to the party leadership and organization. He took a sip of whiskey and poured more over the melting ice cubes, spilling a little on the table.

Zeke Archer came in without speaking, closing the door behind him. "Tell it, Zeke," the governor said without looking up.

Archer carried a clipboard. "Do you mind if I turn on a light so I can read my notes?"

"Go ahead. Start with Texas, Zeke." The best chance for good news.

Zeke turned on a light and took a chair next to the candidate. "Texas is yours, Juss. One hundred twenty-three delegates." He paused; Tolliver showed no sign that he had heard. "Also Louisiana, twenty-seven, Mississippi, thirty-two, Oklahoma thirty-eight, Tennessee thirty-seven, and the networks just declared you winner in Florida with ninety-eight."

Justice nodded. "Donahue?"

"Massachusetts and Rhode Island. Fifty-three delegates between them to your total today of three hundred fifty-five. Juss, you jumped all over that fair-haired Yankee Irish son of a bitch, and now you got the lead by a hundred forty delegates and we headin' west. Can I get you maybe to let out a little Texas whoop?"

Justice heaved himself out of his chair, staggered forward, caught the mantelpiece, and sagged. Zeke jumped up and steadied him. "Everybody did a hell of a job," Tolliver said, his voice soft and slurred. "Gotta go downstairs and thank them."

Zeke turned the governor back to his chair. "Most everyone's gone home," Zeke lied. The campaign coordinators and many volunteers were downstairs but it wouldn't do to have them see the candidate drunk. "It was a long day for everyone, and we all need sleep," he added pointedly.

"OK. Thank 'em tomorrow. Thank you tonight, Zeke. Have a drink with me."

"No thanks, Juss," Zeke said, looking down at his friend. "I'm beat, and you must be exhausted."

"Have a fucking drink, Zeke." He held out his glass. "And freshen mine up. We still got business."

Zeke made two drinks with more ice than the governor liked. He sat and looked at Justice's sweaty, sagging face. "It'll wait till morning, Juss."

"Can't. Who did it, Juss? Had them niggers whomped in Baton Rouge?"

"That kinda worked out for us."

"Who, Zeke?"

Zeke sighed. "I spoke to the Mormon. He says they're kind of an undercover wing of the Witnesses. He calls them the New Zealots and says they're extra security. He also says he had your authorization to set them up."

"He's a lying bastard, he said that. I want to see him in this room at seven-thirty sharp."

"Right." Zeke got up. "See you in the morning, then."

"Seven-thirty sharp."

JIM BOB SLATE stared at the ceiling of the tiny apartment the campaign had rented for him in Austin. Clarissa ran her cool fingers across his damp chest hair as he felt his breathing and heartbeat slowly return to normal. She was always cool, he thought, even in her passion. She tortured him with her coolness, her seeming detachment while driving him to frenzy. He knew and she knew that what they were doing was sin, not only against God but also the governor. Clarissa Alcott was the wife of Rupert Justice Tolliver. Jim Bob burned in his soul with shame, but he couldn't refuse her. She took him places he had never been growing up as a good Christian farm boy. She gave him such exquisite pleasure laced with pain that he lived in hourly fear that he might displease her and she might take it all away.

Clarissa's fingers outlined his washboard-hard abs and down to his spent, sore sex. He closed his eyes against temptation on top of temptation, but his sex rose anyway. "Again, lover," she purred. "Do me with your tongue."

He whimpered, shook his head no. She held his head and guided him, and he complied.

Cobra followed the American presidential campaign in the *Rand Daily Mail* that came up from Cape Town in bundles about once a week. He remembered the boy Tolliver in Cuba, what a silly shit he had been, and he remembered as well the boy's boast that one day he would be President of the United States. Cobra didn't understand the nominating system in detail, but it seemed that Tolliver, at first written off by the press as a hopeless long shot, had drawn ahead of his better-known and better-funded rivals and eliminated all but one, the Connecticut Senator Donahue.

Cobra opened the early files in his memoirs. He wondered if anyone in the United States knew that the very right-wing governor of Texas had once visited Cuba and had, for a short time, direct access to the brothers Castro.

Cobra closed the file, turned the little computer off, and went down to the stables where one of his grooms would have his favorite horse saddled for an afternoon ride.

9

1968

AT THE END OF January, the sharpshooter Jack Chance, promoted to corporal, was ten months into his second tour in Vietnam and looking forward to going back to the world and out of the Corps. He had returned to his old outfit, the Second of the 26th Marines, but the turnover had been nearly a hundred percent, so he knew practically no one. They spent time in and around the Leatherneck Square, in the mountains near the coast near the Demilitarized Zone, or Dead Marine Zone, as it was called. They joined large-unit sweeps and clearing actions from the coast west along Highway 9 that led into Laos. By December of the previous year, the battalion and several others had reached the western end of the road, the besieged, blasted market town of Khe Sanh. Dug into the hills surrounding the airstrip, the marines were rocketed on some nights and subjected to human wave attacks on others. The recon platoon leader, a deceptively soft-eyed, handsome first lieutenant named Tom Shanley, got himself a reputation, a Purple Heart, and a Silver Star for calling in artillery on his own position as it was being overrun, then remaining outside the bunker to correct fire.

At the end of January, in the middle of the unofficial annual cease-fire around the Tet lunar new year celebration, the North Vietnamese sent their surrogates in the South, the Vietcong, to attack the stood-down garrisons of U.S. and ARVN forces from one end of the country to the other. The marines at Khe Sanh, already under heavy attack for ten days and nights, were suddenly cut off from resupply as troops along the coast fought to drive the Cong out of the cities and off the airbases. Cobra's company was sent out to relieve one of the artillery firebases near the airstrip that was being hard pressed, and Cobra shinnied up a tall palm to get a look into the enemy position. In the racket of battle he managed to shoot most of a rocket crew with the bolt-action Remington without being spotted. At dusk he saw masses of Viet Cong in their black pajamas, backed up or maybe herded by North Vietnamese regulars in their green uniforms, preparing to attack. He shouted a warning down to his security detail that should have been waiting beneath him on the ground, but got no answer. He shinnied down; there was no one in sight. The platoon had pulled back and left him, and soon he heard the attackers sliding through the empty bush, flowing around his AO. He had nowhere to go but back up the tree.

The battle raged all night. Cobra couldn't see much because of the thickness of the canopy, but he could hear and feel the bombs and rockets dropped by night-attack aircraft flying from the airbase at Da Nang and carriers in the Gulf of Tonkin. The attackers withdrew near dawn around Cobra's tree as he sat still as a mouse. There seemed to be many fewer than the night before, and many were being carried in ponchos. No one looked up until the last man—it had to be the last man—looked straight up at Cobra, pointed, and let out a startled squeak.

There was nothing for it. His tree surrounded, the sharpshooter corporal slid down and surrendered his weapon. His hands were roughly bound behind him at the wrists and elbows and he was marched into North Vietnam, and later sent to one of the remote camps in the limestone mountains in Laos where prisoners of war grew opium poppies for the heroin processors in Hanoi who supplied cheap smack to the American soldiers in the South. Weakened by poor food, parasites, and disease, the prisoners wasted, went mad, or slowly starved to death.

Rupert Justice Tolliver completed his studies at Divinity School at Houston Baptist University in February, and was ordained the same month. His draft board in Uvalde had kept tabs on his progress, prodding him whenever it appeared he was taking less than a full academic load. Rupert hated the studies, hated the way the Bible had become his life while loving its words, both comforting and frightening. More, he hated his dreary life of night-clerking in a Piggly-Wiggly store and living in a tiny furnished room over some mean old gal's garage.

Now he was ordained, a real-live minister of the Gospel, and the draft board wanted to know his plans. His deferment could be extended or he could be excused completely from the draft if, and only if, he had a permanent preaching position. Churches were hard to come by with divinity schools cranking out many graduates much like Rupert, who heard their calls suddenly and late. The little country churches couldn't pay, and the big, prosperous churches in the cities filled their junior positions easily. Rupert despaired; he had never expected Lyndon Johnson to hang on to this dirty little war so long, but the end seemed nowhere in sight. Five hundred fifty thousand men, Westmoreland wanted, and every day the television news was full of dead and wounded being shipped to the rear as the army and marines fought fierce battles to take back the cities and bases overrun by the Vietcong during what was being called the Tet Offensive.

Nothing for it, Rupert thought. Either find a church and continue starving, or surrender to the draft board, the last two years wasted. Every day he went to the placement office at Houston Christian and looked through lists of openings. He drove around south Texas in his rusty pickup, looking at weathered clapboard churches with leaky roofs and broken windows. Today he was on his way to tiny Batesville, in nearby Zavala County. Batesville, population 632, had a church whose pastor was ailing and wanted to retire. The pay was two thousand dollars a year, and housing in a tiny rectory behind the church. Rupert parked the truck and got out, greeted as he pushed open the door by the rising strains of quite a good choir singing "Amazing Grace," a hymn Rupert knew was written by a repented Scottish slave trader.

Rupert listened to the choir as his eyes became accustomed to the dim light. He saw a stooped, gray-haired man sitting in a pew in the middle of the church. He wore a threadbare suit of black serge, and Rupert took him for the pastor. Seated next to him was a man in a fancy western-style shirt fastened with mother-of-pearl snaps. He had a tape recorder beside him on the pew and held a boom microphone pointed at the choir.

When the hymn ended, Rupert bent and identified himself to the minister. The man smiled, got up, and led Rupert back outside as the choir began to sing "Shall We Gather at the River?" "Very sweet choir," Rupert said, as the door closed behind him.

"Yes, we're proud of them," the Reverend Lovelace said. "Man in there taping is from KSAN in San Antonio. They're considering putting on a Sunday morning gospel hour."

"On the radio?" Rupert's interest shot up suddenly.

"At first. You give a good sermon, boy?"

"I believe I have the makings," Rupert said modestly.

"Man in there says they like the preachin', they may do it on television. Myself, I got the emphysema, can't hardly make myself heard any more."

Television! Rupert thought. A way to get noticed, to get into politics. What a windfall! "You suppose you'd let me preach beside you this Sunday? I'd be glad for your opinion."

"Why, sure," the old man said. "Let the deacons and the search committee have a look at you, and also the TV people; they'll be here." The minister looked cunning. "Mighty fine opportunity for a young man starting out."

"Well, as long as the television thing didn't take a man away from his duties to his flock," Rupert said humbly.

The Reverend Lovelace gave him a look of a man not easily fooled. "Not just local television neither. You know who owns that station and half the rest in Texas?"

"No, sir."

Lovelace smiled, a twinkle in his eye. "Why, Claudia King Travis, of the famous King Ranch family that once owned a ranch bigger than some eastern states."

10

June 2000

THE TOLLIVER CAMPAIGN swept toward the convention in Orlando on a ragged wave of unpredicted triumphs, but increasingly vocal critics said it was a dirty wave. Justice won primary after primary in the West while Donahue remained strong in the Northeast and Midwest. There were stories of intimidation in battleground states, of ballot tampering and outright fraud. Joseph Donahue denounced Tolliver for running goon squads disguised as Get Out the Vote campaigns, and many of Donahue's rallies were disrupted. Justice Tolliver ignored the charges and pounded his principal theme: Washington was a cesspool of corruption and Donahue was a comfortable man of Washington.

The primary campaign went all the way to the fifth of June with Donahue once again leading in the seesaw battle for the nomination. Donahue had 951 delegates and needed 40 more to be nominated. Tolliver had to take all the big states with small populations to overcome Donahue's strength in liberal California, which he won in late March to leapfrog over Tolliver's lead after Super Tuesday.

There were 119 delegates up for election on June 5, and Justice needed essentially all of them. He had 892 delegates in hand, needing, like his opponent, to finish with 991 or better. He needed 99, Donahue only 40, but geography was likely to help as it had on Super Tuesday. Primaries on June 5 included Alabama, Montana, and New Mexico, 71 delegates believed secure for Tolliver. The other primary on that summer day, the battleground, the toss-up, was New Jersey, one of the hardest states to read politically because in many ways it wasn't a coherent political or economic entity at all.

Wags said New Jersey had no head, because that was New

York City, and no asshole because that was Philadelphia. In the grimy north were container ports, old, smelly refineries, shuttered industrial plants and blighted cities. Moving south one found bucolic market gardeners and some new high-tech labs and small businesses near Princeton University. Further south were more farms, inhospitable pine barrens and salt marshes, bedroom suburbs and rusty docklands fronting Philadelphia across the Delaware, and the island of glitter and skin-deep prosperity that was Atlantic City.

New Jersey should have been an easy win for Joseph Donahue, with its urban concentration of blacks and Catholic ethnics. Baptist and Evangelical churches, organizing points for Tolliver's campaigns in southern and western states, were few and far between. The rural vote was too small and market gardening was sure and profitable, not like cash-commodity farming of the South and West with its crop failures, poverty, and government subsidies. Justice Tolliver visited the state five times after Super Tuesday gave him life, and he sent the Witnesses in to spread the word house to house. Justice knew the grass-roots campaign wouldn't be enough; that he could still have his victory snatched away by that smooth prick Donahue.

Find out who hates that prick in New Jersey, he instructed Ezekiel Archer. Archer gave the job to the Mormon, Jim Bob Slate. The answer was deceptively simple.

Archer waited in the New Jersey capital of Trenton on the eve of the climactic primary after Tolliver left the state and flew to Mobile, Alabama, to be among friends for good television if things went right. Archer remembered the morning after Super Tuesday when he and a tortured-looking, sweaty Jim Bob had awaited the candidate's wrath at seven-thirty in Justice's formal office in the mansion. Justice appeared at eight, looking gray and haggard, but his eyes and hands were steady. He'd demanded an explanation of the incident in Baton Rouge: who had ordered the attack on the black ministers and who had carried it out.

Clarissa had come into the office with her husband and stood beside him. Jim Bob caught her eye but her bland expression didn't change. The Mormon thought he was about to be forsaken, and he thought he deserved whatever the governor might mete out, and would accept it without protest. Jim Bob cleared his throat. "I anticipated disruption at that rally, and in future rallies. The Witnesses are too identifiable to do more than protect your person, Governor; I had to find another instrument to defend you from just such an attack as those niggers intended, in front of television. Those boys what attacked the preachers are good Christians; I tell them to look a little rough."

"African-Americans," Justice grated. "We in the big leagues now, boy."

Jim Bob gulped. "Yes, sir."

"Who are these people?" the governor asked.

"They like to call themselves the New Zealots. None of their names are on any of our paid or volunteer lists."

Justice looked at the clean-cut, muscular young man, a New Zealot indeed. He was intelligent and devoted. Justice had thought of the Mormon as a blunt instrument, but perhaps he was more capable. "If any damn reporter ever got wind of this, it could erase this campaign overnight, Jim Bob."

"Yes, sir." The boy hung his head like a twelve-year-old who had lost his homework for Sunday school.

Justice slammed his palms down on the solid wood of his desk hard enough to rattle pens and pencils in an old artillery shell and make the phone give off a startled ring. "How the hell you take something like this all on yourself, boy?" he shouted, flushing scarlet.

Jim Bob looked up at Clarissa with entreaty. She smiled at him, and placed her hands on the governor's flaming, stiff neck. "Jim Bob came to me, Rupert," she said soothingly, caressing his tension. "He was concerned, and he didn't want to bother you when you were so busy getting ready to bust out on Super Tuesday. I thought I mentioned it to you, but perhaps I forgot. Anyway, I told him to go ahead, so it's my fault."

Justice didn't turn around. His wife had been running him for years and was de facto manager of all his campaigns. She had the organization skills he lacked, and the ruthlessness of the Texas tort lawyer she was. Clarissa was cold brainpower to his passion. Justice loved his wife, but he also feared her. He wanted to push her hands away from their strangling caress on his neck, but did not. He addressed Jim Bob as though she had never spoken. "I should fire your ass, Jim Bob," Justice said evenly. "But you got away with it and it made good television. I don't want to hear any more about these New Zealots, and I don't want you doing anything like that again without Zeke's approval." He stood, put his arm affectionately around his wife's slender waist, and kissed her cheek. "Come on, honey," he whispered. "Let's have us a chat over breakfast."

ZEKE ARCHER HELPED himself to a glass of bourbon and flipped on the television. The polls would close in New Jersey in a few minutes; later in the West and South. The Mormon had found out who hated Donahue, the victims of his crusading Senate Select Committee on Organized Crime. Jim Bob had added the muscle of the New Zealots to the money and influence of the Mafia to suppress the votes in the northern cities, especially among blacks and Catholic ethnics, and to stuff ballot boxes in the corrupt south of the docks of Camden, across the river from the port of Philadelphia.

The networks reported light voting in the north, and a near-riot in Newark when two polling places were torched. The south voted heavily, with busloads crossing the Delaware from Pennsylvania. Buses arriving at black churches to pick up voters throughout the state had mysterious mechanical failures. One was overturned and burned in the middle of the Newark disturbance.

At nine-thirty ABC News called New Jersey an upset for Tolliver. Alabama came in ten minutes later, and Montana put Justice over the top at half past ten.

Zeke spoke to the governor at his noisy party in Mobile, had another drink and packed his bag for the trip back to Austin in the morning.

Now the serious shit begins, he thought. He had another drink, and another.

What the hell have I unleashed? he asked himself, his eyes wet, his breath coming in gasps. He felt suddenly ill, feverish, and nauseated. He ran into the bathroom and vomited, shuddering and weeping until he was empty.

On television, large fires continued to burn in downtown Newark.

11

December 1968

COBRA FELT THE MOST oppressive thing about life in the camp in Laos was the silence of the men. The Vietnamese guards did not permit the prisoners to speak to each other as they went to slurp their never-changing, tasteless chow, or washed in the cold, rushing river, or worked in the NVA's poppy gardens or the small rice paddies that provided prisoners and guards alike with their meager rations.

Any prisoner talking was shouted at, beaten with the long bamboo staffs the guards carried in addition to their weapons, or locked down in one of the reeking punishment pits dug into the soft, wet earth and covered with a grill of lashed-together bamboo. The guards talked constantly, in their singsongy language punctuated with giggles and laughter. Cobra learned that laughter, derision, was a great insult in the Vietnamese culture. The listless prisoners were ridiculed for how they looked, ate, slept, worked, and failed to resist. Cobra picked up a few words and phrases; all the prisoners did. *Bui moi* made savage, brute, and was a favorite taunt.

Once the guards had locked the prisoners in their sleeping

hootches and moved away, the prisoners could have talked, but mostly they didn't. Cobra was used to working alone and wasn't bothered by silence, but he felt that in the others the silence was a manifestation of surrender, of loss of will.

Different prisoners reacted to the camp in different ways, but resignation was by far the most common response. Men who arrived sick or wounded often wasted and died in a month or so, despite the primitive but sincere efforts of the Pathet Lao barefoot doctor who made the rounds of the camps and stations with her knapsack of native herbal medicines and occasionally some captured Western antibiotics.

One man was different. A huge, muscular man six feet three or four and over two hundred fifty pounds with sunburned skin, black hair, and hard black eyes, he had been brought to the camp from North Vietnam at the same time as Cobra. He wasted like the others because of the poor food and the ravages of parasites, and became gaunt and stooped, but his eyes remained hard and flat, giving away nothing. The Viets called him *con trau,* water buffalo, because of his great size and strength, and they stayed clear of him with their bamboos, though he never gave them cause to use them.

The Viets gave all the prisoners the names of animals, another insult. They called Cobra *con ran da,* black snake, and that amused him.

Water Buffalo's real name was Moser. Just Moser, Cobra didn't know if it was a first or last name. Moser spent a lot of time looking at the river running swiftly in its gorge below the camp, and one night he slipped out of camp, mounted a primitive raft, and joined the river on its journey south.

Each day after the big man left, the prisoners did talk to each other, and took their beatings from the angry and embarrassed guards. Spirits long absent rose in the shambling men, and many tried to stand a little taller. Moser would get out, they told themselves. Moser would find his way to Thailand and send back rescuers to the camp.

Nine days after he escaped, Moser did return to camp, not with a rescue team but a ragged squad of Pathet Lao guerrillas, allies of the NVA when they got paid. The guards beat Moser, mutilated him, and strapped his body to the water pump that irrigated the rice paddy by the river. A greater gloom than ever gripped the horrified prisoners, and illness, madness, and black despair increased.

Cobra drove himself deep within, resolved to keep his sanity and survive.

RUPERT JUSTICE TOLLIVER preached side by side with the Reverend Lovelace for barely three weeks before the search committee and the deacons asked him to become pastor of Batesville Church of Jesus Present and granted Lovelace his pension and retirement to his poor, dusty ranch. KSAN radio broadcast the choir for a half hour, then decided they liked Rupert's preaching and expanded the broadcast to an hour, forty-five minutes of hymns and fifteen for the sermon. By December the program had moved to television as well as radio, and expanded again to include the entire worship service, ninety minutes in a television market of over a million people.

Rupert—Brother Rupert Justice on the air—didn't give the uplifting speeches of sacrifice and reward or the fire-and-brimstone jeremiads of sin and inevitable damnation that characterized radio preachers who had grown out of the old tent revivals of the thirties and forties. He used the same lessons and stories from the Holy Scripture, but his message was increasingly political. The smug, Godless Eastern establishment, allied with the moneyed interests around the world who answered to no God or government, had stolen control of the world economy and the U.S. government, ruined the schools, bowed to the moneybags of big business and the corrupt, powerful leaders of the unions. Poor God-fearing people were left aside while the fat pigs controlled the trough. His message was populist: give the people access, take the foot of the bankers off the neck of the honest farmer, the laborer, the small businessman. Make the government the helpmeet of the poor widow, the helpless child, the good man down on his luck.

In February 1969, Brother Rupert Justice's tiny church was visited by a middle-aged woman in black glasses. Rupert recognized her from the pulpit despite the harsh TV lights shining in his eyes. She was dark-haired around an incongruous pillbox hat, large-mouthed, and ugly if you ignored the softness of her smile. She was Claudia King Travis, who owned all the radio and television stations in south and central Texas. Brother Rupert Justice held his eyes on her dark glasses and delivered his sermon to her alone, mixing his fire with compassion, almost singing at times.

At the end of the service, Rupert stood by the door on the broad porch added on with money from the TV program. The little church was freshly painted and the roof sheathed with new asphalt shingles. Brother Rupert Justice shook hands with each parishioner in turn, and each thanked him and blessed his heart.

Claudia King Travis kept her seat in a back pew. After the last worshiper had gone, one of her retainers came out to the porch and beckoned Rupert back inside. He told Mrs. Travis what an honor it was—

"I want to move this program to a studio in San Antonio," she said, interrupting, a woman with little time for small talk. "Better lighting, a much larger studio audience, broadcast over most of Texas and Oklahoma."

"Uh, the choir—"

"Will be taken care of. When can you move?"

"Well, it's a great honor, a great calling, but my flock—"

She took off her glasses. Her eyes were hard. "Get someone to help you with the flock; you'll be making enough. Or should I find me another TV preacher?"

"I'd be proud to come to San Antonio," he said smoothly.

"Isn't pride a sin, Reverend Tolliver?" Claudia said sharply. Then she smiled, stood, and gave him her white—gloved hand. She was a small woman but radiated great confidence. Rupert bowed over the hand and accepted her will.

12

July 2000

JUSTICE ARRIVED IN Orlando on July 4, three days before the convention of the Republican Party was to begin. He felt confident that this was his last stop before the prize, the move to 1600 Pennsylvania Avenue in what he always called Godless Washington, D.C. (D.C. for the Devil's Cloister) on January 20, 2001, the true beginning of the new millennium.

Justice held the slimmest margin of any major party candidate since primaries took over from state conventions to dominate the nominating process. After winning New Jersey and going over the top, he had added North Dakota a week later and finished with 1,029 delegates to Senator Donahue's 951. Joseph Donahue had neither conceded nor endorsed his rival, and had angrily promised a fight over each plank in the Republican platform. Ezekiel Archer urged Justice to make peace with Donahue to avoid a fight over policy on nationwide television; Justice refused.

"Fuck him," Justice said into a large glass of bourbon. "Candy ass, Pope-loving, soft-handed, Yankee liberal! What's he got to trade?"

Zeke sighed. The suite in the Marriott Hotel, close by Disney World, was cramped, smoke-filled, and littered with room-service leavings. "Juss, you don't win general elections the way you win nominations. You've proven yourself in the South and West, but that's Republican territory. To beat Vice President Sandman, you need at least some of the Northeast, most of the Midwest, and above all, California."

"Donahue's states," Justice said to his glass. "Shit, Zeke, here I am on the verge of a major triumph, a Texas poor-boy preacher about to receive the nomination of our party to carry the standard forward to victory in November, and you're about to tell me I got to kiss that pretty boy's ass? I won't do it."

"No, Juss, you shouldn't."

"Damn right." Tolliver went to the bar and rebuilt his drink, and poured out a dark one for Archer, even though his confidant had an untouched full one on the table beside his chair. "Fuckin' A right."

"Unless," Archer said, studying his fingernails, "you want to win."

Justice wheeled, his face flushed and blotchy with anger. "Just say your piece, Zeke."

"Let me meet with his people. Cut them some slack on the platform. Unify the party, Juss."

"That'll do it? The stupid platform that nobody remembers a week after it's done? Sure."

"Juss, ask Donahue, *implore* Donahue, to run with you as vice president."

Justice drained his glass. "We back to kissing his ass."

It was Zeke's turn to show a little anger. "Juss, we're talking New England or at least Massachusetts, New Hampshire, Rhode Island, and Connecticut, plus Illinois, Indiana, and California."

"But I'd have that sneaky, disloyal bastard hard on my heels for four years. And what, by the way, would be his price? He doesn't love me as we both know."

Zeke spread his large hands. "Juss, what do you care? Promise him anything. I believe it was Vice President John Nance Gardner who said the vice presidency wasn't worth 'a bucket of warm spit.' "

"Promising's one thing," Justice said with a sudden grin. "Paying off's another."

"Exactly," Zeke said. "Do I have permission to talk to his people?"

Justice refilled his drink. "Yeah, talk, but don't sign any deal without getting back to me."

Clarissa Alcott Tolliver entered the suite's living room from the bedroom. She was flushed from the shower and wrapped in a hotel terry robe that showed a lot of leg and more cleavage. She bent and kissed Justice on his bald spot. "Find out what they want," Tolliver said, caressing his wife's thigh. "Let me and my manager here have the final say."

Archer turned at the door, wanting to say a final word about Donahue's probable demands. Clarissa had dropped the robe and stood, pink and glowing, caressing Tolliver's hair and pressing her sex into his upturned face.

Zeke closed the door softly and went back to his own room to think about how to knit up a deal with Senator Donahue's people.

THE MEETING WAS held in one of the smaller meeting rooms on the ground floor of the Marriott. Six people were present; by agreement, Tolliver, Donahue, and two aides each. Tolliver brought his wife and Ezekiel Archer, Senator Donahue brought his strategist, James "Wild Man" Rochefort, and the banker Colonel Alfred Thayer. "Thank you for coming on such short notice, Senator," Justice said graciously. He stood at the head of the shabby cloth-covered table; he was, after all, the nominee-apparent.

Joseph Donahue nodded but said nothing. He took the chair at the foot of the table, his aides on either side. Clarissa and Zeke took their places while Justice remained standing. There were many empty seats on both sides of the table between the two delegations.

Justice sat, grinning at the Senator from Connecticut. He hates this, Juss thought, but he's here. The deal had already been worked out between the candidates' staffs and needed only ratification in this meeting. "I've asked Zeke here to prepare a short statement we might issue jointly, Senator, if you approve," Justice said. He nodded to Zeke, who got up and passed out copies to Donahue and his two assistants. Everybody had seen the statement, but Rochefort read it again to make sure nothing had been changed. He nodded at Donahue, who pushed the paper away. "Agreed," he said, the only word he had spoken since entering the room.

"Let's review," Rochefort said. "As vice president, Joseph Donahue will head the National Security Council and be the administration's chief architect of foreign policy."

"Chief adviser to the president, yes," Zeke said softly. "We'll be glad of Senator Donahue's experience in this critical area."

"The platform is as agreed," Rochefort continued. "No endorsement of same-sex marriages but no more gay-bashing either. Right to Life but muted. Welfare for unwed mothers limited by time but not eliminated. School prayer on a voluntary basis to be left to the states. Welfare reform—"

"The platform," Clarissa said evenly, "has been agreed."

"Senator Donahue," Justice said, rising and extending his hand. "In the interest of a unified party, in the interest of winning back the White House, will you accept the nomination as vice president? Believe me, sir, though we have our differences, we can and should work together."

Donahue let the offer sit on the table a long minute. His mouth was as pursed as if he had just sucked a lemon. Hell, he thought, and shrugged. It was a done deal. "Yes, Governor, I will, and thank you." He did not rise from his seat to reach for Tolliver's hand twenty feet away. Tolliver reddened and Donahue smiled.

Zeke jumped to his feet and all but ran to shake Wild Man Rochefort's hand. High fives and back slaps were exchanged all around as the handlers sought to celebrate a deal both principals loathed. Both delegations left the meeting as quickly as they decently could.

Before the Republican convention, Vice President Gene Sandman, anointed by the sitting president and unopposed in the

Democratic primaries, enjoyed a lead in nationwide polls of 16 percent. The Republican convention proved to be a surprisingly (and for the journalists covering it, disappointingly) peaceful affair dominated by Justice Tolliver's upgunned but largely unchanged stump speech on his acceptance of the nomination. Zeke and Clarissa had gone down to the floor to watch the speech among the rank-and-file delegates, and Zeke was awed by how good the speech sounded and how well Justice gave it after five months of endless repetition. After the convention, Sandman's lead in the polls slipped to five points.

Senator Donahue kept up his end of the Faustian bargain he had accepted in Orlando, campaigning vigorously in New England, the Midwest and California, sometimes with the candidate and sometimes on his own.

The Democrats convened in San Francisco in mid-August and their convention was even more boring than the Republicans'. Sandman's lead stayed at five to eight points right up to Labor Day as the nation largely ignored the tired campaigns.

"Zeke," Justice said, pulling his aide aside after a day of dark skies and thin crowds in Colorado and California. "We need more TV, a lot more, especially here in the West." Clarissa, at the governor's side as they boarded the chartered airliner, frowned and nodded emphatically.

Zeke shook his head. "Juss, the stations won't book us until we pay the bills for earlier time. We're damn near out of money."

"Book the damn time," Clarissa rasped. "The money will be there."

13

THE CAMPAIGN TURNED ugly. A Tolliver rally in Anaheim, California, was disrupted by Latinos protesting his exclusionary stand on immigration, and his declared intention to prevent illegals from receiving any government services, not even access for their children to public schools. Chanting demonstrators were set upon outside the hall by booted bikers in gang colors and many were hurt. A Mexican-American woman who weighed over three hundred pounds was knocked to the pavement and stomped. She went into cardiac arrest and died in the street when the ambulance and police cars responding to the riot could not get through the crowd to help her.

Justice Tolliver met reporters later that day in his plane and deplored the incident, saying he would pray for the victim and her family. He was asked whether his position on closing the borders to immigrants might have contributed to the mood of the crowd and the violence; he replied that as a youngster in south Texas, most of his friends had been Mexicans.

In San Jose, California, a journalist shouted a question about "bullyboys" attached to the governor's campaign intimidating the press and protesters. The governor cupped his hand to his ear and shrugged, but kept moving. The same evening the journalist was run off the road on his way home; his car wrecked, and him dragged out and badly beaten.

The buzz continued. Black demonstrators were kept away from rallies, also homosexuals, Latinos, and pro-choice women. Stories were written about a shadowy group called the New Zealots. A Denver radio talk show host who had taken up the issue of New Zealots and complained to his audience about phoned-in threats was beaten to death in the underground garage beneath his studio after he ended his show at two in the morning.

Justice continued to deliver his simple message of faith, family, and cleaning up corrupt politics. By October 15, he had drawn even in the polls, and more important, ahead in California.

At the end of a fourteen-hour day of campaigning in dozens of gritty midwestern cities by bus, Justice summoned Ezekiel Archer to his suite in the Fremont Hotel in Chicago. Zeke found the governor dressed in a hotel robe, his skin pink from hot water, a bottle of Wild Turkey whiskey, glasses, and an ice bucket beside him as

Clarissa, herself also wearing a robe with a towel over her hair, admitted him. Zeke was dead tired and felt grubby from the bus and wished he had had time to shower, but he was still in his wrinkled suit and sticky shirt he had been wearing for twenty hours and four states. It was past two in the morning.

Justice, beaming, waved him to a chair. Clarissa made a dark drink for him and one for herself, then rebuilt the governor's. "Great day, Zeke," Justice said. "Good crowds all along the way."

"Lots of demonstrators, Juss," Zeke said gloomily. "Lots of scuffles, many of them on television."

"Best there is, Zeke. Clarissa here and the Mormon think we should get more of that stuff videotaped."

"But why?" Zeke asked, taking a gulp of his drink. "You don't want to look like a racist, or a homophobe, or any of the other names you're being called."

"No, sir, I don't," Justice said, and cackled.

"Justice looks just fine," Clarissa purred. "His message is positive and his audiences are real mainstream Americans. The television audience sees that in contrast to a bunch of rude, noisy niggers and queers and longhaired, ratty-looking people getting a little push back to the fringe where they belong." She smiled and dipped Zeke a little leg. "It's working, and the polls show it."

"So you're saying we *should* be looking like racists." Zeke felt like he had been kicked in the stomach.

"Hell, Zeke," Clarissa said, bending over, patting his knee and treating him to a deep peek at her breasts beneath the loose robe. "We look damn good; it's them as looks ugly."

14

June 1969

RUMORS BLEW THROUGH the camp along with the warm rain of the summer monsoon. The guards whispered that the camp was to be evacuated, the prisoners scattered. No one knew where or why, and there was speculation that the prisoners might be returned to North Vietnam, exchanged and sent home, or simply led into the bush and shot.

Activity around the isolated camp increased. Dirty, ill-uniformed Pathet Lao guerrillas marched through, taunting the few Vietnamese guards and stealing ammunition and food. Villagers with trade goods appeared. Someone, some authority, was taking an interest in the hidden hills and fields of poppies.

Cobra was selected as one of fourteen men to be marched across country with Major Peters, the camp's senior officer, and three guards. The men were roped together and marched through Lao and Meo villages and fields. Cobra felt the hostile stares of the villagers, and he suspected the hill people hated the Vietnamese guards as much as they did the Americans. Both had brought destruction into their peaceful land.

The men selected were the healthier ones, the ones likely to survive a march of several days. The gaunt giant Moser was left lashed to his crude pump to continue his endless march toward death. Cobra wished Moser was with them; he was a totem, a powerful, unbreakable spirit.

In five days the prisoners reached a town on a bigger river, a town called Pak Sane that was teeming with North Vietnamese soldiers, all of whom appeared about to move out. The Americans were locked away in dark cellars, their filthy rice balls and weak tea thrown at them through the barred windows. Seven of the prisoners who had left the camp as the healthy ones died in the rank, drainless cellars.

Six weeks after they arrived at Pak Sane, Moser appeared in the early hours of a rainy morning. He was gaunt, feverish and hollow-eyed, but he was strong. He carried an AK-47 carbine, an NVA canteen, and hundreds of rounds of ammunition. Cobra was one of the few men who recognized Moser, and he helped herd the others down to the river and onto a sampan Moser had commandeered. Moser took them to Thailand across the Mekong, and returned them to American control.

Cobra rested up in the hospital at the American base at Udorn, then at the naval hospital in Oakland, California. The day he was released from the hospital, he received a visit from the sergeant who had accompanied him when he had shot the sniper and saved the platoon on his first tour. The man gave him a present, wrapped in a marine seabag.

"This be the rifle you used that day, Jack," the sergeant said. "I had the armorer write it off as lost, and have been keeping it for you ever since."

In May 1970, Cobra was discharged from the Marine Corps. He used his military ID to obtain a passport and his considerable back pay to buy a first-class air ticket. After two weeks in Paris he returned to Southern Rhodesia and found work on a farm.

15

1971

RUPERT JUSTICE TOLLIVER'S "Radio Mission to South Texas" became a television franchise worth tens of millions of donations and millions in profits as it spread through sharing agreements into Oklahoma, Louisiana, Arkansas, Kansas, Nebraska, Iowa and eastern Colorado. Claudia Bird handled the business end, treating her preacher well by her lights. After a year in the studio in San Antonio, the program was so flush with cash that a special tabernacle, a thirty-thousand-seat auditorium, was built outside Dallas. Rupert hired preachers to share the load, and accountants and lawyers. The sweet-sounding amateur singers from Batesville were augmented, later replaced, by a red-robed choir of three hundred professionals.

In May of 1972, Brother Rupert Justice asked God's permission on the air (after obtaining Claudia Bird's permission in private) to take a rest, a sabbatical, in Europe. He told his vast flock in TV land that he wished to reflect in the gloomy grandeur of Europe's cathedrals and monasteries, that, despite the popish grip, remained the monuments of Christianity's struggle to stave off barbarism in the Dark Ages.

Brother Rupert Justice began his Grand Tour in Paris. There was a lot going on in Paris in May 1972.

16

2000

THE CAMPAIGN GROUND on through September and October. Zeke Archer watched the polls and scheduled the candidate's appearances but shut himself out of the "content" meetings that were run by the candidate's wife, Clarissa and held in check by the glowering countenance of the Mormon. Tolliver's message didn't vary, but the emphasis changed, leaning more and more on the theme of government corruption and what to do about it. Demonstrators continued besieging Tolliver's speeches, and the mysterious toughs the press called, albeit softly, New Zealots, continued to confront them. Vice President Sandman, Tolliver's target as the symbol of everything wrong with the government and losing ground in the national polls, suggested in a TV interview that the demonstrations and confrontations appeared to be staged, as no group ever acknowledged organizing either side. Confronted with that charge, Tolliver laughed, and said all were welcome to see him and hear his message.

Two days later a Sandman rally was invaded by thirty men chanting anticorruption slogans. Despite the efforts of unarmed security volunteers, the men reached the temporary stage from which the vice president was speaking and managed to knock it down. Sandman was pitched into the crowd, surrounded by Secret Service agents with guns drawn, but the thugs slipped away in the pandemonium. Sandman climbed back onto the tilted platform, straightened his clothes and smoothed his hair, and gamely resumed his speech to a shaken and much-diminished crowd.

November 6 arrived cold and rainy in the Northeast and Midwest, fine in the rest of the country. Voter turnout was predicted to be light, and was light. Zeke Archer set up his Death Watch in a basement conference room in the Governor's Mansion in Austin. He had direct feed from the networks' exit polling computers; the networks were committed to report no state's results before the polls closed but in fact had results far earlier, and so did Zeke.

Governor and Mrs. Tolliver were watching movies upstairs in the family quarters; Justice's favorites, old Clint Eastwood Westerns. Justice was depressed; the last polls placed him two percentage points behind across the nation, and left the whole game in the hands of the fickle voters of California, where the race was too close to call.

Zeke liked light turnout, and had been praying for blizzards across the land. Tolliver's supporters were passionate, committed, and would drive through snowdrifts to vote if they had to. Sandman was a boring policy wonk who looked like everyone's bland, overweight brother-in-law. At the end of the campaign, Tolliver's message had sharpened but was still repetitive and approached boredom as well. But Zeke was convinced Justice's voters would care enough. They had to.

Zeke had it all laid out before him. Tolliver needed, absolutely needed, Florida and Texas, for 56 electoral votes. He had to carry the Old South: Alabama, Georgia, Louisiana, Mississippi, North Carolina, South Carolina, and Virginia, for 73 more. Then he needed all of the West: Alaska, Arizona, Idaho, Kansas, Montana, Nebraska, Nevada, North Dakota, Oklahoma, South Dakota, Utah, Wyoming, and of course, mighty California. One hundred ten electoral votes in the West. That would get Justice to 239—31 short of victory. Justice had to gather those votes out of the 53 available in states even harder to predict than essential California: Colorado, Delaware, Indiana, Iowa, Kentucky, Missouri, and New Hampshire.

Early exit polls gave Zeke everything he needed in the Northeast and South. Florida teetered as did Indiana, even though its polls closed first in the nation. Results looked good in the West, although California held at fifty-fifty long after the polls closed.

Zeke sweated it out with the Mormon and just three aides until three in the morning, Central time, when California came in for Justice and Vice President Sandman gave a choked but nonetheless boring concession speech. Zeke stood up, rubbed his sore back and eyes smarting from the computer screen, and went upstairs to congratulate the president-elect.

17

Julia Early arrived at her desk in the Credit Department of Capital National Bank thirty minutes late and hungover on the morning after the election. She had gone to a series of press parties with Charles Taylor, who, unlike her, disparaged Governor Tolliver, but like her had predicted his victory. Justice had won the narrowest victory since 1960, near dead even with Sandman at 49.1 percent of the popular vote. Tolliver's margin in the Electoral College was just twelve votes.

But Justice had won and Julia had celebrated through breakfast. She hung up her raincoat in the closet, got herself a cup of coffee from the urn in the supply room and sat at her desk. She felt weary, her head ached and her mouth was as dry as cotton. She took a sip of bitter coffee, fought down the urge to gag, and turned on her computer monitor. "You have new e-mail," the screen reported.

Julia rubbed her temples. She liked Charles, but she felt he squired her around largely because she thought she had some insight into Rupert Justice Tolliver that she didn't. His calls became less frequent, not the least, she believed, because she wouldn't sleep with him. Julia wasn't ready for any commitment, and she was a Texas country girl with a strong family and a lifelong center on the Baptist Church. She was also a virgin and had no hurry to alter that.

Besides, Charles had slept with Judith, and that was a little close to home, although Julia had no illusions that either Charles or Judith would care.

Julia downloaded her e-mail. Six items, five of them administrative notes from the head of training and the head of Credit Policy. The sixth was a reminder from the Americas and Caribbean Lending Group that she was overdue on her review of the Uvalde County Savings and Loan Society.

Oh God, Julia thought. She considered getting her coat and going home, pleading illness. She certainly felt bad enough, and a review of the poorly organized and neglected credit file would only give her eyestrain and add to her headache. Instead, she took two aspirin from her purse, swallowed them with cold coffee, and trudged to the Credit Library to draw out the hated file.

The file had increased in size from a single manila folder and a thin correspondence file to two brown expanding files and another labeled "Communications." One of the bored clerks in the library got a cart and placed the files on its top shelf. Julia reckoned she was looking at four linear feet of documents. The clerk, a pallid girl with dirty red hair and pimples, offered to wheel the files back to Julia's desk. Julia thanked her but said she would take it herself.

"I'll need that cart back," the girl said suspiciously.

"As soon as I can," Julia replied. "I won't be able to put all this stuff on my desk."

"We only got three carts," the girl whined.

"As soon as I can," Julia said firmly, and lurched off from the door of the library.

By the time she pushed the heavy cart through the carpet back to her desk, she was sweating and dizzy. She ran to the ladies' room, skipping, hurrying, thinking she might be sick. She didn't want to be sick. She splashed cold water on her face and neck, then drank about a pint from her cupped hands. Her face in the mirror shocked her; she hadn't looked that bad when she had got up to her shrilling alarm barely an hour ago.

Julia went back to her desk. There were many empty places and the room was very quiet. Smart ones stayed home, she thought bitterly. Neither of her roommates was at her desk. I guess they know better than to think Washington would be business as usual the night after a dramatic, close election.

Julia selected the thickest accordion file, labeled "Deposits, Transfers and Line Usage," and opened it to the first page.

The paper file was two weeks out of date and showed infrequent, but increasingly large, transfers from the Nassau, Bahamas, and George Town, Cayman Islands, branches of Capital National Bank, into and out of European and Asian banks, and—

And back to Uvalde Savings and Little Cheyenne Development.

Julia keyed the account numbers into her computer to get the current activity. The screen, originating at the current date and flashing backward, was full of entries back to the first of November. Julia kicked it back a screen and found the entries had begun to accelerate around the tenth of October, the time—

The time Tolliver's massive ad campaign had kicked in, the time Tolliver had buried his opponent in accusations and innuendo the vice president had no time to refute.

As much as Julia supported Justice Tolliver, she had felt uneasy. More than uneasy.

Julia keyed the Little Cheyenne file. Identical transfers in, and mirror transfers to a hundred individuals and companies, mostly in Texas but some offshore. Transfers Julia was sure would have become contributions to the Tolliver campaign in the closing weeks.

Of course, she thought. Tolliver needed television money to break Sandman's late surge.

But where had it come from?

Julia began to dig a backtrace on the computer. She felt angry and betrayed. Money-laundering was difficult to trace, but not impossible.

* * *

COBRA READ OF Justice Tolliver's victory in a week-old edition of the *Rand Daily Mail.* He was amused, but he had more immediate problems. A wet spring and early summer had brought blight to his vines and smut and insects to his wheat fields. He had to plow crops under and buy feed for his thinning livestock. There would be no grape harvest worth collecting.

Cobra hadn't worked in his old business since 1981, and over the years since had invested nearly his entire stash of money in the farm, violating a rule of many years to leave the money in Switzerland and Belgium alone as guarantee of his peaceful retirement. But he began to love his land, and his crops and his relations with his workers and the seminomad Zulu herders who grazed their cattle across his grass and recompensed him by trading through him, cattle for sale, goods to be purchased. South African wines became sought after in Europe and the United States, and Cobra brought his money in and bought more good land and cultivated it.

Then came the international boycott against the white rulers of South Africa, and his wines stayed in their cellars. His farms, bought with cash from Swiss banks, acquired mortgages. His aging stock of wines became collateral for more debt. He despaired of losing all, and wondered what he would do next.

Then Nelson Mandela made his peaceful revolution, a war not of guns but of flowers, songs, and dances. The boycott fell, and suddenly it all seemed possible again. Cobra continued to hang on, aided by his bankers, who had too many farms under mortgage to foreclose any that had any chance of deliverance. Cobra hung on, but he had no reserve.

Cobra thought back to his last years in loyal service to any who could pay.

COBRA HAD BEEN HIRED, by the gun broker Rokovski, to go to Rio de Janeiro in 1973. He was met by a man in plain clothes who took him to a small hotel. The Brazilian identified himself as Coronel Suares of the *Serviço Nacional de Informaceos,* Brazil's secret police. There were other officers in the room, in uniform. Cobra was told, obliquely, that a secret operation was planned, that no one expected would be a secret for long. Brazil, whose national motto was *Ordem e Progesso,* was ruled by a military government. The colonel explained that Brazil felt increasingly threatened by the rise of leftist regimes in Argentina, Peru, and especially Chile. The Brazilians had decided to teach a lesson, and the place to do it was Chile, with its democratically elected (wink), highly visible president, Dr. Salvador Allende Gossens.

"You see, senhor," the colonel said. "Brazil respects its neighbors, and all the countries of Latin America have common frontiers with Brazil save two: Ecuador and Chile. If we reach out to Chile, the continent will know we are here and we will not tolerate leftist radicals to infect our continent."

"What is the military situation?" Cobra asked. "I confess to be ignorant of this continent."

"The Chilean military is united in the need to topple this mad professor, but he is clever. Three months ago, Chilean truckers went on strike because their prices are fixed by the government, but the price of fuel has skyrocketed. So Allende, already suspecting trouble from the army and especially the air force, sent the entire air fleet to Arica, in the far northern desert, then took all military stocks of fuel and sold it to the truckers, who generally support his syndicalist madness, at low prices. Most of the army's tanks are restricted to barracks in the north and also without fuel.

"What we will do is refuel and rearm that air force and army. We have the cooperation of the Government of Bolivia, who thinks much as we do. Nothing on paper, nothing official, but our tanker trucks and munitions trucks will travel unimpeded across Bolivia to Arica and other locations. We have no intention of being subtle, although of course we will issue the usual denials. The fuel trucks will be borrowed from Petrobras, and will have the normal yellow paint job with the green 'BR' on the sides. The operation will begin in seven to ten days."

Crazy, Cobra thought. It's better to strike from darkness and without warning. "What do you wish of me?"

"Go to Santiago de Chile. We will furnish papers and money, and of course your payment. The Hilton Hotel is across the central plaza from the *Case de Moneda,* the presidential palace. You will stay at the Hilton, on the top floor. The Moneda will be precision-bombed; it's sufficiently isolated that the Chilean air force expects little collateral damage. The armor, however, will be late arriving, since they can't leave their cantonments before the air force flies at the risk of tipping the government and allowing it to flee.

"We have therefore engaged three shootists, all untraceable foreigners like yourself, to cover the exits from the Moneda. You will be in your room or on the roof of the Hilton with a view of the main entrance, and also of the balcony from which Allende likes to make speeches, and may appear to rally his supporters, the underclasses of Santiago. If he appears at either the door or the balcony, he is not to speak or depart."

Cobra nodded. "*Claro,*" he said. Understood.

Seven days later the coup exploded from the north. The bombing was precise and devastating. Salvador Allende Gossens did indeed appear on the balcony, wrapped in the Chilean flag. The plaza had been emptied by the bombers, but he began to speak anyway, into a microphone Cobra presumed to be radio or television.

Cobra dropped him with a single shot from a German Mauser SP66 sniper rifle supplied by the Brazilian SNI. Cobra left the roof immediately; state television, in the hands of the military under General Pinochet, the new president, later reported Allende had been shot by a Chilean paratrooper while armed and trying to flee.

Cobra didn't care about the lie. His business did not benefit from press cuttings.

Cobra was back in Africa in a week, his bank account once again flush.

* * *

For several years, 1974–1981, he stayed home in Africa, a continent that continued to create great wealth for a few based on grinding poverty for the masses. Cobra hadn't been proud of his service with Idi Amin Dada and Mad Mike Harris, but Amin had paid well for a while, and it was possible to overlook the madman's excesses as being nothing more than the continental norm. Both Harris and Cobra had been forced to run, unpaid, from Amin's anger after they failed to prevent or defeat the Israeli raid on Entebbe Airfield in 1976, although they were later invited back. When Milton Obote invaded from Tanzania in 1979 to reestablish his own cruel rule over the tortured citizens of Uganda, Harris went to South Africa while Cobra returned to Southern Rhodesia. He was badly wounded in a raid into Mozambique two years later, but at least collected most of his pay. In the same year he bought his farm in the hills near Stellenbosch.

He invested, more than he should, he knew, of his reserves. Perhaps it was a vanity when he acquired his own presses and winery and started marketing his own label, the fixed costs of which nearly drove him under during the boycott. Then things began to ease, and when the opportunity came along to take his shot in St. Petersburg, he banked the money in Europe, once again swearing to put no more into the land.

But when his neighbors, a young Boer family he liked very much, decided to emigrate with their young children to the white haven of Australia, he had to buy their farm. It was a lovely piece of bottomland that had been cultivated for three hundred years along a river that never failed even in droughts. Cobra planted the hillsides with vines from California and the Loire, and planted fruit trees as well in the lush soil. His Russian windfall dwindled but the farms prospered.

Cobra stopped his musing. Last dry season the river had shrunk to pools strung together by a thread of flowing water, and the vines had shriveled. The deeper rooted trees survived but bore little fruit. This year, the river had dried to a few water holes and buffalo wallows. Cobra was once again up against it with the banks.

Cobra rode around the farm on his favorite walking horse, a shiny-coated bay gelding. Another extravagance, he reflected, patting the horse's shoulder. He stopped and talked to each of his field bosses; the news was universally bad.

I'm fifty-five, he thought. Four years since the Russian job, the one he'd thought would be the last. He hadn't even hunted game since then, hardly ever fired a rifle. It had been fully twenty years since he'd fought as a soldier.

I'm still fit enough, he thought as he rode among dying orchards. But the world was distressingly peaceful, and he had no idea how to reestablish contacts with the shadow world of killers for hire.

Maybe I'll go up north and guide tourists after elephant and lions, he thought bleakly. God only knew how many guides, more experienced than him, had little or no work.

Nonetheless, he decided to make a few careful contacts. He would not lose his home.

Something would present itself. Something always did.

III

A RECKONING

1

JANUARY 20, 2001, dawned fine and bitterly cold in the nation's capital. Washington is a southern town and usually maintains a mild climate through the winter, but for some reason inauguration days were nearly always cold. At least this year there was no snow, although a biting wind swirled among the grandstands erected in front of the Capitol, lifting trash and dust and rattling the many flags and thousands of yards of bunting.

Rupert Justice Tolliver awoke at dawn as he always did, full of energy and purpose despite a mild hangover. *I rise today for the last time as Brother Justice from the windy dry hills of south Texas,* he thought as he chased Clarissa out of bed and chivied her to hurry and dress. *Tonight when I go to bed in that old white house over yonder, I will be the President of the United States.*

They were staying in the grand old Willard Hotel, just two blocks from the White House. The Willard would be the site of the grandest of fourteen Inaugural Balls Justice and Clarissa would have to at least look in on, take a slow dance around for the invited fat cats who had paid (and would continue to pay) the freight. People Justice didn't know and didn't care about, but it had to be done. There'd be time enough to change the pompous rituals once he began governing.

Clarissa finally emerged from the bathroom, looking pretty but pissed off in a dark blue suit and red silk blouse. The skirt was daringly short. "Catch your death," Justice remarked. "Leastway your pussy will."

Clarissa shot him a black look. She hated to be awakened before midmorning, inauguration or no. "What the hell's the hurry? We don't get sworn in until noon."

"We got to go to church first, darling."

"At the crack of dawn?" she asked, primping her shiny dark hair in front of a long mirror.

"Why sure, honey. Don't forget we be God-fearing. We thanking the Almighty twice, in fact, first at the National Cathedral with all the congressmen and ambassadors and others of quality, then a prayer breakfast at the African Methodist Episcopal up Fourteenth Street; show off my new solidarity with the niggers."

"To think you promised an administration free of hypocrisy," Clarissa said tartly, buttoning a long wool coat that matched her suit. "Let's go, then. It's going to be a very long day of praying and swearing and dancing the night-away."

It's the first day of the dream, Justice thought. Don't forget God sent you here, another thought intruded as Zeke Archer beckoned them from the door of their suite toward the elevator and the waiting line of black limousines below.

Julia Early tapped listlessly on her computer keyboard in the vast bay of the Credit Department on the eighth floor of the bank. Inauguration Day coincided with the official birthday of Dr. Martin Luther King Jr., so the bank was closed and the Credit Department nearly empty. Julia and a few others behind on their reviews of customers under their purview were scattered around the larger room, staring at computers or getting paper cuts. Julia planned to take a break from her work to watch Tolliver sworn in on the television set in the conference room. The good news was that once the reviews were completed and accepted by the lending officers, most of the trainees would move on to permanent jobs.

Julia couldn't wait to finish training; she had a tentative offer from the bank's European Division, with a hope of an eventual posting to London or Paris. Imagine, she thought, from Uvalde and Austin to London or Paris!

Her toughest problem was the one she wished she had never seen, Uvalde County Savings and Loan and its major client, Little

Cheyenne Development Corporation. She analyzed the fourth-quarter financial statements; they were at least in standard SEC format, a major improvement from when she had first seen the file. She spread the statements and signed off; she didn't know how much she believed them, despite comforting assurances from Preston and Martinez of San Antonio, certified public accountants and auditors to the bank. The grindy part of the analysis was the flurry of money transfers, all conducted through, or at least touching on, overseas branches of Capital National Bank. Money sticking in Uvalde accounts and in accounts belonging to Little Cheyenne had slowed to a trickle after the election but had picked up again right before the first of the year, and a dip into the Money Transfer Department's computer area confirmed payments were ongoing.

Somebody ran a bunch of money into Rupert Justice Tolliver's campaign in the closing weeks, Julia thought as she tapped her teeth with a pencil eraser. And somebody was still paying the President of the United States.

She looked at her watch; nearly noon. She went into the conference room to hear the oath, and to see what the new president, a man she had once admired but now doubted, had to say.

MY FELLOW CITIZENS," Justice boomed. The wind that had been blowing flags and bunting around and ruining costly hairdos dropped suddenly as the new president began to speak, and a hole opened in the scudding gray clouds to allow brilliant sunshine to fall on the podium. "My brothers and my sisters. Today we begin a new century, a new millennium, and a new national renewal. Today we cast off limits imposed by a political system that has grown old and stiff as the nation has grown young and supple. Today we revere our history of peaceful changes of government, a tradition that dates to the beginning of the republic and the hand-over of power two hundred and four years ago from George Washington, a man beseeched by many to make himself a king, to John Adams, his elected successor." Justice turned and extended his hand to President Blythe, the man he had just succeeded. "I congratulate my predecessor, and applaud his help with the transition, given freely even though our philosophies and policies are very different." Blythe took Tolliver's hand, a startled look on his face, shook it once and dropped it.

"I come here with a mandate to clean house, to renew and rebuild," Justice said, looking over at the section of the grandstand reserved for senior editors and news anchors. The press had hounded him since November about the thinness of his victory providing no mandate. "And I will clean and rebuild, but on the solid foundation of work of the men and women of this glorious republic.

"Expect great change amid reverence for great tradition. Be prepared to answer President Kennedy's call to do more for, and ask less from, your country. Remember what President Truman said about responsibility: the Buck stops here." Tolliver paused for applause; the media assholes like it I cite two Democrats, he thought, but who would he quote of modern Republicans? Bush? Hardly, and even Reagan the Great Communicator had left little of memory. Lincoln, of course.

"We will reform, but with malice toward none and charity for all. We will bind up wounds of race and poverty. We will defend our borders and our lives from illegal immigration while striving to knit the many rich and diverse traditions of our people into a strong, many-colored fabric, a choir of many different but equally sweet angels and not a jumble of angry and unheard voices. This we promise.

"We will deal fairly with the people of all nations. We will share with those that love us and try to reach out to those that wish us ill. We will chastise those that harm us only with the greatest reluctance and regret. This we promise.

"We will bring our brothers and sisters, and most importantly, our sons and daughters, into a community with God. We'll force religion on no one, but we'll deny its benefits to no one." Justice took off his glasses and dabbed his eyes. "With God's help, all these things we promise."

The president left the podium to thunderous cheers. He

embraced the Reverend Louis Mohammed-Ali, the preacher who had given the invocation preceding his speech, then descended the steps of the Capitol and walked, arm in arm with his wife, into the crowd and on up Pennsylvania Avenue to the White House from whence he would review the parade.

Julia Early dabbed her eyes and clapped, as did most of the junior bankers in the conference room, then went back to her desk. Judith Langtry, her roommate, passed by, and reminded her the credit library closed at one-thirty, so they might's well go get a drink.

A few minutes more, Julia replied. There were some interesting new entries in the files coming up from Money Transfer Research.

Brilliant damn speech, she thought. He is the hope of a great nation.

Julia opened the correspondence file. The blurry numbers on the Xerox copies danced before tired eyes. She clasped her hands together and put her head down for a second, to rest her eyes.

She was instantly asleep.

2

COBRA WATCHED THE NEW American president sworn in on his little Japanese television when the inauguration came on at 7:00 P.M., South African time. He'd spent the day with bankers in Cape Town; they were sympathetic but able to do little for him. The drought and the blight continued; the river continued to dry. Rain was still months away if it came at all, then there would be the expenses of tearing out the shriveled vines and fruit trees and replanting. The Zulu headman had come by to talk after lunch; Cobra had asked him for some payment on the supplies he had delivered. The chief had no calves to sell, and no money, and he asked Cobra for a loan.

And there was no word from old acquaintances in Brussels or Lisbon. Cobra felt very alone, old, and tired.

* * *

JULIA AWOKE WITH a start. The credit department was empty and the sky outside the windows was nearly dark, with just the orange smear of the sunset over Virginia to the west. Christ! She thought, looking at her watch. Nearly five. She ran over to the entrance to the Credit Library but of course it was locked and dark. She went back to her desk. The overhead lights were dimmed and her computer cast a cold glow from its screen saver. How could everyone, especially Judith, have just left her here asleep at her desk? And what was she going to do with the credit files? Bank policy specifically forbade keeping files anywhere but in the Credit Library.

There was nothing for it. She crammed the bulky files into her desk and locked it. The last one, the correspondence file, wouldn't fit, so she put it in her briefcase. She knew she shouldn't remove it from the building, but she couldn't very well leave it on top of her desk. She got her coat from the closet, picked up the briefcase, and headed for the elevators. I hope I'm not locked in, she thought as the elevator took her to the lobby. But the security uniform was on station by his monitors. He made her sign the Late Log, then unlocked the front door and let her out.

She woke up the following morning with a fever of 103 degrees Fahrenheit. She called in sick and went back to bed.

PRESIDENT TOLLIVER WALKED into the Oval Office at 10:30, looking puffy, disheveled, and pissed off. Ezekiel Archer, now the president's chief of staff, waited as he had since the appointed hour of eight o'clock. The president fell into the leather chair that had been made for the fatter ass of his predecessor and said, "Coffee."

"Certainly, Mr. President," Zeke said, buzzing for the duty steward, a navy petty officer. "Breakfast?"

"Yeah, maybe. A Bloody Mary made with real blood, then some tea and toast."

The steward, a navy sailor in dress blues, stood at the door to the pantry, heard the president's request, and backed out without a word. Zeke took a stack of papers from his briefcase and laid them gently on the president's desk. Tolliver held his big head in his hands and rubbed his throbbing temples. "We need to make some decisions on the cabinet, Mr. President, and on legislative priorities."

"Aw, shit, Zeke, cut the crap. When we're alone, use my damn name."

"Sure, Juss." Zeke paused as the black steward entered silently, placed the president's breakfast before him, and departed immediately. "Shall we start with the cabinet?"

"We already named the damn cabinet."

"We'll have some trouble getting them all confirmed, Juss. The Democrats are complaining that while many are able men, they don't reflect the diversity of the nation."

"Fuck the Democrats. We have a majority in the Senate."

"Only two votes, and not all Republicans are immune to pressure from advocacy groups."

Tolliver took the large Bloody Mary in both hands and raised it carefully to his lips. He took a long swallow, closed his eyes, and sighed. "This is all the doing of that dickhead who just left this office. Diversity, my ass. Everybody in *his* cabinet had to be a woman, a nigger, a spic, a Jew, gay and an academic, and look at the messes they had, the scandals. Zeke, if you can bring me a list of black Jewish women that are half Mexican, hold professorships at Ivy League schools, need wheelchair access, and sleep with their sisters, I'll put 'em in office, but somehow I don't think it'll turn out that way. Let's see how many of my choices we can keep."

Zeke sighed. "All white men, Juss. All Christian."

"And all able, Zeke. Top lawyers, former legislators, chief executives of big corporations, men who can run complex organizations. That's what we learned down in Austin, Zeke, get able men to run the big departments, then you and me can have the fun of shaking things up."

"I'll go back to the Capitol this afternoon and see what we can get."

"Yeah. Give 'em that old Roosevelt shit about 'having a mandate from the people.' "

"Roosevelt had rather larger mandates than forty-nine percent of the vote," Zeke said unhappily.

"Yeah, but I got you, Zeke, the finest horse trader in Texas, which means in the world." He took another slug of his drink, needing only one hand this time, and ate a bit of toast. He managed a grin. "Now leave me be to think up what hornet's nest to kick over first."

Mr. Hollis?" the sweet voice of Amanda Schwartz came softly through the speaker-phone of Reginald Hollis, the head of Credit and Training.

He immediately snatched up the receiver; Ms. Schwartz, known as Dragon Mother, was the executive secretary of Alfred Thayer, Chairman of the Board of Capital National Bank, and spoke to no one on a speakerphone. "Yes, Ms. Schwartz, good morning," smarmed Hollis. Bad news with no possible doubt.

"Good morning. Could you please arrange to retrieve a couple of customer credit files? And send them up to me?"

"I'll get them at once, Ms. Schwartz, and bring them up myself," Hollis fawned. "What files were you wanting?"

"Only two," the Dragon Mother crooned. "Uvalde Savings and Loan, and Little Cheyenne Development Company. I believe both are in Texas."

Hollis stood to attention. A little bell of fear tinkled in his brain. Why were those names familiar? "At once, Ms. Schwartz."

Julia felt a little better by noon and got up to make some tea and toast. She sat in the tiny kitchen, poured the tea, and

CALGARY PUBLIC LIBRARY

W.R. Castell Central Library

Self Checkout

March 18,2017 13:52

39065144303128 4/8/2017

Adult paperback - Central - 2016

39065060381173 4/8/2017

Behold a pale horse

Total 2 item(s)

You have 0 item(s) ready for pickup

To check your card and renew items

go to www.calgarylibrary.ca

or call 403-262-2928

looked around for the newspaper. Hilda had taken it to work; she always did. Then Julia noticed her briefcase in the front hall where she'd dropped it the night before, and remembered what was in it; the Correspondence File from Uvalde Savings and Little Cheyenne. She yawned. Might's well get into it, she said to herself.

An hour later she was shivering, and not from her flu. Some of the letters, money transfer covers, mostly, had been stamped "DESTROY." All should have been.

How could anyone have allowed the filing of such incriminating documents? she wondered. She read on because she had no idea what else she ought to do.

WHAT DO YOU MEAN, the files are unavailable?" Reginald Hollis demanded, his reddening face contradicting his calm voice. "Where else can they be but here in the library?"

Monica Croft, the Credit Librarian, stammered, more than usual because she knew Hollis's horrible temper never stayed hidden for long. "I'm looking at the log, Mr. Hollis. They must have been checked out."

"Checked *out?*" Hollis said, his voice growing at once more softer and more urgent. "Policy clearly states—"

"Of course it does," Monica said, gathering some courage from the asshole's petty fit. "But analysts come in on weekends to catch up, or on holidays, like yesterday's, and we have only a volunteer junior clerk on duty." She stabbed her finger at the logbook for yesterday and looked up over her half glasses, pinning the fat little man with hard eyes. "Uvalde Savings and Little Cheyenne were checked out yesterday and not returned when the clerk locked up at one. It was missed."

"Who has them?" he asked. Who fucked up? He wanted to ask, and would he avoid the blame?

Monica Croft pushed her glasses up her long nose. "Julia Early."

Hollis took a deep breath. Early, the pretty, bright one, too country to get the hint that he wanted to help her along if she would only sleep with him. "Come with me to her desk, Monica," he said, calming, trying a little smile. "We'll sort this out."

"Yes, sir. But she's out sick today."

Hollis paled. "Come along anyway."

JULIA READ ON through the afternoon. Money had poured into the Little Cheyenne accounts at Uvalde Savings from all over the country and all over the world, but most had come from banks in Panama and the Caribbean, or had at least been routed through such banks. Julia created a worksheet on her own personal computer and listed the contributions by paying bank, its location, date, and amount. She correlated the payments with notations in the correspondence from Uvalde Savings and determined that between October of 2000 and the end of the year, "downpayments" summed to $30 million, more than three times the *total* value of all lots available for sale at Little Cheyenne, and that since January 2001, payments listed for "utility connections, common facilities, and pre-construction expenses" totaled another $18 million.

Deep in the file was a brochure showing aerial photos of the site, an unimproved wooded valley around an oxbow lake and the slender, slow-moving Little Cheyenne River. Next to the photos was a map showing sixty-two homesites, space for a "central core" containing utilities, security and fire-fighting services, and common facilities such as a riverside marina, tennis courts, and a pool. But no photos of these, or any evidence of even the beginnings of construction of any kind.

Sixty-two building lots, and an average of $775,000 spent for "down payments" and "improvements." Julia couldn't believe the audacity of it, hidden away in an obscure file in a closely controlled bank. What should she do? Destroy the file? It wasn't her responsibility and was probably illegal, and besides, might there not be copies? She never should have brought it home; she never should have looked at it, just spread the numbers and written the usual single-sentence memo on the Credit Department brown sheet: "Statements spread and reviewed, client in compliance with all requirements of policy and agreements," and sent the file on to the lending officer.

But now she knew, and you can't "unknow" something.

The phone on the kitchen wall rang loudly, and she jumped. She picked it up. "Julia Early," an angry male voice said. "This is Reginald Hollis. Unless your illness is serious, it is imperative you come to the bank, my office, right away."

"Mr. Hollis—"

"Bring any and all records you may have removed from the bank. All. I'm sending a car; it will be at your door in ten minutes." Hollis abruptly hung up.

Julia's heart raced. Fine, I'll just give it back. But they'll know I read it, even if I deny it. God, what to do?

She shoved the bulky file into her empty suitcase and locked it and shoved it to the back of the messy closet she shared with Hilda. She hurried to shower and dress.

REGINALD HOLLIS AND Monica Croft had found Julia's desk locked. Hollis had a wild thought of getting a hammer and a screwdriver from maintenance and breaking the drawers open, but that would show panic. What did Old Man Thayer want with the damn file anyway? Ms. Schwartz hadn't expressed any real urgency. "What do you want to do, Reginald?" Monica asked.

Hollis looked at his watch. Nearly eleven-thirty. "Please call Safe and Lock over at the Operations Building in Southeast. Try to catch them before they all knock off for lunch; get them to unlock the desk but then not let anyone near it until I get back." He sighed. "I'll call Ms. Schwartz and tell her we have a little problem, then I have a lunch myself; be back around two."

It was after Hollis returned from lunch, a couple of martinis in him for courage, that he found the missing files in Julia Early's desk that prompted his angry call to Julia that sent her scurrying into the shower and jumping into her clothes and down the stairs to the waiting black limousine.

3

Zeke Archer spent the entire day wandering the gloomy halls of the Capitol, visiting committee chairs and other powerful senators of both parties. Zeke was indeed a fine horse trader, and he had every detail of each senator's wants and needs, ambitions and embarrassments, committed to memory just like a man who practiced the art with real horses would know bloodlines, ailments, gaits, and temperaments. Zeke promised action on self-serving legislation, no use of the line-item veto on pet pork projects, federal jobs, just about everything he would like to have saved for later if he could get Justice to replace just a few of those white faces in blue suits with a woman or two, an African-American, and maybe at least one member of the growing and increasingly assertive Hispanic community.

Zeke finished his rounds at four-thirty and climbed wearily back into his limousine for the short trip to the White House.

Julia hurried to the eighth floor and to her desk. All the drawers were open and the files gone; her personal articles and files were dumped in a messy circle around the workstation. She booted up her computer, tried to log on, and received a message, "Code discontinued; access denied; contact Network Supervisor."

She hung up her coat and went to Mr. Hollis's corner office. His secretary, a pleasant and usually very helpful black woman named Tyra, frowned and beckoned Julia close. "Your tits are in the wringer, girlfriend. I'm to send you right upstairs to seventeen, the chairman's office."

"Jeez, Tyra, just because I didn't return a file on time?"

"I don't know. Hollis is jumping out of his skin. Good luck."

Julia went into the ladies' room and straightened her skirt, tried to brush some order into her damp hair, and reapplied her makeup. She rode the elevator up to the executive floor, lofty seventeen, a place she had never before been. She asked the uniformed security guard for the chairman's office. He made a call from his console and asked her, quite courteously, to wait. After about three very long minutes, a young woman, also in uniform but, unlike the seated guard, unarmed, came and got her and led her to another reception area, where a hard-eyed woman of middle age with improbable red hair sat at a computer. The page departed. The red-haired woman did not look up from her work for another long three minutes as Julia fidgeted. "There," she said, ending whatever she was doing with a flurry of keystrokes. "You must be Ms. Early. I'm Ms. Schwartz, the chairman's executive assistant."

Julia bobbed her head. The Dragon Mother was a legend, a destroyer of careers, even those of senior vice presidents. Julia could think of nothing to say.

Ms. Schwartz frowned. Oh shit, Julia thought, I haven't shown proper respect, or whatever it was. The Dragon Mother snatched a white phone off her console. "Ms. Early is here." Julia gritted her teeth. Ms. Schwartz gave her a smile that looked more like a grimace. "You're to go right in," she said, pointing to double doors of solid oak.

The secretary made no move to open the doors, so Julia drew herself into an erect posture, marched to the door and gripped the brass handle. It failed to yield. "The other door, dear," Ms. Schwartz said with ill-concealed malice. Nearing panic, Julia fumbled for the other handle, and almost fell into the room as the heavy door swung silently inward, balanced by counterweights.

Julia expected to be impressed by the office of the Chairman of Capital National Bank, but instead she was awed. The corner room must have been fifty feet on a side, with panoramic views up and down Pennsylvania Avenue, from the Capitol in the east to the Treasury, the chimneys of the White House, the Mall, the Lincoln Memorial, and even the Arlington Mansion backlit by low sunlight to the west. The walls were paneled with rich dark wood, decorated with portraits of old white men, the carpet was a rich blue with a fine Oriental rug over it. The chairman's huge desk, the size of a Buick, was in the corner of the window walls. The man himself was silhouetted by the setting sun. He looked small and old, with a fine head of silver hair. Reginald Hollis stood next to the desk, at rigid attention. Another man, younger, languid, with a bored look on his face, sat in a low leather couch. Alongside the paneled wall to Julia's right as she entered was a polished conference table that matched the dark paneling. The files from Uvalde County Savings and Loan and Little Cheyenne Development were stacked neatly on the table, and Monica Croft, the credit librarian, sat poring through them, apparently counting pages. The Correspondence File was, of course, missing. Julia's heart raced.

To her left was a group of chairs and couches around a low table that looked like what Julia imagined a gentlemen's club in London might appear. The room smelled of lemon-oil wood polish and old cigar smoke. No one spoke as Julia advanced halfway across the thick carpet and stopped, her hands clutched in front of her crotch, her heart pounding.

The chairman rose slowly. "Ms. Early, I'm Alfred Thayer. Would you be so kind as to have a word with Mr. Hollis, over there?" he gestured at the club chairs to her left. "I'll be just a few minutes, then I'll join you."

Now I'm going to get it, Julia thought grimly as she turned to the chairs and waited for Hollis to march over. He looks like he's had a broomstick rammed up his ass, she thought irreverently. Maybe he had.

* * *

ZEKE REACHED THE OVAL Office and was told by Mrs. Carradine to go right in. Jenna Carradine had been Governor Tolliver's executive secretary in Austin, and onetime mistress. Now in her mid-forties, with the strawberry-blond dyed "big hair" popular in Texas, the early-lined face of a heavy smoker, and the loud voice and laugh of a good ol' girl, she didn't fit in with Washington's quieter tones and Zeke thought her something of an embarrassment.

Zeke found the president sprawled on a leather easy chair in front of the marble fireplace. A fire blazed cheerily and made the office stuffy. Since the president was in shirtsleeves, Zeke shucked his overcoat and suit jacket. "Make yourself a drink, and refresh mine," Tolliver said without looking up from the yellow legal pad he was scribbling on.

Zeke took the president's glass from his hand, went to the sideboard and filled it with bourbon and ice. He mixed a light scotch and soda for himself; he was too tired to trust himself with anything stronger. He went over and took a chair opposite the president, as far from the fire as possible. "How'd the trading go today?" Tolliver asked.

Zeke sipped his drink before answering. The trading was just beginning. "In order to get your cabinet list approved, you'll have to give nearly every committee chair and ranking minority member his or her pet project. Do that and you'll never get a budget passed."

The president looked up from his writing. Zeke had expected anger, but Tolliver looked merely calculating. "What if we turn it around? Give them some minor cabinet posts, some number-two jobs? Make them owe us."

Zeke thought about it. "President Blythe insisted one of the 'big four' cabinet posts be a woman. There are now over a hundred women in Congress, and they and the women's groups would like that seen as a precedent."

"Look what he got for his trouble," Justice sneered. "A prominent liberal lawyer and a New York judge thrown out because they hired illegal aliens to watch their kids, and finally a cracker county prosecutor from some awful place in the Everglades. Zeke, that was a mistake not worth repeating."

"True, but we Republicans have many better qualified woman candidates, some of whom are bulletproof in the Senate."

"Like who?"

"Carolyn White. A professor of history at Stanford, advised both the Reagan and Bush administrations, considered a top foreign-policy mind. Put her in State or Defense."

Justice leaned back, sipped his drink. "She's black, right?"

"Yes, she is."

"Two points. But Jesus, Zeke, do you think a college professor could run State? Those career diplomatic service assholes would eat her alive."

"Better Defense. We'd get her a strong number two to run the day to day."

Tolliver pondered. "I intend makin' some serious changes in foreign and military affairs. You know that, Zeke."

"All the better you have a Secretary of Defense the Congress can't beat up on."

"Well, I'll think on that. That be enough to get the rest of the list?"

"What I'd recommend," Zeke said carefully, "is toss a few bones in some of the lesser departments. I have a list of safe Republicans, some Hispanic, some black, that you might appoint to head departments like Education, Health and Human Services, Housing, Transportation."

Tolliver slapped his knee and guffawed. "You know what I got in front of me? My first major piece of legislation to throw at those squirrels up yonder in the Capitol as soon as we get a budget agreed. My Reorganization of Government Act."

Zeke was startled. "That's heavy lifting, Juss. Second-term stuff. You don't have the votes, the mandate."

"I ran on a platform of cleaning the stables, and clean them I will. No pussyfooting, Zeke. We're not going to close a few pissant agencies and eliminate the honey-bee subsidies, we're gonna ax whole departments."

Zeke shook his head. "Which ones first?"

"You just named all of them. Education, Health and Human Services, Housing, and Transportation. So go ahead, Zeke, give those jobs to minorities, women, spics, whatever. They won't be around long enough to do any harm."

"This isn't Austin, Juss. The system will stop you at every turn."

The president stood up and stretched. "Zeke, old buddy, people, including you, been telling me that my whole damn life. I'll get it done."

"What about Professor White?"

"Call her. I'll set with her, see how it feels, see if we can do business."

"I'll do that, but I want to sound her out first. If we propose her, we can't have her turn us down."

"Yeah, go see her, whatever," Justice said, sitting and going back to his notes. "She's said to be pretty."

REGINALD HOLLIS SAT opposite Julia across the low table. His body language indicated extreme anxiety; legs clamped together, arms tight across his chest. He leaned forward. "I have to know what you were doing with that file," he said in a strangled whisper.

"I first saw it shortly after I started training," she said carefully. "It was incomplete, a mess. The lending officer instructed me to request a complete update from the correspondent bank and to re-review in six months. A couple of months ago I got a reminder from the lending officer, so I began a normal review."

Hollis thought about it. "How much analysis did you complete? Have you sent your report to the lending officers?"

"I was almost finished. It's on my computer."

No, it isn't, Hollis thought triumphantly. He'd seen to the erasure as soon as he found the files locked in Julia's desk. "Nothing printed?"

"No. I wasn't finished. I—" She almost said she hadn't finished with the Correspondence File. "I would have finished today if I hadn't got sick."

"Mr. Hollis? Ms. Early?" the chairman called in his low but carrying voice. "Could you both come over here, please?"

Hollis leaped to his feet like a scalded dog and hustled to the chairs in front of the chairman's desk. Julia followed more slowly. Thayer smiled benignly and waited until both were seated. "What have we discovered, Mr. Hollis?"

"Ms.—Ms. Early became ill and fell asleep yesterday," Hollis explained, trying to breathe normally and failing. "The Credit Library closed early because of the holiday. The clerk on duty apparently did not close out her log—retrieve all files—before she went home."

Alfred Thayer looked across his vast office at Monica Croft. "Monica?"

Monica stood, and approached the huge desk, bobbing her head as though approaching a king on his throne. "Mr. Thayer."

"Is the file complete?"

"It appears to be. Even a draft Brown Sheet from Ms. Early, in longhand."

"All accounted for? The Correspondence File?"

Monica shifted uneasily. "The Correspondence File is not here, nor is it in the library." Julia's heart seemed to stop and she struggled to breathe through clenched teeth. "But the Correspondence File was never signed out," Monica concluded, looking at Julia. "It's just missing."

"Missing." Thayer directed his icy gaze at Hollis, who shuddered. "Ms. Early?" Thayer asked, his voice kindly.

No guts, no glory, Julia thought. It was her father, a retired Texas Ranger's favorite expression. "I did my review based on the numbers. I don't recall seeing a correspondence file."

Thayer seemed to ponder that for a very long minute. "How far along were you with your analysis?" he asked Julia.

"Pretty well along," she stammered. "The computer stuff: balance sheet, income statement, cash flow." Account history, she should have added, money transfers, she should have added, but didn't.

Thayer smiled thinly. "Perhaps we're making too much of this. But confidentiality and security of clients' information is of the highest priority in this bank, Ms. Early. Ms. Croft. Mr. Hollis."

"Yes, Mr. Thayer," Hollis and Croft chorused. Julia said nothing.

"Lessons," Thayer said, his bony index finger touching the side of his ample nose, "will be learned, I trust?"

"Yes, sir," chanted Hollis and Croft. Julia intoned the same, a moment later.

"Good," Thayer said with another bloodless smile. "Ms. Croft, find the missing Correspondence File. Mr. Hollis, find useful work for young Ms. Early." Thayer looked to his left, toward the White House. "That will be all."

ALFRED THAYER WATCHED his terrified subordinates scurry from his large office. He liked his people afraid; he paid over the market at all levels to buy loyalty, and loyalty was best maintained by fear.

Thayer motioned to the man from the White House, who had remained seated behind the conference table, a commanding gesture that got the too-relaxed young man out of his couch and across to one of the chairs in front of the great desk. "Sit," Thayer said, and the man sat. Duane Callendar worked for Zeke Archer, who worked for the improbable new president, Justice Tolliver. It was Archer who had called early in the morning of this very long day and asked for whatever records the bank held on Uvalde County Savings and Loan and "any affiliates" that had caused all the scurrying around after the credit files. "Well," Thayer said. "There you have it. A minor breach of bank confidentiality, quickly contained."

"I'll so report," Callendar said skeptically. "Although some concerns remain about what may have been filed as correspondence."

"The file will turn up," Thayer said wearily. "They always do." He looked at the smooth young man who looked to have been polished and buffed to a hard, arrogant shine.

"What do you think might be in the file that is of concern to the White House?"

Callendar waved the thought away, an exaggerated gesture. "Who knows? Loose lips, all that. Perhaps something a reporter could inflate into a story."

"About what?" Thayer demanded. "Are we going to find any irregular activity in that bank? Hell, we only took them on at the request of the Republican National Committee."

"Quite," Callendar said crisply. "Because your bank has a long and proud tradition of protecting client confidences."

"We'll review the file," Thayer grated. "What are we going to find?"

Callendar shrugged. "The president—really the first lady—had an interest in Little Cheyenne, and a lot of their friends bought in, you know, kinda to be near the Tollivers, the prestige, etc. So she made a couple of bucks."

Thayer sighed. He had worked hard for Vice President Donahue's campaign, but not hard enough. Like most other mainline Republicans, he had not taken Rupert Justice Tolliver seriously until much too late, and he and his friends were now struggling to gain some influence over the rube. "How well did they—did the first lady—do?"

"Quite well," Callendar said coolly, studying his nails. "It was just an investment."

Thayer shook his head. "The money came in during the campaign."

"Well, yes, some of it."

"Most of it, if Hollis can still add and subtract."

Callendar stood up. He could take just so much of this pompous old man, whatever his influence. "Look, Mr. Thayer, you know this town, better than any of us on the president's team. You know how any rumor, any hint of impropriety, gets immediately blown out of all proportion."

Thayer allowed himself a ghost of a smile. "That bad, is it?"

Callendar frowned. "The White House's concern is simply to keep the private business of the first family private. The White House would like your assurance that that is the concern—the primary concern—of your bank as well."

Thayer stood, signaling he was through sparring with this puppy. "We'll do our part, keep our confidences."

"Thank you." Callendar extended his hand, which Thayer shook with great reluctance. "We'll owe you one."

"You will indeed," the old man said. "And I won't forget." Thayer dropped his hands to his sides and waited silently as the young man left the room.

JULIA AND HOLLIS rode the elevator down to eight. Hollis said nothing, but his face was flushed with rage. When the doors opened, he bolted from the car, nearly colliding with her. She went back to her desk and sat, began putting her personal items away, wondering if it was worth the bother. She still felt quite ill but thought she had better wait the last hour to five o'clock before departing, in case anybody wanted to fire her.

Why had she concealed the Correspondence File and lied about it? She had taken it because there simply wasn't any more lockable space in her desk. She'd lied because she was scared, but that wasn't all of it. Julia didn't scare easily. She'd lied because she felt she had been exposed to terrible secrets, and didn't want anyone to know what she knew. She wondered who the smooth-looking, cold-eyed man in Thayer's office who had not been introduced might be. He had the look of law enforcement about him;

Julia's father was a retired captain of the Texas Rangers, once head of the governor's security detail. Julia knew the look of cops. Could the man be a Secret Service agent? FBI?

Julia tapped her access code into the computer terminal and was instantly rewarded with the same flashing "Code discontinued; access denied" message. She walked over to Hilda's desk near the window and asked her to bring up Uvalde County Savings and Loan.

"Nothing on record," Hilda said, puzzled. "You've been working on that for weeks."

Julia shrugged. "I know. I guess maybe the account closed."

"Come on, Julia. Hollis was prowling around your desk like a caged lion this morning, then Safe and Lock came by and picked the lock and all the files were piled on Old Lady Croft's trolley and hustled off to the elevator. What were you working on? What did you find?"

"It might be better for your career if you didn't know," Julia whispered, catching sight of Hollis pop out of his office, look around like an annoyed squirrel, then head straight for her and Hilda. "Forget I asked you to look it up," Julia told Hilda.

"Oh, Julia," Hilda laughed. "Don't be melodramatic. It's only a *credit* file, for goodness sake."

"Ms. Early," Hollis rasped from three desks away. "My office, please." He about-faced and marched back the way he came without waiting for an answer.

Hilda immediately lowered her head to her screen and began typing furiously. Julia followed, wondering whether she would try for another job in Washington or head on back to Texas.

Hollis had just come from the seventeenth floor, his third bollocking of the day, this time from the president of the bank, Max Berlin, whom Thayer let do the real thumping. Asked what he intended to do about a credit trainee who had violated what amounted to the bank's first commandment—protect the privacy of the client—Reginald had of course volunteered to fire Julia Early. Berlin had called him an idiot; actually, the president had said: "Fucking idiot. Of course you don't fire her; you have no idea what she really knows."

"Mr. Berlin, *I* had no idea what was in that file. I called Dan Coates, the lending officer, and he hadn't seen it in seven or eight months. It isn't an active account, they don't borrow except occasionally in the form of a daylight overdraft on money transfers or foreign exchange transactions—"

"I know that, and you may be sure I'll know a lot more in a day or so, as will Dan Coates, as will you. You are aware that they were the bank's highest volume money transfer customer last autumn? Right before the election?"

"I know now," Hollis gulped.

"And you want to fire the only person who might have figured this out before we can?" Berlin shook his head vehemently. "Hell no, we need her where we can watch her." Berlin opened Julia's file, on his desk. "Evaluations are good."

"She's done well, until this fuckup," Hollis said viciously.

Berlin looked up and locked his pale blue eyes on Hollis for a full minute without speaking. "Perhaps she just needs closer supervision."

Hollis felt light-headed and wished the president would invite him to sit down. He was a vice president with only three more years to retirement, and now, because some stupid bitch—

Berlin closed the file. "We'll transfer her to security. Frank Simmons is putting together a small group of people to sell security systems to overseas banks. Apparently the girl has exceptional computer skills and presents herself well; be wasted as a junior on the lending platform."

Hollis took the first breath in half a minute. "Yes, sir. Shall I tell her to report to Frank?"

"Yes, right away. And don't make it sound like punishment even though those nerds do work below street level down near the vault. We want her sweet." Berlin gave Hollis a last cold look. "Frank Simmons runs a very tight ship."

JULIA WAS CALLED to report to Reginald Hollis's office exactly at five P.M. Bank lore held it that firings were always held at five, usually on Fridays but often on other days. But always *a las cinco de la tarde,* the hour of the beginning of the bullfight in Spain and Mexico. Julia knew the bullfight from the ring in Monterrey, Mexico, a grubby industrial provincial capital a hundred eighty dusty miles south of Laredo, a favorite weekend run when she was in college.

Julia waited until exactly five, doing nothing, thinking nothing, staring at the screen saver of her computer terminal that had denied her access. She felt weary, sad, and scared as she crossed the bay toward Hollis's corner office. Her fellow trainees watched her go with hooded eyes. Everybody knew.

Hollis's door was open so she knocked gently on the jam. He looked up from his work, his face impassive, his anger under tight control. "Please come in," he said as pleasantly as he could. "Close the door behind you." Julia did. "And please sit down. I have some reasonably fresh coffee, or ice water?"

"Ice water would be nice," Julia said, her throat suddenly dry. She clenched her teeth. She had heard the drill; severance pay was presented and the victim told not to return to her desk but to leave immediately; any personal items would be sent. She wished Hollis would just get on with it.

"Well." Hollis rose, poured two small glasses of ice water from a thermos, spilling a little. He placed them in front of Julia, sat and seemed to sag. "A long day for us both."

Julia was suddenly furious. She had done everything she could! The patronizing bastard—

"Julia, mistakes were made, but that is why we have training. And supervision. We all have . . . supervision." He looked more pained than angry. "But on the whole, you've done well, very well indeed, in Credit Training. You've learned to do analysis, you're very quick and innovative with the computer." Hollis paused. So I get a decent reference, maybe? Julia flashed between anger and faint hope. "There's an opening in a new unit, just in formation, that might suit you better than becoming a lending officer. When first we met, you expressed an interest in travel, and there would be travel, a lot of it, and you would be involved in an area of banking the Board thinks of as very important to development of relations with foreign correspondent banks, not to mention that this new area is expected to become a profit center in a very short time."

Julia was afraid to breathe. Hollis sat and stared at her, puffy, saturnine. "You're being offered a position in the new unit Frank Simmons has established. I hope you won't think that, after what happened with the Uvalde County file, this appointment is in any way intended as ironic. In fact, I was instructed some time ago to look for the best people as candidates for the new Bank Electronic Security Services Support unit, and you were at the top of my list. Frank Simmons and I have discussed it, and he would like to have you on Monday morning."

Julia had no idea what to say. It felt like having a blindfold taken off and watching the firing squad march away, eyes averted. What would it be like? What was Simmons like? Who worked in this new unit?

Shit, who cared? She'd try it. She'd try anything. She hadn't been fired. "Of course. Monday. Where are they?"

"Basement A, near the mainframes," Hollis said, sitting up, obviously relieved. "But that's for Monday; take tomorrow and Friday off; get the taste of this afternoon's unfortunate unpleasantness off your tongue."

Julia got up, said a plain thank you, shook hands, and left. She walked home in a daze, not wanting the human press of the bus.

Judith was waiting at the door of their apartment, her face twisted in anger. Hilda sat on the floor, in tears. "Look at this, will you, Julia?"

The apartment had been completely trashed, drawers emptied onto the floor, bookshelves upset, beds overturned, mattresses and upholstered furniture slashed. Julia walked slowly into the room she shared with Hilda and crossed to the closet. All their clothes had been torn off the hangers and tossed onto the floor. Her suitcase, where she had hidden the Correspondence File, was gone.

The phone rang. Judith hastened to answer it. "For you, love," she said, handing the receiver to Julia.

Julia took the instrument with dread. "Hello?"

"Charles Taylor," the man said smoothly. "Dinner?"

4

August 1972, Paris

RUPERT JUSTICE TOLLIVER rented a walk-up flat on the Rue Vavin, in the Sixth Arrondissement, near the Luxembourg Gardens. The area was expensive, though the flat was not much above a closet with a single bed, a stained mattress, and a rickety chair and table. The shared bathroom was down the hall. Brother Justice had plenty of money, but wished to live anonymously; Claudia had advised it, especially as she knew he intended to contact students and others opposed to America's war in Vietnam, a war she hated because it had broken her friend, President Lyndon Johnson.

Claudia had nonetheless been against Brother Justice talking to antiwar types, especially Frenchmen whose country had taken U.S. aid, then cut and run. She gave a grudging consent when Rupert promised that he would do nothing or say anything that would embarrass the president or criticize his decision not to seek reelection. Justice promised, gladly. He thought Johnson was right, and had only come to the knowledge too late.

Justice had become obsessed with the war he had labored so hard to avoid; it needed to be over before he could begin his dream of political power beyond the pulpit. What a little voice in his head insisted was God's work.

Justice did visit the grand old churches of Paris; Notre Dame of course, Saint Germain des Pres, Saint Sulpice, and the grand if cold Basilica of Sacre Coeur. He made day trips to Versailles and Vincennes. He also visited many smaller churches, incredibly ancient by the standards of a Texan, and was moved by all of them. Their smoky walls and cold stone seemed so steeped in faith that his own, so recently acquired, seemed shallow and, he knew, born of cynicism. He was humbled.

At nights he found the student bars near the universities and on the Montparnasse, and talked of politics with superior French youths who sneered at America and mocked his rudimentary French.

He met Van Trinh, a Vietnamese girl struggling to afford her studies at the Sorbonne on the little money her middle-class family was able to send from Da Lat in the highlands of Vietnam. Justice liked Van, and she him, and they went places together, and ate together and slept together in his flat. She told him things about her tortured country, and he felt better about his refusal to rush to the colors. Van hated the French while studying in their capital, hated the Americans more because she thought they might actually win, then depart as they always did after they won a foreign war, and leave her debilitated country at the mercy of its ancient and eternal enemy, the Chinese.

There was an underground of leftist Vietnamese students in the universities of Paris. One of the right as well, but Justice had no interest in them. Van could find things out, and she was willing to share information with the ugly long-nose, because she was fond of him, found him absurdly naive, and because he always paid.

One of the things she found out was about secret negotiations going on at the Crillon, a luxurious hotel across the Seine and next to the American embassy, between the Americans and the North Vietnamese. She also knew the head of the Vietcong delegation, a minor player but a legend in Vietnam, a woman known only by her nom de guerre, Madame Binh.

Van thought perhaps she could arrange an introduction. Justice suggested she share his modest flat—a palace in comparison to her filthy, noisy, smelly dormitory garret. She would of course contribute her share of the expenses, she insisted.

There would be no need, Justice replied. That evening he bought her a fancy dinner at the famous bistro Deux Magots, and they walked home beneath the chestnut trees. Justice carried all of Van's worldly goods in her backpack, and she never went back to the dorm.

5

March 2001

President Tolliver's multiracial, bi-gender, multicultural cabinet was finally complete. His choice for Treasury—the party's emphatic choice, given the need for sound money and given as well Justice's reputation while Governor of Texas of spending rather freely from the public purse—the venerable banker Alfred Thayer, withdrew his name from consideration abruptly and without explanation before his confirmation hearings could begin. His replacement, also at the insistence of the party, was some Jew from Wall Street named Levin whom Justice detested, but his appointment got the cabinet issue out of the way. The president didn't care; he didn't plan on listening to his cabinet secretaries anyway.

On the fifteenth of the month Justice instructed Zeke Archer to launch his legislative assault. Justice announced his restructure of government initiative in a rousing speech before both Houses of Congress, then stumped for it around the country like an election campaign. It sounded so good in the president's speeches, the committees of Congress were cowed into breezing it through hearings, calling hardly a critical witness.

Justice was creating a mandate where none existed. Even Zeke Archer was amazed.

JULIA EARLY TOILED on in the basement of Capital National Bank, studying bank computer security and marveling at how primitive and porous it was. She learned more programming skills from the nerds around her, whom, she discovered with amusement, actually knew less about banking and transactions between banks than she did. She had System Manager access to the bank's computer network, far more than she had had on the eighth floor. It went with the job, and no one on eight or seventeen had thought to restrict her.

In slow times, she began to reconstruct the files she had built on Uvalde County Savings and Loan and Little Cheyenne Development. She decoded and recovered the files Reginald Hollis thought he had deleted. Julia learned it is in fact very difficult to "erase" a file on a modern computer. She also downloaded the worksheet on the payments into and out of the two companies from her home PC, the ones before the election and before inauguration, and added them to her file. As a system manager, Julia had her own files, and knew how to protect them.

Julia knew a little Spanish, as did most south Texans. She named her growing record of money movements through Capital National and Uvalde "Plata Negra."

Plata Negra meant Black Money in Spanish, a euphemism for corruption.

PRESIDENT TOLLIVER WAS fifteen minutes late for his first meeting with his national security team; far more prompt than usual. The Cabinet Room was crowded with the vice president, Joseph Donahue; the Secretary of Defense, Carolyn White; her chief deputy, Barney Wilson, the former Chairman of Chrysler

Corporation; the National Security Advisor, Henry Amos, a rock-ribbed Republican from Connecticut selected as a sop to Donahue's backers; and the Joint Chiefs, a bunch of ordinary-looking men in uniform led by the somewhat extraordinary-looking Admiral Josephus Austin, barely five feet tall and fit as a twenty-year-old, a Texan chosen by Tolliver from low down on the list; so low that sixty senior admirals and generals had been forced to retire. Austin was a controversial figure, nearly forced to retire himself near the end of the Blythe administration because he had repeatedly called for the reversal of policies that allowed homosexuals to serve in uniform and women to serve in combat. He was a naval aviator, call sign "Cowboy," and an outspoken advocate of hitting any little dictator the moment he raised his head. Tolliver's choice of him had been unpopular in the military, ridiculed in the liberal press, and viewed with caution even by the conservative republicans on the Senate Armed Services Committee who voted to send his nomination on to the full senate with obvious unease.

"Well, Carolyn. Gentlemen," Justice began after everyone had stood up and shaken hands and sat back down, and the newspaper and TV cameras had been shooed out. "Time we got after our adversaries, who have ceased to fear us as they should, and our friends, who have ceased to obey us as they should."

Justice looked around, grinning. He got no reaction but stunned silence. Fine, he thought. "Admiral, how many carrier battle groups I got?"

Admiral Austin looked across at Admiral Marc Mitchell, the Chief of Naval Operations, who cleared his throat. "Ten, Mr. President, nine really, because *Enterprise* is in dry dock. Plus the training carrier."

"How many we got in reserve? Including escort and support ships?"

Mitchell leaned forward. He had never expected to be asked the question, but every senior naval officer knew the answer. "We could reactivate *Ranger, Independence, Constellation,* and *America*. They're all conventionally powered but very capable ships.

We have plenty of cruisers and destroyers mothballed way before the end of their useful lives, including *Spruance, Kidd,* and *Virginia* classes. We have plenty of support ships in the reserve fleet."

"Aircraft?"

"F-14s, older F-18 C and D versions, plenty of other variants."

"How long?"

"Four to six months, plus training. Maybe a little longer for the older carriers."

"What about ballistic-missile submarines?"

Admiral Mitchell smiled. "Well," he said cautiously.

"Don't be coy, Admiral," the president said sharply. "The peoples' business awaits."

"We retain, in the *Ohio* class boats, the ability to obliterate the world."

"But not to save it," the president said dryly. "I want my carrier battle groups."

"Aye, aye, sir!" the admiral said with enthusiasm.

"And my battleships. Get 'em out of mothballs and to sea."

Admiral Mitchell frowned. "The *Iowa* is being cannibalized for parts, since her number-two turret blew up. We could have *New Jersey, Wisconsin,* and *Missouri* active in four months."

The president nodded approval. "General Dassault?" General Frank Dassault was the Chief of Staff of the Air Force. "What I got for air wings?"

"Thirteen fighter wings, down from twenty-four ten years ago. Seven in reserve. Twelve only B-2 bombers; twenty B-1s, all in reserve. The last B-52s are parked at Davis Monthan, in the Arizona desert."

"What do I need?" Justice asked.

Dassault squirmed. "Depends on the mission, sir."

"The mission is to defend ourselves and our friends, and if need be, chastise our enemies. With certain effect. The need is to be what we once were but that my predecessors pissed away: to be the world's only superpower."

Daussault went for it. "I'd like twenty-four fighter wings, all active, plus my twelve reserve. I'd like advanced cruise missiles for my available bombers. Tankers, AWACS, JSTARS—"

"Give me a plan," the president said with an upraised palm. Today was not for details. "General Brown?" Harrison Brown was Chief of Staff of the Army.

"Well, since this seems to be wish-list day, I would like to get back to the force levels I had for Desert Storm. You may remember, Mr. President, that at the time of the land battle, two-thirds of all American active-duty soldiers and nearly all the Marine Corps were in theater. General Schwarzkopf had at his disposal eighteen divisions plus fifty-seven reserve component brigades. Today I have ten active divisions, many under strength, and forty-two reserve component brigades."

"Would you activate reserves, if you could?"

"We have some very fine units in the reserves, performing specialty functions like communications, command and control, medical, logistics, the like. But the heavy hitters, infantry, armor, artillery, have to be regulars because the training cycle is so intense. Also, infantry grunts have to be young and physically strong, tankers and artillerymen have to handle heavy ammo and break track. Many reserve units are manned by people not as hard-bellied as they once were."

"How long to make up eight regular divisions?"

"I'd want do a little staff work, but we have many fine officers and senior NCOs who are in the reserve, involuntarily, because of the cutbacks. They could be cadre for the returning units. There's a lot of equipment, most of it only ten or so years old, garaged and maintained by the National Guard. Getting the foot soldiers through Basic and Advanced Infantry Training, or Armor, or Artillery—maybe five months if I had everything I needed."

The president nodded and took notes. "That leaves you, General Jones."

General Jackie Robinson Jones, the only black among the chiefs, was Commandant of the Marine Corps. "I have one-hundred seventy thousand marines, Mr. President. Three active

Marine Air-Ground Task Forces—divisions, if you will, with their air—and one reserve. I'd like another twenty thousand marines to rebuild the Fourth Division as an active force, and redesignate the Fourth, now in reserve, as the Fifth."

"Why not just reactivate the existing Forth?"

Jones glanced over at the Army Chief, General Brown. "Same reason as the army, Mr. President. Lots of good officers and NCOs, but we need young men to hump the ruck."

The president seemed pleased as he wrote on his yellow pad.

The vice president, supposedly the senior authority in the administration on foreign policy, had received no advance notice of any of this. He sat in stupefied silence. The Secretary of Defense cleared her throat and spoke softly. "Mr. President, where are we going to get the money for all this? And what do you intend to do with such a massive force? Surely the Russians, with whom we have Conventional Force Reduction Agreements, and the Chinese, with whom we have problems, will become alarmed."

The president put down his pen and looked at the attractive black woman he had allowed, with great reluctance, to become Secretary of Defense. "Carolyn, I'll take your questions in reverse order. The Russians and the Chinese *should* be alarmed, even terrified. So also the Iraqis, Iranis, and North Koreans. We were the world's only superpower before my two predecessors forgot their responsibilities and gave that great might away.

"We're a great and upstanding Christian nation, and Jesus said many times he came not in peace but with a sword. I want that sword."

But you're not Jesus, Carolyn White thought darkly.

"Edward the Black Prince of England," the president continued, "while campaigning in the southwest of France in the fourteenth century once attacked a town; I don't remember the name. As was customary at the time, he sent an emissary to Rome to get the Pope's blessing as a crusade, because many in that part of France were members of a heresy called the Albigensians, or Cathars. The Pope blessed the crusade. Edward's commander asked the prince how he was supposed to tell the heretics from the faithful, and Edward replied, 'Kill them all; let God sort the Godly from the ungodly.' "

The president immediately rose. The chiefs and their aids struggled to their feet. "As to the second part of your question, Madame Secretary, getting the money is your job and mine. But I swear to you all, I will have my legions to do the Lord's work."

The secretary, admirals, generals, and staff stood in stunned silence as the president marched from the Cabinet Room. The vice president kept his seat, color rising in his cheeks.

6

August 1972, Paris

RUPERT JUSTICE TOLLIVER met Madame Binh in a dreary concrete apartment building in a working-class block of the Eleventh Arrondissement. Van Trinh had arranged the meeting, saying that Tolliver was a prominent and influential preacher from the great state of Texas. Madame Binh had heard of Texas; to most Vietnamese not well traveled, Texas was America.

The small apartment was crowded with young people, mostly Vietnamese, Cambodian or Laotian, but some French, other Europeans and Americans. Madame Binh chain-smoked Gauloise Bleu unfiltered cigarettes that smelled to Tolliver like dirty socks. Many of the others smoked hand-rolled cigarettes that smelled like a prairie grass fire. Tolliver realized it must be marijuana, a substance he had heard much about but never before encountered. He accepted a joint from Van, inhaled deeply, and choked on the harsh smoke. Justice had never smoked cigarettes, but he took another hit on the joint before passing it on, and immediately felt a sense of tranquillity.

Madame Binh held court, answering questions with terse blasts of French or Vietnamese. Van sat by Justice and whispered translations of the Vietnamese. The Americans were demoralized nd beaten. Vietnam and especially the southerners of the Vietcong had suffered horribly but would win because they had to. The Americans couldn't win because they didn't have to, and their own people had lost the *dau tranh,* the political struggle.

Tolliver thought it all rote and commonplace. Madame Binh seemed nothing more than the peasant she claimed to be, although Tolliver knew she had been educated in Paris. Justice was ready to leave when he felt a tug on his sleeve. A Latin-looking man, short, thin and dark, pressed his face close. *"No me recuerdas, gringo?"* he whispered.

Tolliver started. "You're the Cuban policeman. Caballero?"

"Carvahal. You made a fine target on that day; Fidel was most impressed."

Justice stood and shook the little man off. "I've not forgotten."

"Nor should you," Ramon Carvahal said evenly. "I am glad you still see the light of our global cause."

"I only see you laughing, along with the brothers Castro, as I rolled in the dust, the bullet ringing in my ears." Justice turned to Van. "Let's go. I need some air."

Justice had not noticed that the framed posters adorning the walls of the drab apartment all had tiny holes in their protective glass. The proceedings were being filmed by North Vietnamese Military Intelligence, South Vietnamese Central Intelligence, the KGB, the French Sûreté, and the Cuban Servicio Nacional de Informaciones.

The American CIA had its own sources and couldn't be bothered. Besides, they had never trusted Kissinger, or Nixon.

The camera teams all knew each other, or at least recognized each other. Everything was cool as long as the local police prefect captain got his *"pour boire."* Everybody paid the same, except of course for the Sûreté that paid no one.

The Sûreté therefore received the least desirable peephole.

Security for Madame Binh and her entourage was provided by officers of the *Compagnie Republicaine de Securité*—the CRS, France's elite riot police—in plain clothes. Their costs were offset by a grant from the American CIA. There you have it.

France considers itself the cradle of modern European democracy. It is also the most efficient police state in the world.

7

April 2001

"DAMMIT, ZEKE," THE president thundered. "Our defense budget is less than three percent of Gross Domestic product. That's less than Sweden spends, and they haven't fought anybody since the seventeenth century. This country needs its troops and tanks and airplanes and ships to do its duty around the world." Tolliver paced the Oval Office like a caged tiger. "Read those damn congressmen their history: the North could have bought and freed every nigger slave in Maryland for the cost of the Battle of First Manassas; bought and freed every damn one of them throughout the Confederacy for the costs of Shiloh and Fredericksburg, and there were twenty other battles in the War Between the States of the same or greater size. Peace is not won by chanting and wearing flowers in our hair, Zeke. It is won by intimidation, by credible, and if need be, deliverable force!"

Ezekiel Archer sighed. "It's still two hundred fifty billion we don't have in the budget."

The president whirled, pointing his finger like a pistol. "Find it. Squeeze the medical frauds, the teachers' lobby. Beat it out of business welfare; the ag programs. It's there, Zeke, and you and I both know it. We played the game well enough from the other side down in Austin."

Archer rose. "I'll get right on it, Mr. President."

"Results!" the president shouted. Then, more softly, "Results, Zeke."

* * *

CONGRESSIONAL HEARINGS TOOK more than two months. The Democrats railed against the increases in military spending, especially as they were to be funded, dollar for dollar, by the reduction of social programs. The administration made no secret of that. Squeeze, Justice said, and he meant it.

The Republicans seemed bemused, caught off guard. They were on record for stronger defense, modernization, new high-tech gear, better education and training, but to blow the force back up to the Cold War level? It was a hard sell, but Carolyn White, Admiral Austin, and the chiefs sold it, or almost did. They were a few votes short in both houses, and they knew it.

Two days before the House scheduled its vote, the president addressed the nation.

The speech was long, and dealt with threats few knew about, or perhaps had thought about. The Koreas, central Asia, the Caucuses, the oil-rich Caspian Sea, the Balkans, China and Russia themselves and in their conflict with each other. Iran and Iraq, Syria and the Lebanon. As long as it was the speech was fiery and eloquent, and kept its share of the TV audience through its full hour and ten minutes.

As he got ready to close, the president mopped his brow and took a sip of water. He then laid his worn family Bible on the podium but didn't open it. Just let it lay there in plain view. "My fellow Americans," he said, his voice hoarse and soft from the long oration. "This is the first year of the third Millennium, a time of great portents. I want to remind you of one tiny verse of scripture, from the Revelation of St. John the Divine. It's the last book of the Bible and speaks of last days. I'm here to tell you that we must be strong if we're to continue into the new millennium free of the scourges of the earth that are not the monsters Saint John saw through the vision of the Lamb of God, Lord Jesus, but the tyrants, great and small, the modern Atillas, the modern Genghis Khans, who will feel free to threaten even the United States of America if we do not show them our might and our will to use it."

The president was interrupted by gentle applause that gained courage and then swelled and lasted two minutes until Justice put up his hands to quell it. "Let me finish." He laid his hand on the Bible but still did not open it. "Let me finish with a Revelation from the Divine: Chapter six, verse eight."

The chamber was deadly silent; a few coughs as when a symphony orchestra pauses between movements.

"Listen, my brothers and sisters, but a moment more," Justice said softly. "Revelation six-eight. 'And I looked, and behold a pale horse, and the name of him that sat upon him was Death, and Hell followed with him.' "

The joint session of Congress was quiet, and then applause began from the Republican side, and gradually, the senators and congressmen got to their feet, all of them, and cheered.

The *New York Times* and the *Washington Post* railed against the speech and the policy. All four major television networks denounced the buildup. Even the *Wall Street Journal* expressed skepticism. The foreign press from London, Paris, and Berlin to Moscow, Tokyo, and Beijing all protested American bullying and recklessness in the strongest possible terms.

The House voted, then the Senate, and the president got his money. That was just as well, as he had already begun bringing ships and planes and tanks out of mothballs using discretionary funds.

After he signed the appropriations bills, Justice had a drink with Zeke Archer in the Oval Office. "In three to six months, Zeke," the president said, raising his glass, "I'll have my legions."

8

ALFRED THAYER CONVOKED a conference of the Republican old guard at his summer home in the Shenandoah Valley of Virginia. No member of the administration was invited or even informed; not even the vice president, who was known to share Thayer's alarm about Tolliver's almost uncanny seizure of the national initiative. Six of the most powerful Republican governors and one Democratic were flown in, all by private jets owned by the most loyal corporations. In most cases the chief executive officers came with them. Committee chairs from both the House and Senate came in anonymous rented minivans with dark tinted glass. No active-duty military men were invited, but many retired admirals and generals were.

Security was tight around the estate, provided by a private service retained by the Capital National Bank. All the arrivals were timed between three and five A.M. The sleepy conferees were given rooms in the vast house, and time to rest before breakfast was served in the Great Hall at exactly eight A.M.

"We're at the brink of a national crisis," Thayer began as second cups of coffee were served. "To quote Lenin, 'What is to be done?' "

"It's not all bad," said the Chairman of Lockheed-Martin. "We've weakened the military far too much, and reconstruction will produce much-needed jobs, especially in key states like California and Texas."

"The Joint Chiefs support the buildup," said a retired admiral, once Chairman of the Joint Chiefs. "We've all studied history; deterrence is always cheaper in blood and treasure than war."

Senator Lodge, Chairman of the Committee on Foreign Relations, spoke softly. "My concern is, and surely ours should be, what's he going to do with such an enhanced military capacity?"

"Exactly," Thayer said.

"What of domestic programs?" Governor Feinstein of California said. "We're suffering, with more and more federal programs dropped in the states' laps with no adequate funding. California bares a huge burden of caring for, educating, and integrating wave after wave of immigrants. The strong economy left by the Blythe administration has helped, but if all this money is suddenly diverted to rebuilding a military that always took more from the economy than it gave, who's to pay?"

The chairman of Lockheed harrumphed. "California can't lose. How many computer programmers, how many engineers, are being produced by universities in your state? How many immigrants? They need jobs. High-paying jobs. Defense jobs."

The senior senator from Mississippi, the Majority Leader, spoke with easy confidence. "Bringing those old ships back and building new ones can't hurt Pascagoula, in my state. Or Newport News, Virginia, or Bath, Maine, or Groton, Connecticut, or Bremerton, Washington. Why not wait and see what happens?"

"He's building that force," Thayer said softly, "because he intends to use it. I've spoken privately with Secretary White. He means a war against the states he views as not only enemies of the United States but of his self-derived image of God's will. He'll use the force to commit a bloody jihad, as our Muslim brethren would call it. He would risk not only world trade, or world peace, but the very survival of civilization."

A retired general laughed nervously. "You can't be serious."

"I would welcome," Thayer said, "any more reasonable explanation."

The chairman of Boeing, a former Secretary of the Air Force named Sheila Quinn, said, "But that's madness. Strength, yes, but to deter, not to fight. We trade with everybody, and in high-tech military, we're the only game in town. We'll be able to produce the new aircraft and missiles at much reduced costs because we can sell to allies and friends. The enemies he identified in his speech are stuck with outdated and hard to maintain Russian and Chinese crap and overpriced and underperforming stuff from the Europeans. A defense buildup is a win-win for the U.S. economy, but wars? Nobody since Bismarck actually won a war of conquest, and the results were reversed in less than fifty years, resulting in the destruction of Germany. Our modern weapons are so much more potent as to make war unthinkable."

"That's why we're here," Thayer said. "I'll ring for more coffee."

9

December 1972

RUPERT JUSTICE TOLLIVER felt he had completed his work in Paris. Kissinger's negotiations with Le Duc Tho of the North Vietnamese government were beginning to move, largely due to a massive defeat inflicted by American and South Vietnamese forces against the NVA's best heavy divisions earlier in the year. The NVA, especially Vo Nguyen Giap, the commander and a national hero since battles against the French, had become convinced they could never win unless the Americans—not only their soldiers but their air power—could be talked out of the war. The NVA fought like an army out of World War I; before it could launch a major attack it had to concentrate its divisions and then supply them with streams of coolies more numerous than the soldiers themselves. Such concentrations were perfect targets for American bombers and were destroyed outside every South Vietnamese city where they massed for assault.

Kissinger would give it away, Rupert knew. By now he had many sources close to the North Vietnamese/Vietcong negotiators beyond the bombastic Madame Binh. The Americans would abandon the war rather than lose it, and a Democrat would succeed Nixon in the White House. Rupert's opposition to the war would be vindicated, and he could start on his path to become a New Republican, unstained by the failed venture.

He flew home to Texas, consulted with Claudia King Travis in Austin, and resumed his ministry. Wait ten years, she counseled, even twenty. Get around the country; get more television. Become big in Texas and known all around the nation.

Rupert Justice Tolliver chafed at the delay of his ambitions, but he knew his employer and mentor's advice was good, and he heeded it.

10

September 2001

THE PRESIDENT CALLED his Secretary of Defense to his office on a steamy day in the capital. The air-conditioning in Carolyn White's limousine failed halfway between the Pentagon and the White House, and traffic was heavy along Pennsylvania Avenue. She arrived hot, sweaty, her hair frizzed. Ten minutes she allowed herself in the ladies' room did little to help. She went up to the Oval Office and was offered a seat by the president's overblown and often rude secretary. She sat, glad of a chance to compose herself, but the door opened almost immediately, and she was waved in by Admiral Austin, the Chairman of the Joint Chiefs.

As Carolyn entered, the other chiefs stood from chairs in a semicircle in front of the president's huge desk. The president did not rise but merely nodded. Carolyn took the chair in the middle of the semicircle, as offered by Admiral Austin. Carolyn noted the absence of the vice president. Coffee was offered by a uniformed navy steward. Carolyn declined and asked for ice water. As soon as the steward served it and withdrew, the president looked up from his notes and smiled. "Carolyn."

"Mr. President."

"I believe it's time to begin the lesson."

" 'The lesson,' sir?"

"That God is love. That the United States is love, but like God, even acting in God's place, love must be honored with obedience."

Carolyn had become used to the president's speaking in sermons. She waited silently, knowing he would come to the point. She glanced at the military chiefs, who looked pained. Justice smiled more broadly. "I want the fleets at sea, in all oceans. Call it exercises but make it awesome. I want sea lanes of communication to see our fleets—any choke point where there are agreements of international passage, from the Suez Canal to the Persian Gulf to the Taiwan and Malacca Straits.

"I want air force bombers on alert, in flight and armed, as they used to be. I want missiles fired from Point Mugu and shot out of space from Kwajelein, using weapons we don't admit we have. I want joint exercises of soldiers and marines with our allies, even if no allies show up. That is the first lesson."

The president paused and took a drink of water. Carolyn did likewise. Her throat was very dry.

"Then we'll begin the second lesson: that peace must be kept and agreements adhered to. We'll begin with three countries that have lied to us for years, North Korea, Iran, and Iraq, but we will not shrink from confronting the bigger bullies, China and Russia. The chiefs here tell me the forces are ready to carry out these missions; as you're in the chain of command, I need you to confirm that."

Carolyn took a deep breath. "Ready, yes, but sir, to what end? Russia, China, even Saudi Arabia, have protested modest buildups in areas they consider theirs to influence. No one is threatening us or our trade; the buildup alone has seen to that."

The president looked down at notes. "The first exercise visible by satellite will begin in two weeks in the area of Midway Island in the central Pacific. Six carrier battle groups. No one in Asia will miss the symbolism of that. Will you see that the rest of the plan is worked out and executed?"

Carolyn stood. "Mr. President, I consider this plan unwise, costly, and very dangerous."

"You are my moderate conscience, Carolyn. Will you carry it out?"

"I must, or tender my resignation, right now?"

"A resignation that would be accepted with great regret."

Carolyn glanced at Admiral Austin beside her. She knew he wanted her job, and the thought frightened her to the point that she knew she couldn't quit. "I'll stay at your pleasure, Mr. President," she said with a firmness she didn't feel. "As long as you'll at least listen to my misgivings."

"Of course," the president said blandly. He looked down at his notes, nodded to himself. "Now let's get cracking."

11

October 2001

The Pacific Fleet began its massive exercise in the area of Midway Island on the tenth of the month. Six carrier battle groups around *Reagan, Constellation, Nimitz, Stennis, Independence* and *Theodore Roosevelt* sailed as the Fifth and Seventh Fleets. That was three more giant warships than the small and inadequately supported carriers that the shattered American Pacific Fleet sent out in 1942 to oppose Admiral Yamamoto's vastly superior force under Admiral Nimitz's famous order "Fleet Oppose Invasion." Carrier aircraft flew hundreds of sorties over millions of square miles of the Pacific, then moved rapidly westward and spread south, overflying the island nations in the Marshalls and Carolines, the Bonins and Belau, all battlegrounds in World War II. Battleship Division 1, *New Jersey* and *Wisconsin,* accompanied by ultramodern destroyers of the *Arleigh Burke* class and cruisers of the *Ticonderoga* class, plus some of the *Virginias* returned to service, crossed the Philippine Sea, pressed through the Bashi Passage between Luzon and Taiwan in the midst of a typhoon, and forced the Taiwan Strait. They carried on into the East China and

Yellow Seas, barely observing China's twelve-mile limit. When they neared the port of Namp'o in North Korea, they stopped, well within sight of shore.

The carrier groups spread out between Japan and Taiwan, where they were joined by Amphibious Ready Groups Three and Five, eight ships surrounding the huge aircraft-carrier–like LHAs *Tarawa* and *Belleau Wood,* with eight thousand marines, all their equipment and aircraft, from the First and Third Marine Divisions.

Navy and Marine pilots flew sorties at a wartime intensity. Any satellite could see the planes were armed.

THE SIXTH FLEET, expanded from one to three carrier battle groups around *Vinson, Eisenhower,* and *Lincoln,* and accompanied by the battleship *Missouri,* sortied from Naples a day after the Pacific exercises began, and headed east at high speed, conducting flight operations and gunnery exercises in international waters. They passed to the Lebanese port of Tyre, paused, then raced south through the Suez Canal, informing, but not asking permission from, Egyptian authorities. The fleet steamed close to the coast all around the Arabian Peninsula, and sailed through the Strait of Hormuz into the Persian Gulf. Once inside, the ships deployed in a spread-out, defensive formation, and waited.

Air Force B2 and B1 bombers, fully armed, flew circular patterns in the high Arctic. Fighters based in England and Germany conducted noisy low-level exercises from Norway to Poland.

Armor and infantry divisions in Europe and the United States went on high alert. Marines practiced amphibious landings at Camp Pendleton in California, Little Creek in Virginia, and on Midway Island.

IN CALIFORNIA, MICHIGAN, Illinois, and New York, riots broke out as welfare payments shrank or stopped completely. Hospitals, many unreimbursed from the Medicare and Medicaid programs for months, refused to admit those injured to emergency rooms. Federalized National Guard troops, on alert for weeks, quickly backed up police and quelled the disturbances, but not before much looting, arson, and murder. Troops in body armor and riot gear patrolled the streets of nearly every large city, but sporadic violence continued.

Juss is beginning to worry even me," Clarissa Tolliver said to Jim Bob Slate, the Mormon, as she lay in his arms in his modern flat in Southeast, behind the Capitol.

Jim Bob waited for his heart rate to slow, asking Jesus silently for the thousandth time for forgiveness of his sin of adultery, all the while knowing he was as powerless to stop his lust for Clarissa as to halt a tornado. "He wants the riots. The New Zealots make sure no insult to the wretched of the cities goes unnoticed."

Clarissa knew Justice thought of the whole process as "cleansing." "The U.N. goes back into session tomorrow. There'll be pandemonium as delegates line up to condemn the United States, and the president too."

"He wants that also," Jim Bob said, with a hint of sadness. Then he felt Clarissa's hand stroking his scrotum and he lost his mind. He needed to pray for relief from the torments of Satan, but he couldn't as she smothered his mouth with hers.

The United States," the U.N. ambassador, Christine Whitman, shouted over the riot of noise in the Security Council Chamber, "is doing no more than exercising the right of innocent passage in international waterways and airspace. We threaten no one." She sat down, maintaining icy composure in the face of angry condemnation of the American actions. When the motion condemning the United States was brought to a vote, thirteen nations voted for it; not even Britain supported her position, although the British ambassador abstained, refusing to condemn the United Kingdom's ally and protector. Ambassador Whitman vetoed the resolution, and walked out.

THE SENATE AND Congress met in open session and demanded the president explain what he was doing and why he had not consulted the Congress.

There was no reply from the White House. "We got 'em runnin' around like chickens in the sudden presence of a fox, Zeke," the president crowed over a dark glass of bourbon whiskey. "How many calls we got from foreign leaders today?"

"Twenty-four, Mr. President," Ezekiel Archer replied over his coffee cup. He was dead on his feet. "Four from the Russian president."

"Fuck him; he's got no cards to play. Fuck them all; let them rail at us; they can't live without us." He slugged back his drink. "I'm going to bed, Zeke. You get some rest too."

FOUR HOURS LATER, at three A.M. Washington time, the North Korean submarine K-19 slipped out of Namp'o harbor and approached Battleship Division One. The submarine, an improved Russian-built Kilo, was detected immediately after she passed the breakwaters by the American destroyers *Burke* and *The Sullivans*. They were instructed to interpose themselves between the sub and the battleships but take no other action unless the submarine did. The entire task force sped up and began antisubmarine maneuvers. The North Korean sub continued her course toward the American force, defying all common sense, then launched a spread of six torpedoes at the battleship *Wisconsin*. The *Whiskey* turned into the spread as the *Burke* launched antitorpedo weapons by the dozens. Five of the incoming torpedoes were destroyed and the sixth driven to the surface, where it porpoised, but still managed to strike *Wisconsin* near her starboard bow. *The Sullivans* immediately dispatched the K-19 with three Mark 52 torpedoes.

* * *

Zeke Archer awakened the president at four A.M. to report the attack. "What happened to my battleship?" the president roared.

"Admiral Jackson reports no significant damage. The torpedo hit the sixteen-inch armor belt; smudged the paint. No loss of operational capacity."

"North Korea? He's sure?"

"He's sure."

The president thought a long moment, rubbing sleep from his eyes. "Get Admiral Austin out of bed, and Carolyn White. Tell 'em to flatten the fucking place."

Archer fidgeted. "Mr. President, Juss—"

"You heard me, Zeke. Flatten it." The president of the United States rolled over and went back to sleep.

Carrier-based F/A-18 fighter bombers swept over North Korea in waves, attacking military installations and airfields in the south and hitting road and rail junctions, communications facilities, and power stations around P'yongyang and Wonsan. *Wisconsin* and *New Jersey* pounded the docks and ship repair facilities in Namp'o with their sixteen-inch guns, each shell over a ton in weight. They sank most of North Korea's tiny navy, including two more Kilo class submarines as they huddled at their docks. The battleships fired incendiary rounds at the oil refinery and power station, setting both burning furiously. BatDiv 1 then raced south through the Strait of Tsushima and rejoined the carriers in the Sea of Japan, off Korea's east coast.

Air Force B-2 bombers flew at 60,000 feet from bases in Alaska and North Dakota, barely skirting Russian airspace, and dropped precision-guided weapons on the hydroelectric dams near the Chinese and Russian borders. In a matter of hours after submarine K-19 had sailed her suicide mission, all of North Korea was cold and dark. But it wasn't to end there.

EVER SINCE THE armistice that had halted, but never truly ended, the Korean War in 1953, the North Korean army and much of its air force had lived in deep bunkers blasted out of the mountains only a few kilometers from the Demilitarized Zone that separated the poor North from the prosperous South. Some of these bunkers were hit by precision guided weapons fired by navy bombers and air force fighters flying from bases in Japan, but the bunkers were deep enough and the troops, all their tanks and guns, and supplies were protected. The commanding general, unable to reach any authority in P'yongyang by landline or radio, sent four divisions, two armored and two mechanized infantry, across the border preceded by air and artillery attacks.

THE HEADQUARTERS OF the Joint U.S. and Korean Command and the Eighth U.S. Army is at Uijongbu, north of the South Korean capital of Seoul and very near the DMZ. The fighting units closest to the border were the U.S. 2d Infantry Division, augmented by troops from the reactivated 4th Infantry flown in to Kimpo Airport near Seoul from Fort Collins, Colorado, and the ROK 14th Division. Even before the naval buildup had begun, they had withdrawn to defensive maneuver positions on the broad plains north and east of Seoul.

Between the DMZ and Seoul is a long series of steep-sided rocky valleys called the Uijongbu Corridor. Dug into its walls are heavy artillery pieces and rocket launchers. The valley floors were carpeted with buried antitank and antipersonnel mines. It is the most heavily fortified place on earth, and the only place the U.S.

Army has mounted a static defense since the Civil War. For the North Korean 4th, 11th, 18th and 22d Divisions, the Corridor was a meat grinder, a killing ground, a valley of death.

The North Korean air force, on paper the fourth largest in the world, had its obsolete MiGs and Sukhois swept from the skies by much higher-performing and better flown American navy and air force fighters. Many NK aircraft could not even fly because of lack of parts, and were destroyed in their concrete and stone revetments by two-thousand-pound concrete-penetrating bombs. No NK planes flew after the second morning of the battle.

The four NK divisions committed to the assault were the best in the army. The troops were well trained and heavily indoctrinated, but poorly paid and fed. Their equipment was old and hard to maintain, and many tanks and other vehicles broke down even before falling prey to the artillery and mines in the Corridor. The easy victory they had been promised against the "soft, decadent" troops of the Americans and South Koreans turned into a nightmare in the Corridor.

The battlegrounds were littered with propaganda leaflets. Many NK soldiers surrendered to the first units of the 14th ROK Division that attacked their flanks north of the Corridor, trading their weapons for the brimming bowl of rice promised in the leaflets. Others stayed in the Corridor and died.

The 14th ROK Division advanced cautiously up the flat coastal plain, with the U.S. Second and Fourth Infantry providing logistical and tactical support. They took the important railhead of Kaesong after a brief, sharp tank and infantry battle. As the ROK 14th moved north, there was little opposition from demoralized second-rank NK units, and the 14th captured P'yongyang on the fifth day of fighting. South Korean and U.S. Marines took the major port of Wonsan with little resistance. North Korea's Dear Leader Kim Jong-il and his generals fled across the Chinese border. The President of South Korea, Kim Keung-buk, declared the North liberated and reunited with the South, and asked the world for aid in feeding their starving northern brothers and sisters.

* * *

SEND FOOD," PRESIDENT Tolliver said to Zeke Archer. He had not spoken in public since the torpedo attack. "Send missionaries also. Korea has a large Christian community; ensure they get moved up and supported. They can handle the distribution of aid and preach the gospel as well."

Zeke, shaken, took notes and nodded.

"Who is the next to receive the lesson?" the president asked.

"Iraq, or Iran," Zeke replied, heartsick. "According to your plan."

"Do both. Sub pens, antiship and antiaircraft missiles, airfields, army concentrations if you can find them, suspected nuclear or chemical sites. And all the Iraqi dictator's palaces."

"Mr. President, Juss, the whole world opposes this, even our staunchest allies."

" 'And Hell followed with him,' Zeke. Make it so."

AIR STRIKES FROM the Persian Gulf were launched from the carriers *Lincoln*, *Vinson* and *Eisenhower* beginning at four in the morning that North Korea surrendered. More than sixty ships surrounded the carriers, including cruisers, destroyers, replenishment ships *and* three amphibious ready groups with over twelve thousand marines, all their gear, and their aircraft. Submarines patrolled the shallow waters of the Gulf, and *Connecticut* popped the first Iranian Kilo to venture out of port, providing the incident, or excuse. Air attacks were intense as were missile launches from the surface warships and submarines. The admiral commanding the task force reported complete success of the mission in less than thirty-six hours.

12

"You're not going to send the marines ashore, are you?" Carolyn White said at the morning briefing.

"Not unless they move toward Kuwait, Carolyn," the president, immensely pleased with himself, drawled. "Hell, those camel jockeys get CNN; they saw what happened to the North Koreans. They ain't gonna do shit."

"Mr. President." Zeke Archer cleared his throat. "The Secretary of State has been waiting an hour."

The president sighed. He found the Secretary of State, seventy-year-old Malcolm Japes, a former senator from Alabama, a bore and a windbag. He had been another appointment forced down Justice's throat by the Republican old guard, and the president rarely consulted him, barely tolerated his pronouncements at Cabinet meetings. "All right, Zeke," Justice said. "Let's get this over with."

Malcolm Japes was thin, handsome, and courtly. He was over six feet tall, ramrod straight despite his age. His eyes were pale blue, his face patrician. His longish silver hair was wavy. Justice suspected it was permed. Justice hated the man. "Mr. Secretary," he said warmly, not rising from behind his desk but extending his hand.

The old man had to lean forward across the president's desk to take the hand, a posture that hurt his lower back. He was sure the president knew this. Malcolm Japes hated the Texas mountebank who sat in the chair that should have been Joseph Donahue's, or perhaps his own. "Mr. President," he responded in warm tones.

"Please sit," Justice said. "May I ask the steward to get you anything?"

"Nothing, sir. I know your time is precious, so may I come straight to the point?"

"Always the best," Justice said, taking a thin Cuban cigar from a silver box and lighting it. He shoved the box toward the secretary who shook his head. The president really didn't like cigars but he knew Japes suffered from asthma; it would keep the meeting short. "What can I do for you?"

"Mr. President, we've had protests from all over the world about the recent military actions in Korea and the Gulf."

"Can't please everybody." The president puffed.

"We're not pleasing anybody, sir. The Russians and Chinese are bitching, and sure, that's dangerous enough. They have both placed their military forces on high alert. But we're also getting howls from the British, the Germans, the Japanese, even the Saudis. All of the latter protesting the use by our forces of bases in their countries for launching our attacks."

The president puffed again. "What do they want?"

"The Japanese and the Saudis have suggested they may close their bases; force our ships and aircraft to leave. The British and the Germans haven't been so direct, but suggest the same sort of thing."

The president leaned forward, his cheeks reddening. "Mr. Secretary, you tell those assholes in your best diplomatic kiss-ass way that if they want us to leave, we will. But we won't be back. Those European cocksuckers couldn't even put a fence around Yugoslavia when it fell apart, and how bad do the Japs and the Saudis want to be left to the mercy of their neighbors? We don't need the oil from the Gulf; it goes to Europe and Japan. We can get all we need right here in our own Western Hemisphere, especially with huge new fields coming in Venezuela, Peru, and Ecuador." The president paused and took another puff. The stinker was beginning to bother even him. The Secretary of State was ashen pale and breathing shallowly. "Tell 'em that, Mr. Secretary. Tell them it's a new day. Tell them to fuck off, and to support our just and righteous position in restoring peace to an uncertain world."

The president leaned back. His color returned to normal and suddenly he grinned. "Tell them that in your best diplomatic style, Mr. Secretary."

Malcolm Japes rose slowly to his feet. "Mr. President, these are our oldest friends and staunchest allies—"

The president took another puff of his cigar and blew it toward his Secretary of State. "I'm sure you'll do fine, Mr. Secretary."

THERE WERE NO FURTHER responses from Korea or any of the Gulf states. The fleets, air forces, and ground troops were withdrawn to normal operating areas and tempo. The world calmed, but angry buzz continued. International travel, and more important, international trade, virtually ceased. Stock markets crashed all over the world, led by Wall Street, where the Dow-Jones Industrial Average declined 30 percent in a week and a half.

The president kept his silence another few days, seeing almost no one. Then he summoned Zeke Archer. The Chief of Staff found the president haggard, drawn, but upbeat.

Manic, Zeke thought, and his worries increased.

"Zeke, call over to the Capitol. I'd like permission to address a joint session. Make sure there is plenty of room for the world's press."

"Of course, Juss." Zeke felt a surge of relief. "When?"

"Tomorrow would be convenient."

13

"MR. SPEAKER, I HAVE the high honor and distinct privilege to introduce the President of the United States," shouted the Speaker of the House of Representatives as the usher led Rupert Justice Tolliver into the packed House chamber. Senators and congressmen rose and clapped politely, but without enthusiasm.

The diplomatic corps and the press in the gallery remained seated and silent. Even the cabinet, seated behind the Justices of the Supreme Court, could manage only a lukewarm welcome.

The president marched to the podium, turned, and shook hands with the Speaker of the House and the vice president, behind the podium in their high chairs. Justice approached the microphones, squinted at the TelePrompTer screens, and laid his speech upon the podium. The chamber fell as silent as is possible for several hundred people to do.

Justice looked around, studying faces. He saw hostility and fear; it was what he had wanted and expected. The lesson had been taught, and now it had to be explained. Justice was ready, his mind right and righteous.

"Mr. Speaker, Mr. Vice President, Members of the House and Senate, Justices of the Supreme Court, Ladies and Gentlemen of the Diplomatic Corps, representatives of the American and foreign media, the American People and the people of the world," Justice said in a loud, clear voice as he changed his distance glasses for his reading ones. "The events of the last few weeks, when our gallant military and naval forces appeared around the globe, exercising, training, and affirming our right—any sovereign nation's right—to innocent passage of international waterways and airspace, have caused a great crying out, by governments and the media. Our own cities have become turbulent; our people distressed. And I have been accused, not only of acting precipitously, but of doing so without regard to national and international law. Worse, some have said, in this Capitol and in the press, I have failed to explain my actions to the Congress, the nation, and the world. Now I stand before you all to explain, and to urge support.

"I'm an ordained minister, bound to God. I saw a world falling into chaos because of the withdrawal of leadership of the United States, a nation bound to God. I'm not talking only of the Christian God, but the God of all of us, whether we call him Buddha, or Allah, or Vishnu, or simply Lord. The Holy Spirit that inhabits us all, even those who do not believe. The Spirit that binds us together, every human being on the planet. The Spirit, some have said, who has turned his face away, because we have sinned, made wars, committed genocides in Germany, Bosnia, Russia, Cambodia, and Central Africa. Turned his face, or perhaps her face, away because we human beings, blessed by God with knowledge and compassion, have shown little intelligence and less compassion in dealing with the world's tragedies and injustices.

"A dozen or so years ago, the Soviet Union fell of its own weight, its burden of corruption and failed ideology. The Russian people got their church back, a thousand-year-old church taken away for seventy years. The Russian people, magnificent in soul, are returning to their roots and flocking to their churches. We're helping them.

"The Chinese people are gaining freedoms lost for fifty years, including, very gradually, freedom of worship.

"Islam spreads across half the world, from Morocco to Indonesia, and Muslims live among us in Europe and America. There are many differences among us, but the presence of God is being felt as it has not for many years."

Justice paused and took a sip of water. The chamber remained completely silent. "My friends around the world, I believe God loves us, but hates our wickedness. I believe He wants us to live in peace and brotherhood. But I also believe He expects us to act to achieve His Kingdom on earth. There are rogues among us, tyrants and slaughterers, many of whom cloak themselves in one religion or another, or even in the failed religion of communism. These rogues must change their ways, cease their offenses against God's peace on earth, or they will be chastised.

"I sent our fleets to some of the areas where the countries' leaders have flouted God and threatened His peace, although most of their people remain devout, if fearful. What was their leaders' response? To attack our ships. We had no choice but to defend our rights as a nation, and in turn the peace of the world. We did so, and we will again. Jesus said many times he came not in peace but with a sword, but he sought peace. We seek peace, not only among nations but within them. Tyrants who oppress their people, even kill them, deserve the fate of Herod and Holofernes, and will receive it. God, by whatever name you call Him, created men and women to be free beings. The Muslims say we can only be free if we first give ourselves completely to God. I believe this also.

"But freedom isn't only the right not to be oppressed; it's also the right to prosper, and raise a family, and grow crops and create goods and trade those goods. The United States cannot and will not police the world, but we will right wrongs when we can, and help when we can. That's why our fleets and armies defend our rights, and all of yours. We will not turn our faces away from human suffering and misery, just as God of any name has not turned his face away. We'll fight injustice, and disease, and corruption, and poverty however we can, however we must. We'll fight to elevate the human spirit in Cambodia and Rwanda, and also in Chicago, New York, and Los Angeles. We'll root out the Beast wherever he appears. We'll make a better world in this new millennium.

"The press has condemned me, the U.N. has condemned me, and the sense of the House and Senate in this room is that I've acted rashly. Think of the other choice, the other path, the path of the unrestrained Beast. Nuclear wars among nations too poor to feed their people. Great plagues in Africa that go unchecked because the dictator has taken the national treasure to build palaces in Geneva or the south of France. Mountains of skulls in Cambodia, ethnic cleansing in the Balkans, tribal slaughter in central Africa, starvation everywhere in a world filled with riches of every variety.

"The United States." Justice felt a knot in his throat, and tears start. He took another sip of water and dabbed at his eyes with a handkerchief. "The United States wishes to lead the world, not to dominate it. We are the messenger, but the message is God's. You all must choose in this, the first year of the Third Millennium, if the early calculations are accurate. Let us find our humanity as a common thing, undivided by religion, race or culture.

"I speak from my heart." Justice placed his hand over his breast. "Here endeth the lesson."

Justice walked down from the podium. Most of the audience rose, and applauded politely. The applause grew louder as the president, surrounded by Secret Service and members of his staff including the Mormon, swiftly left the chamber, stopping not even once to shake an outstretched hand.

JULIA EARLY WATCHED the speech in her apartment with her two roommates, Judith Langtry and Hilda Chu. "He's bloody mad, isn't he?" Judith said, moving to the small bar to refresh drinks.

"He frightens me," Hilda said. "What he did to Korea threatens all Asia, and what threatens Asia threatens the world."

"You knew him," Judith said, passing out the drinks, a dark whiskey for her, white wine for Julia, and as always, orange juice for Hilda. "Was he always crazy?"

"We have a saying," Julia said carefully. " 'Crazy like a fox.' He's put the world on notice that the only superpower is back, and gotten away with it. But I am afraid. He seems to see himself as the last hope of the world, and how will that be perceived?"

"Who will stop him?" Judith asked.

"Someone," Julia said. "Probably the wrong someones."

"What will their motivation be?" Hilda asked. "Sure, he paid lip service to other religions and nations, but this will be read as his taking up the white man's burden. But what nations can restrain him?"

"Only the United States itself, and the quiet, faceless men who run things here and in the rest of the world," Julia said.

"Such men are capable of moral outrage?" Hilda said derisively. "The big industrialists? The bankers? They're making millions out of the military buildup. They will care for the poor, not only in the world but in the inner cities of this rich nation?"

"They'll stop him," Julia said carefully. "Because he's bad for business. Every stock market in the world has tanked, and global trade has nearly come to a stop."

"What'll the loony do next?" Judith asked.

"Are either of you religious?" Julia asked.

"No," Judith said. "Not at all."

"I am Buddhist," Hilda said.

"There is a Bible in my room. Read the last book, the one the president keeps quoting. The Revelation of Saint John the Divine. When Rupert Justice Tolliver says God has warned us to mend our ways, he means it."

"I still say the man's daft," Judith said. "I'm going to bed."

"Me too," Hilda said, rising from a lotus position on the shag carpet in a single smooth movement.

Julia yawned. "I have something to finish on the computer. Good night."

14

JULIA LEFT CNN on low as she typed. She looked at the television, distracted by an aerial camera shot of a huge city in flames. She turned up the volume and was thus one of the first people in Washington to learn that the city of Los Angeles and many surrounding communities had been torn by a vast earthquake whose epicenter was a mile south of downtown at the intersection of three deep faults of the San Andreas system. Huge fires erupted as gas mains broke all over the city, and efforts to fight fires and rescue people from collapsed buildings were rendered practically impossible by the collapse of nearly all elevated sections of freeways. Julia wept.

THE LOS ANGELES earthquake, measured at 8.1 on the Richter Scale, brought all government business to a halt. The president met with advisers at 5:00 A.M. He telephoned the governor of California, reaching her in her helicopter as she flew south from Sacramento. None of the airports in or around Los Angeles were operating. The promise of all aid and assistance was made and accepted. Governor Feinstein said the devastation was very bad and that huge aftershocks continued. Gas supplies were gradually turned off at sources, but one refinery in Long Beach continued to burn, too hot to approach.

The president put the Secretary of Defense in charge of the assistance operation, to aid the Federal Emergency Management Administration, whose own resources were quickly overwhelmed.

The president addressed the nation at noon Eastern time, asking all people of goodwill to do what they could to aid the devastated city and promising the full resources of the federal government. The air force began flying into military bases in the region with emergency supplies and medical teams. Army Combat Engineers and Navy Seabees restored airports and used their heavy equipment to plow pathways through the rubble. Civilian crews from the heavy construction companies of Flour and Bechtel, both headquartered in California, moved in to help. Firefighters and construction crews began arriving almost as soon as the president spoke. The president announced that he would be flying to Los Angeles later in the day. He concluded his remarks by asking the nation to help him to succor, restore, and rebuild.

After his advisers left to carry out their various assignments, the president studied a map of the region that had been marked with areas of greatest damage. South Central and West L.A., older areas with frame houses and older concrete apartment buildings, poor areas. In the affluent community of Palos Verdes, a six-mile section of bluff had slid into the ocean, taking many large homes with it.

The president shook his head in disbelief. If this was not a sign from God, what was?

IT TOOK JULIA a week to finish her report on Uvalde County Savings and Loan, Little Cheyenne Development, and the laundering of money into the president's campaign. The bank was busy, especially in operations, as banks all over the country tried to straighten out transactions with California banks that had lost all access to their own records and records of transactions passing through them. Julia e-mailed the forty pages of facts and figures to the Chairman of Capital National Bank, Alfred Thayer. She had traced much of the money, some from Cuba, some from Colombia, some from Taiwan and South Korea, and some from Saudi Arabia.

Most of the rest of it came from organizations she suspected were controlled by international crime cartels. She was sure Thayer could find out if he cared.

She sent the file in such a way that it could not be traced back to her by anyone less expert than Clifford Stohl, the famous Berkeley mathematician, and even he or one like him would need months.

Julia went out during lunch and purchased a ream of cheap printer paper from Staples. It was nothing like the bank's fine stock. She printed the report, put it in a plain brown envelope, and mailed it to the reporter, Charles Taylor. She was careful to handle the report, the envelope, and the label only by the edges.

On her way back to the apartment, she mailed the package from a Mail Boxes USA, using a completely false name and return address and paying cash. She dumped the rest of the Staples paper in a sidewalk trash barrel.

When she got back to the apartment, she phoned her daddy and asked if she could come home for a few days. When he said, "Sure, baby," she burst into tears.

ALFRED THAYER'S SECRETARY stopped him as he returned from lunch. "You have an e-mail, sir," Ms. Schwartz said. "Very long; marked for your eyes only."

"Who's it from?" Thayer barked. No one sent him e-mail; he hated infernal desktop computers and refused to have one in his office. He also hated long reports by any means.

"No signature, and no origination code," Ms. Schwartz said. "Very odd, but from within the bank."

"What's the subject?"

"Uvalde County Savings and Loan and Little Cheyenne Development."

Damn! Thayer thought. That was supposed to be buried months ago. "Can you print it out?"

Ms. Schwartz handed Thayer a thick folder. "I did, and a damn good thing I did."

"Why's that?" Thayer said idly, opening the file and reading the first few lines of the Executive Summary.

"Because right after it finished printing, the report vanished from the computer."

The president returned to Washington after two days touring Los Angeles. When the fires died and the smoke blew away, the devastation seemed less than the first pictures had suggested. Tall buildings downtown had withstood the temblor with little damage beyond broken windows, as had most structures built to earthquake-resistant codes after 1970. Most of the damage was very near the fissure itself. A crack like an inverted L had opened from Santa Monica in the north to East L.A. and bending down to Seal Beach in the south. West of the fissure the land had settled and slid as a block thirty meters toward the Pacific. Another crack went west from the bend in the L and ran nearly all the way east to Pomona. Both fissures filled with seawater that steamed from the internal heat below. The city had literally been broken into three parts.

The president grieved on his flight back to Washington. Tens of thousands dead or maimed, billions of dollars to rebuild. What could happen next?

15

THE KUWAITI-FLAGGED 500,000 dead-weight-ton oil tanker *Abu Musa,* outward bound and fully loaded, began a transit of the Strait of Hormuz, the narrow choke point between Iran and Oman that restricted all shipping in and out of the Persian Gulf. Because of the narrowness of the passage and the amount of traffic, she had a full crew on the bridge, including the captain. At just past four A.M, the sky off to port of the thousand-foot-long vessel began to light up with bright flares. The first Silkworm missile, with a six-hundred-kilogram incendiary warhead, plunged straight down through the deck and the forward hold. The captain ordered the ship to speed up and turn right in the narrow channel. The quartermaster logged the order, and the missile strike, but as four more missiles struck in quick succession, he fled the bridge with everyone else as the ship burst into flames from end to end. Most of the crew made it off, even the engine room gang, as the ship's great diesels were located aft, beneath the bridge and the crew spaces. The bow of the ship grounded on a rock off the Omani shore. *Abu Musa* swung across the channel and burned until she sank. The waters around her would burn for days, a lake of fire.

AT ELEVEN O'CLOCK in the morning a rented truck filled with barrels of a mixture of fuel oil and common fertilizer detonated with a force equal to seven tons of TNT in front of the federal building in Little Rock, Arkansas. The whole front of the concrete and glass structure collapsed, as did the roof and many of the twenty-two floors. There would be no estimate of casualties for many hours. A muffled voice called the ABC Television Network in New York and claimed responsibility on behalf of the Blood

Urban Brotherhood, saying that a government that could not provide for the poor of the cities should be destroyed and would be. The network's sophisticated tracing equipment got a pay phone near Jacksonville, north of Little Rock on Highway 67.

RUPERT JUSTICE TOLLIVER canceled his schedule for the next two days immediately after the news came in from the Strait of Hormuz and Arkansas. He asked for time from the four major networks that was immediately granted. He mourned the loss of the federal workers—including children in a day-care center in the federal building—and condemned the terrorists. He promised the nation they would be rooted out and punished. He promised as well the assistance of the U.S. fleet in the Indian Ocean and within the Persian Gulf in reopening the Strait of Hormuz and restoring the flow of oil, as well as punishment of the Iranis who had fired the missiles. He asked the nation and the world to remain calm and firm.

WHEN THE CAMERAS had been wheeled out of the Oval Office, the president turned to Zeke Archer. His face was weary and ashen. "It's starting, Zeke, and we're not ready."

"Mr. President—Juss—what're you going to do? You lit a fire, and somebody just poured gasoline on it."

The president's hand shook badly as he took a sip from the drink Zeke handed him, spilling most of it. "Nothing I did can explain Los Angeles, unless it's the wrath of God himself against a man with too many sins to wash away who has taken a high office. We must be firm, Zeke. Things will get worse, far worse, then the promise will be kept."

ACROSS AMERICA, RIOTING and looting began in large cities and small. Violent demonstrations flared up in Europe, Japan, and Hong Kong.

* * *

JUSTICE HAD JUST two meetings the afternoon of the bombing in Little Rock, the day after the sinking of the *Abu Musa*. One was with the vice president, the Secretary of Defense, and the Joint Chiefs, and the other with the Director of the FBI.

He told his defense advisers retaliation against Iran must be swift and sure, and asked for a list of targets to be prepared. After the generals and admirals filed out, the vice president remained. "You're mad!" he seethed. "What became of our bargain before the convention? I'm supposed to advise you on foreign policy, and you don't even keep me informed!"

The president sighed. "Vice President Donahue, you bore the hell out of me, and I haven't time to listen to you whine."

"Mr. President!" Donahue bellowed.

"Get out of my office, Donahue," the president said icily. "Now."

THE PRESIDENT TOLD the Director of the FBI to find out who had blown up the federal building in Little Rock and bring them in body bags.

"You mean arrest them, sir," the director said nervously. "We have leads, good leads."

"Let's save the people the agony and expense of a trial," the president said, and waved the startled director from the Oval Office. God's wrath must be swift, he thought.

ALFRED THAYER READ Julia's report with great care. He knew Capital National Bank had handled accounts for the Republican National Committee, but was totally unaware that it did any business at all with the Tolliver campaign, if the writer was right and that is what the huge money flows meant. But something was wrong with the picture. Very large transactions were reported daily on a sheet called the Significant Balance Change Report that was circulated to all department heads and above, including of course the office of the chairman. He should have known, and the fact that he didn't wouldn't save his bank if this was what the writer said it was.

Thayer knew that because the report existed—he had it in his hands—it would get out. Anything recorded always got out, especially anything on a computer.

Thayer buzzed Ms. Schwartz. "Get Max Berlin in here, please, and Frank Simmons." She acknowledged the request and made the calls.

Berlin, the bank's president, arrived immediately; his office was only a few steps away. It took Frank Simmons five minutes to emerge from the computer warren in the basement. The Dragon Mother brought coffee as the two men sat. Thayer had slid the report into his top drawer and closed it. "Uvalde County Savings and Loan Society," Thayer intoned. "Little Cheyenne Development."

"Never heard of it," Frank Simmons said. "But I don't look at individual accounts unless something gets messed up in the computer."

"I remember something from about last January," Berlin said. "Some credit files went missing, and there was a squeal from the White House."

"It seems the First Lady is involved directly, and the president at least indirectly," Thayer said.

"Yes," Berlin said. "But we recovered the files, all of them, and flagged them 'No Access.' "

"But why didn't we see the huge transfers? Nothing in the daily reports."

Simmons carried a soft briefcase. He withdrew a tiny laptop computer and asked the chairman, "May I?"

"Go ahead," Thayer snapped, eyeing the loathsome thing. "I suppose you have to plug it in somewhere; there's a jack around here somewhere, but I never use it."

Simmons knew the old man's disdain for technology. He

would have to tread softly to avoid getting the blame for whatever had gone wrong. "No, sir, it has internal power and a wireless modem."

Whatever the fuck that was, Thayer thought darkly. He watched as Simmons typed away. "What period are we looking for, sir?" Simmons asked.

"October and November, last year. January, this year."

Simmons typed some more, then he gave a low whistle. "Your source is good, Mr. Thayer. Huge fund movements, but all in overseas branches and affiliates, mostly overnight or within one clearing day, so no report in the dailies." He typed some more. "I'm looking at the last credit review of Uvalde County S. and L. No substantial increase in assets, so the money moved on."

"What about Little Cheyenne?"

"We don't have a direct account relationship," Simmons said, scanning. "Uvalde County is their bank, and they give us information because loans to Little Cheyenne are such a large portion of Uvalde's assets."

Thayer took a deep breath, and blew it out slowly. His stomach hurt. "I have received a report—a tip, really, but very detailed, that our bank may have been used to launder money, including huge amounts from overseas, into the hands of the Tolliver campaign."

Simmons winced, and Berlin shifted uneasily in his seat.

Thayer buzzed Ms. Schwartz. "Ruth, call the White House; the loathsome Mr. Callendar. Tell him I want to speak to him and his boss, the equally slimy Ezekiel Archer."

"Yes, Mr. Thayer. Will you be going over there?" *There* meant the White House, a few blocks away.

Thayer considered it. "No, tell them to come here. The matter is very urgent and very sensitive."

16

Julia Early flew to San Antonio, where her father, Jubal John (J J) Early, met her in his high-axle, four-wheel-drive Ford Bronco. J J was a retired captain in the Texas Rangers, still rangy and fit at sixty. He had been chief of Governor Rupert Justice Tolliver's security detail until the governor hit the big time and headed off to Washington. J J embraced his daughter, rocking her as she wept. After he got her into the truck and gave her a tissue from the box on the dash, he asked softly, "What's the matter, Julia May?"

"I'm scared, Daddy," she said. "And maybe ashamed."

"Tell."

"While I was at the bank, I was given two files to examine. Uvalde County Savings and Loan and Little Cheyenne Development."

J J gave a low whistle. "I been up there a couple of times with the governor—the president, now. Ambitious deal; kinda remote."

"I want to go see it."

"Now, girl, why ever would you want to do that?"

"Because I think the development was a sham. A way to funnel money to the Tollivers, and later to the campaign."

J J shook his head. "Some things are best left unexamined, Julia May. This is Texas, and politicians raise money in different ways." He paused. "It's an awful excuse, but everybody does it; worst of all down here the judges."

"I think a lot of the money came in from foreign sources. I think a lot more was laundered through my bank in Europe and the Caribbean. I'd like to know if there is really a development."

"Why don't we get you on home and get you a nice hot dinner and a rest. We could drive up tomorrow."

"It's almost on the way, Daddy."

"Tomorrow," J J said firmly. "You and me need to have a talk first."

"But, Daddy, the president is acting strange; doing strange things, preaching the Apocalypse to the Congress, making wars, scaring off trade and business. I'm afraid of him, and afraid for him."

"Your mother's making fried chicken. We'll talk after dinner."

CHARLES TAYLOR read the anonymous report that arrived on his desk just as he was leaving on a Friday afternoon. He was both elated and appalled. He examined both the envelope and each page of the report, including the sophisticated graphics in the appendices. Who could have sent it? And why to him? Why not to one of the big newspapers or television networks?

Charles made a copy and put the original in his safe. He called his travel agent and booked himself on the four o'clock American flight to San Antonio via Dallas. He would have to rush to make it, but he wanted to see the place, and photograph it, before he tried to sell the story.

He told the agent he would be needing a car, preferably something four-wheel-drive, grabbed the satchel he always kept in his office. He had two; each with a shaving kit. One contained business attire, the other rugged gear. He took the latter, and called a cab to take him to Dulles Airport.

While Charles Taylor was in the air rereading Julia's report, Julia and her father sat in his study. Her mother had left them with coffee and gone to a meeting at the church. Julia explained what she had discovered, and how, and her strange treatment by the bank, including senior officers' attempts to erase her files. J J listened patiently, interrupting only to ask her to explain some of the arcana of international funds movements, and how the untraceable could often be traced.

"Let's assume you're right," he said, after she wound down to exhausted silence. "He raised money, especially late in the campaign, from questionable sources. Is there any evidence that any of those sources got anything back?"

"What's the level of drug interdiction here in Texas and in the Gulf?" she asked. "Washington's awash with the stuff."

"My friends in Austin tell me it's way down," J J said. "Troops and equipment patrolling the border all ended up in ships at sea or policing up the mess after the riots in the cities. Street traffic is active even down here, and promised assistance and grants from the DEA aren't showing up."

"There was a lot of money that originated in Asia, Daddy. Mostly Korea and Taiwan."

"North Korea gets blown up and China intimidated. Are you suggesting—"

"Who benefits from disruption of trade, especially movement of crude oil?"

"The question there may be who loses." J J scratched the gray stubble on his chin. "People getting oil from the Persian Gulf lose, people producing in the Western Hemisphere win. In the long run, Iran, Iraq, and the Central Asian Republics lose; Saudi Arabia wins because they can pipe crude to the Red Sea." He refilled their coffee cups. "But that don't make up a conspiracy, Julia May."

"There are other losers, Daddy. The powerful men around the world who can't trade in commodities and merchandise because markets are disrupted."

"President Tolliver was never a favorite of the business community."

"They hate him. They backed Donahue and then Vice President Sandman, even though his enthusiasm for environmental protection was viewed as antibusiness. They did everything they could to block Tolliver's election."

J J got up and began to pace. "I worked for the man for years. Can't say I knew his heart, but I always thought he tried to do right."

"But only as he saw it, Daddy. I worked for him too. But he's not down here in cozy, 'you take care of me and I'll take care of you' Texas. He's making wars and ruining markets. He's causing powerful people to lose money. And all that crazy preachiness in his speeches. He's all but said 'repent, the end is near.' "

J J sat on the corner of his desk. "You know, honey, the boys in Wall Street and London and Singapore might not like what he's done, but it plays pretty good out here where the idea of kicking the asses of some of these pesky little countries that don't do as they're told sounds like old-time religion."

"Remember where the money came from, especially the Miami money and the money from Colombia and from crime families."

"He's done nothing for them, except perhaps lighten up on drug enforcement."

"What will the world say when he invades Cuba?"

J J snorted. "Now why in the hell would he do that?"

"Think of all the money from Miami, and from organized crime. They all want Cuba back the way it was before Castro; with gambling and tourism back the island could boom."

J J stood up again, shaking his head. How did his little girl get such ideas? he wondered. Washington afflicted anyone who spent time there with paranoia or delusions of grandeur. "Get a good rest. We'll have breakfast and drive on out there in the morning. I'm bettin' we find a bunch of overpriced houses people bought to help the candidate out, then we can go to the courthouse and see who really owns them."

17

ALFRED THAYER'S SECRET group met again in early October at his estate in the Shenandoah Valley. The group had expanded to include, among others, an Assistant Secretary of the Air Force and the Deputy Director of the FBI, but many of the original participants had declined further participation, including all the politicians. Thayer thought this was best. "Be seated, ladies and gentlemen," Alfred Thayer whispered. He had lost much weight and looked haggard; it was rumored that he had been diagnosed with stomach cancer. The other attendees took seats around the long dining room table, glancing at each other nervously. "The time has come for drastic actions. I regret that this is so, but it is. I would ask the representatives of the air force and FBI to speak first. Madame Secretary?"

The Assistant Secretary of the Air Force, Madeleine Allen, was a petite, pretty woman who, despite her silvery hair, looked far younger than her fifty years. "The Air Force has been ordered to bomb Iran in retaliation to the sinking of the Kuwaiti tanker. The targets, selected by the president, are the refinery and storage facilities at Bandar Khomeni."

"Seems reasonable," grunted Grant Telfer, chairman of Lockheed-Martin.

"We have also been ordered to bomb the holy city of Qom," the assistant secretary continued. "To Shiites, the equivalent of the Vatican."

"What says the air force?" Thayer rasped.

"The secretary says it is an unlawful order, and won't carry it out unless it is confirmed by the Secretary of Defense."

"What says she?" Thayer pressed.

"She's in seclusion. Her son is dying of AIDS."

"The Chairman? General Austin?"

"Is all for it, but legally, he is not in the chain of command."

Thayer turned to the CEO of Exxon, Sam Dunlap. "What is the situation in the Persian Gulf?"

"The Strait is navigable, but navy teams are finding many mines. Commerce has slowed to a trickle."

"But it's manageable?"

"I would say yes. Most of the *Abu Musa* has been blown up on the bottom."

"So the president has given an order sure to inflame the Islamic world and bring chaos—*further* chaos—to the oil and commodities markets. So." Thayer steepled his hands. "When is this attack to be launched?"

"In late November," Madeleine Allen said. "On a Saturday morning. Something is special to the president about that day."

"We must find out why," Thayer said. "Now, FBI?"

The Deputy Director was a chubby, balding man of fifty-six who looked more the rumpled college professor than the top cop he was. His name was Charles Thackery. "The FBI has been ordered to bring in the Little Rock bombers in body bags," he said simply.

"Do you know who they are?"

"We believe we do. Three are in Detroit and one is hiding in Guaymas, Mexico."

"How soon could you have them in custody?" Thayer asked.

The Deputy Director fidgeted. "At any time."

"But you haven't arrested them?"

"Given the president's order, the Director is very reluctant to proceed."

Thayer sat back, breathing deeply, seemingly in pain. After a long pause, he began speaking, slowly, carefully. "It appears clear, regrettably clear, that the president has become sick, or irrational, or deranged. He must be removed before he can plunge the nation and the world into chaos. The bombing of Qom will inflame half the world and starve the rest of oil. The execution of four black militants will fill the streets of our cities with blood and fire. The international trade upon which the wealth of nations—especially poor and emerging nations—depends has dried up. Financial markets are in disarray; even foreign exchange contracts for commercial transactions are impossible to settle."

"And we're all losing our asses in the stock and bond markets," Frank Hannon, the CEO of GE remarked.

"When you say 'removed,' " a retired admiral and former Chairman of the Joint Chiefs said, "of course you mean by constitutional means."

"Of course," Thayer said blandly.

"Impeachment?" Madeleine Allen asked.

"Too slow," Thackery said. "He'll force our hand, and yours, long before Congress could even begin hearings."

"The Twenty-fifth Amendment, then," the former admiral suggested.

"Perhaps," Thayer said.

"This sounds like conspiracy to me," Allen said, standing. "I'll report back to my superior, but she'll have none of it."

"There is no conspiracy," Thayer said, a bit more force in his voice. "Only a discussion. You're all reminded that a condition of your attendance at this conference—each of yours—was on condition of secrecy."

"Nevertheless," Thackery began, rising to his feet.

"Nevertheless, any of you who are not comfortable may leave and no harm done," Thayer interrupted. "Take a moment and consider: the nation and the world face a clear and present danger."

Everyone sat and looked around for about five minutes. In the end, half of the fourteen people in the room got up quietly, gathered their notes, and left.

Those remaining were the industrialists, the bankers, and two retired Chairmen of the Joint Chiefs. Thayer ordered the door locked and drinks were served. Thayer waited until the seven men settled in with their drinks and some canapés brought in by two uniformed butlers who immediately withdrew, relocking the door behind them. When he spoke, he spoke slowly, weighing each word, knowing each was bad news. "There are no constitutional means to do what must be done," he said sadly. "There simply isn't time, although if there were, I believe the president would be removed."

"Why not use the Twenty-fifth Amendment?" asked Admiral Carter Daniels, a decorated, nearly blind veteran of Vietnam, nearing seventy-five years old. "Have him declared temporarily incompetent. Vice President Donahue is an ass, but he can be controlled by the party."

The Chairman of GE, who was also a lawyer, shook his head.

"The president may have committed folly, may indeed have placed the nation and world business in peril for no reason, but it is difficult to argue that he's done anything illegal, beyond his powers, or, legally, insane."

"He acts in the name of religion," Sam Dunlap of Exxon said. "Perhaps a delegation of prominent churchmen—"

"He never showed the slightest inclination to religion in his youth," Admiral Daniels said hotly. "His 'calling' was nothing more than a ploy to avoid service in Vietnam. He's not leading a crusade; he's a simple madman, a Napoleon, a Hitler, a Tamerlane, but with the power to truly destroy the world."

"We agree he must be removed," Thayer said firmly.

Everyone nodded except Dunlap. "I'm afraid I see where this is leading." He rose. "Please have the doors unlocked, Alfred. I can't hear any more."

Thayer pressed a button under the table and one of the butlers unlocked the doors and peered in. The Chairman of Exxon picked up his briefcase and walked rapidly from the room without saying anything further. "Anyone else?" Thayer whispered. "No one will think less of you."

The five remaining men looked at each other, and Thayer, whose face was a granite mask. The Chairman of Citibank hung his head. "I know you're right, Alfred. You've always been right about this man. But I can't do this; I remember 1963 all too vividly."

"It is precisely because of 1963, and the hard decisions that were made then, that we must act as the patriots of the time acted," Thayer said with some heat. "But you all have a say. Do you think I'm wrong? Can we afford the risk of not acting?"

Citibank's chairman walked to the door and out. No one else moved. Thayer nodded, and the door was again locked by the butler. "Now it's time to call a spade a spade," Thayer said. "We're considering the removal of the President of the United States by executive action. For those of you not up to date on the euphemisms of the intelligence community, executive action means assassination." He looked at his four remaining conspirators. Hannon of GE thought he saw a spark of madness in the old banker's eyes, but he kept his seat.

So did the others, Admiral Daniels, General Smith, who had never spoken, and Baruch Rubin, the retired Chairman of the Federal Reserve, who also had never spoken. Thayer continued. "Remember Macchiavelli, my fellows in this awful necessity. 'When you strike at a king, you must kill him.' " He pressed the buzzer under the table again. When the door was opened, he called to the butler. "Bring in our guest, please."

A man dressed all in black including a silk ski mask with narrow eye slits entered the room and took a seat at the foot of the table, as far as he could from the conspirators who had crowded around Thayer at the head. "This is Ramon, who will find us the instrument we require," Thayer said.

"Will he be traceable?" General Arthur Allen asked. He had been Director of Central Intelligence in the early nineties.

"Not to me," the man in black said. "To you, only if you screw it up."

"Then get him," Thayer said. "We'll see that your man has all the information we can supply as to the president's public schedule."

"He'll get that himself."

Thayer looked at each conspirator in turn. No one showed any expression other than sorrow. "Then make it so."

The man in black, Ramon Carvahal of the Cuban National Service of Information, got up and left. Beneath his mask, he was smiling.

Alfred Thayer adjourned the meeting and left his guests to enjoy the pool, tennis courts, and golf course on the estate, or retire to the well-stocked bar if they wished. He went to his study and closed the door, after telling his personal assistant to hold all calls. He sat and looked out the window at the piece of the beautiful Shenandoah Valley that was his. He brooded on what he had done; what he had set in motion. He alone knew the identity of the man in black; none of the others ever would. He alone had the detailed report of Tolliver's money connections to enemies of the United States, both within and without the country. The others had condemned the president on evidence that he was dangerous to business, perhaps crazy. Thayer wasn't sure how crazy Tolliver was, though he was undeniably dangerous. Thayer knew, because of the printout of the financial records of Uvalde County Savings and Loan and Little Cheyenne Development and the money flows into Tolliver's campaign, that the president was corrupt, bought and sold. He was in thrall of all the people in the world who wanted the United States brought low, who would profit from chaos.

He could not reveal the money flows to the others without destroying the reputation of the Capital National Bank; indeed destroying the bank itself. Thayer closed his eyes and brooded. Yes, he decided, the needs of the nation and of his beloved bank coincided, exactly.

If Alfred Thayer hadn't loved the intricately beautiful Shirazi rug beneath his desk, he would have spat.

18

COBRA SAT ON the veranda of his house, watching the sun set into the dark shadowed mounds of the Makapi Hills. Venus brightened, then the sliver of the new moon. Cobra liked the early evening best, when the heat of the day gave way suddenly to the cool of the high plateau. He could put his feet up and have a drink and forget for a while the drought, the condition of the land and stock, and the loom of foreclosure.

The telephone rang, deep within the house. An increasingly rare event as people left the valley as their homesteads failed.

Most moved east, looking for farm work where the rains had come. Many of the whites left the country entirely, bound for Australia, New Zealand, or Canada.

Isaiah, the old houseman who stayed on simply because he had no living family and his home village was too far away to walk, padded softly out of the house carrying the phone on its long cord. He placed it on the table next to Cobra's wicker rocker, picked up the empty glass, and went back into the house without a word.

Cobra picked up the phone. "Yes?"

"This is Quentin. I have something for you."

"I'm a farmer now," Cobra said cautiously. The new black-run government in Pretoria had never discontinued the old apartheid government's monitoring of phone calls, especially calls overseas. The buzz on the line indicated an overseas call, and Quentin, one of Cobra's contractors from the old days, worked from various places in Europe.

"We are told your farm is in some difficulty." Quentin had a strong Afrikaner accent. "Take this and you can either fix it up or simply leave it and retire."

Cobra winced. "Well—"

"Fly to Jo'burg. You'll be met. Fifty thousand rand just to take a look."

"Perhaps."

"And bring your tools."

Cobra paused as Isaiah returned with a fresh Pink Gin. Shooters never carried their own weapons, certainly not across borders. The client always provided the means at or near the site of the act, untraceable throwaways, all too often trash. Isaiah padded away. "That could create difficulties, I'm sure you know."

"Not between where you are and Jo'burg. Read the proposal; it will be sealed, you know my seal. If it is unsealed, take the expense money and go home."

Fifty thousand rand wasn't much, but it would quiet the bank. "I'll go to Johannesburg; no guarantee I'll go farther."

Quentin chuckled. "You'll go farther. Take the flight tomorrow that arrives at seventeen-hundred hours; you'll make your onward connection. Give you a little time to test the gear, and your old formidable skills." Quentin hung up.

COBRA SET THE PHONE down and picked up his drink. "Isaiah?" he called.

"Master," the old man said from just inside.

"Get me my old rifle, the Remington 700."

"Precious little game, master."

"Target practice, for when the game returns with the rain."

"God willing," Isaiah said. He brought the rifle, and the tools and cleaning kit. Cobra set his drink aside and slowly disassembled the old beauty down to its tiniest components.

COBRA ROSE AT SUNRISE, had his simple breakfast of tea and fruit, and took his old Marine Corps Remington Model 700 sniper rifle with its upgraded variable-power telescopic sight and two boxes of ammunition down the dry wash that had been his river. Isaiah tagged along, curious, carrying a burlap sack full of cans and bottles. Cobra had the cans placed in an irregular line along the sandbar, then paced back three hundred meters. He set himself in the parched grass, calm, remembering. He assumed the prone position, and was immediately greeted with stabs of protest from joints and muscles no longer young. Isaiah trudged up the shallow incline with a pillowcase filled with river sand. Cobra sat up, tied off the open end, and pounded the sand into one end, then tied it again. He kneaded a groove across the sandbag with his thumbs and set it in front of his chosen spot in the grass. He resumed his prone position, letting the aches and pains even out then driving them from his mind. He gauged the wind; light, from right to left, stronger down the river valley. He placed the crosshairs on the leftmost tin and slowed his breathing. He had expected it to be difficult to feel the old oneness with rifle and target, but it wasn't. He let the tin blur and focus in his eyes, increasing the pressure on the trigger with each shallow exhalation. The shot broke and Cobra immediately swung to the next can as the first jumped in the air. He worked the bolt action so smoothly he never lost the target image in the scope.

He fired five times in seven seconds. He hit four cans and missed one.

"Set the cans up again, Isaiah," he said to the old man. "And the bottles behind them, in the shadow of the opposite bank."

The old man departed and Cobra marched another two hundred meters up the slope. As soon as Isaiah was clear, Cobra settled himself in a new spot, arranged the sandbag and the rifle, and took aim, swinging the rifle between the cans and the barely visible bottles. He decided to take the center bottle first, then the cans who would be bodyguards, then the rest of the bottles, the target's aides or his generals. He emptied his mind, and began to fire, working the bolt action without thought between each shot while moving to the next target, stopping his heart at each squeeze. Isaiah climbed back and confirmed that every target had been hit.

I wish I had something moving, Cobra thought. He heard the distant *skree-ee* of a hawk, then saw the bird, gliding down the wash, hunting, riding the thermals that rose from the hot sand. Cobra chambered the last round in the magazine and followed the bird effortlessly in the scope. I'm sorry, he thought, to do this to a fellow hunter, then he squeezed off the shot. The hawk exploded from the impact of the heavy military round.

"Reckon that hawk be flyin' 'bout twenty-five kilometers an hour, master," Isaiah said with a grin.

"Faster," Cobra said, not returning the smile. "Let's go back."

19

J J AND JULIA got started just after seven in the morning and drove the forty miles to the dirt road near Knippe that led to the Little Cheyenne River. There was a faded wooden sign at the junction, and J J turned in and drove up the dusty trail. There was a rise, and they could see the river and its oxbow lake below. The office of Little Cheyenne Development was a trailer, jacked up off its wheels, another faded sign, and telephone and electrical wires that ran off into the distance. J J climbed down, then helped his daughter out of the high-wheeled vehicle.

The door to the trailer was locked, but yielded to a vigorous tug. J J had his Ranger's .45 revolver in his hand as he entered, Julia behind. He flipped the light switch and was surprised to see the lights come on; the place looked to have been deserted for a long time.

There were three desk-and-chair sets, file cabinets, and computer monitors, all covered with a thick layer of dust. Every wall had artists' renderings of the houses and common facilities on the broad, curved slope of the ridge that stood over the river and the lake. There was also a chart showing the lots and the roads that would service them. Almost all of them were stamped in faded red: "Sold." "Let's take a look around outside," J J said.

Julia followed him back to the Bronco. There were roads laid out and graded, and connection boxes for phone and electricity. There were no structures other than a large building down by the lakeside, rough-timbered, and a pool, dug out and roughly gunited. The lake glimmered below, still and green with growth. "Shit," J J said. "You said this all was paid for?"

"That's what the bank's records show."

J J turned and spat. "Let's go back to Uvalde and have a look at the ownership records."

Julia followed. It was true, then, the development was a scam, and the money had gone elsewhere, presumably into the campaign. She remembered the cash inflows after the election, and felt a little ill.

When J J and Julia returned to the trailer, they found a Jeep Cherokee, and a tall man taking pictures. Julia and Charles Taylor recognized each other at once.

Shit, Charles thought, she's the source of the report, but who's the guy with the cannon?

Shit, Julia thought. Charles got here too quick. He'll know I sent the report. What to do? "Good morning, Charles," she said. "What brings you all the way out here?"

"Running down an old lead," he said smoothly, taking her hand while watching the big guy with the gun. "Phony land development. Any ideas?"

"No. My daddy and I used to hunt out here and fish when I was a kid. Don't know anything about what's going on."

J J said nothing, but placed his big hand on the small of Julia's back and guided her back to the Bronco.

"WHO WAS THAT man?" J J asked as he negotiated the narrow dirt track back to the state road at a lot higher speed than he had come in.

"Reporter," Julia said. "Strings for the *Washington Times* and others."

"How'd he know about this?"

"I don't know, Daddy," Julia said, realizing it was the first time she had ever lied to her father.

The courthouse in Uvalde was a Depression-era red-brick structure. The Clerk's Office was on the ground floor. The County Clerk was an attractive, gray-haired woman of about fifty who identified herself as Mavis Mills. She accepted the filled-out request form and brought over the land records for Little Cheyenne Development. Julia went through them quickly, with a practiced eye. All corporations, in Grand Cayman, Turks and Caicos Islands, Belgium and Luxembourg. "Who runs the office out there on the site?" J J asked.

"Why, Miss Ida Mae did," Mills said. "Till she had a little stroke about three months ago, then the president's lady moved her down to Florida someplace."

J J and Julia knew Miss Ida Mae was Clarissa Alcott Tolliver's aunt. "Thank you," Julia said, and she and her father returned to the Bronco.

Mavis Mills made an immediate call to Washington, to the office of Ezekiel Archer. His secretary promised he would call back.

Ten minutes later Charles Taylor came in and asked to look at the same files. Mavis Mills accommodated him, and as soon as he left, made another call to Archer, asking the operator to mark the message "urgent."

20

COBRA WAS MET at the airport in Johannesburg by a very pale man whose face was flushed with heat. He led Cobra into the South African Airways first-class lounge, handed him a sealed packet, then helped himself to the free whisky while Cobra read.

The packet included an envelope containing fifty thousand rand in cash that Cobra placed in the inside pocket of his traveling jacket. There were two sets of travel documents, one Belgian, one French. Air tickets, one to Lisbon via Luanda, Angola, departing in an hour. The second set, corresponding to the French passport, departing two days later from Lisbon to Washington, D.C. Both tickets had open returns. Cobra doubted he would use either, but one-way tickets attracted scrutiny. A reservation at the Ritz Hotel in Lisbon for tomorrow night, marked for early check-in. Nothing else.

Cobra sat next to the courier, who had given no name. "Why European documents?" he asked. "I haven't spoken French in many years, and besides—"

"Look at the birthplaces. Leopoldville, Belgian Congo, as it was when you were born. Now Kinshasa, Congo. All the Belgian records have been lost so it's untraceable. On the French document, born Martinique so you're as French as any citizen of Paris, but can be expected to speak the language atrociously. All their old records were lost to a hurricane twenty years ago. You'll destroy the Belgian document in Lisbon. As the citizen of a European Union country, you'll not receive much notice in Washington." The fat man handed over another envelope. "Once inside the U.S. you'll become Frank Hayes, an American born in Los Angeles."

Cobra took the packet and dumped out a driving license, Social Security card, credit cards, and other wallet litter. "All good forgeries?" Cobra held each document up to the light in return.

"All genuine. You're working for top men."

"What's the mission? And what about this?" he pointed to the holdall at his feet that contained his rifle and hand-loaded ammunition.

"You'll be met and handed off in Lisbon and in Washington. The mission will be explained when you get there. That"—he pointed to the holdall as though he thought it might strike him—"you leave with me. You won't see it again until you're briefed and accept the commission."

"And if I refuse?"

Another envelope, fat. "Fifty thousand American dollars in cash. Certainly enough to get home on."

"But surely not the entire payment."

"Not even a tiny fraction."

It had to be political, and someone either dangerous or well protected. Not many dictators left in the world. "Can you tell me who it is?"

The fat man stood, and reached for the holdall. "I have no

idea. You know everything I do. Will you take the flight and have a lovely dinner at the Ritz?"

"Why not?" Cobra said, pushing the holdall with his toe. He got up, tucked the French passport, the Lisbon–Washington tickets, and all the money in a concealed compartment in his carry-on bag. "See you round, mate."

"You'll never see me again," the man said, picking up the holdall with the weapons. He pointed up at the monitor over the bar. "Your flight's checking in."

The courier hurried out of the lounge. Cobra gave him a full two minutes to disappear, then sauntered over to the Air Portugal counter.

IV

REVELATION

1

"WHAT'RE YOU GOING to do now, Julia May?" J J Early said as he drove toward home.

"Go back to work. They only gave me the long weekend."

"I mean about Little Cheyenne."

"I have no idea. If I told anyone, they would think I was mad."

"Who knows about this in your bank?"

"Several people have to," she said cautiously. "Transactions of these sizes are reported to senior management." Unless somebody decided that they shouldn't, she thought, remembering the reaction of the seventeenth floor before she had been buried in the basement, her files, as far as Hollis and presumably Alfred Thayer himself knew, erased from the computer. "But if this stuff is as illegal as I think it is, they may do nothing."

"Maybe that's best," J J said.

"Why? This is evidence of massive corruption that is ongoing."

"Probably true, but we don't know whether Rupert Justice even knows about it. His wife's the business sense, and if I have to say so, the ruthless sense as well."

"But Daddy—"

"Baby, I think he's a good man, and the job will settle him down, just like it did in Austin. He's kicked up a lot of dust in the last few weeks, but like I said earlier, people outside of Washington might just think he was right to do it. As to the fund-raising, it's dirty, but it always was. Remember all the chest-beating the Congress did about the last president? Renting out the Lincoln Bedroom? Taking money from Buddhist nuns who are sworn to poverty? In the end Congress didn't do shit, because they're all in on the deal."

"But, Daddy, you said yourself he's already paid off the South Koreans, the Saudis—"

"We don't know why he did what he did, but he went to the Congress and the people, and his approval rating is up, albeit from a dismal level right after the fighting stopped. I think he'll be more cautious now, and think, Baby, just maybe, he's right."

"It's still corruption," she said softly.

"Do you want a President Donahue? Think about it; let me ask some friends."

"All right." Julia felt guilty. She should have asked her father first; he knew all the Texas insiders on the president's staff. Maybe there was an explanation for all that money that had surely not been spent in the Hill Country of Texas. But how could there possibly be?

But she couldn't stop it now. She had tipped Charles Taylor, and the cat would soon be out of the bag.

CHARLES TAYLOR CALLED Brad Bentley, senior political editor at the *Washington Post*. He supposed he owed the *Times*, but he might never have an opportunity like this again to get into the big leagues. He called from a booth in the Dallas–Fort Worth Airport while waiting for his connection back to Washington, having driven to San Antonio International directly from the County Courthouse in Uvalde.

The *Post* had broken Watergate, for investigative journalism, *the* story of the last century. *Post* people considered their paper the best in the business at finding out the secrets of Washington's powerful, and every lead was pursued.

Taylor called Bentley because, since he had been promoted to senior editor four years before after the retirement of a legend, nothing really big had come across his desk. The Blythe administration had had a host of scandals, but nothing earthshaking, and most had broken out of town. The *Post*'s hated rival, the *New York Times*, had got the FBI files in White House closets story out first, and led the way on uncovering corruption in the raising of campaign funds. Neither story had got very far, but Bentley didn't have a big one at all. Charles Taylor had the story, and if he could prove it up, it could mean a permanent job at the *Post,* and perhaps a Pulitzer.

Bentley accepted the collect call without hesitation. He thought Charles had talent as an investigator, although he needed more time in Washington before he would develop the confidence of the most informed and influential leakers of the leads that made the great reporters. Bentley listened to Charles's story, briefly summarized.

"What's the source?"

"Not sure yet. I think I know; I'll get it confirmed."

"What makes you think you have this exclusively?"

"Because you didn't already know about it."

Bentley chuckled. "All right, go get your plane. Have your film processed downstairs and leave me a copy of the story. I'll protect you, and call you the minute I've read it."

Charles hung up, grabbed his bulky camera bag and his travel bag and ran for the gate. He was the last passenger to board, and the American Airlines 777 began taxiing before he had his seat belt on.

Now, he wondered, accepting a double scotch from the flight attendant, how do I get the rest of this out of Julia Early? Or how do I get this verified independently?

In this business you had at best days, sometimes only hours. How?

EZEKIEL ARCHER RETURNED to his cluttered office after hours of meetings with congressmen, senators, and very worried Wall Street types. He saw the two messages from the clerk of Uvalde County and immediately dialed the number. Mavis Mills answered her own phone. "Mavis, Zeke Archer. It's been too long."

"Why thank you, Mr. Archer. I'm surprised you remember my first name, but thank you."

Normally in Texas even the most important conversations

were begun with elaborate small talk about family, friends, and the weather, but Zeke had hours of work to do and he felt sure that Ms. Mills wouldn't have called for no reason. "How can I help you, Mavis?"

"You remember that land deal, on the Little Cheyenne River? Mrs. Tolliver—hell, the First Lady now—set up a few years back? Well, after a flurry of deed recordings right around the election, nobody has been in here to look at anything, record any mortgages, nothing like you'd expect for such a big development. But today I had two inquiries within minutes of each other."

Zeke thought his heart had stopped. He didn't know much about Little Cheyenne; it had been Clarissa's project from the start. Zeke knew Clarissa had pressured a lot of local fat cats to buy options on the lots, and he suspected some of that money had found its way into Tolliver's last campaign for governor, and maybe the owe for president as well. Zeke, took a ragged breath. "Who did these people say they were?"

"The first two were J J Early, who used to guard the governor? And a young woman I kinda thought was his little girl. The second was a man who didn't say who he was. They don't have to, you know, the records are public, though I did think it rude he wouldn't introduce himself."

"Well, thank you for calling, Mavis. Please call me if anything like this happens again. Did anyone take any copies?"

"The man with no name did, copies of about sixty pages of recorded deeds. Paid cash and took his receipt."

Jesus, Zeke thought. "Mavis, thank you again. I have to take another call."

"I'm sure you're busy. You take care, now."

"You too, Mavis. Good-bye." Zeke immediately dialed the White House telephone exchange in the basement. "Find a retired Texas Ranger named Jubal John Early. He headed up the president's security detail when he was governor. It's quite urgent."

"Should be no trouble, Mr. Archer. A man giving that name just tried to reach you."

Zeke's phone rang again, the secure line. "Mr. Early, sir," the operator said, and immediately made the connection. "J J?"

"Howdy, Zeke. Sorry to bother you, but someone's digging up bones out at Little Cheyenne and hereabouts in the courthouse."

"I heard, from the county clerk."

J J chuckled. "Shoulda figured. Anyway, there was a reporter, name of Charles Taylor. I didn't talk to him."

Zeke wrote the name down. He didn't recognize it. "What's your involvement, J J?"

"Well, Zeke, I heard a rumor that maybe the development was a funnel for campaign contributions to the president. Took a ride out there, and there ain't nothing but a few unpaved roads and some utility connections."

"What was the source of the rumor? You been retired seven months, as I recall. What made you take a look?"

"Hell, Zeke, we known each other a long time. You know how it works; no source." J J paused. "Is there going to be a problem?"

"J J," Zeke said, "Let me call you back. I'll need to know everything you can tell me."

"Fine, but no source." J J hung up, thinking these good old boys get up to Washington and lose all their manners.

Zeke thanked J J and rang off, then called Callendar, who told him of Colonel Thayer's demand for an immediate meeting. There was no question in Zeke's mind that something had come unstuck with the Uvalde County–Little Cheyenne matter. Zeke told Callendar to set the meeting for tomorrow, as early as the chairman would see them.

THAYER'S UGLY SECRETARY served coffee and withdrew, closing the big double doors behind her. Thayer handed the forty-page report across his desk, and Archer read each page, passing them to Callendar as he finished. There was no conversation at all until both had finished. "Where did you get this?" Zeke whispered. It was devastating.

"I can't tell you that. I'm not sure I would if I could, but I truly don't know; it just showed up on Ms. Schwartz's computer yesterday."

"It should be traceable," Callendar said. "Nothing is ever truly erased; we have very good people—"

"My people are also very good. They say it's gone," Thayer snapped. "Now, let's get to the substance. Inevitably this'll find itself into unfriendly hands. What are you going to do about it?"

"We'll . . . have to ask the president," Zeke said. "And the First Lady."

"You won't spin-doctor yourselves out of this one."

"We have to contain it, by whatever means," Callendar said.

"You're assuming it's true," Thayer said flatly.

There was no point lying to the man, Zeke thought. "All I know is that we did need a lot of money near the end of the campaign, and we got it. I know Jerry Earl and Susan McCray, who own Uvalde, have always been close to Clarissa."

"Damn!" Thayer pushed himself out of his big chair and placed his hands flat on his polished desk. "This will be worse than Watergate, and the party took years to recover from that."

"We have to think about the president," Archer said desperately.

"Yes, we do," Thayer said, "have to think about the president." He sat; the meeting was over.

"Is this our copy?" Callendar said as he rose.

"No. It's the only one I know to exist, but when it surfaces again, we'll all know it didn't come from me." He reached for it. Callendar reluctantly handed it back, and he and Archer filed out.

EZEKIEL ARCHER SUMMONED a hasty meeting in his office. The White House counsel, Barney "Big Dog" Jonas, a lawyer and rancher who had been Justice's Attorney General in Texas, and the First Lady were invited. Jonas showed up, big, red-faced, and rumpled; the First Lady sent her chief of staff, a hard-eyed woman in a severe gray suit named Mary-Kate Houston. Zeke was angered that the First Lady couldn't be bothered to attend in person; Mary-Kate wouldn't know anything useful.

Zeke laid out the information he had received from Mavis Mills. Mary-Kate shrugged; said she'd ask Clarissa. Big Dog whistled. "If'n you think this is bad campaign stuff, you're going to need a sharper knife than me."

"We need Clarissa's input," Archer said pointedly. "We need to know, *know*, whether this is corrupt or not."

"Well," Mary-Kate said breezily, "I'm sure there's no problem, but perhaps I could call Clarissa?"

"Please do," Zeke said, handing her his phone. Mary-Kate looked a bit miffed by the abruptness of his tone, but dialed a number and spoke a few soft words. She hung up and pushed the phone back toward the Chief of Staff. "She'll be down in a minute," Mary-Kate said triumphantly.

THE FIRST LADY made her entrance, arms crossed over her ample breasts and a thoroughly pissed-off look on her face. "What?" Clarissa all but shouted. Zeke buzzed his secretary for refreshments while Big Dog and Mary-Kate looked at the carpet.

"Little Cheyenne Development, Clarissa," Zeke said, holding his temper. How I hate this woman, he thought. "A reporter is digging; looking for some connection to the president or his campaign, or both. What can you tell me?"

Clarissa preened her glossy black hair. "That was years ago. I set up the corporation for Jerry Earl and Susan McCray, who, as you well know, own Uvalde Savings and have a lot of property in the area. I did some early closings when we were in Austin. I hardly remember it."

"You remember J J Early?"

Clarissa did, but not with favor. He had, she knew, in addition to his other services to the governor, arranged trysts for Justice and a host of women of low degree. "Of course I do."

"He drove out there after hearing a rumor that the money collected had never gone into the ground. Apparently it hasn't."

"Judas priest," Big Dog whispered. "How much money?"

"I don't know yet, but I will," Zeke said. "The information I do have suggests tens of millions."

Clarissa leaped to her feet. "I won't be interrogated by you, Zeke Archer. My work on Little Cheyenne was over years ago, and completely proper." She stalked out of the office, Mary-Kate scurrying behind.

"How bad's this going to be?" Big Dog almost whispered.

"Bad, I guess. We better think about damage control."

"The president's not flying too high right now."

"Don't I know it." Zeke rose from his chair and rubbed his aching back. "You know how to find the Mormon?"

"Yeah, he's technically on my staff. But he's, well, close, to the First Lady."

"Find him anyway. We need to know what we can about a reporter, presumably from Washington but maybe not, named Charles Taylor."

Big Dog Jonas pulled his bulk from the chair with a sigh. "Why not use the FBI? They do this stuff better than the Mormon and his New Zealot thugs."

"Think about it, Big Dog."

"Right," Big Dog said, after a momentary hesitation.

"I'll find Jim Bob."

2

Cobra was met at the airport in Lisbon by a man with a crudely lettered sign with the name from his Belgian passport. The handler was dressed as a limousine driver, and he did indeed have a dusty Mercedes waiting at the curb. Limo drivers were a favorite dodge in the intelligence business, because nobody noticed them around airports or hotels.

The driver slid the big car into light early-morning traffic and soon deposited Cobra at the sixties-era tower that was the Ritz Hotel, to Cobra's eyes the only ugly Ritz in the world. The driver took Cobra's light case and his carry-on out of the trunk and handed them to a porter. He then climbed back into his car and drove away without having said a single word.

Cobra had slept reasonably well on the plane as it flew all night over the dark expanse of West Africa, so he checked in, showered and changed, and went down to breakfast.

He bought an *International Herald Tribune* and went into the nearly empty dining room. He ordered tea, fruit and a soft-boiled egg in passable Portuguese. The two lead stories in the paper concerned the continuing buildup of American military power in the Persian Gulf area, and an account of how two unarmed aircraft flown from Miami by a Cuban exile group had been shot down over international waters. On the inside was an excerpt from a speech by Cuban leader Fidel Castro's grandson and successor, Ernesto, called by his people simply "Nieto," made to the U.N. General Assembly hours after the crash. Nieto had called the flights "provocative invasions of Cuba's sovereign airspace." A smaller article said that one of the American carrier battle groups on its way home from the Mediterranean had been diverted toward the Florida Strait.

Cobra turned to the worldwide weather page. Nothing on the map to indicate rains in southwest South Africa. He finished his breakfast and walked out into bright sunshine. He was about to ask the doorman for a taxi when the black Mercedes that had brought him from the airport slid into position in front of the hotel.

Cobra would have preferred to be on his own, without watchers, but he figured he'd be less conspicuous in the limo than being tailed by it. Besides, he'd done nothing yet. He climbed into the backseat as the driver held the door, and described where he wanted to go: the old citadel for a view of the Portuguese capital, then the monument to Prince Henry the Navigator on the beach across the harbor from the busy commercial port, then on to lunch at the best fresh fish and shellfish restaurant the driver could find.

The driver nodded, but didn't speak. Cobra wondered whether he could.

Cobra made an easy day, ended with dinner in the old city and entertainment by the *Fado*, a haunting, romantically sad but beautiful song style unique to Portugal.

In the morning, he paid his bill with the Belgian's credit card and asked for a car for the airport. One was waiting, the concierge said. He went outside; a different but similar Mercedes with a different driver. He had been handed off.

When he reached the terminal for Air Portugal, where the driver had dropped him without instruction, he went to the men's room. Using a very sharp pair of scissors he carried with his shaving gear, he cut up all the Belgian documents including the credit card into tiny pieces and flushed them down the toilet.

He emerged as a Frenchman from Martinique, and walked the hundred or so meters to the adjoining terminal, where he checked in for his Continental Airlines flight for Washington/Dulles. He saw no one watching him, but he would have bet they were there.

Cobra's plane touched down at Dulles, fifteen minutes early. He took his bags from the overhead locker and filed off the plane. Immediately after he cleared customs and immigration with barely a glance at the French documents, he went down through baggage claim, where he was met by a uniformed chauffeur and another man in plain clothes. The limousine, a Lincoln this time, waited at the curb with a third man in the driver's seat. Cobra tried to get a look at the license plate but was hustled into the car. The uniformed man got in front and the plainclothesman got in back and the car pulled out immediately into the vast parking lot of

Dulles Airport. The plainclothesman wore a cheap and sweet cologne. He opened a briefcase and extracted a black hood. "Put this on, please. Normal security."

Cobra complied without protest. It was sound tradecraft; Cobra didn't want to know these men.

Moments later the car pulled over and stopped, and Cobra heard doors opening, low voices, and the doors slammed. Cobra was not touched. The limo accelerated onto a highway. Cobra had never been to Washington, but he knew the locals called the expressway that really went to Dulles and nowhere else, "the driveway."

The sweet cologne was gone. Cobra had been handed off again.

After an hour, as best Cobra could guess, the limousine turned off high-speed roads onto a paved but rougher track. He had no idea where he was being taken, but he noticed he smell of flowering plants and trees, and the air, blowing in from the driver's window, grew cooler.

Mountains, he thought, thinking of home. Maryland? No, Virginia, he guessed, west of the capital. Cobra relaxed and dozed.

3

CLARISSA ALCOTT TOLLIVER was the daughter of a dirt-poor cotton farmer in the Nueces Valley of south Texas and a fourteen-year-old Mexican girl who had waded the big river. Neither of these details were in her official biography, but she wasn't ashamed of her heritage. Her mother, Luz Ruiz, was beautiful until the hard work made her old before she was thirty. She taught her only daughter, made her go to church and study at school even though her father, a kindly man but nearly illiterate, would have preferred the child to work in the fields.

Clarissa grew up fast. Her friends teased her for her "hot Mexican blood" because her breasts and hips grew round and womanly when she was barely twelve. Her father began to look at her in a different way, and to hug and fondle her more than he had when she was little. One day her mother caught the farmer stroking the girl's breasts through her thin cotton T-shirt. Luz grabbed her daughter and hustled her to her room at the back of the shack, pulling the curtain behind her. Clarissa didn't understand; wasn't Daddy just being nice? Clarissa heard her parents' loud argument through the thin wall, and the sound of blows and breaking furniture. Clarissa pressed herself into a corner of the tiny room and sobbed. The fight subsided but nobody came to let her out, and there was no supper that night.

In the morning, her mother, with two black eyes and bruises on her arms and throat, packed Clarissa's few belongings in a cardboard box and took the girl out to the dusty red pickup. Clarissa didn't see her father. Luz drove the rickety old Ford faster than she should have to Loma Alta, where she and Clarissa went to Mass every Sunday. She left the child sitting in the nearly empty church and went off to find the priest.

An hour later Clarissa was enrolled in the parish school as a boarding student. She wouldn't know it for years, but Luz had given the priest the family's life savings for tuition.

Clarissa graduated at the top of her class and received a full scholarship to the University of Texas at Austin. Her parents came to graduation. Clarissa's mother wept and embraced her; her father shook hands stiffly and looked at his cracked boots.

Clarissa stayed in Austin right through law school, going home only once for her mother's funeral. Luz died at the age of thirty-seven from abuse and overwork. After the funeral, Clarissa never saw her father again.

Even with scholarships and student loans, Clarissa had to work part-time to support herself. Despite her striking good looks—olive skin, perfectly smooth, her mother's hair as black and shiny as a raven's wing, her face set off by her father's striking blue eyes—she made few friends; she had so little time. She passed the bar on her first try in 1986 and was recruited by the law firm of Henry and Villard, one of Austin's best regarded. In

1990 she became the only woman and the youngest person ever to be made partner. Her specialty was real estate law, and one of her new clients was the Uvalde County Savings and Loan Society. She met and became friends with the freewheeling couple who ran the bank and its many subsidiaries, Jerry Earl and Susan McCray, who were often in Austin, doing deals with the state government. Susan introduced Clarissa to Rupert Justice Tolliver, a darkly handsome man who had done well for himself while preaching the word of the Lord. Susan whispered that Rupert had political ambitions and powerful backers, and would go far. Clarissa started to see more and more of Brother Justice, and when he told her of his plan to run for governor and maybe reach higher than that, she ended her longtime clandestine relationship with Henry and Villard's married senior partner, and married the Hill Country preacher.

CLARISSA WENT DIRECTLY from her meeting with Zeke Archer to the Oval Office. She glared at Jenna Carradine and demanded, "Who's he got in there?"

"The Secretary of Defense."

"Buzz him. Telling I'm here and it can't wait."

Jenna did as she was told. Clarissa was the only person in Washington she truly feared. Clarissa paced like a caged cat for ten minutes, then the Secretary, Carolyn White, looking very upset, emerged and hurried away without a word. Clarissa shot past Jenna's desk and into the Oval Office.

BIG DOG JONAS waved the Mormon into his West Wing Office on the third floor of the White House almost directly above the Oval Office. "Sit down, Jim Bob. Coffee? No, of course not. Something else?"

Jim Bob Slate helped himself to a glass of ice water from the stainless steel thermos on the sideboard and took a seat in front of the White House Counsel desk. "We got us a problem," Big

Dog continued. "How much do you know about Little Cheyenne development?"

Jim Bob gulped. More than he cared to, was the truth. "Very little. Clarissa—the First Lady—did some legal work, way back."

Big Dog opened a large folder. "There's been a reporter, we think from right here in the capital, down there looking at the land records. These are copies of what he had copied. See the signature where it says 'attorney for the seller'?"

Jim Bob leafed through the copies. The attorney for the seller was always Clarissa Alcott; she'd kept her maiden name for her legal work. "I see it."

"Look at the dates on these last few."

"October 2000."

"Not so way back, Jim Bob."

"No."

"No. Now we know what this damn reporter's got. What do you suppose he can make of it?"

"I don't know," Jim Bob lied.

"Zeke Archer got a call from a local banker. Republican bigwig, but no friend of this administration. Says money came into that development through Uvalde County Savings, that scoundrel Jerry Earl McCray's little bank. Big money, Jim Bob, right before the election and right around the inauguration."

The Mormon knew all that. He knew all the dirty tricks of the campaign; all the shady finances. He had been Clarissa's errand boy; her bag man. "What's this banker going to do?"

"Nothing, we guess. He seems to see this as our mess and he's concerned about the party if not about us. We're more concerned about the reporter, and his source."

"You want this—looked into, Big Dog?"

"Yes. The name the reporter uses is Charles Taylor. Nobody I know or Zeke knows, so he's nobody big. But we don't want any young gunslinger doing a Woodward and Bernstein on us."

Zeke Archer walked into the office and sat next to the Mormon. "Hello, Jim Bob. Big Dog explain our problem?"

"Yes, sir."

"Find the reporter. We'll have to buy him or discredit him."

"What about the source?" Big Dog said. "I'm guessing the reporter has whatever the banker has; why else he hightail it down to south Texas?"

"I have a thought about that," Zeke said. "Should have come to me earlier, but here it is. J J Early—you know him, ran security for the president when he was governor—called me. Said he heard a rumor, so he drove out to Little Cheyenne and found two things: nearly no work done and none in progress, and this Charles Taylor snooping around. Asked J J where he got the rumor; he refused to say. But before he called, Mavis Mills, the County Clerk down Uvalde, called to tell me people been out to look at the land records. One didn't identify himself; we make him Taylor. The other was J J, and someone Mavis thought might be his daughter. Ring any bells?"

"Yeah, Julia," Big Dog said. "Worked on the governor's campaigns. We got her a job after she graduated—Jesus! I recall it was with some bank here in town."

"That's my thinking. Why she would have dug this up I have no idea, but we got to be real careful. J J Early is as loyal to Justice Tolliver as any of us, but he's a mean son of a bitch. He gets wind we're leaning on his daughter, he'll help her before us."

The Mormon rose. "I'll look into it."

"Carefully," Zeke said.

"Very carefully," Big Dog said.

"Very carefully," the Mormon echoed, and left the room.

4

CAROLYN WHITE RETURNED to the Pentagon, where the Joint Chiefs awaited her, along with Malcolm Japes, the Secretary of State, and Mary-Ellen O'Hearn, the Secretary of the Air Force. They all looked strained, except the chairman, Admiral Josephus

Austin, who looked like the cat who had swallowed the canary. "How did it go?" asked the Secretary of the Air Force, before Carolyn could even take her seat.

Admiral Austin grinned. He fully expected Carolyn to be cleaning out her—soon to be his—desk.

Carolyn sat, and smoothed her hair with her hands. "He listened, more than I expected. He agreed to reconsider the bombing of Qom."

"But didn't cancel it, I trust," Austin said, his good mood dissolving. The bitch hadn't resigned after all.

"He agreed to reconsider. I argued that the naval attacks on the Silkworm and other sites had sent the message. He agreed to wait and see what the Iranis actually *did* beyond the bombast."

"What about the rest of the world?"

"The fleet is sailing toward home waters. The army and marine expeditionary forces are returning to bases, and the air force bomber and missile forces have returned to DefCon Four." Defense Condition Four was a lower state of readiness than the DefCon Two prevailing during the crisis. DefCon Two had rattled the world, perhaps even more than the actual military and naval deployments, because DefCon Two meant the nuclear forces of the United States were on alert and targeted. "All except the *Vinson* battle group, that continues toward Cuba."

"I have a bit of bad news to inject," Admiral Austin said. "The Miami Cubans sent two more Cessnas of the *Fuerza Aerea de Libertad* to drop leaflets; one was shot down by a MiG."

"Jesus," Japes exploded. "We don't need this! The Dow-Jones was down another three hundred points yesterday, and markets around the world are following."

"Why are the Miami people doing this, at this time?" Carolyn asked pointedly.

"State doesn't know, despite our extensive contacts within the major revanchist organizations. CIA doesn't know either, or won't tell me." Japes sighed. "I suspect Cubans associated with the narcotics traffic may be pushing the fringe groups like this Freedom Air Force, but I can't prove it."

Carolyn's phone rang, the red one that had to be answered. She reached over the console of her regular phones and picked it up. "Yes?" She listened quietly for five long minutes, a smile spreading slowly across her pretty face. "Keep me posted, no less than hourly." She hung up. "A piece of good news, or at least I hope it is. That was the Defense Intelligence Officer in our embassy in Saudi Arabia. He's heard through confidential sources that the army in Iran has overthrown the government of Ayatollah Tabtabi and issued a proclamation: free elections within six months, an end to religious government, and the wish to enter into peaceful dialogue with all states in the region to assure the security interests of all and an end to foreign intervention."

"They're telling us to butt out," Austin blustered. "Fat chance."

"Or, my dear Admiral," Japes said quietly, "they may be suing for peace."

Carolyn's red phone rang again. She listened briefly and hung up. "The Secretary of Commerce. Stock market's way up, especially those companies with heavy international trade."

"Then perhaps y'all might concede the president's policy of strength might just have done the trick," Austin said, trying to make the best of a bad afternoon.

"Then, Admiral," Carolyn said sweetly, "you'll support me when I ask the president to stand down further?"

"Let's see what shakes out," the old sailor said.

"What about the battle group on the way to Cuba?" Malcolm Japes asked, rising from his seat. No one responded. "I have to get back to my office. Carolyn, please keep me apprised."

5

CLARISSA TOOK A SEAT facing her husband, who sat in front of the dead fireplace. He looked exhausted. "Rupert, we have problems you have to address. Two of them major."

The president looked at his wife with no recognition in his eyes. She waited, then said, "Rupert!"

His eyes cleared. "Clarissa. Jenna told me you were waiting; I'm sorry. The Lord's work is very taxing these days."

"Rupert, there's a reporter digging up bones down home, the Little Cheyenne Development."

"Every time I close my eyes I see Los Angeles in flames, or that federal building in Little Rock blown to bits."

"Little Cheyenne Development," Clarissa said through clenched teeth.

Justice shook his head. "Something with Jerry Earl and Susan? I don't really remember."

"Money, Rupert, at the end of the campaign and since. I told you."

"I don't remember," the president said weakly. "Money from whom? Friends, Texans—"

"Rupert, our friends were as tapped out as we were. I had to take money from other sources. Some foreign."

Justice became more alert. "Illegal?"

"Yes. I thought I hid it in Little Cheyenne, but apparently not well enough."

"Sweet Jesus, not now, Clarissa! We're in trouble, we're sore afflicted, but we're winning."

"I think we may be able to contain this thing; it's only one reporter, nobody big. But the Cubans are making their play; they contributed massively when we needed it, along with some of their . . . friends."

"I sent a battle group, scare El Nieto off—"

"Rupert, they want their island back. We promised."

Justice sat up straight. He had developed a tick under his right eye, and it started up. "Surely they don't expect me to invade the place?"

"They do. They want freedom."

"Shit," Justice hissed. "Fuck 'em."

Clarissa sighed. She had long ceased to love her philandering husband, but she felt his pain, so far in over his head in the presidency. She also knew his future, rise or fall, contained hers. "Justice, the Cuban money didn't come without a price. They have videotapes of you in Cuba, albeit thirty-five years ago, with the brothers Castro. They also have tapes of you consorting with North Vietnamese sympathizers and even officials, in Paris in the early seventies. How's that gonna look, you sending American sevicemen to fight all over the world? Tapes of you consorting with an enemy you made every effort not to have to fight?"

"You believe that?" he whispered.

"It was before I knew you. But I've seen the tapes; I have copies if you want to see them."

"How the hell could the Miami exiles have obtained such tapes?"

"My Miami contact—originally Zeke's, but he no longer trusts Zeke—a fellow who styles himself as Coronel de la Hoya, says he got them recently from the *Servicio Nacional de Informaciones*."

Justice, like Clarissa and most south Texans, spoke passable Spanish. "That's Castro's secret police. Why would they cooperate with the Miami Cubans?"

"Nieto Castro has to fall sooner or later; the country is broke. I suspect someone—probably someone high up—in the SNI wants to make a deal for a quiet but elegant exile. Or maybe he wants a piece of the action in the new Cuba you'll soon restore to freedom."

"I can't do that now."

"What else can you do? Those tapes, you consorting with the enemy in a war many think you avoided and being chummy with the Castros, coupled with the reports of fund-raising illegalities—a bought election, the *Wall Street Journal* will trumpet—the Justice Department will be forced to appoint a special counsel, Congress will go holier-than-thou and impeachment hearings will follow after."

Justice covered his face in his hands and bowed as if in prayer. "Jesus, sweet Jesus."

"Rupert! What are you going to *do?*"

The president raised his head, wiping away tears. His tired

eyes grew cold, his gaze distant. "Clarissa, you're my most trusted adviser in addition to being my staff of support. Squash this reporter and his story; bury Little Cheyenne deep. Stall the Cubans; we'll rattle El Nieto Castro's cage, but only a little."

"What will *you* be doing all the while?" she asked sarcastically.

"My mission will be to complete the Lord's work much sooner than I'd planned." He threw his head back and closed his eyes.

She stood. "Rupert. Rupert!"

He didn't move. It was almost as though he had entered a trance. Clarissa had an inkling of concern that Rupert Justice Tolliver was beginning to believe his hokey preaching. She got up and stalked out.

6

COBRA WOKE UP fully—he had learned over the years to nap like a cat, ears alert—as the big Lincoln drew to a crawl, then a stop on a gravel road. Front doors slammed, then his door was opened. He was assisted from the car by a big man with gentle hands. No threat, Cobra thought, no intimidation. He heard the car drive off as he was escorted into a building. The air smelled heavily of pine.

Cobra was seated in a chair, and he heard his handler leave. Moments later his blindfold was removed, and he was confronted by an elderly couple who looked both friendly and concerned. "We're to look after you," the woman said. "We're not to say our names, and we don't know yours."

"Fine," Cobra said, grinning. "Call me John, after the Baptist, who hid his face and those of others in the waters of purification."

The man, seventy or so but powerfully built, chuckled. "We'll be Mary and Joseph, then. We're to see to your every need, but you can't leave. The place is guarded outside around the clock."

Cobra would have betted he could have slipped out, but why? He was here for a big payday. "Fine. Just now my every need is a hot shower, a large whisky, and a steak dinner with a decent claret."

"All easily done," the woman said, her face relaxing into a pretty smile. "Jason—Joseph, put the man's bags in the guest room and I'll start working on dinner. You'll do the drinks."

Cobra returned her smile as the man went out to get his bags. Cobra appreciated good trade craft; these people knew nothing and never would, but they also knew enough not to ask. He was being iced for a while; probably his handlers thought he would feel vulnerable because he was isolated and unarmed. Cobra had no illusions, but he also knew the game. If someone wanted to kill him they would have done it in South Africa, not gone through this long and expensive journey. He believed without question that the grounds were patrolled, most likely to protect him and preserve his anonymity rather than to prevent his escape.

ADMIRAL CARTER DANIELS met Colonel Alfred Thayer at the Sulgrave Club, an exclusive Washington haunt favored for very private conversations. "The *Vinson* battle group will reach the Cuban operating area in fifteen hours. She has with her an amphibious ready group—nearly two, actually—around *Tarawa* and *Saipan.* Do you think Tolliver will invade?"

"Is that enough force for the job?"

"No, but he could blockade. The Cuban military is in shambles; those old MiGs are a fine match for unarmed Cessnas, but would be flying a suicide mission against the *Vinson* air group. The marines could land at various points, kill people, break things, and withdraw, leaving Cuban guerrillas behind. El Nieto Castro runs a very great risk if he doesn't back down."

"How does he back down from the killing of four pilots, all U.S. citizens, in unarmed aircraft, Admiral? Especially since the mighty of the world in Europe and Asia have protested mightily about what Tolliver's done in Asia and the Persian Gulf, but done nothing. Cuba's just the pretext Tolliver needs to carry out more of the Lord's work against Godless communism."

Daniels pondered. "Have you spoken to the vice president?"

"Yes. Noncommittal, but not shocked either."

"He's weak."

"But not crazy."

"A poor choice," Daniels said. "Did you know that the contractor is here?"

"I heard. You're in charge of his custody; I don't need to know anything else."

"Actually, your friend in black has him stashed about twenty miles from here, not far from your farm."

Thayer wondered if Daniels had found out the identity of Ramon Carvahal. The old man was very resourceful. "Has your thinking changed? I really wish there was another way."

"You? You have doubts?" Daniels whispered. "You've driven this forward from the beginning."

"I know. I'll take that to my grave and to hell beyond."

"My answer is no," Daniels said softly. "There's no other way. Tensions around the world are on the boil: India, Pakistan; Iran, Iraq and Turkey; even Russia and China."

"The pressures on the American and European stock markets and foreign exchanges have eased, but Latin America and Asia are reeling," Thayer said.

"We have to know the mind and heart of Vice President Donahue," Daniels said. "We need to know if he has the stomach for this thing."

Thayer sighed. "He's due here any minute. Why don't you stay?"

Daniels heaved himself out of the deep club chair with a groan. "Better I don't. Remember Benjamin Franklin: 'Three people can keep a secret if two of them are dead.' "

Thayer ordered a cognac to ease his headache as the old admiral shuffled out, tapping his red and white cane.

7

VINSON AND HER escorts sailed through the narrow Windward Passage between Cuba and Haiti and took up a position west of the Cayman Islands, about 140 miles south of Havana. *Eisenhower* and her group sortied from Norfolk and moved toward a blocking position in the Atlantic northeast of the Bahamas. The Florida Strait itself was too narrow and had too many shallow banks and reefs to be suitable for carrier operations.

The Cessnas from the *Fuerza Aerea de Libertad* returned to the north coast of Cuba, flying high and tossing out leaflets they hoped would blow onshore in the Northeast trade wind. U.S. Navy F/A-18Fs from *Vinson* catapulted off the deck and established control with an air force AWACS that had flown two thousand miles from Offutt Air Force Base in Nebraska. The AWACS had side-looking radars similar to the JSTARS aircraft that allowed it to track vehicles on the ground. "Tango Strike," the AWACS controller called the navy fighters. "MiGs rolling at Matanzas and Camaguey." Matanzas, near the capital, and Camaguey in the southeast were Cuba's biggest air bases.

"Tango Leader rogers," said Commander Richard "Snapper" Tuttle, commanding officer of the Super Hornet squadron flying the mission. His radar intercept officer (RIO), seated behind him, relayed the instructions to the other seven aircraft on Squadron Net.

The mission was tightly scripted; no shooting unless the Cubans did. The jets had full loads of cannon shells and air-to-air missiles, and a couple of Maverick air-to-ground missiles each in case they had to shoot anything moving on the ground.

Snapper lead his four in a tight echelon formation down to the deck over Camaguey. Two bullet-nosed MiG 21s were indeed rolling, with four more behind them waiting to take off. Snapper's four roared over the runway at one hundred feet and Mach 1.2, creating deafening sonic booms and turbulent jet wash.

One of the Cuban pilots lost control in the downdraft and skidded off the runway into soft sand. The other, Major Raul Sanchez, like Snapper a squadron commander, got off, barely controlling his gyrating fighter, and almost immediately wished he hadn't. His missile warning radar warbled, indicating the Americans were acquiring him as they made a sharp turn back toward the field. Sanchez kicked in his afterburner, turning away from the airfield, and as he banked he could see none of the rest of his aircraft had moved. The missile warning radar changed to a steady tone, indicating lock-on. Major Sanchez was moments from death, and since his hands were very full, he mentally crossed himself.

Sanchez saw one of the Americans drop on him, only meters from his right wing. Another joined up on the left. The ones he feared were the ones he could not see; they would be behind in firing position. *Pobre Cuba,* he thought. Not a day to die for a *boludo* like Castro Nieto. The American on his right wing waved, then pointed straight down. Holding the stick between shaking knees, Sanchez raised both hands above his head.

"Big Eye, Tango Strike," Snapper called the AWACS. "Only one got off at Camaguey and he seems disinclined to play."

"Same story in Matanzas, Tango," the controller said. "One got off and the pilot immediately ejected. We have their frequency; we'll tell your pigeon to land."

"Rather tell him myself, make sure he understands."

Big Eye gave Snapper the frequency and he dialed it in. "*Piloto de la Fuerza Aerea Cubana, vuelva a su base, ahorita.*"

"Arrogant *yanqui* bastard," Sanchez shot back in flawless English. "Cuba is sovereign, and you are in my airspace."

"Land, *Cabron,*" Snapper said amiably. "Or my friends and I will land you. Turn left, slow glide, right on in. We'll grade your approach and touchdown."

Sanchez shot Snapper the finger, but then immediately dropped his wheels and flaps, turned, and landed. The navy jets made another supersonic pass over the field, breaking windows and eardrums, then climbed out of Cuban airspace.

"Bigeye, Tango Leader. Next?"

"Return to mothership. The air force from Homestead has the next watch."

AFTER DARK ON the same day, Cuban Freedom Fighters were landed by Marine Force Recon units both on the southwest coast and inland, near the Sierra Maestra Mountains, from which Fidel Castro had come more than thirty years ago. Make a go of it, they were told, show genuine support among the people, and we'll support you.

IN HAVANA, CROWDS filled the streets shouting anti-American slogans, burning crudely stitched American flags, and marching on the Swiss Embassy that contained a U.S. interests section. Riot police and soldiers barely prevented the demonstrators from storming the building.

Reaction in other Cuban cities was far more muted, but anti-American demonstrations rocked cities from Mexico to Argentina.

8

ADMIRAL DANIELS WAS finishing his simple lunch of beef broth, pears, and cottage cheese in his house in Alexandria, Virginia. He moved a tetrapod-mounted magnifying glass down a very satisfying piece in the *Washington Post* about Cuban insurgents attacking and capturing a remote police barracks in the mountains when his nurse came in and said there was a messenger waiting with a letter. "He doesn't look threatening, Admiral," the retired navy medical corpsman said. "I think he works for Colonel Thayer, but I didn't ask."

"Please show him in," the old admiral said, standing and putting on his suit jacket.

A man in a black chauffeur's uniform came in, followed by the burly nurse, who stayed by the door of the dining room. The chauffeur greeted Admiral Daniels, and handed him an unsealed envelope. Daniels shook out a single sheet of paper and put on his thick glasses. He recognized Thayer's shaky hand, large letters to aid Daniels's near nonexistent vision. "The Keyman wants one more day. Come as soon as you can and bring your technician."

The Keyman was their informal code for Vice President Donahue. The technician was the mysterious man-in-black's shooter, hidden someplace and known to Daniels through a cutout phone in the District. Daniels looked up at the blurred face of Thayer's man. "I'll have to arrange a car and driver, then I'll do as Colonel Thayer asks."

"Colonel Thayer said I was to take you anywhere you directed, Admiral," the chauffeur said.

Daniels held the letter up before tossing it into the blazing fireplace. "Did you read this?" he asked.

"Of course not, sir."

"Then let's go to his house in the Shenandoah."

9

ERNESTO CASTRO, EL Nieto to his people, summoned el coronel Ramon Carvahal to his office at the old Pardo Palace in central Havana. News of the raid on a police barracks had made him very angry, and he wanted answers. Regular army troops had retaken the place, but only after the rebels had stripped it of weapons and supplies and slipped back into the forest. El Nieto was badly scared.

Colonel Carvahal knocked, entered, came to attention before Castro's desk, and saluted. Carvahal's relations with El Nieto were correct but distant. Carvahal considered El Nieto a pompous dilettante who had lived a soft and luxurious life while his grandfather had ruled in the name of socialism and sacrifice.

"Sit down, please, Colonel," Castro said. "Coffee?"

"No thank you, my president."

"What is the news from—from the mountains?"

"There are at least two bands, maybe three. A few hundred in each. It is hard to know more because the Americans are keeping our air force grounded. We do know the Americans are landing supplies by boat and helicopter from ships in the area."

"Is there any sign of popular support?"

"That area is very poor," Carvahal said, looking at his hands. "It was there that your grandfather began his revolution, recruiting peasants by giving them food and boots he got from the Russians. I can only assume the rebels will recruit the same way."

El Nieto slammed a pudgy fist on the desk, rattling his coffee cup. "We must crush these insurgents! If they can take a province, a city, and hold it, the Americans will recognize a provisional government. Then they will come and bring more *gusanos* with them."

"We drove them back to the sea in 1961, my president," Carvahal said softly. "At the Playa de Cocinos. The revolution's finest hour." Carvahal didn't believe El Nieto had a finest hour in him.

"The *gusanos* could have succeeded if the Americans had used their vast air power," El Nieto snarled. "President Kennedy feared to do so because he feared the Russians. President Tolliver shows no such reluctance."

"He has no international support. I think he will leave his Miami friends in the lurch."

"He has God on his side," Castro sneered. "Tolliver is the problem; one man. Remove him and the world will breathe again."

Carvahal studied the fat little man. He was trying to grow a beard, the better to look the part, and had affected the green utility uniform of his grandfather, hiding away his extensive wardrobe of

Italian suits. He looked like a clown, one of the sad ones. "Is that an order, my president?"

Castro jerked in his chair. He hated decisions. "Could it be done? Done without anyone knowing it was us?"

Carvahal kept his face expressionless. How nice to be paid for the same job twice. "It could be. Very expensive, though."

"Look into it," El Nieto said cautiously. "Someone must rid the world of this ranting preacher."

" 'Look into it?' " Carvahal goaded.

Castro drew himself up. "Do it, but don't get caught. Do it soon before this insurgency becomes a real threat to the Cuban revolution."

More of a threat to your lazy ass, Carvahal thought as he left.

10

The Vice President of the United States, Joseph Donahue of Connecticut, was surprised when his executive assistant informed him that the president wanted to see him in the Oval Office at his earliest convenience. He had not been invited to national security meetings nor even informed of them, since the president had rudely thrown him out after he objected to the Persian Gulf raids. He thought the president was dangerous and getting more so. He had listened to the dark predictions of Colonel Alfred Thayer. It was obvious that Thayer and others were preparing to assassinate the president, though of course the old banker hadn't said so in so many words.

Donahue was torn. He wanted the job; he thought it was legitimately his, since he firmly believed Tolliver had stolen the election through voter intimidation and massive spending far beyond that allowed by the campaign finance laws. But could he countenance murder?

Thayer had made the "good of the nation" argument—that Tolliver's increasing rashness was ruining world markets, shattering the wealth of entire nations, and perhaps bringing the world closer to catastrophic wars. Donahue was getting more of his information from increasingly alarmed cabinet members, notably Carolyn White, Malcolm Japes, and the Ambassador to the U.N. Christine Whitman. Carolyn was particularly concerned about the Cuban situation, where American air and naval forces remained, in contrast to their rapid withdrawal from Korean waters and the Persian Gulf after the raids.

It's only a matter of time, Carolyn said, before one of those Kilo-class submarines the Russians sold the Cubans in the early nineties pops an aircraft carrier. What then?

Joseph Donahue straightened his tie, put on his suit jacket, and walked across the West Wing to the Oval Office.

COBRA WAS INTERRUPTED at his dinner by a loud knocking on the cabin door. "Mary" answered, and immediately brought him a blindfold. He put it on with a shrug. The guards had let him walk around the compound blindfolded during daylight for a modicum of exercise, guided by Mary or Joseph. He had been locked away for a week, but hardly mistreated. Mary had turned out to be an excellent cook with a range of dishes he wouldn't have expected from a country woman, and Joseph brought him books and newspapers. He was getting tired of American television that seemed even more mindless than South African, and he was bored, but he knew the game and how much of it was waiting. Waiting for the split second when he completed his contract.

Two of his keepers came in and guided him outside. He was helped into a van that smelled of stale cigarette smoke. Soon they were rolling along a winding road. He heard the rustle of dry leaves under the tires, and felt the air coming through open windows grow chillier and drier; the van was climbing into low hills.

* * *

Vice President Donahue was admitted to the Oval Office by a uniformed marine guard. The awful Jenna Carradine had apparently left for the day. Donahue found the president seated at his desk, slumped over his Bible, open before him. The president looked as though he had aged ten years in the two weeks since their last confrontation. "Please be seated, Joseph. Better yet, pour us both a drink and then take a seat."

The president's voice was soft and toned with sorrow. The vice president poured generous tumblers of bourbon and brought them to the desk, and sat. The president had never once called him Joseph during the whole time he had known him.

"Mr. President?" Donahue said, when Tolliver sat silent, turning the pages of the big Bible.

The president nodded, and looked up. "We never got to know each other, Joseph, and that's my fault. Please call me Justice, or Juss, when we're alone. I need your help and there may be little time."

"Of course, Mr.—Justice."

"I've never shared my vision with you, because I knew you'd oppose it."

Donahue shifted in his chair. "I still do, Mr. President."

"Then I must convince you. You must believe so you can carry on."

"Carry on?"

"I sense I may not be able to complete the nation's and the Lord's work. I sense I'll not have time."

Donahue looked hard at the man, holding his face expressionless. Could he have found out about Colonel Thayer's plot to kill him? Did he suspect Donahue's guilty knowledge?

Justice studied the man he had accepted as vice president with disgust. What is he thinking? Can he know already what Clarissa knows about the reporter digging up the money-laundering scheme of Little Cheyenne, his contacts with Castro and

Madame Binh, and Clarissa's prediction of impeachment and disgrace? He turned a page in his Bible. "Joseph, I believe God has ordered a reckoning. I believe it's here, in Revelation. The earthquake that destroyed Los Angeles, literally splitting it into three burning cities, is precisely foretold in chapter sixteen, although the city in the prophecy is Babylon, but who could but argue that Los Angeles, with its license and violence, has become Babylon?" The president turned pages back. "Revelation describes plagues, and the reasons. Chapter nine, verse twenty-one. 'Neither repented they of their murders, nor of their sorceries, nor of their fornication, nor of their thefts.' Sound like central Africa, or Bosnia, or Iraq? Are the plagues AIDS, or Ebola, or some new horror?

"Last month Iran tested a weapon of great power, almost certainly nuclear, if crude. Chapter nine, verse one, 'And the fifth angel sounded and I saw a star fall from heaven unto the earth and to him was given the key to the bottomless pit'; verse two, 'and he opened the bottomless pit and there arose a smoke out of the pit as the smoke of a great furnace and the sun and the air were darkened by reason of the smoke of the pit.' Joseph?"

"Mr. President—Justice, these are ancient words, written, it is thought, while the Divine was consuming narcotic mushrooms—"

The president continued, ignoring the interruption. "Chapter sixteen, verse eight. 'And the fourth angel poured out his vial upon the sun and power was given unto him to scorch men with fire.' What does that sound like to you? Chapter sixteen, verse ten. 'And the fifth angel poured out his vial upon the seat of the beast, and his kingdom was full of darkness, and they gnawed their tongues for pain.' Chapter twenty, verse one. 'And I saw an angel come down from heaven, having the key of the bottomless pit and a great chain in his hand.' Verse two. 'And he laid hold of the dragon, that old serpent that is the devil and Satan and bound him for a thousand years.' Then, verse three. 'And cast him into the bottomless pit and shut him up and set a seal upon him, that he should deceive the nations no more, *till a thousand years shall be fulfilled, and after that he must be loosed a little season.'* Think of it, Joseph."

The vice president shook his head. Alfred Thayer was right; the man was clearly deranged.

" 'And when the thousand years are expired, Satan shall be loosed out of his prison, and shall go out to deceive the nations which are in the four quarters of the earth, Gog and Magog, to gather them in battle, the number of whom is as the sand of the sea.' What is that, Joseph? St. John the Divine knew only Asia Minor, yet the prophecy looks east, always east. Gog and Magog, with numbers like the sand of the sea? China? Russia? India? Pakistan? From the *east,* Joseph. The end of the world will come from the east if God is denied His reckoning, and who will prevent that if we do not?"

Donahue took a deep breath. He fought down an urge to flee the presence of this madman. "Mr. President, do you believe the Bible is literal truth?"

Justice shook his head. "No, Joseph, and I'll admit something to you I've admitted to no one, although I know many say it. I answered the call to preach to avoid service in Vietnam. But I did study the scripture as a fundamentalist, and preached as a fundamentalist. The words go deep inside the more they are said, and are accepted by the congregation in front of you yearning for comfort and guidance. More and more I began to believe in the warnings, the threat of reckoning, the wrath of God. What I see here is a pattern that cannot be coincidental."

Donahue didn't know whether to laugh or weep. "The millennium was a thousand years ago. Nothing happened then."

"Much happened then. There were outbreaks of bubonic plague all over the world, including the one in Venice that foreshadowed the great plague of the fourteenth century. There were religious revivals and the burning of priests and heretics. There was the never explained frenzy of St. Vitus's Dance. Monasteries were besieged and some were destroyed. Mystery cults flourished and defied the church. And darkness—ignorance, disease, and depopulation—descended upon the earth. Much happened, Joseph, but not a full reckoning."

"And now?" the vice president said in a small voice.

"And now the second millennium has come and gone. Mankind is polluting and destroying the world. Genocide and exploitation are everywhere. Every little dictator has nuclear weapons and germs and poison gases. Who stands before the Beast? Only the United States, and she, I challenge you, sir, reluctantly."

"I'm speechless," Donahue said.

"Go and reflect, Joseph, and pray. See if the pattern I see is not revealed to you."

The vice president mumbled his assent. When he stood his knees nearly buckled, but he got out of the room.

He's mad, utterly mad, the vice president thought. He hurried back to his office and called Colonel Alfred Thayer.

THAYER PUT THE PHONE down just as Admiral Daniels came into his office. The Admiral took his usual seat as the butler who had brought him in poured a snifter of Armagnac and set it on the table beside him. "That was Donahue," Thayer said, his voice just above a whisper. "He just spent a half hour with the Reverend Tolliver, receiving a lecture about the end of the world as described in the Revelation of Saint John the Divine. The bottomless pit, Gog and Magog, the whole nonsense. Keyman is finally convinced that the president is mad and must be removed."

Daniels shook his head slowly. "Then it must be done."

"And done quickly. What is the status of the technician?"

"His handlers have collected him. He'll be brought to one of the hunting cabins up on the ridge a mile from here. We shall then instruct him."

Thayer pondered; sipped his Armagnac. "An interesting

development. Donahue was very evasive in the past; no personal involvement; deniability, all that."

"And now?"

"Now he's very frightened, and he's coming here."

11

U.S. AIR FORCE and navy aircraft continued to range over Cuba, and the marines continued their insertions of eager but poorly trained Cuban exiles in the southeast of the island, with tons of supplies of war. Guerrilla units expanded influence and support, if not control, in the province of Granma, near the Sierra Maestra, and raiding into the neighboring province of Las Tunas. The marines were sending more supplies, by air and sea but also directly from the naval station at Guantanamo Bay. The Russians were too poor and too busy with their neighbors to help, but they thundered nonetheless against American aggression.

COBRA WAS BROUGHT to a small cabin and locked in a Spartan but comfortable bedroom. He was given dinner. At 10:00 P.M. he heard a helicopter land close by, then take off almost immediately. Shortly thereafter, he heard two vehicles arrive on the gravel road, doors slam, and voices.

Cobra heard voices and the noise of furniture being shoved around in the main room of the cabin. He got off his bed and put on his half boots; considered a shave, but there was a knock on the door. Cobra put on his blindfold. "Come," he said, and the door was unlocked and opened.

He was led out and seated in a straight wooden chair. To his surprise, his blindfold was removed and he was given a glass of water. Three men sat at a table facing him, about fifteen feet away. The only light in the room was from behind and above them; they were dark silhouettes casting long shadows past his chair. Cobra sipped his water and waited.

"You have been brought here," a whispery voice said, "because a man must be killed."

Cobra nodded, and waited some more. He wasn't here to talk.

"We propose to pay you four million dollars, deposited according to your instructions anywhere in the world. Half now and half on completion of the mission."

Cobra still said nothing.

"Is that a fair price?" the raspy voice said.

Cobra shifted his chair a few inches to the right. He was establishing his own space. "That would depend on the target, the location, and the time," he said.

The three men bent their heads together, murmured, and nodded. "We know of your successes," the whisperer hissed. "We know all about you. The target is the President of the United States."

Cobra forced his body to remain still, the discipline of a shooter. But he was shocked. Twice in one lifetime? He thought to himself. "The price is far too low. The man is the best guarded in the world."

"Better than Zhirinovsky?" the whisperer wheezed.

They did know everything, Cobra mused. "One assumes."

"Then what is the price?"

"Twenty million, all up front."

The man to the right cleared his throat. "What if you fail, or just run off?"

"If I fail and survive, I'll refund half. If I run off, well, you found me once."

There was another murmured exchange. Cobra had very keen hearing but he couldn't make it out.

"It's what we expected," Admiral Daniels whispered to Alfred Thayer. "Plus the ten percent to the agent."

Thayer nodded. The third man listened, but said nothing.

"All right," the man in the middle said. He handed an envelope to a masked aide, who materialized out of the darkness. "This's a money transfer instruction to a bank in Brussels. Fill in your account information, and the payment will be made tomorrow at New York's opening. I'm sure you have ways of confirming that the money is received?"

"Of course," Cobra said, taking two envelopes from the masked man, who melted into the darkness.

"The second envelope contains your escape route and documents."

Cobra slipped it into his jacket, knowing he would use it only to plan a totally different route out.

The man in the middle rose. "Then our business is concluded. You must act on or before the last Saturday in November."

The masked aide returned and laid the nondescript duffel that contained Cobra's rifle case at his feet.

"One last thing," the man on the left said, his first utterance. "If it's possible, we would prefer not to have a grieving widow."

Cobra laughed. "One attack, not two. If it's all one action, OK."

The other two men stood and filed out. The aide handed Cobra his blindfold and gestured for him to put it on. Cobra complied and was led out of the cabin and into a car that drove away immediately.

The masked aide laughed loudly. Ramon Carvahal would get two million from the yanqui conspirators, and demand another ten from El Nieto Castro, who could hardly refuse. None of that, of course, would go to the shooter.

Cobra was driven down out of the hills and into the noise of suburban, then urban, areas. After about an hour he felt the limousine dip into an underground parking garage. He was led out, his bags including the weapon set on the concrete beside him. "Give us two minutes to drive away," a voice he didn't know whispered. Cobra nodded. He heard the car's doors slam and it move off with a squeal. He counted to one hundred and removed his blindfold. The garage was nearly full of cars but devoid of people, at least people he could see. Cobra was standing next to an elevator; he pressed the lighted button. Inside the box the only choices were four levels of parking and "Lobby." Cobra selected the lobby. In a few seconds he emerged into the opulent lobby of the Willard Hotel in downtown Washington. A bellboy rushed up and took his cases, and led him to reception, where he gave the name on his American documents. "Of course, Mr. Hayes," the manager said. "Your suite is ready. Please follow George." The manager handed a key-card to the bellboy and Cobra was whisked to the main elevators and up to the twelfth floor, a very nice suite with a view of the Treasury Department, and beyond it the White House.

Cobra shaved, showered and dressed in his only business suit. He went downstairs and had a large and excellent meal. He would rise early the next morning, check that his payment had been received in Europe, and immediately move the money by coded instructions. Then he would check out using Hayes's credit card, and disappear.

12

BILLY BOB SLATE, the Mormon, located Charles Taylor within hours, using no government resources. The Mormon had Taylor's apartment, in a run-down section of upper Connecticut Avenue in the District, watched around the clock. The subject was reported arriving at ten-thirty the morning after the heads-up from Big Dog Jonas and Zeke Archer. The watchers didn't know he had gone directly from Dulles to the *Washington Post,* been let in by the night security, and taken his film to the photo lab that worked around the clock. Charles went up to the editorial floor and booted up a computer terminal outside Brad Bentley's office. He downloaded his entire story from his laptop and printed out one copy for Bentley and another for himself. He then took himself out to a triumphant breakfast at the Willard Hotel.

The dining room was nearly empty at nine-thirty, and Taylor couldn't help noticing a dark man in clothing more appropriate to a safari than to Washington seated in a far corner reading what appeared to be an Official Airline Guide. There was something striking about the man, and Charles thought to call a source he had in the Willard's management and try to get a line on him. Just a hunch: who actually read the OAG?

Charles might have remembered to inquire about the man had he not been met at the door of his apartment, shoved inside and punched around by two men in black ski masks while two more ransacked his apartment. They took the copy of his story from his briefcase, all the film from his camera and camera bag (all blank; Taylor wondered what they would do when they discovered that), and also the laptop. The biggest man braced him against the wall of his bedroom and told him in a low voice to forget "everything you saw in Texas." He then threw the two-hundred-pound reporter across the room hard against a bookcase that collapsed to the floor. Charles slid down like a rag doll as books rained down on him, and the big man led his team out.

Charles gasped for breath, nearly blacking out. He had been hit hard in the solar plexus, and his ribs, groin, and face were dully painful. His stomach rolled as he crawled desperately for the bathroom, barely reaching the toilet before vomiting up his Eggs Benedict.

He leaned back against the tub, the porcelain cool against the back of his neck. The pain grew worse as he forced himself to take slow, shallow breaths. He probed his face and rib cage and felt nothing broken. The beating had been administered quickly and efficiently; a warning, a threatening, carefully executed not to do serious or permanent damage, but certainly a promise of far worse if his attackers chose to return.

For the first time in his life as a journalist, Charles Taylor was truly frightened. He'd heard stories throughout the presidential campaign about the shadowy New Zealots and their involvement in intimidation, assault, and even the killing of troublesome journalists.

He was thrilled also; he'd hit the big time, if he could stay alive. Charles Taylor had no illusions about his courage; he might well have ditched his best-ever story if he could, but by now, Brad Bentley would have received the copy he'd left on his secretary's desk, the photos would be there as well, and the story was in the Post's computer. There was no going back.

Charles had to find Julia Early, get his scoop confirmed, then get out of Dodge.

COBRA HAD NOTICED the pale, nervous-looking man in the Willard dining room, if only because the fool kept staring at him. He returned to his suite at ten o'clock and phoned his bank in Brussels. The money was all there. He immediately faxed coded instructions to transfer the money to three other accounts, one each in Geneva, Turks and Caicos Islands, and Grand Cayman. He checked out, using Frank Hayes's credit card, and took a cab to Dupont Circle. He entered the Metro and jumped on the train north into Maryland, reversed his track in Bethesda, made several other changes and finally arrived at Ronald Reagan National Airport across the Potomac in Virginia. He locked away his gun case in a locker, and walked slowly toward the Delta Airlines counter, holding the ticket he had purchased at the Willard with Frank Hayes's credit card for the 11:10 flight to Atlanta. He saw no pursuit, but wondered if his skills were still what they once were. When he reached the counter, he asked to change his destination to Miami, and paid the difference in cash. The flight had already been called, and he rushed to the boarding gate, his head down. The 11:00 Miami flight was two gates before the Atlanta departure, and he was last to board.

At Miami's awful airport, he used forged British documents and credit cards of his own to get on Cayman Airways 1600 departure for Grand Cayman.

13

"He transferred the money," Frank Simmons said to Alfred Thayer. "Inside Europe; all coded."

"How do you know?" Thayer asked.

"Friend of mine at NSA," Simmons replied. The National Security Agency had the capacity to monitor any telephone, radio, or fax entering or leaving the United States and many other countries. "As a courtesy."

"Could the NSA break his codes?"

"Almost certainly, Colonel Thayer. But they'd need a reason."

"Leave it, for now," the old man whispered.

Julia Early reported for work at the Capital National Bank on Tuesday morning, nervous and unrefreshed from her four days at home. She straightened out her desk and read and returned her e-mail, then reopened a file she had begun on a new security program for Banque Bruxelles's Western Hemisphere operations. Banque Bruxelles had many private clients in the U.S and Latin America. They all were assured by the bank that their accounts were secure from the prying eyes of their governments. Julia knew the system leaked badly as she had penetrated it in less than half an hour and read some very interesting transfers from prominent businessmen, legislators, and government officials of numerous nations, many of whom stridently maintained a public image of rectitude. She yawned as Frank Simmons crossed the open bay and entered his office.

Simmons answered his ringing phone. The Dragon Mother, the inevitable pause, then the voice of Alfred Thayer. "Did the Early woman return from her holiday yet?"

"Just this morning, Colonel," Simmons said. "I haven't said anything to her yet."

"Don't. What's she working on?"

"Several projects. One for the Bank of Thailand, one for the Belgians—"

"Thailand is too far; Belgium is about right. Get her back pronto via Concorde from Paris if we have to. Do you think she has enough done for a preliminary presentation in Brussels? Guided by an appropriately senior officer, of course."

"That could be arranged. In fact, Arne Olafsen, my senior operations man in London, is due to travel to the Low Countries and Germany beginning Monday."

"Good. A little field experience; get the cobwebs from your dank cave out of her head."

"May I ask why, Colonel? There are many down here more deserving of a junket."

"It's better you don't, although I'm sure you'll figure it out in time and realize the need for secrecy."

Simmons shrugged. "I'll arrange it then."

"Do so," Thayer said, and hung up.

Frank Simmons began to doodle on a pad. What did this have to do with the telephone instructions sent from the Willard Hotel to Europe he had been asked to trace? Why did the chairman want Julia Early out of the country, but well supervised? Thayer ran a very tight, very compartmented operation, and the fastest way out the door for an employee at any level was to snoop, ask, or speculate. He would do none of these. He had never been given the slightest hint why Julia had been sent to him from the credit training program, and he hadn't asked. When, to his relief, she had turned out to be a real asset, he forgot about the why, as he would now. He called Julia in and gave her the good news.

14

At the Sheraton Hotel on Grand Cayman's Seven Mile beach Cobra registered as Richard Thomas, a British subject born in St. Johns, Antigua in 1944. It was early for the Scuba season and the hotel was nearly empty. Cobra preferred to hide in large hotels where no one was ever remembered by the numerous, impersonal staff. He changed and took a van-taxi to a famous restaurant called Chef Tell's Grand Old House on the southern tip of the island. He arrived early to observe, as was the custom of Tell's repeat patrons, the spectacular tropical sunset of gold into red into blue and starry black, all within a few minutes. He then went in and dined well on conch chowder and lightly fried grouper, washed down by a crisp chardonnay from California's Napa Valley.

He rose early the following morning and walked to Grand Cayman's tiny capital, George Town, with its hundreds of branches of banks from all over the world. Some of these were full-service branches, like Barclays, Gulf Bank, and the Bank of Nova Scotia; some were independent or quasi-independent entities like Cayman Islands Trust Company; and most were merely mail drops, brass plates outside the offices of the many law offices in town.

Cobra opened new accounts with new numbers in several banks, each time piously signing government forms swearing that the funds were not the proceeds of any crime. He moved his money again and again, burying it deeper and deeper. He knew it could be found by the best sleuths of the U.S. Treasury Department, the Bank of England, or the Swiss police, but given his commission, he doubted anyone like that would be after the money for years, and by then he would have moved it again, if he was still alive.

Cobra completed his business in time to catch the 6:00 P.M. flight to Atlanta, where he made his connection to Washington National.

15

JERRY O'HEARN, THE Chairman and President of Executive Alert, Inc., a detective and protection agency incorporated in Chevy Chase, Maryland, stood at parade rest in front of Alfred Thayer's big desk. Capital National Bank was practically Executive Alert's only client, providing 90 percent of the firm's revenue. The bank, through a subsidiary in Luxembourg, also controlled the 75 percent of the stock not owned by O'Hearn.

Thayer steepled his hands in front of him. O'Hearn, lean, hard, fifty, with a military short haircut turned completely gray, looked like the Green Beret major he once had been. "Sit down, Major," Thayer offered. "Have some coffee."

O'Hearn sat, barely less stiffly than he had stood. "Thank you, Colonel. No coffee, thank you."

Thayer had invited no one else to the meeting. "So where is he?"

"He checked out of the Willard two days ago, having purchased a ticket to Atlanta. He then led our tail team on a hare-and-hounds through the Metro, and they lost him. It wouldn't have been difficult, sir. As you know, we aren't the FBI or even the detective bureau of a good-sized city police force. We've only thirty operatives, and most of them aren't trained in close surveillance. I'd have been surprised if your asset couldn't have ditched a two-man team in a crowded subway system. Frankly, Colonel, that wouldn't speak well of his credentials."

Thayer smiled. The same thought had occurred to him. O'Hearn had no idea of Cobra's identity and no inkling of his commission, other than it was something clandestine in which the chairman of Capital National took a personal interest. "What next?" Thayer asked.

"We sent another operative directly to National Airport with a description of the man and a ticket on the same Atlanta flight.

She waited by the Delta counter until the flight was called, then proceeded to the gate in case he had gone there directly; we knew from the concierge at the Willard that he had a preassigned seat and a boarding card. No one matching the description you gave us boarded the Atlanta flight, so our operative didn't either. It would be surer, of course, if we'd taken photographs while he was still at the hotel, or at the lodge on your estate."

"Absolutely no photographs," Thayer said sharply. "As you've been instructed, Major."

"Quite so, sir. When I heard from the agent at the airport, I called friends in Atlanta, Miami, and a few other cities that had departures from National at about that time. I asked them to observe only; don't contact, just report. Nothing."

He moved our money and simply vanished, Thayer thought, color rising from his throat to his cheeks. But somehow, he didn't believe it. He knew Carvahal would gladly hunt the man down for his 10 percent, and the shooter would know that too. Besides, Thayer had sensed a dignity, a pride of profession in the assassin during their brief encounter at the lodge. As mad as it seemed, Thayer felt sure the shooter would come back and complete his commission. "Anything further?"

O'Hearn drew himself up proudly. "Yes, sir. We kept a watch on National; had three teams of agents meeting every likely flight. Your man turned up at 2313 last night, coming in from Atlanta after all. He removed a bulky holdall from an airport locker and rented a car from Hertz. One of our operatives charmed a look at the rental contract; he's still using the Frank Hayes documents. We followed him to a small motel in Alexandria; he made no attempt to lose the tail, that now, of course, had three teams."

"Good. So he's returned, and is close by."

O'Hearn shook his head wryly. "My people sat on the place all night, watching his car and his room. When he hadn't emerged by ten this morning, my guy bribed the maid to let him into the room. The bed had been slept in, the lock on the rear window had been carefully removed, and our pigeon slipped us again."

COBRA HAD CAUGHT the tail as soon as he emerged from the jetway. Two teams; doubtless more. He collected his weapon from the locker, noting that the bag had not been moved from the precise alignment in one corner as he had left it, and that locks of his hair were still wound around the two zippers. He drove to the motel in Alexandria he had examined the day after his interview with the three judges, as he thought of them. He got three hours of sleep, then bailed out the back window as soon as he was sure his minders had set up one sleepy team outside and let the others go home.

Cobra took a bus west along Route 50, dropping off at a used-car dealership that was just opening for business at 6 A.M. He paid cash for a two-year-old blue Chevy van, and took himself across the Potomac through Maryland into Pennsylvania, ironically following Robert E. Lee's route of march to the Battle of Gettysburg in 1863. Cobra found a small, run-down motel on Route 30 near Seven Springs and paid cash for a dingy room for two days. Cobra had been prepared to say he intended to visit the battlefield, but the proprietor asked no questions, required no identification, and barely glanced at the signature Cobra scrawled on the register.

He carried his bags to his room. He would move again tomorrow, abandoning his second-night's payment. He couldn't help but marvel at how easy it was to travel in America, compared to Europe and especially South Africa. He had plenty of cash and wouldn't need to show his passport until he was ready to leave the country by air. If he attracted the attention of police, he had the British driving license and another from California, but he had no intention of attracting attention.

Cobra did indeed walk the famous battlefield, following the guide and map he obtained from the visitors' center. He enjoyed feeling the terrain and imagining the clash of mighty armies in the hot summer of 1863. There were discreet plaques along the walking paths, describing the many small battles within the great one. The most interesting to Cobra was the engagement at a low hill called Little Round Top. The plaque described the charge of Texas cavalry against a Federal artillery battery protected by trees and earthworks. The cavalry had been thrown back with staggering losses, and the battery continued to pound the Confederate lines. Brave boys, those Texans, Cobra thought, but the commander who ordered that attack should have been relieved for sheer stupidity.

There was a copse of trees near the High Water Mark, where Federal troops awaited Pickett as he began his famous charge. Walking north, Cobra reached the Brian Barn, another Union strongpoint. From there he could see the quiet beauty of the cemetery, the site of Lincoln's dedicating address on November 19, 1863. Cobra watched as workers assembled grandstands to the right and left of a covered platform draped with red, white and blue bunting. The lectern was faced with the blue and gold seal of the President of the United States. Cobra estimated the distance at between seven hundred and seven hundred fifty meters.

The President of the United States was to speak at Gettysburg the day after tomorrow, November 19, the one-hundred-thirty-eighth anniversary of Lincoln's famous speech. Cobra would be there; it was nice open country.

16

JULIA EARLY RUSHED into her apartment clutching a bottle of cheap champagne. Judith and Hilda laughed as she popped the cork and made a mess, but gladly joined her in the frothy wine served in their odd assortment of glasses. "I'm going to Europe!" Julia whooped. "An escape from the tombs, and a chance to present my own ideas, rather than let those pompous asses of relationship managers fuck them up."

Judith and Hilda were lavish in their congratulations, although Judith felt more than a twinge of envy. Both Judith and Hilda had been placed in the bank's Asia Department, the fastest growing in terms of business, but had yet to set foot out of Washington. Hilda, of course, Judith thought bleakly, couldn't miss. She spoke two Chinese dialects. Judith spoke only English, and Hong Kong was gradually suppressing the language of its success for the Mandarin Chinese of its new owners that even most Cantonese-speaking Hong Kong Chinese had to learn nearly from scratch. "When will you leave?" Judith said, pouring Hilda's untouched glass into her own and getting a six-pack of Lowenbrau from the fridge.

"Friday night. I get the weekend in London," Julia said, refusing to lose her ebullient mood to her friends' lukewarm congratulations. "Business class!"

The phone trilled. Hilda answered. "Charles Taylor, for you," Hilda whispered, holding her hand over the mouthpiece. "He left about five messages on the machine."

Julia waved her hands. "Not here," she whispered. Christ, why had she sent that report to the reporter she had no reason to trust. How she wished she had it back!

Hilda relayed the message, then covered the mouthpiece again. "He says he saw you come in ten minutes ago; he's calling from his cellphone. He says it's very urgent and he'll wait in the lobby until you'll see him."

"Call security," Judith advised. "Have that lard-ass cracker throw him out."

Julia raised her hands in front of her face. Give me a minute, the gesture pleaded. "All right. Tell him the Brew Pub on the corner; ten minutes."

"What's he want?" Judith asked. "He's a shit."

Which means he hasn't called her, Julia thought sourly. The only thing Charles Taylor could want would involve Little

Cheyenne Development. Could she get him to drop it? She doubted it. "I'll just wash my face and go. Shouldn't be long."

"Take your time," Judith said acidly. "Might's well get fed at least for whatever he wants of you."

Julia brushed her teeth, ran a comb through her hair, and took the creaky elevator to the lobby. The lard-ass security guard was fast asleep and snoring at his desk. Julia went out into the rain, rounded the corner to the Brew Pub, and went in. Charles Taylor, wet, rumpled, and with two awful black eyes, waved her to a corner booth, and rose to greet her. "Julia, darling, sorry to press, but we need to talk."

17

THE PRESIDENT OF the United States, flanked by aides and Secret Service agents and carrying his big Bible, rushed into the Cabinet Room and took his seat at the center of the long table. It was after seven P.M., late for formal meetings.

The president never appeared anymore without the Bible, and he had his Secret Service detail close even within the White House itself. Cameras began whirring and popping, and reporters shouted questions. The president heard many queries about his health. There had been much speculation in the press because he appeared frail and disoriented; the president smiled and answered in a firm voice. He'd had a mild flu, but felt fine now. He thanked the press for their concern.

"Mr. President, what about the rebellion in Cuba? It seems to be spreading rapidly westward, and the Cubans insist we are sustaining the rebels who have no popular support."

"What else would they say?" the president asked, to general laughter. "I've said time and again our naval forces in the area of south Florida and Cuba are there for defensive purposes only, to stop Nieto Castro from exporting refugees and drugs to our shores.

He jams radio and television signals from the United States, including Free Radio and TV Marti, that seek to tell the Cuban people the truth. His air force shoots down brave Cuban-American pilots flying slow airplanes the Cubans know are unarmed, and does it in international airspace. So we're showing we cannot be provoked, taunted even, without response. Once the little tyrant begins to behave, we'll leave, and then let's see who has the support of the Cuban people." More questions were shouted, but the president nodded to the usher by the door, the signal that the reporters were to leave so that business could begin. The TV and press reporters and cameramen all knew the signal, and left quickly.

"Well done, boss," said Big Dog Jonas, from the end of the table.

Carolyn White slipped in past the usher as the last reporters left the hallway. She took her customary seat at the president's right; the White House media people liked to have her pretty black face in as many shots of the president as possible. The door was firmly closed.

"Mr. President," Carolyn whispered, leaning close and gripping his arm. "I've just left the Russian ambassador. We should have a private word."

The president turned. He had never been so close to Carolyn, and he marveled as the silky smoothness of her skin and her subtle perfume. "Something the cabinet shouldn't know?" he said mockingly.

"I'd rather tell you first, then you decide who hears what, when."

The president understood. The cabinet secretaries, so seldom consulted about anything, leaked whenever they could to try to impress the media. "Ladies, gentlemen," he said, rising. "Enjoy your coffee for a few minutes more. Carolyn has something urgent for me." With no further explanation, he strode from the room, Carolyn trotting behind. The president stopped in the middle of the empty hall and turned to the Secretary of Defense. Two Secret Service agents dropped back discreetly out of earshot. "What is it, Madame Secretary? What business have you with the Russians? Isn't that State's job?" He smiled.

"The ambassador brought his military attaché. The purpose of the meeting was to avoid any misunderstanding or overreaction on our part or on the part of NATO allies."

The president's smile vanished. "What have those bastards done? Invaded Western Europe?"

"They say not, but Russian airborne troops have landed in their enclave on the Baltic around Kaliningrad—do you know it? It's a piece of Russia surrounded by Poland and Lithuania."

"I know it." European history had been a passion of Rupert Justice Tolliver since boyhood. "The ancient Prussian city of Königsberg. What else?"

"Follow-on forces are coming by road and rail through Belarus and Lithuania. The Russians claim they have rights of passage by treaty, but the Lithuanians are screaming."

"Do the Russians say why they're doing this?"

"To reinforce the fleet for, as Ambassador Zlotkin put it, 'defensive operations in southern waters.' "

President Tolliver smoothed his black hair. "Does that mean what I think it means?"

"It means they are sending a naval task force, presumably with heavy ground forces embarked, to Cuba."

"I won't allow it." Tolliver said.

"Mr. President—"

"As soon as that fleet sails, I want to know its composition and strength. Make sure the Atlantic Command has whatever it needs to kick the Russians' asses if it comes to that. I won't have a Russian fleet ninety miles from Key West. And where the hell is that old fruit, Japes?"

"The Secretary of State is traveling in the Middle East. Syria today, I believe. The switchboard—"

"I know; the White House switchboard can find anybody, anywhere. Let's not say anything to the cabinet. You go back to work and plan this thing. I'll go wrap up that meeting of empty suits, then I'll speak to Japes, tell him to get his ass up to Moscow and preach the word."

* * *

SECRETARY OF STATE Malcolm Japes flew to Moscow directly from Damascus, arriving at midnight, Moscow time. His aircraft was not met at the airport by any high Russian official, only by the American ambassador, who escorted the exhausted man and his small entourage to the embassy in the center of the city. The President of Russia, Alexandr Lebed, would not receive the American secretary, the ambassador related, but the foreign minister, Dmitri Shepilov, would, at nine o'clock in the morning. The meeting would take place not at the ministry, but at Shepilov's small office in the presidential complex inside the Kremlin. Japes suspected that might mean Lebed might attend the meeting "unofficially."

Before Japes could get to bed, there was a call from the Assistant Secretary for Far Eastern Affairs in Washington. "Yes?" Japes said querulously. What couldn't wait a few hours?

"Sorry to disturb you so late, sir," the assistant said. "We've just received a request, more of a polite demand, actually, from the government of Korea, that we begin withdrawing our troops and aircraft from the country as they are no longer needed with the peninsula united and at peace."

"Oh, God," Japes said. "The military will hate that, and so will the president."

"So he informed me when I called. I would've called you first, but CNN is already broadcasting the story as a lead."

Maybe Tolliver isn't so crazy after all, Japes thought as he hung up the phone. Maybe the world *is* unraveling.

18

CHARLES TAYLOR INSISTED that Julia let him take her to a better restaurant. Julia selected a bistro that was only a block away, and they hurried there in the windblown rain. Charles ordered a bottle of white wine, a Muscadet de Sevres et Main he couldn't really afford, and they looked at menus. Julia had spoken barely a word. Charles tasted the wine, pronounced it good, and they ordered: vichyssoise for both, poached turbot for Julia, and trout almondine for Charles. When the vichyssoise arrived in chilled cups embedded in miniature coolers filled with shaved ice, he began. "Julia, the material you sent me about Little Cheyenne Development could be the basis for the story of the decade, but I need a way to confirm key facts, and I need to get it before anyone else does."

"What information?" Julia said lamely. "I didn't send you anything."

Charles took her hand but she snatched it away. Charles took a deep breath. "OK, maybe we can work it that way. Maybe your name need never come up; I can see why that could be awkward for you."

Julia almost choked on her soup. "Are you threatening me?"

"Me? No," Charles said smoothly. "Give me a way to confirm the details of the transaction, and I'll try to keep you out of it." This was a bald lie; if the story ran Julia would be getting subpoenas from congressional committees by the basketful, and doubtless from a grand jury as well. Then there would be the interrogations from Treasury and likely the FBI. Julia was in for a rough time.

Julia felt trapped. She believed that the corruption of the campaign, the corrupt money still flowing to the Tolliver administration, had to be exposed. She wondered if her father was right, that knowledge, at least specific knowledge, might stop with the First Lady. She should have let her father handle it. She shouldn't have lied to him. She should never have thought Charles Taylor wouldn't have figured out who had such access, even though running into him at the development site was just plain bad luck. "How could you keep me out of it?" she pleaded.

"Remember Watergate? Woodward and Bernstein had a source, unknown to this day, called Deep Throat. You could be my confidential source, talk only to me. Only one other person would have to know your identity and roughly how you got the story."

Julia didn't remember Watergate; it had happened before she was born, but she knew the story about Woodward and Bernstein's exposé in the *Washington Post.* "Who would have to know?"

"My editor. He would never reveal the identity of a confidential source. This is Washington, Julia, the press lives on leaks from never-revealed sources."

"But I gave you the whole thing. Can't you check it yourself?"

"I'll need your help. Banking operations are opaque to me but I need to prove them up to make the meat of the story, the illegal foreign funding of the Tolliver campaign, stand up."

Julia looked up as her soup was cleared and the fish placed before her. Maybe there was a way, but she needed time to think. "Let me think about it. Maybe I can help."

Once again Charles took her hand. She didn't pull it away, but she didn't return the squeeze either. "We don't have much time. If some other reporter gets to this before me, I'm dead. Aren't you better off working with me, who you know you can trust, than risking someone else exposing your involvement?"

Like I trust scorpions and rattlesnakes, Julia thought, withdrawing her hand to pick up her fork. She began eating, barely tasting the perfectly poached turbot, and said no more. Charles could tell she was working out how vulnerable she was, and he said nothing either. He tried a few amusing stories about the foibles of Washington's giants, but got no rise from Julia, so they finished the meal in near silence.

Charles and Julia left the restaurant early, before ten. The rain had stopped, and Julia said pointedly that Charles needn't walk her back to her building. He insisted. At the corner, a black van with dark-tinted windows slid to the curb in front of them, and a dark sedan pulled to a stop behind. Two large men in dark clothes and ski masks got out of each vehicle and moved quickly to encircle them. Julia gripped Charles's arm, but he was pulled away, almost lifted, and shoved into the back of the van as the door was opened from the inside. The two men from the van jumped in, the door slammed, and it sped off.

One of the men from the sedan touched her arm gently. "We'll drive you home, miss."

"No-no, thank you," she squeaked. "I live just around the corner."

The man's hand on her arm tightened slightly. "Nevertheless, these streets aren't safe." He chuckled as he guided her into the backseat of the sedan and the car moved off rapidly, speeding right past her building. "Stop!" she shouted. "I live right there."

"We mean you no harm, miss," the man beside her said softly. His accent was like hers before she had shaken most of it off, Texas Hill Country. "Friends of yours—good friends—want you to know that the man you were with is a liar, and anything you do to help him is likely to place you in jeopardy."

"But he knows—"

"We know what he knows." The man's voice took on a menacing edge. "He needs you to make it stick. Don't help him, miss. Don't do that at all."

The car careered around corners in the quiet neighborhood, and soon slid to a rubber-burning stop in front of Julia's building. "Let your friends look after you, miss," the man said, his tone soft again. "We'll always be with you." He opened the door, got out, and handed her out. Before she even reached the steps to the lobby of the building, the car door slammed and it sped away.

Julia fumbled with her keys as tears ran down her cheeks. If she didn't help Charles, he would blackmail her. If she did, she'd have those scary men to contend with. Julia had heard the stories; she was almost sure they must be the New Zealots who protected the president by any and all means.

She took the elevator to her floor and let herself into the apartment. Hilda and Judith had gone out, and Julia felt another jolt of fear in the dark and empty place. She turned on every light, then made herself a stiff scotch. She desperately wanted to call her daddy, but she would have to tell him she'd lied to him. She finished her drink and made another. In the morning I'll decide, she thought.

THE NEW ZEALOTS in the van drove out to Fort Marcy Park and pulled Charles roughly from the back, rolling him onto the muddy grass. "You bin warned once, boy," the big one who had led the team at his apartment, kicking Charles sharply beneath the ribs. Charles gasped as his breath rushed out. "You got a story that don't want to be told."

Charles got a breath tried to sit up. A boot pushed him gently back down. "I'd stop the story if I could, but it's already filed."

"Then why you need that girl?"

"She knows certain details," Charles said, hating his cowardice.

"Where's the story filed?"

"The *Washington Post*."

"Shit," the big man spat and turned away. "You really stuck your foot in it, boy. I'm tempted to drag your ass over to Vince Foster Corner and kick you to death. Won't be no story without a reporter."

"They'd print it if I was murdered," Charles said quickly, his guts turning to water. "They'd figure out the missing pieces quickly enough, and the murder itself would make it news."

"Maybe yes, maybe no. You ain't big enough to be remembered long, boy," the big man said. "You figure out some way you can help me with my problem?"

"I'll rewrite. I'll tell the *Post* I couldn't prove the most damaging parts. It'll run on page thirty if at all."

"That's a start. Now, who was that girl? By now the boys will have dropped her home, so we know how to find her."

"Her name's Julia. I-I don't know her last name. I don't know her well at all." The man kicked him in the stomach, much harder, and Charles doubled up and vomited. When he was empty, he began to sob. "Please—"

The big man turned Charles over with the toe of his boot, and squatted beside him, careful to avoid the mess. "Tell me," the man said, just above a whisper, "that the name is not Julia Early."

"Yes," Charles sobbed, waiting for the next kick. "Yes."

"Boy, you are one troublesome little cootie, you know that?" he rose and called to his team. "Get him up."

"Hell, no," one of them said. "I ain't havin' him back in my van smellin' like that."

The big man looked down at Charles, who was still sobbing. "Then you got a walk ahead of you, boy. Make you feel better. And you got no need to be looking over your shoulder to see if we be around for a while, because we will be."

The Mormon got into the front seat of the van and they drove off, leaving the reporter in the deserted park. Jesus Lord, I hope them others didn't rough up Jubal John Early's kid. There'd be hell to pay if they had.

19

Malcolm Japes and Ambassador Collins were ushered into one of the Kremlin's great dining halls exactly at nine. The Russian Foreign Minister, Dmitri Shepilov, stood to welcome them, while a uniformed steward served tea in silver-bottomed glasses. Shepilov was a short, fat man who frequently mopped his brow in the overheated room. Behind him stood a tall, balding man in an ill-fitting suit. Shepilov introduced him as his interpreter as they all took seats at the head end of the long polished birchwood table.

Strange, Japes thought, sipping the sweet tea. He had met with Shepilov on several occasions, and the minister spoke perfect, unaccented English. Japes, for his part, spoke passable Russian. The two diplomats exchanged bland courtesies in both languages; the interpreter, if so he was, did not interrupt.

After Japes thought they had danced around long enough to be polite, he came right to the point. "You're reinforcing the Kaliningrad District, and readying a large fleet for sea. May we ask why?"

Shepilov shrugged. "Our brothers in Cuba complain they are being attacked by bandits, inserted, supplied, and protected by your naval and air forces. Surely you wouldn't have us abandon our brothers."

"In fact," Japes said dryly, "that would be our strong recommendation. They may be your brothers, or have been before you abandoned the creed of International Communism that they still preserve. But brothers or no, they're a thorn in our side."

"Does that mean, dear Malcolm, that your fleet will interpose itself between a Russian friendship mission and the Cuban people, who have asked our aid?"

"We must protect our national interest. Surely you would feel the same if NATO forces were to march into Belarus or Ukraine to greet our many friends there."

"Perhaps. But you're suggesting a direct conflict between Russian and American forces, on the high seas; international waters that belong to neither of us."

"We'll not allow Russia to land troops in Cuba," Japes said, abandoning any pretense of diplomatic nicety. "That's the message of my president. You know perfectly well your fleet wouldn't last ten minutes if hostilities begin near our shores."

"A grave threat, my friend, against a peaceful, humanitarian mission. There would, of course, be the risk of miscalculation, and escalation of the conflict, even to the level of nuclear exchange."

"Russia won't risk that to defend Cuba's bankrupt revolution," Japes said bluntly. "The United States will defend its near seas, including the Caribbean Basin."

"You're relying on your antimissile system. The one you built in contravention of the ABM treaty you piously say you honor."

"We've conducted a few tests," Japes lied carefully.

"In contravention of the treaty," Shepilov repeated.

"Technically," Japes admitted. "Russia also builds its antimissile forces, and has for years."

"We don't," Shepilov said, wide-eyed.

"Of course we do," a loud, hoarse voice called in Russian from the back of the hall. Shepilov leaped out of his seat. The interpreter came to attention and translated.

Japes watched as Alexandr Lebed, President of the Russian Federation, marched the length of the room. Lebed was a compact man who looked as fit as the paratrooper he had been. His face was badly scarred and his black hair was thinning, but his eyes, so deep in their sockets as to be in shadow, gleamed with energy as if they had their own light source. He wore a perfectly tailored, certainly not Russian, double-breasted gray suit. He continued speaking in Russian, pausing between sentences to let the interpreter catch up. Japes caught nearly all of what the president said, and realized the interpreter was toning it down.

"Russia has always opposed antimissile defenses," Lebed said in his parade-ground voice, "because they make the unthinkable inevitable. Suppose your navy attacks my fleet and I decide to retaliate with a single nuclear missile, perhaps fired from here or from a submarine. I could fire that missile at your carriers, or at a city, perhaps one of your ungovernable ones like Miami, from whence I suspect this current madness proceeds. But I can't do that, because your Aegis-system cruisers and destroyers would detect a submarine-launched missile as it broke the surface and shoot it down, and a missile launched from here to Miami would be shot down by your antimissile-missiles that don't exist. Similarly, your President Tolliver couldn't risk a surgical retaliatory strike at, say, one of our naval bases: Sevastapol, Kola Peninsula, Vladivostok, because our few antimissiles might get yours. So what alternative do we have, Mr. Secretary? The one nobody wants or has ever wanted: a full, overwhelming, nuclear exchange."

Japes used the time while the interpreter spoke to collect his thoughts. There was much logic in what Lebed said. Lebed, a former general, understood military realities and options; Japes knew that Tolliver did not. "The United States," Japes said carefully, "wishes no conflict with the Russian Federation."

"Then quit fucking with Cuba!" the president shouted, after the interpreter translated Japes's bland statement. The translator rendered the Russian's outburst as "Please exercise restraint in respect of Cuba."

"I'll consult with my president today," Japes said. "If he agrees to reduce the interdiction of Cuban drug shipments and refugee boats, would there be anything our Russian friends could do to restrain President Castro?"

Lebed waited for the translation, then barked, "We'll tell that fat sack of shit Castro to shut the fuck up. But if the Americans don't cease the blockade and the overflights, much less the obvious support of so-called freedom fighters, our fleet will sail and there *will* be risk of war."

The interpreter stumbled through the president's statement. Japes wondered: surely Lebed must have been told I speak Russian. Is he using the interpreter as a foil so he can say it as he likes and let the interpreter protect the niceties? To let me know he is serious?

The president stood up. "A military secret, Mr. Secretary, so you won't have to wait for your satellite photos. The load-out for the task force will take another four days. Then it sails to join submarine squadrons already in the Atlantic. Ten to twelve days at sea to reach Cuba, Mr. Secretary, so we have two weeks to reach an agreement or incinerate the earth. A happy result would be highly publicized joint maneuvers of our two fleets for training." Lebed marched from the room while the translator droned.

Japes, Collins and Shepilov shook hands all around, then Japes and Collins made the short drive to the U.S. Embassy to use the secure satellite link to Washington.

THE MORMON REPORTED to Clarissa Alcott Tolliver at 8 A.M., as instructed, the morning after the roust of the reporter Charles Taylor and the brief detention of Julia Early. The First Lady's office in the West Wing was small but elegantly appointed. Jim

Bob sat on the visitor's chair in front of her desk; Clarissa sat on the forward edge of the desk itself. Her skirt was leather and very short; Jim Bob couldn't help noticing she wore panty hose but no panties. He felt an urgent pressure in his groin.

"A fuckup," Clarissa said evenly. "You were specifically told to stay away from J J Early's daughter. J J knows everything, and he's the meanest man in Texas, including you."

"We didn't know who she was, but she was in earnest conversation with the reporter. She had to be checked," Jim Bob explained again. "She wasn't hurt."

"But doubtless frightened," Clarissa said, allowing her thighs to separate a few inches more. She could tell he was looking. "You're going to find a way to lean on the *Washington Post*."

"Lord Jesus, Clarissa," Jim Bob whined, watching her shifting legs. "Nobody leans on them; they brought down Nixon, and his people were a hell of a lot better organized than we are."

"Then kill the reporter."

Jim Bob squirmed. "I suggested that to him and he said that his death might kick the story onto the front page even without proof."

"Bullshit. Kill him and they'll have nothing."

Jim Bob swallowed. Clarissa's thighs parted farther. "What about the girl?"

"Nothing. Leave her the hell alone."

"I don't like this, Clarissa."

She kicked off her shoes and slid off the desk. With deliberate slowness, she hiked up her skirt and peeled off her sheer panty hose, then sat again. "Come here, Sugar Bear. Come get some honey." She spread her legs wide.

Jim Bob slid to her on his knees and pushed his head between her thighs. She was silk and warmth as he probed with his tongue. She moaned and gripped his curly hair, pressing him to her, and soon began to move to him. When she was finished, she pulled him to his feet. "Do it," she said.

"Dear God, Clarissa," he said. His erection was painfully pressing against his fly. Clarissa seemed to notice it with surprise, but she deftly unzipped him and freed it. She touched the swollen tip with fingers that felt like feathers. "Save this for later, when it's done," she said, and turned away.

Jim Bob Slate shoved his aching member back into his pants and fled toward his own tiny office in the basement. He went into the men's room at the end of the hall, locked himself in a stall, and relieved himself with the sin of Onan, his face streaming with tears and red with shame.

THE PRESIDENT BARELY waited until the navy steward left the Oval Office. Seated in a half circle in front of his desk were the vice president, Joseph Donahue, the Secretary of Defense, Carolyn White, the Chairman of the Joint Chiefs, Admiral Josephus Daniels, and the Chief of staff, Ezekiel Archer. The Secretary of State, Malcolm Japes, was present via the secure video conference net from the embassy in Moscow. He looked tired and haggard; in fact, in the president's eye, all his advisers did. "So what do we have?" the president asked. "The Koreans are telling us to leave; fine, money saved. The Russians are sending a fleet to Cuba."

Admiral Austin spoke first. "Let's start with Korea. We cannot allow them to throw us out; Korea is our hinge in northeast Asia. If we go, they'll integrate the best units of the old North Korean Army, including missile troops, into the already potent Republic of Korea Army. That'll frighten the Japanese and the Chinese into increasing already large commitments to rearming and modernizing their forces."

"Comments?" the president said. All agreed, including the video image of Secretary of State Japes. "So what do we do? We're in Korea at their request and they've asked us to leave."

"The Second Infantry Division and its supporting air must stay," Carolyn White said. "We can't let the Koreans become a new Hermit Kingdom with nuclear missiles."

Admiral Austin smiled. She's finally getting to know her job, he thought. "We stall. Talk, talk, fight fight, like our old North Vietnamese adversary."

"And the Russians," the president said, pointing at the camera that relayed the Oval Office meeting to Moscow. "Are they serious?"

Japes cleared his throat. He had sent his report of his meeting with Lebed and Shepilov hours earlier via secure teletype. "I believe they are, Mr. President. Lebed's position here, especially with respect to his military, is too precarious to allow him to back down. My gut says he doesn't want to anyway."

The president stood and paced, rubbing his aching back. "So we stall the Koreans. Ungrateful bastards. What about the Russians?" He looked around the room.

The vice president cleared his throat. It had been a long time since he had been asked for advice in this office. "The Cuban freedom fighters aren't worth nuclear war, Mr. President."

"Bullshit," Admiral Austin exploded. "The Russians can't risk it. Their missiles haven't been maintained for years, and neither God nor the Russians know whether they will fire at all or if they do where they might land. Any fleet they may cobble together in the Baltic would last less than ten minutes against even one of our carrier battle groups, and we have two in theater. Half their ships will never leave port, and another quarter will break down on the way across the Atlantic."

"I won't let them send a fleet here," the president said, once again pointing at the camera. "I won't, Mr. Secretary."

"Why," Carolyn suggested softly, "not offer half a loaf? Declare a two-hundred-mile exclusion zone around Cuba for drug interdiction; get the word out before the Russians can sail. Then invite their fleet to conduct joint exercises with ours, including port visits in Cuba and other Caribbean nations. Call their bluff, but not aggressively, and make Nieto Castro squirm as well."

"Brilliant," Malcolm Japes said from Moscow.

"We could live with it," growled Admiral Austin. "But we should be prepared to bloody them if need be."

"Prudent," the vice president said cautiously.

"Recall," Japes said. "President Lebed said he would restrain Castro."

"I like it," the president said. "Carolyn, be sure the forces are ready. Secretary Japes, sell it, then come home."

WHEN THE VICE president reached his own office, he telephoned Alfred Thayer. "He's being reasonable today. Perhaps we should delay."

"We can't. Remember the security arrangements; the artist cannot be recalled."

"Surely his movements are known. You had people—"

"He slipped them, several times. He's as good as we wished."

"But—"

"The die is cast," Thayer said. "As it should be."

20

JULIA WAS STILL AGONIZING about whether to call her father the morning after the attack when the phone on her desk rang and there he was. "I been anxious about you, Julia May."

She took a deep breath, and the story poured out of her in a whisper that couldn't be overheard from the desks on either side of her. She apologized for lying to him; he said nothing about that. "Maybe you better come home and visit your Momma while I take a trip to Washington and sort a few things out," J J said quietly. Julia could detect menace in his voice, danger.

"Daddy, I'm going to Europe the day after tomorrow, for the bank. It's a big break."

"How can you trust the people at that bank? You got to believe they know what you did."

"I'm guessing, but I think they want to keep me away from Charles—from the reporter."

"President Tolliver is a good man, though temperamental at times, but that Clarissa is utterly ruthless, and she has some mean sons of bitches working for her."

"I think I would be safe in Europe. All those people said was don't help the reporter."

"All right. Don't go out by yourself until you go to the airport. Hire a limo; don't drive yourself. I'll pay for it. While you're gone, I'll fly back and rattle a few cages. By the way, what's this Charles Taylor to you?"

"Nothing," she said angrily. "He threatened to blackmail me."

"Keep well clear. Enjoy Europe; call me at the Mayflower Hotel in D.C. if you have any problems. I got friends in Europe."

"Thank you, Daddy. I'm sorry I lied."

"Tan your hide later for that one, young lady. Just now be careful."

JULIA FLEW TO LONDON on British Airways nonstop. The flight was crowded, even in business class, and an hour late taking off, but she enjoyed it nonetheless. She departed Dulles at nine P.M. in darkness and landed at Heathrow in a watery pink dawn. She had been told to take a taxi to her hotel, the Basil Street in Knightsbridge. She couldn't believe the fare; well over one hundred dollars U.S, but Frank Simmons had insisted, telling her when he handed her the tickets and an envelope full of five-pound notes that the buses were confusing for one who didn't know the British capital, and the Underground painfully slow.

Julia was relieved to find her request for early check-in had been honored, and she was shown to a clean but very small room with bath *en suite*; 130 pounds Sterling a night; truly unbelievable.

She hung up her things, took a shower, and put on fresh clothes; her smartest black suit, then phoned Capital National Bank's branch on Bishopsgate Street in the City and asked for Arne Olafsen. He suggested she take a nap and come in around twelve-thirty for lunch. She was tired but had been told by Simmons, who made the trip often, that the jet lag went away much more quickly if one stayed awake all the daylight hours the first day, so she said she would be in by eleven. Then she went out to take a walk.

The rain had stopped, and a few blue patches appeared through low gray clouds. She passed restaurants and read menus posted in windows, went into a "Chemist," what the British called a drugstore, and bought some aspirin to counter the hangover from British Airways' plentiful champagne, then found herself at Harrods, the most famous grand store in the world. She browsed through the food court, then past displays of clothing. Once again she was amazed at the prices. If they had been in dollars, they would have compared with the better shops on Wisconsin Avenue in Washington, the ones she couldn't afford. But they were in pounds, and every pound was worth $1.66 at today's rate. How could working people afford to live?

She continued to walk east, through the Green Park past Buckingham Palace, then down The Mall to Trafalgar Square and the Strand beyond, marveling at all the Victorian buildings and statues. It was hard to believe the British Empire had become so vast and built these monuments, then once again become a small island nation.

Determined to experience the Underground, she entered on the Strand and with no difficulty found herself at the Broad Street Station. After a few minutes gazing at street signs and the small map provided by the hotel, and managing to avoid being run over by a hurtling red double-decker bus that came from an unexpected direction, she found the small, old limestone building that housed Capital National Bank, identified by a highly polished but discreet brass plaque.

She felt safe. Surely the New Zealots wouldn't follow her here.

21

J J EARLY LANDED at Dulles at 11:30 the day after his daughter had departed. He made several calls to Austin and Washington, and had secured an audience with the president's Chief of Staff, Ezekiel Archer. J J took the hotel bus to the Mayflower on Connecticut Avenue, dumped his light luggage, and walked to the White House. The security guards at the southwest entrance had his name on the daybook, and he went right through. Once inside the building, he waited at a security desk until Archer's secretary came down and signed for him, then escorted him to the Chief of Staff's surprisingly modest office. J J remembered Archer's digs had been much grander at the state capitol in Austin.

Archer rose and greeted the retired lawman. Big Dog Jonas had forwarded the Mormon's report, so Zeke wasn't surprised to see anger on J J's face. Archer offered coffee or whiskey; J J declined both. "Speak to me," J J said, without any pretense of friendly down-home preliminaries.

"All right, J J," Zeke said once they were seated. "We have a problem, it touched Julia but we didn't know it. She was warned off but not harmed; I apologize. It was a mistake."

"I called you about that," J J said.

"But didn't say anything about Julia. We were hunting the reporter and she happened to be with him. She was warned to stay away from him; that's all."

"Leave her alone, Zeke."

Archer held up his hands. "We will. But she really should stay away from the reporter. He wants the president's scalp to enhance his own career."

J J shifted in his seat in front of Archer's desk. "How bad a mess is Little Cheyenne?"

"Bad." Zeke shrugged. "Maybe very bad. Money came in from

there, or through there, during the campaign and after. I didn't know, and I don't think Justice knew much."

"Clarissa," J J spat. "And her boy-toy, Jim Bob Slate."

"That could be," Zeke said carefully. "We have to smother this thing, J J, surely you can see that."

"I don't see it if you threaten my daughter."

"J J, she never should've gotten involved with this reporter. We'll take care of it one way or another; without her he has no proof."

"You'll leave her the hell alone," J J said, leaning over Zeke's desk. "That animal Jim Bob Slate still around?" J J knew that he was.

"He—he runs errands."

"I ain't above killing a man bothers my girl, Zeke. Him and anybody who orders it. You know that."

"She's safe," Zeke said, trying to meet J J's hard-eyed gaze, and failing. "We know she's in London now; be in Europe a month if we need that long to bury the reporter."

Nice turn of phrase, J J thought. "Why'd she get this trip just now? I didn't ask her, but it seems a bit early in her banking career."

"The bank is run by a friend, a major figure in the Republican Party."

"No friend of Tolliver."

"No. But Tolliver's the only president he's got."

J J stood up and went to the sideboard, a mere two steps in the tiny office. He poured Jack Daniel's into two glasses, not bothering with ice from the bucket on the tray. He placed the glasses on Zeke's desk. "Zeke, I'm going to do you a favor. I'm going to hang around for a while, at your expense. I'm going to look after my kid, and I'm going to help you with the president's security."

Zeke stiffened. "The president is well protected."

"He's pissed way too many people off, Zeke," J J said, taking a sip from the cut-crystal glass. "Jim Bob can take care of a reporter or two, though he's sure to make a mess of it. The reporter's a gnat. My Julia did you a hell of a favor by letting you into the picture of Little Cheyenne; too many people already know, and they'll be coming, and hell coming with them."

Zeke picked up his glass, then put it back on the leather blotter without tasting the whiskey. "What are you saying?"

"They're gonna kill Tolliver, Zeke. And soon."

"Who's they?"

"That's your problem. Could be the bankers and businessmen he's fucked over, could be the Russians, or the Cubans—either flavor of Cubans; they both got grudges. Could be anybody else who dumped money into Little Cheyenne and now doesn't feel they got their money's worth, or perhaps does and wants to cover their tracks. Remember, Zeke, I've seen the land records."

"How do you know this?" Zeke asked. He knew J J had very good instincts.

"Don't, but I feel it. It's why I'll be staying around a few days."

Zeke drank his whiskey, welcoming the burn. "I'll set you up an office."

"Nope." J J stood up. "Just get me some walking-around money, a lot of it. You maintain the president's security; increase it if you can. I'll operate on my own, Zeke. Someone has to look in the shadows."

22

CHARLES TAYLOR STAGGERED out of Fort Marcy Park and was lucky enough to find a taxi after only a few agonizing blocks. Cabs were hard to find cruising in D.C., especially after dark; usually one had to telephone. He thought of having himself taken to a hospital but decided against it. When he reached his apartment, he shoved a twenty-dollar bill at the driver, who sped off without making change. Charles realized he smelled foul and couldn't blame the man. He went upstairs, put his soaked clothing in a black plastic garbage bag and cinched it tight. He had not only vomited but lost control of his bladder and bowel; no dry cleaner or laundry would touch the stuff.

He showered, then let the tub fill with water almost hot enough to scald. He got a bottle of whiskey and a glass from his tiny living room, double-checked the locks on the front door. He took three ibuprofen tablets and lowered himself into the tub.

He hurt all over from the two beatings and felt enough congestion in his lungs to presage pneumonia. His throat was so raw he could barely swallow, but swallow he did, all that remained in the whiskey bottle. After soaking until the water cooled, he took more painkillers and went to bed, after checking the triple dead-bolt locks on the front door one more time. He half walked, half crawled to his bed and tumbled in, and slept through tortured nightmares.

He awoke to the phone ringing beside his bed. The digital clock next to it said 10:12, and Charles knew the phone must have rung a long time to awaken him. It was Brad Bentley. "You sound awful," the *Washington Post* editor said.

"I—Brad, my story—"

"Is *brilliant*. Pulitzer-material. Do you have the proof?"

"No. I may not be able to get it. Brad, I've been threatened and beaten up. I'm afraid I can't give you the story at all."

"But we already have it," Bentley said cunningly. "You were threatened? Beaten? By whom?"

Charles could hear relish in the editor's voice. My best chance, he thought longingly, of the big story. But Brad Bentley wasn't the one with the bruises. "I'm not sure. They told me to forget what I learned in Texas."

Bentley guffawed with joy. "The president's goons! We tried to trace them throughout the campaign but never did. You've struck the proverbial nerve, Assistant Editor Taylor."

God, it was so close, Charles thought. He tipped more ibuprofen into his shaking hand and swallowed them dry. "I'm afraid, Brad. They'll kill me. I have to run."

"Nonsense. We'll protect you; wrap you in the First Amendment, hide you. But we have to have your proof."

"They know who she is, so I'll tell you. Julia Early; works for the Capital National Bank, but I doubt she'll tell you more than what I've already submitted."

"We'll find her," Bentley said importantly.

"What about me? How will you protect me?"

There was a long silent pause. Charles realized to his terror that as far as the *Post* was concerned, he had just become irrelevant. "Come in to the office. As soon as possible. We'll work it out."

"Brad—"

"We've done this before," Bentley said soothingly. "We know how to protect sources."

Against the men in the black van? The men with steel-toed boots? Charles had his doubts, but where else could he turn. "All right. I should come to your office?"

"As quickly as possible. Call a cab; I'll be waiting and I'll call in our security chief." Brad Bentley broke the connection.

Charles hung up and heaved himself out of bed, nearly collapsing because of the pain. His face was too swollen to shave, so he dressed in jeans and a sweater, threw on his jacket and phoned Checker Taxi and Livery. Five minutes, they said. Charles drank some orange juice from a carton in his fridge, and nibbled at a stale bagel, watching from his window for the cab to arrive. When it did, he locked his apartment and hobbled down to the lobby. As he reached for the rear door of the waiting cab, a black van pulled in ahead of it, riding up onto the sidewalk. While Charles was still struggling with the door handle of the taxi, a man in a black ski mask jumped from the van and shot him five times. For good measure, he shot the wide-eyed Nigerian taxi driver twice before jumping back into the van that was already backing into the busy avenue.

23

THE PRESIDENT TRAVELED to the Gettysburg National Military Monument by helicopter, designated Marine One, a souped-up, armored VH-60N Blackhawk painted combat marine green with "UNITED STATES OF AMERICA" in bright yellow letters on the sides and kept highly polished with automobile wax. It was a short, pleasant drive in late autumn but a motorcade would have tied up traffic and Tolliver knew that pissed voters off.

The helicopter landed on a cordoned-off area next to the military cemetery. The grandstands to either side of the podium were filled with invited guests, the press and television photographers were crouched before the podium on the grass, and the casual crowd of onlookers was left to stand or sit behind them. The president, carrying his Bible, strode from the helicopter to the podium, ringed by Secret Service agents and preceded by a military honor guard in dress blues drawn from the Third Infantry, the ceremonial unit that presided over military funerals at Arlington. The Marine Band had been trucked in earlier, and played ruffles and flourishes and "Hail to the Chief." The president waved and acknowledged polite applause.

Cobra stood with the tourists about a hundred meters back from the podium. He carried no weapon, but an expensive video camera equipped with a telephoto lens he had bought in Washington. An earnest young man in a gray suit with a curly telephone wire running from a plug in his ear into his collar had stopped him at one of many checkpoints surrounding the graveyard, set up with portable metal detectors at intervals in metal barriers. The Secret Service agent, for so Cobra assumed him to be, examined the video camera with exaggerated care, pressed its trigger to run off a few feet of tape, then returned it.

This security is awful, Cobra thought. The perimeter is too

small and too close to the podium, the agents too few. Even the military vehicles on the roads could be evaded by a man willing to risk his life for a shot, and the small army observation helicopters buzzing around the outer limits of the battlefield wouldn't be of much use except perhaps to search for the assassin after he struck.

Cobra wasn't willing to risk his life to kill the president. Most U.S. presidents assassinated, or upon whom attempts had been made, had been shot at very close range by fanatics who were apprehended or killed almost immediately. The exception, of course, was Kennedy at Dallas, but the cleanup squad had pinned that on Oswald and had him killed before he could reveal how little he knew. Cobra wondered if there would be a cleanup squad looking for him after this was done.

Cobra also wondered why he was expected to act alone, even to the point of choosing the time and place. Why not a team, as in Dallas? Triangulated fire; make it sure.

If there was a cleanup squad, Cobra would be very difficult to collect, because only he would know where and when he would strike and how he would escape afterward. But he was wary; all that money up front, no supervision. Just kill the president and move on.

The preliminaries concluded and the president began to speak. Cobra listened without great interest; he was here to observe how the man moved as he spoke. He knew the man had been a preacher, and he wasn't surprised to find that he panned the audience with his eyes, right and left, giving the impression that he looked into each individual's heart. He wore a black raincoat that hung stiffly. Kevlar body armor, Cobra had to assume.

"My fellow Americans," President Tolliver began. "I stand on the very spot, as near as historians can determine, where President Abraham Lincoln made a short speech he himself called 'a dud' but that every American schoolchild must hear and most recite at least once in his or her early years. Lincoln was perhaps the greatest man ever to hold this office, at once humble and unbending. He saved the Union. He erased the colossal evil of slavery. And he hallowed this ground, for all his protests that he couldn't."

Cobra watched, and videotaped. The man held his body very still, and pivoted his head almost rhythmically.

"I come here today, on the anniversary of the Gettysburg Address, to speak of things that greatly trouble me. This's a place of memory, of glorious dead from the Civil War and from many later wars. It's a place where one cannot but honor our gallant fallen. It's a place of sacrifice, of horror of war, but also of the need of gallant men and women to stand against injustice or insult.

"When the Soviet Union and its empire collapsed, many wanted to declare victory and bring all the brave young men and women home. But the world of two superpowers had its own mad logic; a move by them, a countermove by us. Third world countries were in their camp or ours, and had to heed us as we restrained them or lose support. Half of Europe was theirs, every other country in Africa, much of Asia. In the Americas into the nineteen seventies, nations from Cuba to Peru to Argentina and Chile fell into the Russians' camp, at least for a time.

"Now democracy marches eastward through the old captive states of middle and eastern Europe, resides in South Africa, and struggles to gain ground in Asia. Democracy has moved through Latin America like a cleansing sword.

"Saving only poor Cuba. She remains in chains."

The president paused; took a sip of water. "Reform and democracy struggle against the old, entrenched, communist past. But the past won't yield. The Russians have informed us that they're preparing to send a fleet to rescue the spiritually and economically bankrupt regime in Cuba. To do this, they've trampled the roads and fields of newly free nations; Belarus and Lithuania. They boast of war and rumors of war. They berate us for protecting our shores from drugs transshipped through Cuba, and for turning away the misfits and criminals Castro empties from his prisons into leaky, overcrowded boats as his grandfather did. We reason, and will continue to try to reason with the Russians. They respond with threats and more threats. I believe the American people are behind me when I say we should not and will not allow Russia to dictate events five thousand miles from their borders but ninety miles from ours."

Carolyn White fought an instinct to shake her head. Malcolm Japes, seated beside her, whispered in anguish. "Why this? Why now? We were *making progress*."

"I've written to President Lebed, just this morning," the president continued. "I entreated him to withdraw his threat of sending a fleet that we might be forced to scatter and destroy. The world, especially the world near Russia, the states broken away from the old Soviet Union, also Iran, Iraq, Pakistan, India, China, Burma, Korea, Vietnam, and all, is racked with instability and the threat of violence, even violence with weapons of mass destruction. We and the Russians must work together to restore the stability we once held so precariously through confrontation, and build a new order based on prosperity and freedom. This I have proposed to President Lebed, and I believe that he, a former commander of troops in bloody conflict, will agree."

The president, ignoring Lincoln's precedent of brevity, went on for another forty minutes. Cobra had what he needed, so he drifted away.

Carolyn White wondered whether the president knew more about the Russians than any of his advisers.

ALEXANDR LEBED WATCHED a tape of President Tolliver's speech and listened to the translation. He was seething; the American had him by the balls. He had just finished chewing a new asshole in the Chief of the Naval General Staff when the latter informed him that the fleet could not sortie, perhaps not in days, perhaps not in weeks, because the ships were undermanned and in poor repair, and because mobs of farmers in Belarus and Lithuania had torn up railways and roads and felled trees across them, halting the convoys of tanks and other vehicles that had been ordered not to shoot except if actually attacked. "Tell the Americans," Lebed told Minister Shepilov. "Something. Anything. We'll accept his offer of joint exercises, but with only a small battle group. Tell that asshole Nieto Castro to back off and say so publicly. He could hold elections, or some damn thing."

"Mr. President!" Shepilov said emphatically. "That amounts to surrender."

"What the fuck would you have me do, Shepilov?" the president roared. "The fucking navy can't sail, and the troops and their equipment are bogged down on ruined, muddy roads in Belarus and Lithuania. What would you do, and fuck your mother!"

Shepilov blanched and stepped back. "I'll make an appointment with the American ambassador," he said. "I'd like a little time to work on the statement."

"Fine, take an hour or two; there's little to say. And tell Admiral Klimov to get at least a squadron underway; a cruiser or two, some destroyers, and that useless aircraft carrier *Kusnetzov*. With a few planes on deck, if he can find any. Do that before you go home tonight."

Shepilov rose. "Exactly so, Mr. President."

PRESIDENT TOLLIVER STRODE into the Cabinet Room, to applause. The president waved away shouted questions from the press, and the reporters and cameramen were shooed out. Tolliver went to his chair and waved at his aides to be seated. "You all have copies of President Lebed's reply. I've just spoken to the man, a very good conversation. He agrees we have much business in common in Europe, Africa and Asia, and asks merely if he may 'know our intentions' in respect of Cuba."

Clarissa, at the end of the table, frowned. The Miami Cubans wanted a lot more than a few overflights and a token force on the ground in the southeastern mountains. She tried to catch her husband's eye but could not.

Admiral Austin cleared his throat. By protocol, he shouldn't speak unless invited to by the Secretary of Defense, who sat directly across from him at the president's side, but he rarely observed the courtesy. "We can reduce the overflights, make them less obvious but still enough to prevent the Cuban Air Force from doing anything effective against the freedom fighters. Our intelligence, plus what we get from our friends in Miami, indicates that very few of their aircraft are in flying condition anyway. In another week, way before the Russians could have anything even out of the Baltic, the rebels should have enough men, beans and bullets to take care of themselves, if they gain popular support."

"And if they don't gain popular support?" Clarissa asked sharply. The question was pointed at her husband, but he stared straight ahead.

Admiral Austin shrugged. "Then it's their problem. We've given them a helluva better start than Kennedy did at the Bay of Pigs; they have to make it work, and unless the Miami leaders are complete liars, they should be able to do so. Fidel gave Cuba nothing but sacrifice, but at least he was a commanding presence. Nieto has nothing holding him up but an army and police that don't have any commitment to his person and seem to have little stomach for a fight."

Clarissa wondered if that would be enough. She would have to talk to a few people in Miami.

"I've decided to speak to the nation after I confer again with President Lebed," Tollliver continued. "We've agreed tentatively to a summit in the next six months, and I want to reassure the people that the steps that we've taken, wrongly, in my view, branded as aggressive, are having positive results. There'll be a rally of antiwar and civil rights groups at the Lincoln Memorial on Saturday. It's kind of a commemoration of the rallies thirty-five years ago. I'll speak; Zeke is setting it up. I'll rebut the notion that I've hidden myself from the people, and do it in front of a less-than-friendly crowd. Zeke, make sure the loudspeakers are really loud."

A ripple of nervous laughter circled the table. Clarissa, stone-faced, wondered why Rupert was wrapping himself in Lincoln. She also wondered what the *Washington Post* would do with the story of the reporter's murder and his Little Cheyenne story. They'd have to report the killing in the Saturday paper, but it was too much to hope for that they would bury the bigger story in the little-read Saturday edition. Front page Sunday, she guessed. Better then that Rupert speak Saturday; it might be the last day anyone would listen.

J J Early sat in one of the chairs away from the table. He'd go down to the Executive Protection Service, as the White House detail of the Secret Service was called, and see what they had put together for security at the wide-open steps of the Lincoln Memorial and the vast Mall that stretched all the way to the Capitol. About as good a spot as a shooter could want, a vast open space with tall buildings along both sides on Constitution and Independence Avenues.

J J figured the Secret Service had to have the area well covered. After all, the Lincoln Memorial shot was nothing but a mirror image of the problem of protecting a president being sworn in on the Capitol steps. J J would have a chat with them, then hit the streets.

Tolliver closed the meeting, panning the room with a gentle smile. J J had an eerie feeling the president knew something violent was coming, and that perhaps he welcomed it.

24

ADMIRAL DANIELS MET Alfred Thayer at the Officers' Club at Fort Myer, Virginia, where both were members. They chose a quiet table far from the lunchtime crowd at the bar. "The mechanic hasn't done it," Daniels said, without offering any greeting. "Does your ex-Green-Beanie know where he is?"

"I don't know, and I've told you I don't want to micromanage this thing. His deadline is tomorrow."

"The president is going to address the rally of aging radicals at the Lincoln Memorial tomorrow," Daniels said. "It won't be announced until an hour before."

"How will the shooter find out?" the old banker asked.

"Beats the hell out of me," Daniels said angrily. "Alfred, we ought to find this man and control him. In the last few weeks, even days, Tolliver's apparent blunders have gone from strength to strength. He's revealed to all the world the Russians' military unpreparedness, set Cuba on a road to perhaps throwing off communism once and for all, and quieted the cities of this country with a few high-sounding but relatively cheap programs. Maybe this thing shouldn't be done."

Thayer looked at the old admiral, his shaking hands, his impossibly thick glasses. "I'm afraid I agree. I'll have my security firm look harder, but so far they've found nothing since they tracked him through National Airport to Alexandria."

"Perhaps we should alert the Secret Service."

"How could we do that without implicating ourselves? And aren't they supposed to be prepared for a lone gunman."

"The answer to your first question is that I may have a way. The answer to the second, is no, they aren't. They're no less complacent than they were in Dallas in 1963."

"But you can do something?"

"Perhaps. Can your people find the assassin?"

"Perhaps."

"He'll have to be terminated, of course, Colonel Thayer. He knows far too much."

"Of course, Admiral. But first we must find him."

Admiral Daniels rose, painfully pushing himself up on his red and white cane. "I'll make a call."

Cobra studied the videotape of the president speaking at Gettysburg from his room in a Motel 6 in Chevy Chase, Maryland, and got the rhythm of his head movement. Cobra had selected the motel because he would have easy access to Washington without having to cross any river bridges or other obvious choke points.

He called the National Park Service to ask about the grandstands and barricades he had seen being set up in front of the Lincoln Memorial on the Mall. Rally, he was told. He called the White House Visitors' Office and was told there were to be no tours offered tomorrow, Saturday, because of the crowd in front of the Lincoln Memorial that might stretch back to the Ellipse south of the White House. He told the helpful young lady he had come from France and hoped to see the president, even at a distance. He'll speak at the rally, around noon, she said. We just found out.

Patrice Lumumba had had better security, Cobra thought. It was time to find a spot, to plan the attack, and then execute it. He climbed into his dented van and drove into the capital.

ADMIRAL DANIELS TELEPHONED J J Early at the Mayflower Hotel. Early had served under Daniels in Vietnam and they had kept in touch. He got the Mayflower address from a quick call to J J's wife in Uvalde. There was no answer in J J's room; Daniels left an urgent message with several callback numbers.

COBRA DRESSED IN coveralls stolen a week ago from a van belonging to Potomac Gas and Electric. He slipped in and out of buildings on both Constitution and Independence Avenues. He had a photo badge stolen with the uniform that looked nothing like him. He carried a large toolbox. No one paid him any attention.

He decided on the roof of the Bureau of Engraving and Printing Building, on Independence Avenue, east of the Lincoln Memorial. The building was still called that, although the Bureau that made U.S. currency had moved years ago to a new facility a few blocks away. The building, a turn-of-the-century brick structure about five stories high, was now occupied by the United States Auditors. Cobra neither knew what they did nor cared, but reasoned that they would have less security than a facility that literally printed money.

Cobra concealed his equipment in a service room in the basement, in a locker that must belong to one of the service workers. He cut off the padlock and substituted one of his own. He went up to the roof, carrying only a laser range finder that had come in with his rifle. He calculated the distance to Lincoln's knees at 1,247 meters. It was a much longer shot than he would like, but the Mall was actually much less surrounded by aiming points than he had thought. Along Constitution Avenue to the north of the Memorial were buildings housing the American Pharmaceutical Institute, the National Academy of Sciences, the Federal Reserve, and the Department of the Interior. Cobra was sure all these buildings would be heavily secured. Then there was the open Ellipse, south of the White House. He had to stay outside the perimeter the Secret Service would establish. He guessed five hundred meters maximum; Oswald in Dallas (or whoever actually took the shot from the rear) had barely a one hundred and twenty meter shot. Cobra's had been sixty or less; dead flat.

Cobra walked around the roof, getting a feel for the place. The wind was mild from the south, but it would be a cold night. He would not leave the building until the job was done.

He surveyed the roof. The building was old and had chimneys, probably long disused. Lots of places of concealment, and places to dump his old rifle when he was finished. The roof, with its clear view of the Memorial, might of course be patrolled, even at so great a distance. If it was he would have to bail out and make another plan. He felt a frisson of fear, but the Cobra was a master of concealment, and escape.

Cobra was willing to bet the Secret Service would have most of their assets in the crowd, close to the podium. John Wilkes Boothe had shot President Lincoln from a foot away. Not much different for Presidents Garfield, McKinley, and Reagan, or for an attempt on Theodore Roosevelt.

* * *

J J Early met Special Agent Matt Blackstone in his shabby office in the White House basement. They howdied and shook, and reminisced a while about how J J had handed the governor of Texas off to Blackstone during the presidential campaign. Pleasantries completed, J J asked, "What special precautions are you making for this speech to the mob in the Mall tomorrow?"

"Nothing special, J J. The usual is very tight. Why might you ask?"

"Gotta feeling, Matt. Can't tell you why; it's a million tiny things. The hairs on the back of my neck feel a shooter out there."

Matt swung his booted feet off his desk and down to the floor with a crash. "We're always on the lookout for that, and this president has pissed off more than most. Any idea who?"

"None."

"Well, you know the drill. Every building with a clear shot at the Memorial will be swept, starting"—he looked at his watch—"about now, as the workers clear out for the weekend. Then the buildings will be sealed, guarded outside, patrolled inside, shooters on the roofs, all along Constitution Avenue. They're damn near all government buildings, so it's no problem."

"What about the south side? Independence Avenue?"

"No good high points within a thousand meters, but they'll be checked and sealed. We only got so many agents, J J."

"A thousand meters," J J thought. "I never had anybody could shoot that good."

"We don't either; nor does the FBI or the CIA. Only ones are the Navy SEALS, with that five-foot-long cannon, the Barrett 82 A1. 50 caliber sniper rifle. They claim accuracy to four thousand meters, but they keep those weapons locked away. Besides, it's not exactly a concealable weapon."

J J fidgeted. "I got me a Big Horn Sheep at about seven hundred yards once, in Idaho, with an old Sharps Fifty my granddaddy owned and I rebuilt. My own loads; I figured I could hit what I wanted at a thousand. 'Course, it was a flat shot across a canyon, and no wind, and I had to adjust the rear sight for a drop of near six feet."

"Not hardly reliable, J J, though doubtless you be a fine rifleman. No, we'll be looking for a sniper from a few hundred yards; likely much less, and the crazies like John Hinkley who'll try to get right up close. The worst nightmare is a lunatic with ten sticks of dynamite taped around his waist and a Bic lighter."

"Or a man with a pistol and a death wish."

"Or a bomb, got up close somehow we don't find it, command detonated. It's a bitch, J J, you know that. We'd like to keep the man in a bulletproof bubble, but you know we can't."

J J got up to go. "You mind I snoop around some of those tall buildings?"

Matt handed him a pass with a red diagonal stripe. "You think of anything, you call me right away, you hear?"

J J took the pass and stuffed it in his jacket pocket. "You bet."

SECRET SERVICE AGENTS Ben Green and Carla Code walked across the Mall after checking buildings along Constitution Avenue as far south as 14th Street. They were one of fifteen agent pairs assigned to the duty, and by seven P.M. they were tired. Their last call was the Bureau of Engraving and Printing Building on Independence Avenue, a site with a clear view of the Lincoln Memorial but three-quarters of a mile away. They took the elevator to the top floor, climbed the stairs to the roof, and admired the view. They could see the Lincoln Memorial brightly lit by floodlights, but the statue was in deep shadow. "From here," Carla said. "The only chance would be a shoulder-fired missile."

"I reckon," Ben said, walking around the roof, expecting nothing and finding nothing. Agent Code followed. "Let's run the floors and get out of here."

They went down the stairs, checking the stairwells and each floor. Upon instruction from the Secret Service, offices had been left unlocked so the checking went quickly. The bottom three floors were where the presses used to run, turning out banknotes. Ben Green was about to suggest bagging it on the fourth floor when the two agents rounded a corner and encountered a black man in coveralls waxing the floor with a big round electric buffer. He pushed along a cleaning cart with a deep canvas bin as he went. The two agents stopped him and politely asked to see his identification. The cleaner held out the photo I.D. hanging from a bead chain around his neck. "Be Rufus Coombs, bawse. Night cleaner."

Code looked at the photo with tired eyes. Even though the picture was in color, as in so many photos of black men the face was little more than a dark dot. "What time you get off shift, Rufus?" she asked.

"I only just started. Be gone five A.M, before the Saturday folks arrive."

"You check out with security in the lobby?" Carla asked.

"Every morning, ma'am."

Ben Green reached down into the bin, shifting dirty towels, rags, and supplies. Carla Code made a note of Rufus's name and I.D. number, so she could alert the guard at the door to make sure Rufus left as scheduled. The building was too far away from the Memorial to warrant a Secret Service detail. "Good night, Mr. Coombs," Agent Code said.

"G'night," Rufus said, grinning, as the agents boarded an elevator and descended.

Agents Green and Code passed the security guard in the lobby. He was all but asleep. Whatever the United States Auditors kept in there, no one was real concerned about guarding it. Carla handed her note about Rufus Coombs to the fat black man in his unpressed black uniform. "Yeah, old Rufus," he said, making no effort to suppress a yawn. "Been here longer than me. I'll see him off in the morning."

Carla preceded Ben from the building. A little buzz in the back of her head: *old* Rufus? Rufus wasn't that old, but maybe it was just an expression.

* * *

COBRA'S WEAPON AND equipment were on the cleaning cart but under the linen bin. The real Rufus Coombs was tied up and gagged with duct tape in the service bay in the second basement. Cobra was somewhat surprised the Secret Service would search a building so far from the Lincoln Memorial, but he felt fairly sure they wouldn't be looking in basements. Coombs would be found in a day or two, dehydrated and scared but not hurt. It was bad news the woman took his name to leave at the front desk, but the fat guard hadn't looked at Cobra coming in, and probably wouldn't miss Rufus not going out.

Cobra pushed the cart and the buffer into the elevator and back down into the service bay, ripped off the duct tape on the scared man's mouth, and gave him a drink of water from a cooler in the corner. He regagged the man, recovered his weapons, and looked for a secure place to wait out the night.

Ironically, it was the same in Africa. Nobody ever figured a black man would be the shooter.

25

BRAD BENTLEY WROTE the article about the murder of Charles Taylor himself, and ran it on the front page of the Saturday paper, below the fold. He felt righteous but a little ashamed. He had offered to protect the boy, and he would have, but perhaps he should have sent a car or two of the *Post*'s security force to pick him up. Judging by the police report of the shooting, the people who wanted Charles wanted him bad, and Bentley doubted whether a few rent-a-cops in gray uniforms armed with ancient .38 special pistols most of the guards had never fired would have accomplished much beyond adding to the body count.

Ashamed or no, Brad Bentley built Charles into a much bigger figure in the world of journalism than he had been in life, the better to punch up the story of Little Cheyenne that would run the following day, front page, above the fold. He was nervous about running the story without proof, but a dead reporter solved a lot of problems. Brad Bentley filed the report of Charles's death, then telephoned Colonel Alfred Thayer, the old bull Republican who ran the bank where Julia Early worked. He had known Thayer for years and although they disagreed violently over everything political, they liked each other. Thayer and Brad Bentley observed Tip O'Neill's rule: politics ended at five o'clock.

Thayer took the call, after his infamous gatekeeper, the Dragon Mother, kept Bentley on hold for two minutes. "Brad Bentley? Not often I hear your voice."

"Colonel. One question. Who is Julia Early?"

"On the record, Brad, she is a trainee employed by this bank."

"And off the record?"

"Nothing."

"Could she be made available for an interview?"

"She's presently traveling abroad."

"Where?"

"Abroad. That's all, Brad. Let me call you for a drink next week."

By that time the story will be on its own, Bentley thought. Thayer knows that. "I'd like that, Colonel."

"I'll call." The banker hung up.

So you go with your gut, and Charles Taylor's splattered guts, Bentley thought. The story would run.

26

COBRA FOUND A lounge area on the top floor of the Bureau of Engraving and Printing that had a television set, a Mr. Coffee, a microwave oven, a small bar and a refrigerator full of microwavable snacks. He dialed up the Weather Channel; tomorrow morning partly cloudy, warm for November, light southeasterly winds coming up the Potomac.

Cobra unpacked the rifle, disassembled it to its tiniest components, and cleaned it. Before putting it back together and attaching the stock and telescopic sight, he donned tight rubber gloves he had bought at a Maryland supermarket. He had fifty hand-loaded rounds in the case, with powder mixes and bullets for different shots, all color coded with Magic Marker. For the range of tomorrow's shot, he would need the hottest load. All the bullets were hollow points, designed to expand when they hit flesh and shatter if they hit bone. For such a long shot, Cobra thought that the increased drag caused by the hollow point would make the bullet's trajectory less than optimally predictable. He therefore set out to modify his hottest, longest-range loads.

He didn't have his loading press with him; it would have been too heavy and bulky to carry. He had a small battery-operated drill, a jeweler's soldering iron with a reel of self-fluxing solder, and small dressing files. Lacking a proper circular vice, Cobra held each cartridge in his left hand, butt-end firmly against the table. He drilled out the hollow points to widen them a fraction, and tapped out the lead shavings. He cleaned the cavities with a pipe cleaner dipped in rubbing alcohol, and let them air out. With a magnifying glass, he examined each cartridge and selected the five he would load, and three backups.

Cobra cut tiny pieces of rice paper from a sheet in his kit, and one at a time he chewed them into dense masses. He forced a tiny ball into each hollow point using the drill bit, then added liquid mercury, a drop at a time from a small bottle. Another rice paper ball went in on top. Cobra heated his soldering iron and dropped molten solder in the remaining opening at the tip of the bullets. When the solder was cool and solid, he dressed each bullet into a slightly dull point with a fine file.

The mercury loads would make the bullets heavier even as they made them more aerodynamic. Cobra refigured the drop on his laptop. He had to compute as well on the drop in altitude between his firing point and the target. Bullets fired downhill tended to float, much as a long pass in American football may seem perfectly thrown by the quarterback and still fly over the receiver's head.

The mercury loads were not designed just to smooth the bullet's shape. Mercury, much denser than the surrounding lead, would decelerate less on impact. Mercury loads did not merely expand on impact, they exploded.

Nasty business, Cobra thought with a shrug. Yet I'm merely the instrument.

He ate a microwave pizza that tasted like cardboard and ketchup, washed down by a diet Coke. He wrapped himself in his overcoat, then stretched out on a worn couch for the night. Cobra slept like a cat, ears alert for any sound of a patrol's footfall. There were none.

ADMIRAL DANIELS CALLED the Mayflower Hotel again at seven-thirty. J J Early was not in, he was told, and he hadn't called in for messages. Daniels pondered; President Tolliver was rotten to the core, corrupt, and foolish. Yet he seemed to be getting results. If it would be possible to give him a reprieve, see what came next, crazy or crazy-smart. But if the shooter couldn't be found, and if he hadn't simply skipped with the money, he would make his attempt, almost surely tomorrow when the president addressed the crowd from the Lincoln Memorial. How could Daniels alert the Secret Service without implicating himself? He could trust J J Early, if he could just find him. J J knew a lot of secrets and was trusted by anyone who knew him to take them to his grave. Daniels had two pieces of information on the shooter the Secret Service lacked, the only things the admiral knew about the man he had seen only once at Thayer's estate. The shooter was a black man, and Daniels knew the profiles on shooters always assumed a white. And the shooter killed from very long range.

Daniels dialed the Mayflower again.

* * *

J J Early walked the Mall, all around the Lincoln Memorial, looked for firing points around the Vietnam Veterans' Memorial and the Washington Monument. He observed the Secret Service teams checking buildings along Constitution Avenue; he didn't follow them. They knew their jobs. He walked across the Mall to Independence Avenue, but there was really no good place within reasonable range of the Memorial.

Would the gunman fire from the crowd and take his chances? J J didn't sense a fanatic but a paid assassin. It had to be; the president would be targeted because he had pissed off powerful men all over the world. Someone who expected to survive and spend the millions such an evil job would command.

Night fell softly, a little fog, a little drizzle. J J continued to walk, to watch, to try to puzzle it out. A mercenary could be anyone, young, old, male, female. Or the killer could be, just might be, a fanatic with a pistol or a bomb. J J rubbed his hands together against the cold and his growing frustration. At four in the morning he retreated to the Mayflower, had a sandwich in the all-night coffee shop, and went up to bed. The message light was blinking on the phone, so he phoned the desk. Admiral Carter Daniels, three messages, marked urgent. J J's old commander must have found out he was in Washington. J J would call in the morning; Daniels must be nearing eighty and needed his rest.

Cobra rose at first light, washed up in the nearby men's room, made himself coffee and a microwaved frozen bagel. He wanted to be out on the roof before any of the day staff, or any Secret Service personnel, arrived. The president was due to speak around noon, a wait of six hours, but Cobra had much to do.

He loaded his five best rounds into the rifle after donning a new pair of the throwaway rubber gloves. He put another three mercury-loaded rounds in his bush jacket pocket. If he couldn't get it done and get away on eight rounds, he reasoned, he'd be dead. He cleaned and loaded a tiny five-shot .380 semiautomatic pistol, an Astra, and shoved it into the opposite pocket. He wiped down all the other equipment, replaced it in the fitted case, and wiped down the case with oil.

Cobra walked down the hall toward the stairs to the roof and threw the case into a trash chute. They'd find it anyway. He climbed the two flights to the roof with the rifle, a tool belt he had taken from Rufus Coombs's locker, and his cleaning cart filled with miscellaneous items. He made a careful reconnaissance, staying well back from the parapet, out of sight of anyone on nearby buildings. He wondered if the Secret Service would have observers, even sharpshooters, in the Washington Monument. He'd bet they would; it commanded the entire area. Did the obelisk have windows at the top that could be opened? He didn't know.

Cobra planned to rest his rifle on the parapet, about two feet high, and shoot from a sitting position. He'd bought a ten-pound ankle weight filled with lead shot from a People's Drug store in Georgetown to steady the rifle barrel in lieu of a sandbag, and carried up a sofa cushion from the lounge to sit on. The cushion was dull green and shouldn't attract attention. Cobra wedged it as close to the parapet as he could, and concealed his rifle beneath it. He then retreated to the shed that topped the stairs to the roof.

Inside the shed was a padlocked tool locker. Cobra unscrewed the hinges and took out a sealed bucket of liquid asphalt and an oil-encrusted broom. It was too cold to apply the stuff to cracks in the roof, but who in a helicopter would think of that? Cobra put the bucket and broom outside and took a last cautious look at the Mall.

At eight o'clock in the morning, there were already police below on the Mall, and helicopters circling lazily in the near distance. The fog was thinning, but the wind was picking up off the river.

If I make this shot, I'll be immortal, Cobra assured himself. Then he forced himself into the shed and closed his eyes to rest them. One thousand two hundred and forty-seven meters. He would be a god.

He had to make the shot, then live long enough to escape his pursuers, then gather his money. He would be a legend with a story he could never tell anyone. Or he would be dead.

Cobra waited as the day warmed, the drizzle and the fog lifted, and the wind died.

AT 9:00 A.M. J J Early called Admiral Daniels at the number he had left and was told the old man was being assisted through his bath. J J left his room number for a callback at the admiral's convenience, then went down to breakfast in the coffee shop. He couldn't figure it, but it didn't feel right; security was tight for such an open space, and the territory was as well known to the Secret Service as any on earth. J J called Matt Blackstone. Bomb-sniffing dogs in and around the Memorial? Of course, in the crowd as well. Buildings sealed? Every one within a thousand yards that commanded a clear view of the Memorial. Sharpshooters on roofs? Yes, and in windows, plus thirty Secret Service agents in the crowd and around the president, backed up by uniformed Washington and National Park police, including SWAT teams and FBI agents. "Don't worry, J J," Blackstone said. "We've been on heightened alert since he sent the fleet to Korea. It's as tight as we can make it."

J J returned to his room. The message light was flashing. He called the desk; Daniels again. He dialed and the admiral answered immediately. "How good to hear your voice," J J began. "How's retirement treating you?"

"Admirals never really retire, J J, but there's no time for that. I understand you're doing some security work for the White House."

"Yeah, 'cause I know the man so well."

"I heard a rumor. Perhaps you could pass it on, or check it yourself."

"Happy to, but why not call the Secret Service yourself?"

"There are reasons. I ask you to respect that."

J J was puzzled, but the admiral had been his commander and he trusted him. Besides, this was Washington. "Whatever you say."

"I've heard there's a hired assassin in Washington. A man who has killed from very long range. A man who won't fit the profile."

"Why not?"

"The man is black. I believe African; a mercenary. They never notice blacks, especially in this city, J J."

"That's it?"

"I can do no more."

J J stood up, almost at attention. "I'll get right on it."

AGENT BLACKSTONE IS not in his office," a courteous government secretary told J J.

"I have to reach him," J J insisted. "Wherever he is. It's a matter of national security, and he knows me."

"I can try his cellphone and his portable radio, Mr. Early. Where can he call you back?"

"I'll hold."

"He'll call you back, Mr. Early," her voice turned flinty. "He's very busy."

"Dammit, miss, tell him J J Early says urgent. The Mayflower Hotel, room 808. He'll call me."

She had already disconnected. J J looked at his watch: ten minutes to eleven. Five minutes I'll give him, then I'll do what? Try to find a black shooter on a roof? What roof? And with what assets? Hell, the best he could do is run to the Lincoln Memorial and try to intercept the bullet with his body.

Instead, he got out his tourist map of central Washington and looked for a building that wouldn't be under control.

AN FBI LOH-6A helicopter made a final circuit of the area around the Memorial and the Mall, checking the surrounding rooftops. Teams of agents and Bureau sharpshooters waved; they were relaxed, the president hadn't yet arrived. They made a long swing south, circling the Washington Monument. "What's down there?" the pilot asked. "On the roof; the old Bureau of Engraving and Printing."

The observer, who had an M-60 machine gun mounted on a swivel in the open door, looked out with binoculars, spotted an gray-haired black man spreading tar on the roof. He didn't look up even as the helicopter hovered a hundred feet above his head. "Just some old nigger feeding cracks in the asphalt."

"We should call that in," the pilot insisted. "That building should have been cleared."

The radio barked. "Bureau 332, check a group of people carrying signs busting through police lines south of the Ellipse."

"Roger," the observer said.

"We should call that black guy in," the pilot said again, even as he turned away from the Bureau of Engraving and Printing.

"Christ, Jake, the radio's going bullshit, and the guy has a broom in his hand close to a mile away from the Memorial. I'll wait for a lull in traffic."

Cobra had gone outside to measure temperature and humidity, and therefore air density, with an instrument called a sling psychrometer. He entered the data in his laptop and barely had time to throw the delicate weather instrument back into the shed and slip the computer back inside Rufus Coomb's coveralls as the helicopter swung overhead. As it hovered, he played step-and-fetchit with the oily broom. He dropped his broom as the helicopter turned away. His heart was racing. It was *time*. He sat on his cushion, his right foot braced against the bottom of the parapet, his left crossed underneath his right calf. His back was bent forward; it was an uncomfortable position but very steady. Cobra sought to will the fear away. He placed the ankle weight on the parapet and steadied the rifle in one of its sewn seams. He closed his eyes and willed his heart to slow, and his breathing. He entered the state of Nirvana that was so familiar.

The President of the United States walked onto the podium beneath the massive statue of the seated Lincoln.

V

THE SEVENTH ANGEL

1

J J WAITED FOUR minutes, studying the map. He figured the buildings on Constitution Avenue had to be under control, so he looked elsewhere. Independence Avenue; more government buildings including the Smithsonian Institution complex. Nearest the Lincoln Memorial was the old Bureau of Engraving and Printing building. He pulled on his raincoat and started for the door. The phone rang and he dove across the bed to answer it.

"J J? Matt Blackstone."

"Matt, I got a believable tip. A black guy; a long-range shooter."

"Every roof within a thousand yards is sealed; within five hundred yards patrolled."

"Figure longer range. I like the Bureau of Engraving and Printing."

"Building was checked last evening."

"But it's not patrolled?"

"No. Too far."

"What about helicopters?"

"We have to pull them back. The president is about to speak, and he doesn't want to be drowned out by helicopters."

"Can you check and see if they saw anything on their last pass?"

"Wait one," Blackstone said. He held his cellphone and pulled the radio from his belt. "All airborne surveillance, this is Blackstone. Anyone seen on rooftops, no matter how far out?"

"This is Bureau 332," came an immediate reply. "There's an old black guy on the roof of the Bureau of Engraving and Printing, pushing a broom."

"Get back over him," Blackstone said. "J J you hear that?"

"Get the president off the podium, Matt."

"I concur." Blackstone hung up and began barking orders into his radio.

J J Early ran out of his room with no idea of where he was going and what he would do.

COBRA WATCHED AS the president waved to the crowd, both arms outstretched, his Bible in his right hand, just as he had at Gettysburg. Cobra could hear applause and boos, even from 1247 meters away. When he drops his hands, he'll pause, and then he'll begin to speak, just like on Cobra's videotape from Gettysburg. He steadied the rifle, felt the slight breeze on his cheek, and made a final adjustment to the gun sight. Even at its highest power, the telescopic sight showed the president's head as a tiny dot. Cobra centered the crosshairs on the president's hairline, right over his nose. He increased the pressure on the trigger every time his heart paused, held steady when it beat. His breathing was as soft and shallow as he could stand. The president dropped his hands and he looked out at the center of the crowd. Cobra was patient, but as the first words came from the president's mouth, the shot broke.

Cobra shook off the bright flash and the deafening report, and kept his sight picture. He rotated the bolt back and forward and fired again. Then again. His hot loads had a muzzle velocity of 950 meters per second, so two if not three were in the air before the first was due to arrive.

MATT BLACKSTONE RADIOED the detail standing right beside the president. "My fellow Americans, God is sending a message," the president said. The Mormon, on the Secret Service net, was closest and dove to tackle Tolliver, while a young Secret Service agent came from the other side. The Mormon had a hand across the president's chest when the bullet struck him in the mouth, only six inches lower than the shooter had aimed it. The mercury load blew the president's brainstem and spine to foam and splinters. The brain stem controls the autonomic nervous system, the automatic pilot that runs the heart, the lungs and other involuntary muscles. Tolliver's heart spasmed briefly, then stopped.

Contrary to popular belief, the brain cortex does not die instantly when the heart ceases to supply blood. The second bullet, arriving less than two seconds later, struck the Mormon on his shoulder, nearly severing his arm. The third hit took a large chunk of stone out of the Memorial's top step.

The young Secret Service agent laid the president down on the cold stone, covering him with his body. He keyed his radio and bellowed for backup. The president held his Bible, and seemed to try to speak even as his eyes dimmed. He had his thumb in the book, toward the back, as the Secret Service agent gently prized it from his grip. Tolliver died, and four minutes later Jim Bob Slate expired from massive loss of blood.

The crowd milled and cried out in confusion, not really understanding what they had seen. Matt Blackstone pushed through to the dead president, and to the young agent. "He tried to speak," the agent said. He held the Bible open to where the president's thumb had left a bloody print. "Revelation," the agent said. "Chapter sixteen, verses sixteen and seventeen. Read it, sir."

Blackstone read: "And he gathered them together into a place called in the Hebrew tongue Armageddon. And the seventh angel poured out his vial into the air, and there came a great voice out of the temple of heaven, from the throne, saying, It is done."

"You will say nothing of this," Blackstone said to the shocked agent, taking the Bible with him.

COBRA WATCHED AS his work was done. The president's wife, a dark-haired beauty, held the body and seemed to peer right back into Cobra's eyes. The conspirators that had hired him had wanted the widow as well, but Cobra didn't fire again.

The Mall was silent; the sirens would start soon. Cobra picked up the three brass shell casings and pocketed them. He took his old Remington 700 and swung it from the stock, hitting the barrel as hard as he could against one of the brick chimneys, sending brick dust and mortar into the air. He did it twice before the stock broke. The heavy barrel was bent, so slightly that even Cobra could barely see the damage, but it was enough; no one would ever fire a bullet through it for ballistics comparison. Who knew whether Cobra's employers might have made tests?

He dumped everything down several chimneys and ran for the stairs. He had made the impossible shot, but he felt no pride.

By now sirens screamed everywhere.

J J SPRINTED ACROSS the Mall, but even halfway to the Bureau of Engraving and Printing Building, he heard a vast sigh rise from the crowd gathered around the Lincoln Memorial. It was done, he thought. He pushed through the doors of the building and ran to the security desk in the lobby. "I'm looking for a black man," J J blurted, panting for breath.

The guard rose and drew his .38 revolver. "You done found one, cracker. Be a bunch of us, this town. Who the fuck are you?"

J J produced the I.D. he had received from Matt Blackstone. "He'd be on the roof."

"He'd be gone, he had a lick of sense," the guard said, picking up his handheld radio. "President's just been shot, over yonder." He pointed west toward the Memorial.

J J struggled for breath against sharp chest pain. "Logs. Anybody in this building that shouldn't be?"

"Not on my shift." He picked up a clipboard and ran a thick thumb down the left column. "Hm. On the last shift, one signature missin' goin' out. Rufus Coombs, a cleaner."

"How do I get to the roof?"

"Elevator, then stairs." A loud siren sounded within the building, and the guard moved rapidly back to his console. "Basement door just opened."

COBRA PUSHED THROUGH the fire exit in the first basement and ran up the stairs to the street. He heard the siren go off inside the building and the big red bell outside. He walked rapidly, resisting the impulse to run, south to D Street, where he had parked the van. He removed a parking ticket from beneath the windshield wiper and pocketed it, started the van and headed left around the block to Independence Avenue, then on to Pennsylvania. He turned onto the Beltway going north, and almost immediately onto the Baltimore-Washington Expressway. Military and emergency vehicles of all descriptions were headed into Washington, and helicopters buzzed around with no apparent plan. Cobra depended for his escape on the confusion lasting several hours, and control spreading slowly outward from the capital to the rest of the nation, then the rest of the world.

In half an hour, he was at the Baltimore-Washington International Airport; he hadn't wanted to risk the Potomac bridges to National or Dulles. He parked the van in a spot near the main entrance marked "Reserved for Senator Barbara Milkulski" and ran inside. His Delta flight to Miami was the last to depart before the FBI shut down the three Washington-area airports.

Cobra sat back and allowed himself several deep breaths. His single small shoulder bag was in the bin over his head; the Astra automatic, the three shell casings, and the last of his conspiracy-supplied documents dumped in a trash container in a men's room just before the metal detectors. He'd flushed the rubber gloves and the parking ticket down the toilet.

HIS EMPLOYERS HAD told him to go to Union Station and take a slow train to Canada, then fly to Europe. No sane fugitive would confine himself in a train, easily stopped and surrounded at any remote point along its route.

Cobra used the phone on the plane to make a reservation on Varig Airline's 6:00 P.M. departure for Rio de Janeiro, using another of his many credit cards, all legitimate if the names on them were not, bills paid by his bank in Brussels. He wanted to go someplace, and on an airline, where black people would be commonplace. He would decide the next step if he got through Miami and be gone.

J J RAN TO the basement and out the door with its still-ringing alarm and the siren within. The fat black guard followed at his own pace, puffing. There was nothing to see. J J walked to the Lincoln Memorial, showed his Secret Service I.D. to an agent, and was taken to the podium where he met Matt Blackstone. Two stretchers, both with faces covered, were being lifted up and carried to ambulances. "They'll take them to Walter Reed to be pronounced, J J," Matt said. "But they're both as dead as St. Peter."

"The president? Who else?"

"The Mormon. His bodyguard; some say other. Jim Bob Slate. He took the second round."

"Matt, I'm almost sure the shots came from the roof of the Bureau of Engraving and Printing."

"We and the FBI have forensics teams combing the place now."

"We won't find the shooter."

"No, not likely. Who's your source, J J?"

"Believe me, Matt, I can't tell you. But I am sure he can do no more good than he tried to do."

"I'm not sure I believe that, J J, but we'll talk later. You ain't going anywhere, are you?"

"No. Not for a while."

J J didn't know it, but he was protecting a ghost. As soon as he heard of the president's death, Admiral Daniels had placed the barrel of his Colt General Officer's Model .45 against the roof of his mouth and pulled the trigger.

VICE PRESIDENT JOSEPH Donahue was picked up by a Connecticut state trooper at his home in Essex within minutes of the call from Walter Reed announcing the president's death. He was wearing chinos and a blue turtleneck; he threw on a sport jacket. The trooper drove at high speed to the airport at Groton, where an air force C-140 VIP transport jet that became Air Force One as soon as Donahue stepped aboard was waiting with engines screaming. The plane took off immediately. Thirty minutes later the new president landed at Andrews Air Force Base in Maryland southeast of the capital. He transferred to the presidential helicopter, Marine One, for the short trip to Walter Reed Army Medical Center. The pilots flew high in case the shooter or shooters were still around. Donahue looked down at the Lincoln Memorial and the Mall, a scene of chaos as police and troops contained the crowd that only wanted to escape the place of death.

It was never my choice, Donahue told himself, rubbing his hands raw as if trying to wipe away blood.

At Walter Reed, Donahue was taken to the president, who was laid out on a gurney in the morgue. Clarissa was with the body, staring at it, dry-eyed. "May I offer my sincerest condolences," Donahue began. Clarissa turned and spat in his face.

Donahue wiped away the spittle with his handkerchief, saying nothing as Clarissa, weeping now, turned back to the corpse. "Rupert, we were so close!" she all but shouted. "You heard the Lord; you were his way."

"Clarissa," Donahue said, still holding his handkerchief ready. "I'm going to Navy House now." Navy House was the vice president's official residence. "The Chief Justice will be there, to administer the oath of office. I think it would be healing if you'd come with me."

She turned back to him. Her face had softened, but the tears still streamed. "Like Jackie in Dallas, with blood all over her pink suit?" She brushed ineffectuality at the bloodstains on her own dress. "At least I'm already wearing black."

"You'll come, then?"

"Will you respect my husband's work, his vision?" she challenged.

Not bloody likely, he thought. "Of course," he said.

PRESIDENT DONAHUE WAS sworn in, a teary Clarissa Tolliver at one side and his wife at the other. He told Clarissa she could have as long as she wanted to vacate the residence section of the White House, but he needed the executive and staff spaces and the sophisticated communications gear, none of which was available at Navy House.

President Donahue convened the cabinet and other senior advisers an hour later. The president pointed a finger at the Director of the FBI. "Any progress on finding the killer?"

"No, sir," the director answered. "We got an anonymous tip that he might be on the Amtrak train that left Union Station at thirteen-ten in the afternoon, to Albany arriving at twenty-oh-five, presumably to make his way to Canada. We stopped the train a mile after it departed; found no one who didn't check out. We stopped departures from National, Dulles, and BWI airports between one and one-thirty; no viable suspects. We recommend we hold all international flights until they can be checked."

Donahue felt a pain in his chest. "Who the hell are we looking for? Do we have any idea at all?"

"The only lead is from J J Early, and he is vague on the source. He says a black man, an experienced shooter-for-hire. We're running the data banks here and at Interpol and all over the world."

Donahue all but gasped. They were closer than they knew. "Any matches?"

"Some worth checking. These people use many names; usually none of them their own."

"I don't want to shut down our air travel system on so slim a chance," Donahue said. "I don't want to telegraph panic to the world."

"Just a few hours, Mr. President," Matt Blackstone pleaded. "If he's running he'll be gone in no time, but if we don't try, we'll never get a clue."

"You said you had the three local airports controlled."

"He could drive," Director Wilson said. "To Richmond, to Wheeling, to Philadelphia. A few hours."

"No," Donahue said. "The business of the nation must be, and be seen to be, running as usual. Now, the funeral."

Zeke Archer cleared his throat. "The First Lady—the widow, sir—demands complete control. He's being prepared, and will be lying in state in the Capitol by tomorrow. A memorial service at the National Cathedral, then interment in the Texas churchyard where President Tolliver first preached. No parade, no Arlington."

The president's eyes flashed anger. "Bury a president behind some outhouse country church? Better a public funeral here, and at Arlington. It heals."

"He'd rest better in Texas," Archer said sharply.

"I'd better talk to her."

"I wouldn't, Mr. President," Archer said evenly. "She doesn't like you, or trust you."

"Who the hell are you to say a thing like that to me?" the president shouted.

"The ex-Chief of Staff," Archer said, taking a single-page letter from his briefcase and spinning it across the polished surface of the table toward the president. Zeke got up and left the meeting without another word.

The president straightened his jacket, determined to ignore the insult. Dora Hollings, who had been his vice-presidential Chief of Staff, tried to defuse the moment, defend her boss. "Mr.

President," she said sweetly, "will there be other cabinet changes?"

"Naturally," Malcolm Japes, the Secretary of State, said, "we'll all offer our resignations immediately."

"After the funeral," Donahue said angrily. "Let's get through the damn funeral."

"Mr. President," Carolyn White said. "Immediately after the president was shot, I placed the armed forces in DefCon Three, not knowing what we faced."

"Stand them down," Donahue said. He knew, as they did not, that no foreign power had murdered the President of the United States.

The word "murder" bounced around in his brain. He couldn't put it away. "In fact, bring the fleets and the troops and air forces home. Let that be our first act: to show we'll no longer bully the world. All forces not normally stationed overseas should be brought home immediately, and the troops and air force in Korea as well, since they aren't wanted."

"Mr. President!" Admiral Austin exploded. "With respect, sir, President Tolliver's deployment of our military might worked! We're the only glue holding the planet together."

"Bring them home," the president said coldly.

Admiral Austin stood. Tolliver had been right. This lily-livered bastard would never measure up. "You may expect many further resignations, sir."

"After the damn funeral," the president growled.

BRAD BENTLEY STARED at Charles Taylor's story on his computer. Of course it couldn't run now; the assassination trumped it completely. He downloaded it onto a disk and erased it from his hard drive. In a year or two, he would turn it into a book.

Charles Taylor was in no position to miss it.

2

COBRA CROSSED MIAMI'S impossibly congested airport carrying his little bag. He was glad of the crowds and saw no lines at the counter; there were few waiting. Three women, two light-skinned Latins who were probably local and a black woman with "Da Silva" on her name tag, waited on the late check-ins. Cobra chose the black woman and presented his Portuguese passport. "*Boa tarde, Senhor de Morais,*" she said, smiling pleasantly.

"*Boa tarde, Senhora da Silva.*"

She tapped at her computer. It spat out a boarding card that she slipped into his passport and handed to him. "*Porta Seis, Senhor. Bem vindo a Varig, muito obrigada e boa viagem.*"

"*Obrigdo,*" Cobra replied, and walked slowly past security, out the pier, and through Gate Six onto the Varig DC-10. It was a long flight, and Cobra would have liked to have indulged himself in first class, but even on Varig, first class was mostly white.

The big plane backed out, taxied, and took off into the twilight. In a few seconds he was out of the United States.

3

PRESIDENT DONAHUE GOT through the funeral, delivering a eulogy that so praised the man who had despised and shamed him he had to fight not to gag. President Tolliver's remains were flown to Texas in an air force transport with a minimal military honor guard and laid to rest behind the Batesville Church of Jesus Present. Clarissa wept at graveside practically alone.

Clarissa had found a note in Justice's Bible, near the bloody thumbprint. "I was a poor husband, dear Clarissa, a poor preacher and a flawed man all my life. Raise up a stone behind the old Batesville church, saying, 'He loved God as only a sinner can.' "

She did so.

DONAHUE REMEMBERED TOLLIVER'S apocalyptic ravings. Lakes of fire, bottomless pits, angels of doom. Within a month he had the military standing down to peacetime routine, the fleets directed to or in port, the older ships back on the way to deactivation, the army divisions and air force squadrons back at their bases, their men exhausted and their parts stores depleted.

Donahue spoke frequently with President Lebed of the Russian Federation; the Russian fleet did not sail from the Baltic. Donahue promised the Russian president that no more aid or protection would be provided to the Cuban *insurgentes,* but they continued to advance out of the Sierra Maestra as the people rallied to them, fed them, and hid them from Nieto Castro's slow-moving, predictable army. By December, they held half the country. Lebed couldn't do anything about that, and Donahue wouldn't.

Donahue wondered when the former president had expected his Armageddon. The new year passed quietly, 2002.

Then it began. A riot in Srinigar, Kashmir, caused the burning of a mosque. Indian paratroops suppressed the rioters, and Pakistani troops crossed the frontier to defend their Muslim brothers. The Indian Army, using a plan they had written in the early 1980s, constantly updated, invaded Pakistan with heavy divisions of armor and infantry covered by fighters and bombers. The Southern Force crossed the Indus River in three days, capturing Karachi and Hyderabad, while the Northern Force advanced on Lahore, Rawalpindi, and Islamabad. The Pakistanis fought fiercely, inflicting heavy casualties, and threatened to use their nuclear missiles.

The Russians rallied to their Indian ally; the Chinese to their

Pakistani. Russia and China joined the two Subcontinent neighbors on full nuclear alert.

The United States called for an emergency meeting of the U.N. Security Council.

The Chairman of the Joint Chiefs of Staff, Admiral Josephus Austin, appealed to the Secretary of Defense, Carolyn White, to get the fleets to sea and place all the armed forces of the United States on high alert. White took Austin's recommendations to the president, recommending immediate approval. The president called the heads of government of India, Pakistan, Russia, and China and advised caution. He did nothing else. Austin declared DefCon Two, ordered the fleets to sea, and placed the air force and navy ICBM forces on high alert. The president fired the Chairman of the Joint Chiefs and countermanded his orders.

ADMIRAL AUSTIN APPEARED to accept his dismissal and forced retirement without rancor. He refused invitations to speak to veterans' groups and rallies organized by both political parties. "The new president is entitled to his own team" was all he would say publicly.

Privately, he began locating old friends, military and political, over the Internet and by phone. A meeting was organized on the large motor yacht of a wealthy banker who had served two terms as governor of Maryland. When the six men and one woman were gathered, the ship set sail from Annapolis and down the Severn River into Chesapeake Bay. Drinks and hors d'oeuvres were served by uniformed stewards in the grand saloon. The stewards withdrew and the hatches were locked. Austin rose immediately and began to speak without notes.

"Lady and gentlemen, I am greatly concerned. Practically from the day of his inauguration, President Donahue has been withdrawing and dismantling the military force President Tolliver built up, and as Tolliver predicted, chaos has rushed to fill the vacuum. We stand on the brink of war, that Tolliver predicted, and indeed the Revelation predicted, would begin in Asia, then engulf the world. My question to you, bluntly put because there is little if any time for planning or politics, is whether Donahue has the wit, the will and simple courage to defend this nation if the need arises?"

"Tolliver was murdered," said Sara McPhearson, a wealthy widow of a prominent Delaware chemical-fortune heir and a former ambassador to France. "Surely we can't have another."

"Tolliver was murdered by an assassin hired by conspirators. We don't know exactly whom; they hid themselves well, although the suicide of Admiral Daniels provides leads that could be followed." Austin paused. "If Donahue should resign or be removed, the Speaker of the House would become president. He retired from the navy as a commander and still holds a reserve commission as a rear admiral. He served under me and he shares my concerns."

"I don't see him among us," retired General Iorio of the marines said.

"Nor should he be," Austin said. "If we agree, I will set plans in motion to change the president's mind, or failing that, seek his removal."

"Without hurting him," Sara McPhearson said firmly. "If my support is wanted."

"He won't feel a thing. Are we agreed, then?"

"Agreed to what?" General Iorio asked. "What would you have us do?"

"Support the action I must take. Those of you with contacts in the active military speak to them, quickly but quietly. This country has a choice of deterring a strike on ourselves or striking ourselves to decapitate the enemies of our nation. Our enemies see no more evidence than we do that President Donahue has the balls to do either of those things.

"Those of you with contacts in the party, especially you, Sara, try to hearten the president, to make him see his duty, and if that fails, support the new government that would be formed to respond to the emergency."

The seven looked at each other and then at Admiral Austin. They nodded. The captain was called and the yacht was turned back to its slip in Annapolis.

PAKISTAN FIRED ITS small nuclear force at India, destroying Delhi, Calcutta, and Mumbai. The Indian counterstrike, much larger, burned all the populated parts of Pakistan to white ash and green glass. A limited nuclear exchange between Russia and China occurred two days later, confined to military targets and troop concentrations near the long common border, and to a few nuclear missile sites including some in southern China and the western highlands around Lop Nor. Both sides threatened massive attacks but secretly began urgent consultations.

The American fleets remained in port, the long-range aircraft grounded. The president finally threatened to intervene and revived Admiral Austin's revoked order. United States and Russian nuclear arsenals were placed on highest state of readiness, and targeted at each other's cities and military and naval resources.

Admiral Austin read the reports and acted the next day. Escorted by a battalion of the 82d Airborne Division, landed by helicopters on the Ellipse, he forced his way to the Oval Office. Admiral Austin took the "football," the launch code computer that was really a modern laptop computer with a wireless modem, from the army major who sat outside the oval office, at gunpoint. The president sat stunned at his desk as the admiral and the soldiers crowded in. "Launch the strike, Mr. President!" Austin bellowed.

"No," Donahue whispered. "We launch, they launch. We must stop the madness, not make it worse. I have just spoken to President Lebed—"

"It's already as bad as it can get." Austin popped open the computer and booted it up.

"You can't," the president said. "I won't give you the code."

Austin sneered, punched in some commands. "Do you really think I don't know it?" He immediately began punching in the complex code.

Donahue leaped to his feet. "Colonel!" he shouted at the senior army officer in his office. "I am the Commander in Chief! Arrest Admiral Austin and take that thing away from him."

The colonel hesitated but a second, then pointed at a sergeant major. The sergeant major approached the ashen Austin, saluted, and extended his hand. The admiral pressed the enter key and handed over the laptop, his hands shaking.

"It is done, Mr. President," Austin gasped. "I suggest you get the hell out of Washington if you want to live."

"I don't think I want to live," Donahue whispered.

The soldiers trooped out, leaving the laptop open in front of the president. He stared at it, at its blank screen. How to countermand the order? He had never had anything to do with the thing while vice president. "Major!" he shouted. "Get in here, please."

The major from whom the "football" had been taken hurried in and saluted. "Mr. President."

"Admiral Austin has ordered a strike. Illegally. How do I reverse that order?"

The major looked at his watch. "There is very little time; ten minutes I think after the launch code is entered. I know you have to begin with an eight-digit code that only you know. Wasn't the computer reprogrammed after President Tolliver's death?"

"No." Jesus, Donahue thought. He abhored the whole idea of nuclear war, but after Tolliver's death, he had allowed himself to be instructed in the codes to launch Armageddon but not how to reverse them. Why had he not? Why had none of his advisers told him?

He was responsible for Tolliver's death. Or at least he could have stopped it. What had he done?

"Then you must find the Secretary of Defense, sir," the major said. "She has the only other viable machine."

* * *

NUCLEAR FIRES IN Asia were so intense that the very soil burned, giving up its oxygen and carbon. Russian missiles, unmaintained for decades, fell way outside their targets but did terrible damage. Forests flashed to ash and pillars of dense black smoke.

Volcanoes, long dormant, erupted from the terrible shaking of the earth, from the Cascades in North America to the Caucuses in Russia, and all around the Pacific Rim. Russian missiles aimed at naval bases in the very south of China skipped off the exo-atmosphere and landed in Indonesia. Volcanoes called to sudden violence split the island of Java into three parts, and two of them submerged into the sea, taking with them seventy million souls.

4

COBRA STAYED IN Rio, first in the Ouro Verde Hotel in Copacabana, luxurious even in the face of catastrophe but too white, then in an apartment he rented in Ipanema. Since few winds or ocean currents cross the equator, the effects of the nuclear fires in the northern hemisphere took a long time to travel to the southern, but every day the skies got darker and the weather colder. The people of Brazil got little news; the explosions of so many nuclear missiles triggered electromagnetic pulses that knocked out all power grids and communications, even satellite communications. No information came from the Northern Hemisphere and the people of Brazil feared that if there was news there was no one up north to tell it to them.

The Catholic churches, the grand cathedrals and the humble chapels, filled and stayed filled. Priests said masses for the unknown dead, and for the comfort of the living. Along the beaches, at low tide, the followers of the old African religions, *Macumba* and *Candomble,* lit candles and laid out offerings of candles, fruit, and flowers, and watched as the waves of the rising tide carried the offerings away to the sea gods who could touch both Brazil and Africa.

The *Maizinhas,* the priestesses, entered trances and allowed themselves to be taken into possession by the ancient gods, begging the spirits of darkness to release the sun. Crossroads in the countryside were adorned with candles shielded by paper shields, and offerings of fruit, flowers, and animal bones. The skies grew darker every day.

Cobra thought of going further south, perhaps to the tip of Argentina, but he did not. He wrote to Isaiah in South Africa, but got no reply. He had no idea whether international mail was functioning at all.

As Carnival neared, in the height of the Brazilian summer, the skies were dark all day. The sun, when it could be seen at all, was a ghostly blue that people could look directly at. Cobra remembered a legend of the Ndebele people of his homeland that a blue sun foretold the end of the world.

Cobra went out into the scared crowds of dancers and drummers of the grand *Escolas de Samba,* bravely clad in their skimpy costumes despite temperatures near freezing as they practiced for the grand parade on Shrove Tuesday. On the Sunday before the parade was to begin, a cyclone hit Rio with high winds and violent rain. Of course there had been no warning, and there was much damage along the beaches and mudslides in the *favelas,* the slums that perched on steep hillsides.

When the storm passed, the skies lightened, and the sun rose weak but golden. The temperature rose into the seventies. On Monday the skies were brighter still, and Brazilian radio and television stations picked up signals from Europe and North America. The Brazilian stations immediately shifted to all news, and *cariocas* crowded into shops and around portable radios to find out what had happened.

Fernando Botelho, Brazil's most respected television newsman, appeared on all six channels. "People of Brazil," he intoned. "The planet escaped death by the narrowest of margins. An American admiral ordered a launch of all her missiles as a preemptive strike on Russia, but the American president was able to countermand the order. The Russians and Americans faced each other, fingers on the trigger, for two days, then the two presidents met hastily and in secret in London. They issued a joint declaration forswearing war between them, and stating that any nation using nuclear, biological, or chemical weapons against any other nation, or even within its own borders, would be attacked by both Russia and the United States. The Chinese refuse to sign, but have fired no more. The wars in South Asia, between India and Pakistan and between Iran and Iraq, have ceased, with all sides exhausted. Russia, the United States, and the European Union have agreed to massive aid projects, and they ask nations of the Southern Hemisphere, especially the prosperous ones such as ourselves, to help as well.

"There will be more news later. Brazilians, enjoy Carnival as never before, then begin forty days of prayer to Almighty God who has spared us."

COBRA SAW THE news in his apartment. He wondered only whose instrument he had been. A single phrase rattled around in his brain: It is done.

Fat Tuesday dawned fine and hot. When the sun went down over the hills to the west, Carnival exploded with fireworks, music, dancing, drinking, sex, and the joy of renewal.